Erema

Or, My Father's Sin

by
R. D. Blackmore

Erema
Or, My Father's Sin
by R. D. Blackmore

Copyright © 2024

All Rights reserved.

No part of this publication may be reproduced, stored in a retrieval system, or transmitted in any form or by any means, electronic, mechanical, photocopying or Otherwise, without the written permission of the publisher.
The author/editor asserts the moral right to be identified as the author/editor of this work.

ISBN: 978-93-67149-31-7

Published by

DOUBLE 9 BOOKS
2/13-B, Ansari Road
Daryaganj, New Delhi – 110002
info@double9books.com
www.double9books.com
Tel. 011-40042856

This book is under public domain

ABOUT THE AUTHOR

Richard Doddridge Blackmore, who wrote under the name R. D. Blackmore and was born on June 7, 1825, and died January 20, 1900, was one of the most famous English writers of the 1800s. He was praised for vividly describing and giving people in the countryside personalities. Like Thomas Hardy, he was born in Western England and his works have a strong sense of where they are set. A poster for R. D. Blackmore's book Perly-Cross. Blackmore, who is sometimes called the "Last Victorian," was one of the first literary writers of the period that other writers like Robert Louis Stevenson followed. People have said that he is "proud, shy, quiet, strong-willed, sweet-tempered, and self-centered." His other books are no longer in print, except for Lorna Doone, his novel, which has stayed famous. In Berkshire (now Oxfordshire), Richard Doddridge Blackmore was born on June 7, 1825, at Longworth. He was born a year after his older brother Henry (1824-1875). His father, John Blackmore, was Curate-in-Charge of the church. His mother died a few months after he was born. She had typhus, which had spread through the town.

CONTENTS

CHAPTER I
A LOST LANDMARK 9

CHAPTER II
A PACIFIC SUNSET 13

CHAPTER III
A STURDY COLONIST 17

CHAPTER IV
THE "KING OF THE MOUNTAINS" 22

CHAPTER V
UNCLE SAM 27

CHAPTER VI
A BRITISHER 32

CHAPTER VII
DISCOMFITURE 38

CHAPTER VIII
A DOUBTFUL LOSS 42

CHAPTER IX
WATER-SPOUT 46

CHAPTER X
A NUGGET 53

CHAPTER XI
ROVERS 58

CHAPTER XII
GOLD AND GRIEF 64

CHAPTER XIII
THE SAWYER'S PRAYER 70

CHAPTER XIV
NOT FAR TO SEEK 74

CHAPTER XV
BROUGHT TO BANK 80

CHAPTER XVI
FIRM AND INFIRM 85

CHAPTER XVII
HARD AND SOFT 91

CHAPTER XVIII
OUT OF THE GOLDEN GATE 97

CHAPTER XIX
INSIDE THE CHANNEL 103

CHAPTER XX
BRUNTSEA 108

CHAPTER XXI
LISTLESS 114

CHAPTER XXII
BETSY BOWEN 120

CHAPTER XXIII
BETSY'S TALE 126

CHAPTER XXIV
BETSY'S TALE—(Continued) 132

CHAPTER XXV
BETSY'S TALE—(Concluded) 137

CHAPTER XXVI
AT THE BANK 146

CHAPTER XXVII
COUSIN MONTAGUE 154

CHAPTER XXVIII
A CHECK 161

CHAPTER XXIX
AT THE PUMP 167

CHAPTER XXX
COCKS AND COXCOMBS 172

CHAPTER XXXI ADRIFT	178
CHAPTER XXXII AT HOME	185
CHAPTER XXXIII LORD CASTLEWOOD	192
CHAPTER XXXIV SHOXFORD	200
CHAPTER XXXV THE SEXTON	206
CHAPTER XXXVI A SIMPLE QUESTION	215
CHAPTER XXXVII SOME ANSWER TO IT	221
CHAPTER XXXVIII A WITCH	228
CHAPTER XXXIX NOT AT HOME	235
CHAPTER XL THE MAN AT LAST	242
CHAPTER XLI A STRONG TEMPTATION	248
CHAPTER XLII MASTER WITHYPOOL	254
CHAPTER XLIII GOING TO THE BOTTOM	262
CHAPTER XLIV HERMETICALLY SEALED	269
CHAPTER XLV CONVICTION	275
CHAPTER XLVI VAIN ZEAL	281
CHAPTER XLVII CADMEIAN VICTORY	288

CHAPTER XLVIII
A RETURN CALL..296
CHAPTER XLIX
WANTED, A SAWYER..306
CHAPTER L
THE PANACEA..313
CHAPTER LI
LIFE SINISTER...320
CHAPTER LII
FOR LIFE, DEATH...327
CHAPTER LIII
BRUNTSEA DEFIANT..333
CHAPTER LIV
BRUNTSEA DEFEATED..341
CHAPTER LV
A DEAD LETTER..350
CHAPTER LVI
WITH HIS OWN SWORD...356
CHAPTER LVII
FEMALE SUFFRAGE..365
CHAPTER LVIII
BEYOND DESERT, AND DESERTS...369

CHAPTER I
A LOST LANDMARK

"The sins of the fathers upon the children, unto the third and fourth generation of them that hate me."

These are the words that have followed me always. This is the curse which has fallen on my life.

If I had not known my father, if I had not loved him, if I had not closed his eyes in desert silence deeper than the silence of the grave, even if I could have buried and bewailed him duly, the common business of this world and the universal carelessness might have led me down the general track that leads to nothing.

Until my father fell and died I never dreamed that he could die. I knew that his mind was quite made up to see me safe in my new home, and then himself to start again for still remoter solitudes. And when his mind was thus made up, who had ever known him fail of it?

If ever a resolute man there was, that very man was my father. And he showed it now, in this the last and fatal act of his fatal life. "Captain, here I leave you all," he shouted to the leader of our wagon train, at a place where a dark, narrow gorge departed from the moilsome mountain track. "My reasons are my own; let no man trouble himself about them. All my baggage I leave with you. I have paid my share of the venture, and shall claim it at Sacramento. My little girl and I will take this short-cut through the mountains."

"General!" answered the leader of our train, standing up on his board in amazement. "Forgive and forget, Sir; forgive and forget. What is a hot word spoken hotly? If not for your own sake, at least come back for the sake of your young daughter."

"A fair haven to you!" replied my father. He offered me his hand, and we were out of sight of all that wearisome, drearisome, uncompanionable company with whom, for eight long weeks at least, we had been dragging our rough way. I had known in a moment that it must be so, for my father never argued. Argument, to his mind, was a very nice amusement for the weak. My spirits rose as he swung his bear-skin bag upon his shoulder, and the last sound of the laboring caravan groaned in the distance, and the fresh air and the freedom of the mountains moved around us. It was the 29th of May—Oak-apple Day in England—and to my silly youth this vast extent of snowy mountains was a nice place for a cool excursion.

Moreover, from day to day I had been in most wretched anxiety, so long as we remained with people who could not allow for us. My father, by his calm reserve and dignity and largeness, had always, among European people, kept himself secluded; but now in this rough life, so pent in trackless tracts, and pressed together by perpetual peril, every body's manners had been growing free and easy. Every man had been compelled to tell, as truly as he could, the story of his life thus far, to amuse his fellow-creatures— every man, I mean, of course, except my own poor father. Some told their stories every evening, until we were quite tired—although they were never the same twice over; but my father could never be coaxed to say a syllable more than, "I was born, and I shall die."

This made him very unpopular with the men, though all the women admired it; and if any rough fellow could have seen a sign of fear, the speaker would have been insulted. But his manner and the power of his look were such that, even after ardent spirits, no man saw fit to be rude to him. Nevertheless, there had always been the risk of some sad outrage.

"Erema," my father said to me, when the dust from the rear of the caravan was lost behind a cloud of rocks, and we two stood in the wilderness alone—"do you know, my own Erema, why I bring you from them?"

"Father dear, how should I know? You have done it, and it must be right."

"It is not for their paltry insults. Child, you know what I think all that. It is for you, my only child, that I am doing what now I do."

I looked up into his large, sad eyes without a word, in such a way that he lifted me up in his arms and kissed me, as if I were a little child instead of a maiden just fifteen. This he had never done before, and it made me a little frightened. He saw it, and spoke on the spur of the thought, though still with one arm round me.

"Perhaps you will live to be thankful, my dear, that you had a stern, cold father. So will you meet the world all the better; and, little one, you have a rough world to meet."

For a moment I was quite at a loss to account for my father's manner; but now, in looking back, it is so easy to see into things. At the time I must have been surprised, and full of puzzled eagerness.

Not half so well can I recall the weakness, anguish, and exhaustion of body and spirit afterward. It may have been three days of wandering, or it may have been a week, or even more than that, for all that I can say for certain. Whether the time were long or short, it seemed as if it would never end. My father believed that he knew the way to the house of an old settler, at the western foot of the mountains, who had treated him kindly some years before, and with whom he meant to leave me until he had made arrangements elsewhere. If we had only gone straightway thither, night-fall would have found us safe beneath that hospitable roof.

My father was vexed, as I well remember, at coming, as he thought, in sight of some great landmark, and finding not a trace of it. Although his will was so very strong, his temper was good about little things, and he never began to abuse all the world because he had made a mistake himself.

"Erema," he said, "at this corner where we stand there ought to be a very large pine-tree in sight, or rather a great redwood-tree, at least twice as high as any tree that grows in Europe, or Africa even. From the plains it can be seen for a hundred miles or more. It stands higher up the mountainside than any other tree of even half its size, and that makes it so conspicuous. My eyes must be failing me, from all this glare; but it must be in sight. Can you see it now?"

"I see no tree of any kind whatever, but scrubby bushes and yellow tufts; and oh, father, I am so thirsty!"

"Naturally. But now look again. It stands on a ridge, the last ridge that bars the view of all the lowland. It is a very straight tree, and regular, like a mighty column, except that on the northern side the wind from the mountains has torn a gap in it. Are you sure that you can not see it—a long way off, but conspicuous?"

"Father, I am sure that I can not see any tree half as large as a broomstick. Far or near, I see no tree."

"Then my eyes are better than my memory. We must cast back for a mile or two; but it can not make much difference."

"Through the dust and the sand?" I began to say; but a glance from him stopped my murmuring. And the next thing I can call to mind must have happened a long time afterward.

Beyond all doubt, in this desolation, my father gave his life for mine. I did not know it at the time, nor had the faintest dream of it, being so young and weary-worn, and obeying him by instinct. It is a fearful thing to think of—now that I can think of it—but to save my own little worthless life I must have drained every drop of water from his flat half-gallon jar. The water was hot and the cork-hole sandy, and I grumbled even while drinking it; and what must my father (who was dying all the while for a drop, but never took one)—what must he have thought of me?

But he never said a word, so far as I remember; and that makes it all the worse for me. We had strayed away into a dry, volcanic district of the mountains, where all the snow-rivers run out quite early; and of natural springs there was none forth-coming. All we had to guide us was a little traveler's compass (whose needle stuck fast on the pivot with sand) and the glaring sun, when he came to sight behind the hot, dry, driving clouds. The clouds were very low, and flying almost in our faces, like vultures sweeping down on us. To me they seemed to shriek over our heads at the others rushing after them. But my father said that they could make no sound, and I never contradicted him.

CHAPTER II
A PACIFIC SUNSET

At last we came to a place from which the great spread of the earth was visible. For a time—I can not tell how long—we had wholly lost ourselves, going up and down, and turning corners, without getting further. But my father said that we must come right, if we made up our minds to go long enough. We had been in among all shapes, and want of shapes, of dreariness, through and in and out of every thrup and thrum of weariness, scarcely hoping ever more to find our way out and discover memory of men for us, when all of a sudden we saw a grand sight. The day had been dreadfully hot and baffling, with sudden swirls of red dust arising, and driving the great drought into us. To walk had been worse than to drag one's way through a stubbly bed of sting-nettles. But now the quick sting of the sun was gone, and his power descending in the balance toward the flat places of the land and sea. And suddenly we looked forth upon an immeasurable spread of these.

We stood at the gate of the sandy range, which here, like a vast brown patch, disfigures the beauty of the sierra. On either side, in purple distance, sprang sky-piercing obelisks and vapor-mantled glaciers, spangled with bright snow, and shodden with eternal forest. Before us lay the broad, luxuriant plains of California, checkered with more tints than any other piece of earth can show, sleeping in alluvial ease, and veined with soft blue waters. And through a gap in the brown coast range, at twenty leagues of distance, a light (so faint as to seem a shadow) hovered above the Pacific.

But none of all this grandeur touched our hearts except the water gleam. Parched with thirst, I caught my father's arm and tried to urge him on toward the blue enchantment of ecstatic living water. But, to my surprise, he staggered back, and his face grew as white as the distant snow. I managed to get him to a sandy ledge, with the help of his own endeavors, and there let him rest and try to speak, while my frightened heart throbbed over his.

"My little child," he said at last, as if we were fallen back ten years, "put your hand where I can feel it."

My hand all the while had been in his, and to let him know where it was, it moved. But cold fear stopped my talking.

"My child, I have not been kind to you," my father slowly spoke again, "but it has not been from want of love. Some day you will see all this, and some day you will pardon me."

He laid one heavy arm around me, and forgetting thirst and pain, with the last intensity of eyesight watched the sun departing. To me, I know not how, great awe was every where, and sadness. The conical point of the furious sun, which like a barb had pierced us, was broadening into a hazy disk, inefficient, but benevolent. Underneath him depth of night was waiting to come upward (after letting him fall through) and stain his track with redness. Already the arms of darkness grew in readiness to receive him: his upper arc was pure and keen, but the lower was flaked with atmosphere; a glow of hazy light soon would follow, and one bright glimmer (addressed more to the sky than to the earth), and after that a broad, soft gleam; and after that how many a man should never see the sun again, and among them would be my father.

He, for the moment, resting there, with heavy light upon him, and the dark jaws of the mountain desert yawning wide behind him, and all the beautiful expanse of liberal earth before him—even so he seemed to me, of all the things in sight, the one that first would draw attention. His face was full of quiet grandeur and impressive calm, and the sad tranquillity which comes to those who know what human life is through continual human death. Although, in the matter of bodily strength, he was little past the prime of life, his long and abundant hair was white, and his broad and upright forehead marked with the meshes of the net of care. But drought and famine and long fatigue had failed even now to change or weaken the fine expression of his large, sad eyes. Those eyes alone would have made the face remarkable among ten thousand, so deep with settled gloom they were, and dark with fatal sorrow. Such eyes might fitly have told the grief of Adrastus, son of Gordias, who, having slain his own brother unwitting, unwitting slew the only son of his generous host and savior.

The pale globe of the sun hung trembling in the haze himself had made. My father rose to see the last, and reared his tall form upright against the deepening background. He gazed as if the course of life lay vanishing below him, while level land and waters drew the breadth of shadow over them. Then the last gleam flowed and fled upon the face of ocean, and my father put his dry lips to my forehead, saying nothing.

His lips might well be dry, for he had not swallowed water for three days; but it frightened me to feel how cold they were, and even tremulous.

"Let us run, let us run, my dear father!" I cried. "Delicious water! The dark falls quickly; but we can get there before dark. It is all down hill. Oh, do let us run at once!"

"Erema," he answered, with a quiet smile, "there is no cause now for hurrying, except that I must hurry to show you what you have to do, my child. For once, at the end of my life, I am lucky. We have escaped from that starving desert at a spot—at a spot where we can see—"

For a little while he could say no more, but sank upon the stony seat, and the hand with which he tried to point some distant landmark fell away. His face, which had been so pale before, became of a deadly whiteness, and he breathed with gasps of agony. I knelt before him and took his hands, and tried to rub the palms, and did whatever I could think of.

"Oh, father, father, you have starved yourself, and given every thing to me! What a brute I was to let you do it! But I did not know; I never knew! Please God to take me also!"

He could not manage to answer this, even if he understood it; but he firmly lifted his arm again, and tried to make me follow it.

"What does it matter? Oh, never mind, never mind such, a wretch as I am! Father, only try to tell me what I ought to do for you."

"My child! my child!" were his only words; and he kept on saying, "My child! my child!" as if he liked the sound of it.

At what time of the night my father died I knew not then or afterward. It may have been before the moon came over the snowy mountains, or it may not have been till the worn-out stars in vain repelled the daybreak. All I know is that I ever strove to keep more near to him through the night, to cherish his failing warmth, and quicken the slow, laborious, harassed breath. From time to time he tried to pray to God for me and for himself; but every time his mind began to wander and to slip away, as if through want of practice. For the chills of many wretched years had deadened and benumbed his faith. He knew me, now and then, betwixt the conflict and the stupor; for more than once he muttered feebly, and as if from out a dream,

"Time for Erema to go on her way. Go on your way, and save your life; save your life, Erema."

There was no way for me to go, except on my knees before him. I took his hands, and made them lissome with a soft, light rubbing. I whispered into his ear my name, that he might speak once more to me; and when he could not speak, I tried to say what he would say to me.

At last, with a blow that stunned all words, it smote my stupid, wandering mind that all I had to speak and smile to, all I cared to please and serve, the only one left to admire and love, lay here in my weak arms quite dead. And in the anguish of my sobbing, little things came home to me, a thousand little things that showed how quietly he had prepared for this, and provided for me only. Cold despair and self-reproach and strong rebellion dazed me, until I lay at my father's side, and slept with his dead hand in mine. There in the desert of desolation pious awe embraced me, and small phantasms of individual fear could not come nigh me.

By-and-by long shadows of morning crept toward me dismally, and the pallid light of the hills was stretched in weary streaks away from me. How I arose, or what I did, or what I thought, is nothing now. Such times are not for talking of. How many hearts of anguish lie forlorn, with none to comfort them, with all the joy of life died out, and all the fear of having yet to live, in front arising!

Young and weak, and wrong of sex for doing any valiance, long I lay by my father's body, wringing out my wretchedness. Thirst and famine now had flown into the opposite extreme; I seemed to loathe the thought of water, and the smell of food would have made me sick. I opened my father's knapsack, and a pang of new misery seized me. There lay nearly all his rations, which he had made pretense to eat as he gave me mine from time to time. He had starved himself; since he failed of his mark, and learned our risk of famishing, all his own food he had kept for me, as well as his store of water. And I had done nothing but grumble and groan, even while consuming every thing. Compared with me, the hovering vultures might be considered angels.

When I found all this, I was a great deal too worn out to cry or sob. Simply to break down may be the purest mercy that can fall on truly hopeless misery. Screams of ravenous maws and flaps of fetid wings came close to me, and, fainting into the arms of death, I tried to save my father's body by throwing my own over it.

CHAPTER III
A STURDY COLONIST

For the contrast betwixt that dreadful scene and the one on which my dim eyes slowly opened, three days afterward, first I thank the Lord in heaven, whose gracious care was over me, and after Him some very simple members of humanity.

A bronze-colored woman, with soft, sad eyes, was looking at me steadfastly. She had seen that, under tender care, I was just beginning to revive, and being acquainted with many troubles, she had learned to succor all of them. This I knew not then, but felt that kindness was around me.

"Arauna, arauna, my shild," she said, in a strange but sweet and soothing voice, "you are with the good man in the safe, good house. Let old Suan give you the good food, my shild."

"Where is my father? Oh, show me my father?" I whispered faintly, as she raised me in the bed and held a large spoon to my lips.

"You shall—you shall; it is too very much Inglese; me tell you when have long Sunday time to think. My shild, take the good food from poor old Suan."

She looked at me with such beseeching eyes that, even if food had been loathsome to me, I could not have resisted her; whereas I was now in the quick-reviving agony of starvation. The Indian woman fed me with far greater care than I was worth, and hushed me, with some soothing process, into another abyss of sleep.

More than a week passed by me thus, in the struggle between life and death, before I was able to get clear knowledge of any body or any thing. No one, in my wakeful hours, came into my little bedroom except this careful Indian nurse, who hushed me off to sleep whenever I wanted to ask questions. Suan Isco, as she was called, possessed a more than mesmeric power of soothing a weary frame to rest; and this was seconded, where I lay, by the soft, incessant cadence and abundant roar of water. Thus every day I recovered strength and natural impatience.

"The master is coming to see you, shild," Suan said to me one day, when I had sat up and done my hair, and longed to be down by the waterfall; "if, if—too much Inglese—old Suan say no more can now."

"If I am ready and able and willing! Oh, Suan, run and tell him not to lose one moment."

"No sure; Suan no sure at all," she answered, looking at me calmly, as if there were centuries yet to spare. "Suan no hurry; shild no hurry; master no hurry: come last of all."

"I tell you, Suan, I want to see him. And I am not accustomed to be kept waiting. My dear father insisted always—But oh, Suan, Suan, he is dead—I am almost sure of it."

"Him old man quite dead enough, and big hole dug in the land for him. Very good; more good than could be. Suan no more Inglese."

Well as I had known it long, a catching of the breath and hollow, helpless pain came through me, to meet in dry words thus the dread which might have been but a hovering dream. I turned my face to the wall, and begged her not to send the master in.

But presently a large, firm hand was laid on my shoulder softly, and turning sharply round, I beheld an elderly man looking down at me. His face was plain and square and solid, with short white curls on a rugged forehead, and fresh red cheeks, and a triple chin—fit base for remarkably massive jaws. His frame was in keeping with his face, being very large and powerful, though not of my father's commanding height. His dress and appearance were those of a working—and a really hard-working—man, sober, steadfast, and self-respecting; but what engaged my attention most was the frank yet shrewd gaze of deep-set eyes. I speak of things as I observed them later, for I could not pay much heed just then.

"'Tis a poor little missy," he said, with a gentle tone. "What things she hath been through! Will you take an old man's hand, my dear? Your father hath often taken it, though different from his rank of life. Sampson Gundry is my name, missy. Have you ever heard your father tell of it?"

"Many and many a time," I said, as I placed my hot little hand in his. "He never found more than one man true on earth, and it was you, Sir."

"Come, now," he replied, with his eyes for a moment sparkling at my warmth of words; "you must not have that in your young head, missy. It leads to a miserable life. Your father hath always been unlucky—the most unlucky that ever I did know. And luck cometh out in nothing clearer than in the kind of folk we meet. But the Lord in heaven ordereth all. I speak like a poor heathen."

"Oh, never mind that!" I cried: "only tell me, were you in time to save—to save—" I could not bear to say what I wanted.

"In plenty of time, my dear; thanks to you. You must have fought when you could not fight: the real stuff, I call it. Your poor father lies where none can harm him. Come, missy, missy, you must not take on so. It is the best thing that could befall a man so bound up with calamity. It is what he hath prayed for for many a year—if only it were not for you. And now you are safe, and for sure he knows it, if the angels heed their business."

With these words he withdrew, and kindly sent Suan back to me, knowing that her soothing ways would help me more than argument. To my mind all things lay in deep confusion and abasement. Overcome with bodily weakness and with bitter self-reproach, I even feared that to ask any questions might show want of gratitude. But a thing of that sort could not always last, and before very long I was quite at home with the history of Mr. Gundry.

Solomon Gundry, of Mevagissey, in the county of Cornwall, in England, betook himself to the United States in the last year of the last century. He had always been a most upright man, as well as a first-rate fisherman; and his family had made a rule—as most respectable families at that time did—to run a nice cargo of contraband goods not more than twice in one season. A highly querulous old lieutenant of the British navy (who had served under Nelson and lost both, arms, yet kept "the rheumatics" in either stump) was appointed, in an evil hour, to the Cornish coast-guard; and he never rested until he had caught all the best county families smuggling. Through this he lost his situation, and had to go to the workhouse; nevertheless, such a stir had been roused that (to satisfy public opinion) they made a large sacrifice of inferior people, and among them this Solomon Gundry. Now the Gundries had long been a thickset race, and had furnished some champion wrestlers; and Solomon kept to the family stamp in the matter of obstinacy. He made a bold mark at the foot of a bond for 150 pounds; and with no other sign than that, his partner in their stanch herring-smack (the Good Hope, of Mevagissey) allowed him to make sail across the Atlantic with all he cared for.

This Cornish partner deserved to get all his money back; and so he did, together with good interest. Solomon Gundry throve among a thrifty race at Boston; he married a sweet New England lass, and his eldest son was Sampson. Sampson, in the prime of life, and at its headstrong period, sought the far West, overland, through not much less of distance, and through even more of danger, than his English father had gone through. His name was known on the western side of the mighty chain of mountains before Colonel Fremont was heard of there, and before there was any gleam of gold on the lonely sunset frontage.

Here Sampson Gundry lived by tillage of the nobly fertile soil ere Sacramento or San Francisco had any name to speak of. And though he did not show regard for any kind of society, he managed to have a wife and son, and keep them free from danger. But (as it appears to me the more, the more I think of every thing) no one must assume to be aside the reach of Fortune because he has gathered himself so small that she should not care to strike at him. At any rate, good or evil powers smote Sampson Gundry heavily.

First he lost his wife, which was a "great denial" to him. She fell from a cliff while she was pegging out the linen, and the substance of her frame prevented her from ever getting over it. And after that he lost his son, his only son—for all the Gundries were particular as to quality; and the way in which he lost his son made it still more sad for him.

A reputable and valued woman had disappeared in a hasty way from a cattle-place down the same side of the hills. The desire of the Indians was to enlarge her value and get it. There were very few white men as yet within any distance to do good; but Sampson Gundry vowed that, if the will of the Lord went with him, that woman should come back to her family without robbing them of sixpence. To this intent he started with a company of some twenty men—white or black or middle-colored (according to circumstances). He was their captain, and his son Elijah their lieutenant. Elijah had only been married for a fortnight, but was full of spirit, and eager to fight with enemies; and he seems to have carried this too far; for all that came back to his poor bride was a lock of his hair and his blessing. He was buried in a bed of lava on the western slope of Shasta, and his wife died in her confinement, and was buried by the Blue River.

It was said at the time and long afterward that Elijah Gundry—thus cut short—was the finest and noblest young man to be found from the mountains to the ocean. His father, in whose arms he died, led a sad and lonely life for years, and scarcely even cared (although of Cornish and New England race) to seize the glorious chance of wealth which lay at his feet beseeching him. By settlement he had possessed himself of a large and fertile district, sloping from the mountain-foot along the banks of the swift Blue River, a tributary of the San Joaquin. And this was not all; for he also claimed the ownership of the upper valley, the whole of the mountain gorge and spring head, whence that sparkling water flows. And when that fury of gold-digging in 1849 arose, very few men could have done what he did without even thinking twice of it.

For Sampson Gundry stood, like a bull, on the banks of his own river, and defied the worst and most desperate men of all nations to pollute it. He had scarcely any followers or steadfast friends to back him; but his fame for stern courage was clear and strong, and his bodily presence most manifest. Not a shovel was thrust nor a cradle rocked in the bed of the Blue River.

But when a year or two had passed, and all the towns and villages, and even hovels and way-side huts, began to clink with money, Mr. Gundry gradually recovered a wholesome desire to have some. For now his grandson Ephraim was growing into biped shape, and having lost his mother when he first came into the world, was sure to need the more natural and maternal nutriment of money.

Therefore Sampson Gundry, though he would not dig for gold, wrought out a plan which he had long thought of. Nature helped him with all her powers of mountain, forest, and headlong stream. He set up a saw-mill, and built it himself; and there was no other to be found for twelve degrees of latitude and perhaps a score of longitude.

CHAPTER IV
THE "KING OF THE MOUNTAINS"

If I think, and try to write forever with the strongest words, I can not express to any other mind a thousandth part of the gratitude which was and is, and ought to be forever, in my own poor mind toward those who were so good to me. From time to time it is said (whenever any man with power of speech or fancy gets some little grievances) that all mankind are simply selfish, miserly, and miserable. To contradict that saying needs experience even larger, perhaps, than that which has suggested it; and this I can not have, and therefore only know that I have not found men or women behave at all according to that view of them.

Whether Sampson Gundry owed any debt, either of gratitude or of loyalty, to my father, I did not ask; and he seemed to be (like every one else) reserved and silent as to my father's history. But he always treated me as if I belonged to a rank of life quite different from and much above his own. For instance, it was long before he would allow me to have my meals at the table of the household.

But as soon as I began in earnest to recover from starvation, loss, and loneliness, my heart was drawn to this grand old man, who had seen so many troubles. He had been here and there in the world so much, and dealt with so many people, that the natural frankness of his mind was sharpened into caution. But any weak and helpless person still could get the best of him; and his shrewdness certainly did not spring from any form of bitterness. He was rough in his ways sometimes, and could not bear to be contradicted when he was sure that he was right, which generally happened to him. But above all things he had one very great peculiarity, to my mind highly vexatious, because it seemed so unaccountable. Sampson Gundry had a very low opinion of feminine intellect. He never showed this contempt in any unpleasant way, and indeed he never, perhaps, displayed it in any positive sayings. But as I grew older and began to argue, sure I was that it was there; and it always provoked me tenfold as much by seeming to need no assertion, but to stand as some great axiom.

The other members of the household were his grandson Ephraim (or "Firm" Gundry), the Indian woman Suan Isco, and a couple of helps, of race or nation almost unknown to themselves. Suan Isco belonged to a tribe of respectable Black Rock Indians, and had been the wife of a chief among them, and the mother of several children. But Klamath Indians, enemies of theirs (who carried off the lady of the cattle ranch, and afterward shot Elijah), had Suan Isco in their possession, having murdered her husband and children, and were using her as a mere beast of burden, when Sampson Gundry fell on them. He, with his followers, being enraged at the cold-blooded death of Elijah, fell on those miscreants to such purpose that women and children alone were left to hand down their bad propensities.

But the white men rescued and brought away the stolen wife of the stockman, and also the widow of the Black Rock chief. She was in such poor condition and so broken-hearted that none but the finest humanity would have considered her worth a quarter of the trouble of her carriage. But she proved to be worth it a thousandfold; and Sawyer Gundry (as now he was called) knew by this time all the value of uncultivated gratitude. And her virtues were so many that it took a long time to find them out, for she never put them forward, not knowing whether they were good or bad.

Until I knew these people, and the pure depth of their kindness, it was a continual grief to me to be a burden upon them. But when I came to understand them and their simple greatness, the only thing I was ashamed of was my own mistrust of them. Not that I expected ever that any harm would be done to me, only that I knew myself to have no claim on any one.

One day, when I was fit for nothing but to dwell on trouble, Sampson Gundry's grandson "Firm"—as he was called for Ephraim—ran up the stairs to the little room where I was sitting by myself.

"Miss Rema, will you come with us?" he said, in his deep, slow style of speech. "We are going up the mountain, to haul down the great tree to the mill."

"To be sure I will come," I answered, gladly. "What great tree is it, Mr. Ephraim?"

"The largest tree any where near here—the one we cut down last winter. Ten days it took to cut it down. If I could have saved it, it should have stood. But grandfather did it to prove his rights. We shall have a rare job to lead it home, and I doubt if we can tackle it. I thought you might like to see us try."

In less than a minute I was ready, for the warmth and softness of the air made cloak or shawl unbearable. But when I ran down to the yard of the mill, Mr. Gundry, who was giving orders, came up and gave me an order too.

"You must not go like this, my dear. We have three thousand feet to go upward. The air will be sharp up there, and I doubt if we shall be home by night-fall. Run, Suan, and fetch the young lady's cloak, and a pair of thicker boots for change."

Suan Isco never ran. That manner of motion was foreign to her, at least as we accomplish it. When speed was required, she attained it by increased length of stride and great vigor of heel. In this way she conquered distance steadily, and with very little noise.

The air, and the light, and the beauty of the mountains were a sudden joy to me. In front of us all strode Sampson Gundry, clearing all tangles with a short, sharp axe, and mounting steep places as if twoscore were struck off his threescore years and five. From time to time he turned round to laugh, or see that his men and trained bullocks were right; and then, as his bright eyes met my dark ones, he seemed to be sorry for the noise he made. On the other hand, I was ashamed of damping any one's pleasure by being there.

But I need not have felt any fear about this. Like all other children, I wrapped myself up too much in my own importance, and behaved as if my state of mind was a thing to be considered. But the longer we rose through the freedom and the height, the lighter grew the heart of every one, until the thick forest of pines closed round us, and we walked in a silence that might be felt.

Hence we issued forth upon the rough bare rock, and after much trouble with the cattle, and some bruises, stood panting on a rugged cone, or crest, which had once been crowned with a Titan of a tree. The tree was still there, but not its glory; for, alas! the mighty trunk lay prostrate—a grander column than ever was or will be built by human hands. The tapering shaft stretched out of sight for something like a furlong, and the bulk of the butt rose over us so that we could not see the mountains. Having never seen any such tree before, I must have been amazed if I had been old enough to comprehend it.

Sampson Gundry, large as he was, and accustomed to almost every thing, collected his men and the whole of his team on the ground-floor or area of the stump before he would say any thing. Here we all looked so sadly small that several of the men began to laugh; the bullocks seemed nothing but raccoons or beavers to run on the branches or the fibres of the tree; and the chains and the shackles, and the blocks and cranes, and all the rest of the things they meant to use, seemed nothing whatever, or at all to be considered, except as a spider's web upon this tree.

The sagacious bullocks, who knew quite well what they were expected to do, looked blank. Some rubbed their horns into one another's sadly, and some cocked their tails because they felt that they could not be called upon to work. The light of the afternoon sun came glancing along the vast pillar, and lit its dying hues—cinnamon, purple, and glabrous red, and soft gray where the lichens grew.

Every body looked at Mr. Gundry, and he began to cough a little, having had lately some trouble with his throat. Then in his sturdy manner he spoke the truth, according to his nature. He set his great square shoulders against the butt of the tree, and delivered himself:

"Friends and neighbors, and hands of my own, I am taken in here, and I own to it. It serves me right for disbelieving what my grandson, Firm Gundry, said. I knew that the tree was a big one, of course, as every body else does; but till you see a tree laid upon earth you get no grip of his girth, no more than you do of a man till he lieth a corpse. At the time of felling I could not come anigh him, by reason of an accident; and I had some words with this boy about it, which kept me away ever since that time. Firm, you were right, and I was wrong. It was a real shame, now I see it, to throw down the 'King of the Mountains.' But, for all that, being down, we must use him. He shall be sawn into fifty-foot lengths. And I invite you all to come again, for six or seven good turns at him."

At the hearing of this, a cheer arose, not only for the Sawyer's manly truth, but also for his hospitality; because on each of these visits to the mountain he was the host, and his supplies were good. But before the descent with the empty teams began, young Ephraim did what appeared to me to be a gallant and straightforward thing. He stood on the chine of the fallen monster, forty feet above us, having gained the post of vantage by activity and strength, and he asked if he might say a word or two.

"Say away, lad," cried his grandfather, supposing, perhaps, in his obstinate way (for truly he was very obstinate), that his grandson was going now to clear himself from art or part in the murder of that tree—an act which had roused indignation over a hundred leagues of lowland.

"Neighbors," said Firm, in a clear young voice, which shook at first with diffidence, "we all have to thank you, more than I can tell, for coming to help us with this job. It was a job which required to be done for legal reasons which I do not understand, but no doubt they were good ones. For that we have my grandfather's word; and no one, I think, will gainsay it. Now, having gone so far, we will not be beaten by it, or else we shall not be Americans."

These simple words were received with great applause; and an orator, standing on the largest stump to be found even in America, delivered a speech which was very good to hear, but need not now be repeated. And Mr. Gundry's eyes were moist with pleasure at his grandson's conduct.

"Firm knoweth the right thing to do," he said; "and like a man he doeth it. But whatever aileth you, Miss Rema, and what can 'e see in the distance yonner? Never mind, my dear, then. Tell me by-and-by, when none of these folk is 'longside of us."

But I could not bear to tell him, till he forced it from me under pain of his displeasure. I had spied on the sky-line far above us, in the desert track of mountain, the very gap in which my father stood and bade me seek this landmark. His memory was true, and his eyesight also; but the great tree had been felled. The death of the "King of the Mountains" had led to the death of the king of mankind, so far as my little world contained one.

CHAPTER V
UNCLE SAM

The influence of the place in which I lived began to grow on me. The warmth of the climate and the clouds of soft and fertile dust were broken by the refreshing rush of water and the clear soft green of leaves. We had fruit trees of almost every kind, from the peach to the amber cherry, and countless oaks by the side of the river—not large, but most fantastic. Here I used to sit and wonder, in a foolish, childish way, whether on earth there was any other child so strangely placed as I was. Of course there were thousands far worse off, more desolate and destitute, but was there any more thickly wrapped in mystery and loneliness?

A wanderer as I had been for years, together with my father, change of place had not supplied the knowledge which flows from lapse of time. Faith, and warmth, and trust in others had not been dashed out of me by any rude blows of the world, as happens with unlucky children huddled together in large cities. My father had never allowed me much acquaintance with other children; for six years he had left me with a community of lay sisters, in a little town of Languedoc, where I was the only pupil, and where I was to remain as I was born, a simple heretic. Those sisters were very good to me, and taught me as much as I could take of secular accomplishment. And it was a bitter day for me when I left them for America.

For during those six years I had seen my father at long intervals, and had almost forgotten the earlier days when I was always with him. I used to be the one little comfort of his perpetual wanderings, when I was a careless child, and said things to amuse him. Not that he ever played with me any more than he played with any thing; but I was the last of his seven children, and he liked to watch me grow. I never knew it, I never guessed it, until he gave his life for mine; but, poor little common thing as I was, I became his only tie to earth. Even to me he was never loving, in the way some fathers are. He never called me by pet names, nor dandled me on his knee, nor kissed me, nor stroked down my hair and smiled. Such things I never expected of him, and therefore never missed them; I did not even know that happy children always have them.

But one thing I knew, which is not always known to happier children: I had the pleasure of knowing my own name. My name was an English one—Castlewood—and by birth I was an English girl, though of England I knew nothing, and at one time spoke and thought most easily in French. But my longing had always been for England, and for the sound of English voices and the quietude of English ways. In the chatter and heat and drought of South France some faint remembrance of a greener, cooler, and more silent country seemed to touch me now and then. But where in England I had lived, or when I had left that country, or whether I had relations there, and why I was doomed to be a foreign girl—all these questions were but as curling wisps of cloud on memory's sky.

Of such things (much as I longed to know a good deal more about them) I never had dared to ask my father; nor even could I, in a roundabout way, such as clever children have, get second-hand information. In the first place, I was not a clever child; for the next point, I never had underhand skill; and finally, there was no one near me who knew any thing about me. Like all other girls—and perhaps the very same tendency is to be found in boys—I had strong though hazy ideas of caste. The noble sense of equality, fraternity, and so on, seems to come later in life than childhood, which is an age of ambition. I did not know who in the world I was, but felt quite sure of being somebody.

One day, when the great tree had been sawn into lengths, and with the aid of many teams brought home, and the pits and the hoisting tackle were being prepared and strengthened to deal with it, Mr. Gundry, being full of the subject, declared that he would have his dinner in the mill yard. He was anxious to watch, without loss of time, the settlement of some heavy timbers newly sunk in the river's bed, to defend the outworks of the mill. Having his good leave to bring him his pipe, I found him sitting upon a bench with a level fixed before him, and his empty plate and cup laid by, among a great litter of tools and things. He was looking along the level with one eye shut, and the other most sternly intent; but when I came near he rose and raised his broad pith hat, and made me think that I was not interrupting him.

"Here is your pipe, Uncle Sam," I said; for, in spite of all his formal ways, I would not be afraid of him. I had known him now quite long enough to be sure he was good and kind. And I knew that the world around these parts was divided into two hemispheres, the better half being of those who loved, and the baser half made of those who hated, Sawyer Sampson Gundry.

"What a queer world it is!" said Mr. Gundry, accepting his pipe to consider that point. "Who ever would have dreamed, fifty years agone, that your father's daughter would ever have come with a pipe to light for my father's son?"

"Uncle Sam," I replied, as he slowly began to make those puffs which seem to be of the highest essence of pleasure, and wisps of blue smoke flitted through his white eyebrows and among the snowy curls of hair— "dear Uncle Sam, I am sure that it would be an honor to a princess to light a pipe for a man like you."

"Miss Rema, I should rather you would talk no nonsense," he answered, very shortly, and he set his eye along his level, as if I had offended him. Not knowing how to assert myself and declare that I had spoken my honest thoughts, I merely sat down on the bench and waited for him to speak again to me. But he made believe to be very busy, and scarcely to know that I was there. I had a great mind to cry, but resolved not to do it.

"Why, how is this? What's the matter?" he exclaimed at last, when I had been watching the water so long that I sighed to know where it was going to. "Why, missy, you look as if you had never a friend in all the wide world left."

"Then I must look very ungrateful," I said; "for at any rate I have one, and a good one."

"And don't you know of any one but me, my dear?"

"You and Suan Isco and Firm—those are all I have any knowledge of."

"'Tis a plenty—to my mind, almost too many. My plan is to be a good friend to all, but not let too many be friends with me. Rest you quite satisfied with three, Miss Rema. I have lived a good many years, and I never had more than three friends worth a puff of my pipe."

"But one's own relations, Uncle Sam—people quite nearly related to us: it is impossible for them to be unkind, you know."

"Do I, my dear? Then I wish that I did. Except one's own father and mother, there is not much to be hoped for out of them. My own brother took a twist against me because I tried to save him from ruin; and if any man ever wished me ill, he did. And I think that your father had the same tale to tell. But there! I know nothing whatever about that."

"Now you do, Mr. Gundry; I am certain that you do, and beg you to tell me, or rather I demand it. I am old enough now, and I am certain my dear father would have wished me to know every thing. Whatever it was, I am sure that he was right; and until I know that, I shall always be the most miserable of the miserable."

The Sawyer looked at me as if he could not enter into my meaning, and his broad, short nose and quiet eyes were beset with wrinkles of inquiry. He quite forgot his level and his great post in the river, and tilted back his ancient hat, and let his pipe rest on his big brown arm. "Lord bless me!" he said, "what a young gal you are! Or, at least, what a young Miss Rema. What good can you do, miss, by making of a rout? Here you be in as quiet a place as you could find, and all of us likes and pities you. Your father was a wise man to settle you here in this enlightened continent. Let the doggoned old folk t'other side of the world think out their own flustrations. A female young American you are now, and a very fine specimen you will grow. 'Tis the finest thing to be on all God's earth."

"No, Mr. Gundry, I am an English girl, and I mean to be an Englishwoman. The Americans may be more kind and generous, and perhaps my father thought so, and brought me here for that reason. And I may be glad to come back to you again when I have done what I am bound to do. Remember that I am the last of seven children, and do not even know where the rest are buried."

"Now look straight afore you, missy. What do you see yonner?" The Sawyer was getting a little tired, perhaps, of this long interruption.

"I see enormous logs, and a quantity of saws, and tools I don't even know the names of. Also I see a bright, swift river."

"But over here, missy, between them two oaks. What do you please to see there, Miss Rema?"

"What I see there, of course, is a great saw-mill."

"But it wouldn't have been 'of course,' and it wouldn't have been at all, if I had spent all my days a-dwelling on the injuries of my family. Could I have put that there unekaled sample of water-power and human ingenuity together without laboring hard for whole months of a stretch, except upon the Sabbath, and laying awake night after night, and bending all my intellect over it? And could I have done that, think you now, if my heart was a-mooning upon family wrongs, and this, that, and the other?"

Here Sampson Gundry turned full upon me, and folded his arms, and spread his great chin upon his deer-skin apron, and nodded briskly with his deep gray eyes, surveying me in triumph. To his mind, that mill was the wonder of the world, and any argument based upon it, with or without coherence, was, like its circular saws, irresistible. And yet he thought that women can not reason! However, I did not say another word just then, but gave way to him, as behooved a child. And not only that, but I always found him too good to be argued with—too kind, I mean, and large of heart, and wedded to his own peculiar turns. There was nothing about him that one could dislike, or strike fire at, and be captious; and he always proceeded with such pity for those who were opposed to him that they always knew they must be wrong, though he was too polite to tell them so. And he had such a pleasant, paternal way of looking down into one's little thoughts when he put on his spectacles, that to say any more was to hazard the risk of ungrateful inexperience.

CHAPTER VI
A BRITISHER

The beautiful Blue River came from the jagged depths of the mountains, full of light and liveliness. It had scarcely run six miles from its source before it touched our mill-wheel; but in that space and time it had gathered strong and copious volume. The lovely blue of the water (like the inner tint of a glacier) was partly due to its origin, perhaps, and partly to the rich, soft tone of the granite sand spread under it. Whatever the cause may have been, the river well deserved its title.

It was so bright and pure a blue, so limpid and pellucid, that it even seemed to out-vie the tint of the sky which it reflected, and the myriad sparks of sunshine on it twinkled like a crystal rain. Plodding through the parched and scorching dust of the mountain-foot, through the stifling vapor and the blinding, ochreous glare, the traveler suddenly came upon this cool and calm delight. It was not to be descried afar, for it lay below the level, and the oaks and other trees of shelter scarcely topped the narrow comb. There was no canyon, such as are—and some of them known over all the world—both to the north and south of it. The Blue River did not owe its birth to any fierce convulsion, but sparkled on its cheerful way without impending horrors. Standing here as a child, and thinking, from the manner of my father, that strong men never wept nor owned the conquest of emotion, I felt sometimes a fool's contempt for the gushing transport of brave men. For instance, I have seen a miner, or a tamer of horses, or a rough fur-hunter, or (perhaps the bravest of all) a man of science and topography, jaded, worn, and nearly dead with drought and dearth and choking, suddenly, and beyond all hope, strike on this buried Eden. And then he dropped on his knees and spread his starved hands upward, if he could, and thanked the God who made him, till his head went round, and who knows what remembrance of loved ones came to him? And then, if he had any moisture left, he fell to a passion of weeping.

In childish ignorance I thought that this man weakly degraded himself, and should have been born a woman. But since that time I have truly learned that the bravest of men are those who feel their Maker's Land most softly, and are not ashamed to pay the tribute of their weakness to Him.

Living, as we did, in a lonely place, and yet not far from a track along the crest of the great Californian plain from Sacramento southward, there was scarcely a week which did not bring us some traveler needing comfort. Mr. Gundry used to be told that if he would set up a rough hotel, or house of call for cattle-drovers, miners, loafers, and so on, he might turn twice the money he could ever make by his thriving saw-mill. But he only used to laugh, and say that nature had made him too honest for that; and he never thought of charging any thing for his hospitality, though if a rich man left a gold piece, or even a nugget, upon a shelf, as happened very often, Sawyer Gundry did not disdain to set it aside for a rainy day. And one of his richest or most lavish guests arrived on my account, perhaps.

It happened when daylight was growing shorter, and the red heat of the earth was gone, and the snow-line of distant granite peaks had crept already lower, and the chattering birds that spent their summer in our band of oak-trees were beginning to find their food get short, and to prime swift wings for the lowland; and I, having never felt bitter cold, was trembling at what I heard of it. For now it was clear that I had no choice but to stay where I was for the present, and be truly thankful to God and man for having the chance of doing so. For the little relics of my affairs—so far as I had any—had taken much time in arrangement, perhaps because it was so hard to find them. I knew nothing, except about my own little common wardrobe, and could give no information about the contents of my father's packages. But these, by dint of perseverance on the part of Ephraim (who was very keen about all rights), had mainly been recovered, and Mr. Gundry had done the best that could be done concerning them. Whatever seemed of a private nature, or likely to prove important, had been brought home to Blue River Mills; the rest had been sold, and had fetched large prices, unless Mr. Gundry enlarged them.

He more than enlarged, he multiplied them, as I found out long afterward, to make me think myself rich and grand, while a beggar upon his bounty. I had never been accustomed to think of money, and felt some little contempt for it—not, indeed, a lofty hatred, but a careless wonder why it seemed to be always thought of. It was one of the last things I ever thought of; and those who were waiting for it were—until I got used to them—obliged in self-duty to remind me.

This, however, was not my fault. I never dreamed of wronging them. But I had earned no practical knowledge of the great world any where, much though I had wandered about, according to vague recollections. The duty of paying had never been mine; that important part had been done for me. And my father had such a horror always of any growth of avarice that he never gave me sixpence.

And now, when I heard upon every side continual talk of money, from Suan Isco upward, I thought at first that the New World must be different from the Old one, and that the gold mines in the neighborhood must have made them full of it; and once or twice I asked Uncle Sam; but he only nodded his head, and said that it was the practice every where. And before very long I began to perceive that he did not exaggerate.

Nothing could prove this point more clearly than the circumstance above referred to—the arrival of a stranger, for the purpose of bribing even Uncle Sam himself. This happened in the month of November, when the passes were beginning to be blocked with snow, and those of the higher mountain tracts had long been overwhelmed with it. On this particular day the air was laden with gray, oppressive clouds, threatening a heavy downfall, and instead of faring forth, as usual, to my beloved river, I was kept in-doors, and even up stairs, by a violent snow-headache. This is a crushing weight of pain, which all new-comers, or almost all, are obliged to endure, sometimes for as much as eight-and-forty hours, when the first great snow of the winter is breeding, as they express it, overhead. But I was more lucky than most people are; for after about twelve hours of almost intolerable throbbing, during which the sweetest sound was odious, and the idea of food quite loathsome, the agony left me, and a great desire for something to eat succeeded. Suan Isco, the kindest of the kind, was gone down stairs at last, for which I felt ungrateful gratitude—because she had been doing her best to charm away my pain by low, monotonous Indian ditties, which made it ten times worse; and yet I could not find heart to tell her so.

Now it must have been past six o'clock in the evening of the November day when the avalanche slid off my head, and I was able to lift it. The light of the west had been faint, and was dead; though often it used to prolong our day by the backward glance of the ocean. With pangs of youthful hunger, but a head still weak and dazy, I groped my way in the dark through the passage and down the stairs of redwood.

At the bottom, where a railed landing was, and the door opened into the house-room, I was surprised to find that, instead of the usual cheerful company enjoying themselves by the fire-light, there were only two people present. The Sawyer sat stiffly in his chair of state, delaying even the indulgence of his pipe, and having his face set sternly, as I had never before beheld it. In the visitor's corner, as we called it, where people sat to dry themselves, there was a man, and only one.

Something told me that I had better keep back and not disturb them. The room was not in its usual state of comfort and hospitality. Some kind of meal had been made at the table, as always must be in these parts; but not of the genial, reckless sort which random travelers carried on without any check from the Sawyer. For he of all men ever born in a civilized age was the finest host, and a guest beneath his roof was sacred as a lady to a knight. Hence it happened that I was much surprised. Proper conduct almost compelled me to withdraw; but curiosity made me take just one more little peep, perhaps. Looking back at these things now, I can not be sure of every thing; and indeed if I could, I must have an almost supernatural memory. But I remember many things; and the headache may have cleared my mind.

The stranger who had brought Mr. Gundry's humor into such stiff condition was sitting in the corner, a nook where light and shadow made an eddy. He seemed to be perfectly unconcerned about all the tricks of the hearth flame, presenting as he did a most solid face for any light to play upon. To me it seemed to be a weather-beaten face of a bluff and resolute man, the like of which we attribute to John Bull. At any rate, he was like John Bull in one respect: he was sturdy and square, and fit to hold his own with any man.

Strangers of this sort had come (as Englishmen rove every where), and been kindly welcomed by Uncle Sam, who, being of recent English blood, had a kind of hankering after it, and would almost rather have such at his board than even a true-born American; and infinitely more welcome were they than Frenchman, Spaniard, or German, or any man not to be distinguished, as was the case with some of them. Even now it was clear that the Sawyer had not grudged any tokens of honor, for the tall, square, brazen candlesticks, of Boston make, were on the table, and very little light they gave. The fire, however, was grandly roaring of stub-oak and pine antlers, and the black grill of the chimney bricks was fringed with lifting filaments. It was a rich, ripe light, affording breadth and play for shadow; and the faces of the two men glistened, and darkened in their creases.

I was dressed in black, and could not be seen, though I could see them so clearly; and I doubted whether to pass through, upon my way to the larder, or return to my room and starve a little longer; for I did not wish to interrupt, and had no idea of listening. But suddenly I was compelled to stop; and to listen became an honest thing, when I knew what was spoken of—or, at any rate, I did it.

"Castlewood, Master Colonist; Castlewood is the name of the man that I have come to ask about. And you will find it worth your while to tell me all you know of him." Thus spoke the Englishman sitting in the corner; and he seemed to be certain of producing his effect.

"Wal," said Uncle Sam, assuming what all true Britons believe to be the universal Yankee tone, while I knew that he was laughing in his sleeve, "Squire, I guess that you may be right. Considerations of that 'ere kind desarves to be considered of."

"Just so. I knew that you must see it," the stranger continued, bravely. "A stiff upper lip, as you call it here, is all very well to begin with. But all you enlightened members of the great republic know what is what. It will bring you more than ten years' income of your saw-mill, and farm, and so on, to deal honestly with me for ten minutes. No more beating about the bush and fencing with me, as you have done. Now can you see your own interest?"

"I never were reckoned a fool at that. Squire, make tracks, and be done with it."

"Then, Master Colonist, or Colonel—for I believe you are all colonels here—your task is very simple. We want clear proof, sworn properly and attested duly, of the death of a villain—George Castlewood, otherwise the Honorable George Castlewood, otherwise Lord Castlewood: a man who murdered his own father ten years ago this November: a man committed for trial for the crime, but who bribed his jailers and escaped, and wandered all over the Continent. What is that noise? Have you got rats?"

"Plenty of foreign rats, and native 'coons, and skunks, and other varmint. Wal, Squire, go on with it."

The voice of Uncle Sam was stern, and his face full of rising fury, as I, who had made that noise in my horror, tried to hush my heart with patience.

"The story is well known," continued the stranger: "we need make no bones of it. George Castlewood went about under a curse—"

"Not quite so loud, Squire, if you please. My household is not altogether seasoned."

"And perhaps you have got the young lady somewhere. I heard a report to that effect. But here you think nothing of a dozen murders. Now, Gundry, let us have no squeamishness. We only want justice, and we can pay for it. Ten thousand dollars I am authorized to offer for a mere act of duty on your part. We have an extradition treaty. If the man had been alive, we must have had him. But as he has cheated the hangman by dying, we can only see his grave and have evidence. And all well-disposed people must rejoice to have such a quiet end of it. For the family is so well known, you see."

"I see," Mr. Gundry answered, quietly, laying a finger on his lips. "Guess you want something more than that, though, Squire. Is there nothing more than the grave to oblige a noble Britisher with?"

"Yes, Colonel; we want the girl as well. We know that she was with him in that caravan, or wagon train, or whatever you please to call it. We know that you have made oath of his death, produced his child, and obtained his trunks, and drawn his share in the insurance job. Your laws must be queer to let you do such things. In England it would have taken at least three years, and cost a deal more than the things were worth, even without a Chancery suit. However, of his papers I shall take possession; they can be of no earthly use to you."

"To be sure. And possession of his darter too, without so much as a Chancery suit. But what is to satisfy me, Squire, agin goin' wrong in this little transaction?"

"I can very soon satisfy you," said the stranger, "as to their identity. Here is their full, particular, and correct description—names, weights, and colors of the parties."

With a broad grin at his own exquisite wit, the bluff man drew forth his pocket-book, and took out a paper, which he began to smooth on his knee quite leisurely. Meanwhile, in my hiding-place, I was trembling with terror and indignation. The sense of eavesdropping was wholly lost, in that of my own jeopardy. I must know what was arranged about me; for I felt such a hatred and fear of that stranger that sooner than be surrendered to him I would rush back to my room and jump out of the window, and trust myself to the trackless forest and the snowy night. I was very nearly doing so, but just had sense enough to wait and hear what would be said of me. So I lurked in the darkness, behind the rails, while the stranger read slowly and pompously.

CHAPTER VII
DISCOMFITURE

The Englishman drew forth a double eyeglass from a red velvet waistcoat, and mounting it on his broad nose, came nearer to get the full light of the candles. I saw him as clearly as I could wish, and, indeed, a great deal too clearly; for the more I saw of the man, the more I shrank from the thought of being in his power. Not that he seemed to be brutal or fierce, but selfish, and resolute, and hard-hearted, and scornful of lofty feelings. Short dust-colored hair and frizzly whiskers framed his large, thick-featured face, and wearing no mustache, he showed the clumsy sneer of a wide, coarse mouth. I watched him with all my eyes, because of his tone of authority about myself. He might even be my guardian or my father's nearest relation—though he seemed to be too ill-bred for that.

"Sorry to keep you waiting, Colonel," he went on, in a patronizing tone, such as he had assumed throughout. "Here it is. Now prick your ears up, and see if these candid remarks apply. I am reading from a printed form, you see:

"'George Castlewood is forty-eight years old, but looks perhaps ten years older. His height is over six feet two, and he does not stoop or slouch at all. His hair is long and abundant, but white; his eyes are dark, piercing, and gloomy. His features are fine, and of Italian cast, but stern, morose, and forbidding, and he never uses razor. On the back of his left hand, near the wrist, there is a broad scar. He dresses in half-mourning always, and never wears any jewelry, but strictly shuns all society, and prefers uncivilized regions. He never stays long in any town, and follows no occupation, though his aspect and carriage are military, as he has been a cavalry officer. From time to time he has been heard of in Europe, Asia, and Africa, and is now believed to be in America.

"'His only surviving child, a girl of about fifteen, has been seen with him. She is tall and slight and very straight, and speaks French better than English. Her hair is very nearly black, and her eyes of unusual size and lustre. She is shy, and appears to have been kept under, and she has a timid smile. Whether she knows of her father's crime or not is quite uncertain; but she follows him like a dog almost.'

"There now, Colonel," cried the Englishman, as he folded the paper triumphantly; "most of that came from my information, though I never set eyes upon the child. Does the cap fit or not, Brother Jonathan?"

Mr. Gundry was leaning back in his own corner, with a favorite pipe, carved by himself, reposing on his waistcoat. And being thus appealed to, he looked up and rubbed his eyes as if he had been dozing, though he never had been more wide awake, as I, who knew his attitudes, could tell. And my eyes filled with tears of love and shame, for I knew by the mere turn of his chin that he never would surrender me.

"Stranger," he said, in a most provoking drawl, "a hard day's work tells its tale on me, you bet. You do read so bootiful, you read me hard asleep. And the gutturals of that furrin English is always a little hard to catch. Mought I trouble you just to go through it again? You likes the sound of your own voice; and no blame to you, being such a swate un."

The Englishman looked at him keenly, as if he had some suspicion of being chaffed; but the face of the Sawyer was so grave and the bend of his head so courteous that he could not refuse to do as he was asked. But he glanced first at the whiskey bottle standing between the candlesticks; and I knew it boded ill for his errand when Uncle Sam, the most hospitable of men, feigned pure incomprehension of that glance. The man should have no more under that roof.

With a sullen air and a muttered curse, at which Mr. Gundry blew a wreath of smoke, the stranger unfolded his paper again, and saying, "Now I beg you to attend this time," read the whole of his description, with much emphasis, again, while the Sawyer turned away and beat time upon the hearth, with his white hair, broad shoulders, and red ears prominent. The Englishman looked very seriously vexed, but went through his business doggedly. "Are you satisfied now?" he asked when he had finished.

"Wal, now, Squire," replied Uncle Sam, still keeping up his provoking drawl, but turning round and looking at the stranger very steadfastly, "some thin's is so pooty and so ilegantly done, they seems a'most as good as well-slung flapjacks. A natteral honest stomick can't nohow have enough of them. Mought I be so bold, in a silly, mountaneous sort of a way, as to ax for another heerin' of it?"

"Do you mean to insult me, Sir?" shouted the visitor, leaping up with a flaming face, and throwing himself into an attitude of attack.

"Stranger, I mought," answered Mr. Gundry, standing squarely before him, and keeping his hands contemptuously behind his back—"I mought so do, barrin' one little point. The cutest commissioner in all the West would have to report 'Non compos' if his orders was to diskiver somethin' capable of bein' insulted in a fellow of your natur'."

With these words Uncle Sam sat down, and powerfully closed his mouth, signifying that now the matter was taken through every phase of discussion, and had been thoroughly exhausted. His visitor stared at him for a moment, as if at some strange phenomenon, and then fell back into self-command, without attempting bluster.

"Colonel, you are a 'cure,' as we call it on our side of the herring pond. What have I done to 'riz your dander,' as you elegantly express it here?"

"Britisher, nothing. You know no better. It takes more than that to put my back up. But forty years agone I do believe I must 'a heaved you out o' window."

"Why, Colonel, why? Now be reasonable. Not a word have I said reflecting either upon you or your country; and a finer offer than I have made can not come to many of you, even in this land of gold. Ten thousand dollars I offer, and I will exceed my instructions and say fifteen, all paid on the nail by an order on Frisco, about which you may assure yourself. And what do I ask in return? Legal proof of the death of a man whom we know to be dead, and the custody of his child, for her own good."

"Squire, I have no other answer to make. If you offered me all the gold dug in these mountains since they were discovered, I could only say what I have said before. You came from Sylvester's ranch—there is time for you to get back ere the snow begins."

"What a hospitable man you are! Upon my word, Gundry, you deserve to have a medal from our Humane Society. You propose to turn me out of doors to-night, with a great fall of snow impending?"

"Sir, the fault is entirely your own. What hospitality can you expect after coming to buy my guest? If you are afraid of the ten-mile ride, my man at the mill will bed you. But here you must not sleep, because I might harm you in the morning. I am apt to lose my temper sometimes, when I go on to think of things."

"Colonel, I think I had better ride back. I fear no man, nor his temper, nor crotchets. But if I were snowed up at your mill, I never might cross the hill-foot for months; but from Sylvester's I can always get to Minto. You refuse, then, to help me in any way?"

"More than that. I will do every thing in my power to confound you. If any one comes prowling after that young lady, he shall be shot."

"That is most discouraging. However, you may think better of it. Write to this address if you do. You have the girl here, of course?"

"That is her concern and mine. Does your guide know the way right well! The snow is beginning. You do not know our snows, any more than you know us."

"Never mind, Mr. Gundry. I shall do very well. You are rough in your ways, but you mean to do the right; and your indignation is virtuous. But mark my words upon one little point. If George Castlewood had been living, I have such credentials that I would have dragged him back with me in spite of all your bluster. But over his corpse I have no control, in the present condition of treaties. Neither can I meddle with his daughter, if it were worth while to do so. Keep her and make the best of her, my man. You have taken a snake in the grass to your bosom, if that is what you are up for. A very handsome girl she may be, but a bad lot, as her father was. If you wish the name of Gundry to have its due respect hereafter, let the heir of the sawmills have nothing to do with the Honorable Miss Castlewood."

"Let alone, let alone," Uncle Sam said, angrily. "It is well for you that the 'heir of the saw-mills' hath not heard your insolence. Firm is a steady lad; but he knoweth well which foot to kick with. No fear of losing the way to Sylvester's ranch with Firm behind you. But, meddlesome as you be, and a bitter weed to my experience, it shall not be said that Sampson Gundry sent forth a fellow to be frozen. Drink a glass of hot whiskey before you get to saddle. Not in friendship, mind you, Sir, but in common human nature."

That execrable man complied, for he began to be doubtful of the driving snow, now huddling against the window-frames. And so he went out; and when he was gone, I came forth into the fire-light, and threw my arms round the Sawyer's neck and kissed him till he was ashamed of me.

"Miss Rema, my dear, my poor little soul, what makes you carry on so?"

"Because I have heard every word, Uncle Sam, and I was base enough to doubt you."

CHAPTER VIII
A DOUBTFUL LOSS

When I tried to look out of my window in the morning, I was quite astonished at the state of things. To look out fairly was impossible; for not only was all the lower part of the frame hillocked up like a sandglass, and the sides filled in with dusky plaits, but even in the middle, where some outlook was, it led to very little. All the air seemed choked with snow, and the ground coming up in piles to meet it; all sounds were deadened in the thick gray hush, and nothing had its own proportion. Never having seen such a thing before, I was frightened, and longed to know more of it.

Mr. Gundry had a good laugh at me, in which even Suan Isco joined, when I proposed to sweep a path to the mill, and keep it open through the winter.

"It can be done—I am sure it can," I exclaimed, with vigorous ignorance. "May I do it if I can? It only requires perseverance. If you keep on sweeping as fast as it falls, you must overcome it. Don't you see, Uncle Sam?"

"To be sure I do, Miss Rema, as plain as any pikestaff. Suan, fetch a double bundle of new brooms from top loft, and don't forget while you be up there to give special orders—no snow is to fall at night or when missy is at dinner."

"You may laugh as much as you please, Uncle Sam, but I intend to try it. I must try to keep my path to—somewhere."

"What a fool I am, to be sure!" said Mr. Gundry, softly. "There, now, I beg your pardon, my dear, for never giving a thought to it. Firm and I will do it for you, as long as the Lord allows of it. Why, the snow is two foot deep a'ready, and twenty foot in places. I wonder whether that rogue of a Goad got home to Sylvester's ranch last night? No fault of mine if he never did, for go he would in spite of me."

I had not been thinking of Mr. Goad, and indeed I did not know his name until it was told in this way. My mind was dwelling on my father's grave, where I used to love to sit and think; and I could not bear the idea of the cold snow lying over it, with nobody coming to care for him. Kind hands had borne him down the mountains (while I lay between life and death) and buried him in the soft peach orchard, in the soothing sound of the mill-wheel. Here had been planted above his head a cross of white un-painted wood, bearing only his initials, and a small "Amen" below them.

With this I was quite content, believing that he would have wished no better, being a very independent man, and desirous of no kind of pomp. There was no "consecrated ground" within miles and miles of traveling; but I hoped that he might rest as well with simple tears to hallow it. For often and often, even now, I could not help giving way and sobbing, when I thought how sad it was that a strong, commanding, mighty man, of great will and large experience, should drop in a corner of the world and die, and finally be thought lucky—when he could think for himself no longer— to obtain a tranquil, unknown grave, and end with his initials, and have a water-wheel to sing to him. Many a time it set me crying, and made me long to lie down with him, until I thought of earth-worms.

All that could be done was done by Sampson and Firm Gundry, to let me have my clear path, and a clear bourne at the end of it. But even with a steam snow-shovel they could not have kept the way unstopped, such solid masses of the mountain clouds now descended over us. And never had I been so humored in my foolish wishes: I was quite ashamed to see the trouble great men took to please me.

"Well, I am sorry to hear it, Firm," said the Sawyer, coming in one day, with clouts of snow in his snowy curls. "Not that I care a cent for the fellow—and an impudenter fellow never sucked a pipe. Still, he might have had time to mend, if his time had been as good as the room for it. However, no blame rests on us. I told him to bed down to saw-mill. They Englishmen never know when they are well off. But the horse got home, they tell me?"

"The horse got home all right, grandfather, and so did the other horse and man. But Sylvester thinks that a pile of dollars must have died out in the snow-drift. It is a queer story. We shall never know the rights."

"How many times did I tell him," the Sawyer replied, without much discontent, "that it were a risky thing to try the gulches, such a night as that? His own way he would have, however; and finer liars than he could ever stick up to be for a score of years have gone, time upon time, to the land of truth by means of that same view of things. They take every body else for a liar."

"Oh, Uncle Sam, who is it?" I cried. "Is it that dreadful—that poor man who wanted to carry me away from you?"

"Now you go in, missy; you go to the fire-hearth," Mr. Gundry answered, more roughly than usual. "Leave you all such points to the Lord. They are not for young ladies to talk about."

"Grandfather, don't you be too hard," said Firm, as he saw me hurrying away. "Miss Rema has asked nothing unbecoming, but only concerning her own affairs. If we refuse to tell her, others will."

"Very well, then, so be it," the Sawyer replied; for he yielded more to his grandson than to the rest of the world put together. "Turn the log up, Firm, and put the pan on. You boys can go on without victuals all day, but an old man must feed regular. And, bad as he was, I thank God for sending him on his way home with his belly full. If ever he turneth up in the snow, that much can be proved to my account."

Young as I was, and little practiced in the ways of settlers, I could not help perceiving that Uncle Sam was very much put out—not at the death of the man so sadly, as at the worry of his dying so in going from a hospitable house. Mr. Gundry cared little what any body said concerning his honor, or courage, or such like; but the thought of a whisper against his hospitality would rouse him.

"Find him, Firm, find him," he said, in his deep sad voice, as he sat down on the antlered stump and gazed at the fire gloomily. "And when he is found, call a public postmortem, and prove that we gave him his bellyful."

Ephraim, knowing the old man's ways, and the manners, perhaps, of the neighborhood, beckoned to Suan to be quick with something hot, that he might hurry out again. Then he took his dinner standing, and without a word went forth to seek.

"Take the snow-harrow, and take Jowler," the old man shouted after him, and the youth turned round at the gate and waved his cap to show that he heard him. The snow was again falling heavily, and the afternoon was waning; and the last thing we saw was the brush of the mighty tail of the great dog Jowler.

"Oh, uncle, Firm will be lost himself!" I cried, in dismay at the great white waste. "And the poor man, whoever he is, must be dead. Do call him back, or let me run."

Mr. Gundry's only answer was to lead me back to the fireside, where he made me sit down, and examined me, while Suan was frying the butter-beans.

"Who was it spied you on the mountains, missy, the whole of the way from the redwood-tree, although you lay senseless on the ground, and he was hard at work with the loppings?"

"Why, Ephraim, of course, Uncle Sam; every body says that nobody else could have noticed such a thing at such a distance."

"Very well, my dear; and who was it carried you all the way to this house, without stopping, or even letting your head droop down, although it was a burning hot May morn?"

"Mr. Gundry, as if you did not know a great deal better than I do! It was weeks before I could thank him, even. But you must have seen him do it all."

The Sawyer rubbed his chin, which was large enough for a great deal of rubbing; and when he did that, I was always sure that an argument went to his liking. He said nothing more for the present, but had his dinner, and enjoyed it.

"Supposing now that he did all that," he resumed, about an hour afterward, "is Firm the sort of boy you would look to to lose his own self in a snow-drift? He has three men with him, and he is worth all three, let alone the big dog Jowler, who has dug out forty feet of snow ere now. If that rogue of an Englishman, Goad, has had the luck to cheat the hangman, and the honor to die in a Californy snow-drift, you may take my experience for it, missy, Firm and Jowler will find him, and clear Uncle Sam's reputation."

CHAPTER IX
WATER-SPOUT

If Mr. Gundry was in one way right, he was equally wrong in the other. Firm came home quite safe and sound, though smothered with snow and most hungry; but he thought that he should have staid out all the night, because he had failed of his errand. Jowler also was full of discontent and trouble of conscience. He knew, when he kicked up his heels in the snow, that his duty was to find somebody, and being of Alpine pedigree, and trained to act up to his ancestry, he now dropped his tail with failure.

"It comes to the same thing," said Sawyer Gundry; "it is foolish to be so particular. A thousand better men have sunk through being so pig-headed. We shall find the rogue toward the end of March, or in April, if the season suits. Firm, eat your supper and shake yourself."

This was exactly the Sawyer's way—to take things quietly when convinced that there was no chance to better them. He would always do his best about the smallest trifle; but after that, be the matter small or great, he had a smiling face for the end of it.

The winter, with all its weight of sameness and of dreariness, went at last, and the lovely spring from the soft Pacific found its gradual way to us. Accustomed as I was to gentler climates and more easy changes, I lost myself in admiration of this my first Californian spring. The flowers, the leagues and leagues of flowers, that burst into color and harmony—purple, yellow, and delicate lilac, woven with bright crimson threads, and fringed with emerald-green by the banks, and blue by the course of rivers, while deepened here and there by wooded shelter and cool places, with the silver-gray of the soft Pacific waning in far distance, and silken vapor drawing toward the carding forks of the mountain range; and over all the never-wearying azure of the limpid sky: child as I was, and full of little worldly troubles on my own account, these grand and noble sights enlarged me without any thinking.

The wheat and the maize were grown apace, and beans come into full blossom, and the peaches swinging in the western breeze were almost as large as walnuts, and all things in their prime of freshness, ere the yellow dust arrived, when a sudden melting of snow in some gully sent a strong flood down our Blue River. The saw-mill happened to be hard at work; and before the gear could be lifted, some damage was done to the floats by the heavy, impetuous rush of the torrent. Uncle Sam was away, and so was Firm; from which, perhaps, the mischief grew. However, the blame was all put on the river, and little more was said of it.

The following morning I went down before even Firm was out-of-doors, under some touch, perhaps, of natural desire to know things. The stream was as pure and bright as ever, hastening down its gravel-path of fine granite just as usual, except that it had more volume and a stronger sense of freshness. Only the bent of the grasses and the swath of the pendulous twigs down stream remained to show that there must have been some violence quite lately.

All Mr. Gundry's strengthening piles and shores were as firm as need be, and the clear blue water played around them as if they were no constraint to it. And none but a practiced eye could see that the great wheel had been wounded, being undershot, and lifted now above the power of the current, according to the fine old plan of locking the door when the horse is gone.

When I was looking up and wondering where to find the mischief, Martin, the foreman, came out and crossed the plank, with his mouth full of breakfast.

"Show me," I said, with an air, perhaps, of very young importance, "where and what the damage is. Is there any strain to the iron-work?"

"Lor' a mercy, young missus!" he answered, gruffly, being by no means a polished man, "where did you ever hear of ironwork? Needles and pins is enough for you. Now don't you go and make no mischief."

"I have no idea what you mean," I answered. "If you have been careless, that is no concern of mine."

"Careless, indeed! And the way I works, when others is a-snorin' in their beds! I might just as well do nort, every bit, and get more thanks and better wages. That's the way of the world all over. Come Saturday week, I shall better myself."

"But if it's the way of the world all over, how will you better yourself, unless you go out of the world altogether!" I put this question to Martin with the earnest simplicity of the young, meaning no kind of sarcasm, but knowing that scarcely a week went by without his threatening to "better himself." And they said that he had done so for seven years or more.

"Don't you be too sharp," he replied, with a grim smile, partly at himself, perhaps. "If half as I heard about you is true, you'll want all your sharpness for yourself, Miss Remy. And the Britishers are worse than we be."

"Well, Martin, I am sure you would help me," I said, "if you saw any person injuring me. But what is it I am not to tell your master?"

"My master, indeed! Well, you need not tell old Gundry any thing about what you have seen. It might lead to hard words; and hard words are not the style of thing I put up with. If any man tries hard words with me, I knocks him down, up sticks, and makes tracks."

I could not help smiling at the poor man's talk. Sawyer Gundry could have taken him with one hand and tossed him over the undershot wheel.

"You forget that I have not seen any thing," I said, "and understand nothing but 'needles and pins.' But, for fear of doing any harm, I will not even say that I have been down here, unless I am asked about it."

"Miss Remy, you are a good girl, and you shall have the mill some day. Lord, don't your little great eyes see the job they are a-doin' of? The finest stroke in all Californy, when the stubborn old chap takes to quartz-crushing."

All this was beyond me, and I told him so, and we parted good friends, while he shook his long head and went home to feed many pappooses. For the strangest thing of all things was, though I never at that time thought of it, that there was not any one about this place whom any one could help liking. Martin took as long as any body to be liked, until one understood him; but after that he was one of the best, in many ways that can not be described. Also there was a pair of negroes, simply and sweetly delightful. They worked all day and they sang all night, though I had not the pleasure of hearing them; and the more Suan Isco despised them—because they were black, and she was only brown—the more they made up to her, not at all because she governed the supply of victuals. It was childish to have such ideas, though Suan herself could never get rid of them. The truth, as I came to know afterward, was that a large, free-hearted, and determined man was at the head of every thing. Martin was the only one who ever grumbled, and he had established a long right to do so by never himself being grumbled at.

"I'll be bound that poor fellow is in a sad way," Mr. Gundry said at breakfast-time. "He knows how much he is to blame, and I fear that he won't eat a bit for the day. Martin is a most conscientious man. He will offer to give up his berth, although it would be his simple ruin."

I was wise enough not to say a word, though Firm looked at me keenly. He knew that I had been down at the mill, and expected me to say something.

"We all must have our little mistakes," continued Sawyer Gundry; "but I never like to push a man when he feels it. I shall not say a syllable to Martin; and, Ephraim, you will do the like. When a fellow sticks well to his work like Martin, never blame him for a mere accident."

Firm, according to his habit, made no answer when he did not quite agree. In talking with his own age he might have argued, but he did not argue with his grandfather.

"I shall just go down and put it right myself. Martin is a poor hand at repairing. Firm, you go up the gulch, and see if the fresh has hurt the hurdles. Missy, you may come with me, if you please, and sketch me at work in the mill-wheel. You have drawn that wheel such a sight of times, you must know every feather of it better than the man who made it."

"Uncle Sam, you are too bad," I said. "I have never got it right, and I never shall."

I did not dare as yet to think what really proved to be true in the end—that I could not draw the wheel correctly because itself was incorrect. In spite of all Mr. Gundry's skill and labor and ingenuity, the wheel was no true circle. The error began in the hub itself, and increased, of course, with the distance; but still it worked very well, like many other things that are not perfect.

Having no idea of this as yet, and doubting nothing except my own perception of "perspective," I sat down once more in my favorite spot, and waited for the master to appear as an active figure in the midst of it. The air was particularly bright and clear, even for that pure climate, and I could even see the blue-winged flies darting in and out of the oozy floats. But half-way up the mountains a white cloud was hanging, a cloud that kept on changing shape. I only observed it as a thing to put in for my background, because I was fond of trying to tone and touch up my sketches with French chalks.

Presently I heard a harsh metallic sound and creaking of machinery. The bites, or clamps, or whatever they are called, were being put on, to keep the wheel from revolving with the Sawyer's weight. Martin, the foreman, was grumbling and growling, according to his habit, and peering through the slot, or channel of stone, in which the axle worked, and the cheery voice of Mr. Gundry was putting down his objections. Being much too large to pass through the slot, Mr. Gundry came round the corner of the building, with a heavy leathern bag of tools strapped round his neck, and his canvas breeches girt above his knees. But the foreman staid inside to hand him the needful material into the wheel.

The Sawyer waded merrily down the shallow blue water, for he was always like a boy when he was at work, and he waved his little skull-cap to me, and swung himself up into the wheel, as if he were nearer seventeen than seventy. And presently I could only see his legs and arms as he fell to work. Therefore I also fell to work, with my best attempts at penciling, having been carefully taught enough of drawing to know that I could not draw. And perhaps I caught from the old man's presence and the sound of his activity that strong desire to do my best which he seemed to impart to every one.

At any rate, I was so engrossed that I scarcely observed the changing light, except as a hindrance to my work and a trouble to my distance, till suddenly some great drops fell upon my paper and upon my hat, and a rush of dark wind almost swept me from the log upon which I sat. Then again all was a perfect calm, and the young leaves over the stream hung heavily on their tender foot-stalks, and the points of the breeze-swept grass turned back, and the ruffle of all things smoothed itself. But there seemed to be a sense of fear in the waiting silence of earth and air.

This deep, unnatural stillness scared me, and I made up my mind to run away. But the hammer of the Sawyer sounded as I had never heard it sound. He was much too hard at work to pay any heed to sky or stream, and the fall of his strokes was dead and hollow, as if the place resented them.

"Come away, come away," I cried, as I ran and stood on the opposite bank to him; "there is something quite wrong in the weather, I am sure. I entreat you to come away at once, Uncle Sam. Every thing is so strange and odd."

"Why, what's to do now?" asked the Sawyer, coming to my side of the wheel and looking at me, with his spectacles tilted up, and his apron wedged in a piece of timber, and his solid figure resting in the impossibility of hurry. "Missy, don't you make a noise out there. You can't have your own way always."

"Oh, Uncle Sam, don't talk like that. I am in such a fright about you. Do come out and look at the mountains."

"I have seen the mountains often enough, and I am up to every trick of them. There may be a corn or two of rain; no more. My sea-weed was like tinder. There can't be no heavy storm when it is like that. Don't you make pretense, missy, to know what is beyond you."

Uncle Sam was so seldom cross that I always felt that he had a right to be so. And he gave me one of his noble smiles to make up for the sharpness of his words, and then back he went to his work again. So I hoped that I was altogether wrong, till a bolt of lightning, like a blue dagger, fell at my very feet, and a crash of thunder shook the earth and stunned me. These opened the sluice of the heavens, and before I could call out I was drenched with rain. Clinging to a bush, I saw the valley lashed with cloudy blasts, and a whirling mass of spiral darkness rushing like a giant toward me. And the hissing and tossing and roaring mixed whatever was in sight together.

Such terror fell upon me at first that I could not look, and could scarcely think, but cowered beneath the blaze of lightning as a singed moth drops and shivers. And a storm of wind struck me from my hold, so that I fell upon the wet earth. Every moment I expected to be killed, for I never could be brave in a thunder-storm, and had not been told much in France of God's protection around me. And the darts of lightning hissed and crossed like a blue and red web over me. So I laid hold of a little bent of weed, and twisted it round my dabbled wrist, and tried to pray to the Virgin, although I had often been told it was vanity.

Then suddenly wiping my eyes, I beheld a thing which entirely changed me. A vast, broad wall of brown water, nearly as high as the mill itself, rushed down with a crest of foam from the mountains. It seemed to fill up all the valley and to swallow up all the trees; a whole host of animals fled before it, and birds, like a volley of bullets, flew by. I lost not a moment in running away, and climbing a rock and hiding. It was base, ungrateful, and a nasty thing to do; but I did it almost without thinking. And if I had staid to cry out, what good could I have done—only to be swept away?

Now, as far as I can remember any thing out of so much horror, I must have peeped over the summit of my rock when the head of the deluge struck the mill. But whether I saw it, or whether I knew it by any more summary process, such as outruns the eyes sometimes, is more than I dare presume to say. Whichever way I learned it, it was thus:

A solid mass of water, much bigger than the mill itself, burst on it, dashed it to atoms, leaped off with it, and spun away the great wheel anyhow, like the hoop of a child sent trundling. I heard no scream or shriek; and, indeed, the bellow of a lion would have been a mere whisper in the wild roar of the elements. Only, where the mill had been, there was nothing except a black streak and a boil in the deluge. Then scores of torn-up trees swept over, as a bush-harrow jumps on the clods of the field; and the unrelenting flood cast its wrath, and shone quietly in the lightning.

"Oh, Uncle Sam! Uncle Sam!" I cried. But there was not a sign to be seen of him; and I thought of his gentle, good, obstinate ways, and my heart was almost broken. "What a brute—what a wretch I am!" I kept saying, as if I could have helped it; and my fear of the lightning was gone, and I stood and raved with scorn and amazement.

In this misery of confusion it was impossible to think, and instinct alone could have driven my despair to a desperate venture. With my soaked clothes sticking between my legs, I ran as hard as they would go, by a short-cut over a field of corn, to a spot where the very last bluff or headland jutted into the river. This was a good mile below the mill according to the bends of channel, but only a furlong or so from the rock upon which I had taken refuge. However, the flood was there before me, and the wall of water dashed on to the plains, with a brindled comb behind it.

Behind it also came all the ruin of the mill that had any floatage, and bodies of bears and great hogs and cattle, some of them alive, but the most part dead. A grand black bull tossed back his horns, and looked at me beseechingly: he had frightened me often in quiet days, but now I was truly grieved for him. And then on a wattle of brush-wood I saw the form of a man—the Sawyer.

His white hair draggled in the wild brown flood, and the hollow of his arms was heaped with froth, and his knotted legs hung helpless. Senseless he lay on his back, and sometimes the wash of the waves went over him. His face was livid, but his brave eyes open, and a heavy weight hung round his neck. I had no time to think, and deserve no praise, for I knew not what I did. But just as an eddy swept him near me, I made a desperate leap at him, and clutched at something that tore my hands, and then I went under the water. My senses, however, were not yet gone, and my weight on the wattle stopped it, and I came up gurgling, and flung one arm round a fat, woolly sheep going by me. The sheep was water-logged, and could scarcely keep his own poor head from drowning, and he turned his mild eyes and looked at me, but I could not spare him. He struck for the shore in forlorn hope, and he towed us in some little.

It is no good for me to pretend to say how things were managed for us, for of course I could do nothing. But the sheep must have piloted us to a tree, whose branches swept the torrent. Here I let him go, and caught fast hold; and Uncle Sam's raft must have stuck there also, for what could my weak arm have done? I remember only to have felt the ground at last, as the flood was exhausted; and good people came and found him and me, stretched side by side, upon rubbish and mud.

CHAPTER X
A NUGGET

In a sacred corner (as soon as ever we could attend to any thing) we hung up the leathern bag of tools, which had done much more toward saving the life of Uncle Sam than I did; for this had served as a kind of kedge, or drag, upon his little craft, retarding it from the great roll of billows, in which he must have been drowned outright. And even as it was, he took some days before he was like himself again.

Firm, who had been at the head of the valley, repairing some broken hurdles, declared that a water-spout had burst in the bosom of the mountain gorge where the Blue River has its origin, and the whole of its power got ponded back by a dam, which the Sawyer himself had made, at about five furlongs above the mill. Ephraim, being further up the gulch, and high above the roaring flood, did his utmost with the keen edge of his eyes to pierce into the mischief; but it rained so hard, and at the same time blew so violently around him, that he could see nothing of what went on, but hoped for the best, with uneasiness.

Now when the Sawyer came round so well as to have a clear mind of things, and learn that his mill was gone and his business lost, and himself, at this ripe time of life, almost driven to begin the world again, it was natural to expect that he ought to indulge in a good deal of grumbling. Many people came to comfort him, and to offer him deep condolence and the truest of true sympathy, and every thing that could be thought of, unless it were a loan of money. Of that they never thought, because it was such a trifling matter; and they all had confidence in his power to do any thing but pay them. They told him that he was a young man still, and Providence watched over him; in a year or two he would be all the better for this sad visitation. And he said yes to their excellent advice, and was very much obliged to them. At the same time it was clear to me, who watched him like a daughter, that he became heavy in his mind, and sighed, as these kind friends, one after the other, enjoyed what he still could do for them, but rode away out of his gate with too much delicacy to draw purse-strings. Not that he would have accepted a loan from the heartiest heart of all of them, only that he would have liked the offer, to understand their meaning. And several of them were men—as Firm, in his young indignation, told me—who had been altogether set up in life by the kindness of Sampson Gundry.

Perhaps the Sawyer, after all his years, had no right to be vexed by this. But whether he was right or wrong, I am sure that it preyed upon his mind, though he was too proud to speak of it. He knew that he was not ruined, although these friends assumed that he must be; and some of them were quite angry with him because they had vainly warned him. He could not remember these warnings, yet he contradicted none of them; and fully believing in the goodness of the world, he became convinced that he must have been hard in the days of his prosperity.

No sooner was he able to get about again than he went to San Francisco to raise money on his house and property for the rebuilding of the mill. Firm rode with him to escort him back, and so did Martin, the foreman; for although the times were not so bad as they used to be some ten years back, in the height of the gold fever, it still was a highly undesirable thing for a man who was known to have money about him to ride forth alone from San Francisco, or even Sacramento town. And having mentioned the foreman Martin, in justice to him I ought to say that although his entire loss from the disaster amounted only to a worn-out waistcoat of the value of about twenty cents, his vehemence in grumbling could only be equaled by his lofty persistence. By his great activity in running away and leaving his employer to meet the brunt, he had saved not only himself, but his wife and children and goods and chattels. This failed, however, to remove or even assuage his regret for the waistcoat; and he moaned and threatened to such good purpose that a speedy subscription was raised, which must have found him in clothes for the rest of his life, as well as a silver tea-pot with an inscription about his bravery.

When the three were gone, after strict injunctions from Mr. Gundry, and his grandson too, that I was on no account to venture beyond calling distance from the house, for fear of being run away with, I found the place so sad and lonesome that I scarcely knew what to do. I had no fear of robbers, though there were plenty in the neighborhood; for we still had three or four men about, who could be thoroughly trusted, and who staid with us on half wages rather than abandon the Sawyer in his trouble. Suan Isco, also, was as brave as any man, and could shoot well with a rifle. Moreover, the great dog Jowler was known and dreaded by all his enemies. He could pull down an Indian, or two half-castes, or three Mexicans, in about a second; and now he always went about with me, having formed a sacred friendship.

Uncle Sam had kissed me very warmly when he said "good-by," and Firm had shown some disposition to follow his example; but much as I liked and admired Firm, I had my own ideas as to what was unbecoming, and now in my lonely little walks I began to think about it. My father's resting-place had not been invaded by the imperious flood, although a line of driftage, in a zigzag swath, lay near the mound. This was my favorite spot for thinking, when I felt perplexed and downcast in my young unaided mind. For although I have not spoken of my musings very copiously, any one would do me wrong who fancied that I was indifferent. Through the great kindness of Mr. Gundry and other good friends around me, I had no bitter sense as yet of my own dependence and poverty. But the vile thing I had heard about my father, the horrible slander and wicked falsehood — for such I was certain it must be — this was continually in my thoughts, and quite destroyed my cheerfulness. And the worst of it was that I never could get my host to enter into it. Whenever I began, his face would change and his manner grow constrained, and his chief desire always seemed to lead me to some other subject.

One day, when the heat of the summer came forth, and the peaches began to blush toward it, and bronze-ribbed figs grew damask-gray with a globule of sirup in their eyes, and melons and pumpkins already had curved their fluted stalks with heaviness, and the dust of the plains was beginning to fly, and the bright spring flowers were dead more swiftly even than they first were born, I sat with Suan Isco at my father's cross, and told her to make me cry with some of all the many sad things she knew. She knew a wondrous number of things insatiably sad and wild; and the quiet way in which she told them (not only without any horror, but as if they were rightly to be expected), also the deep and rather guttural tone of voice, and the stillness of the form, made it impossible to help believing verily every word she said.

That there should be in the world such things, so dark, unjust, and full of woe, was enough to puzzle a child brought up among the noblest philosophers; whereas I had simply been educated by good unpretentious women, who had partly retired from the world, but not to such a depth as to drown all thought of what was left behind them. These were ready at any time to return upon good opportunity; and some of them had done so, with many tears, when they came into property.

"Please to tell me no more now," I said at last to Suan; "my eyes are so sore they will be quite red, and perhaps Uncle Sam will come home to-night. I am afraid he has found some trouble with the money, or he ought to have been at home before. Don't you think so, Suan?"

"Yes, yes; trouble with the money. Always with the white mans that."

"Very well. I shall go and look for some money. I had a most wonderful dream last night. Only I must go quite alone. You had better go and look to the larder, Suan. If they come, they are sure to be hungry."

"Yes, yes; the white mans always hungry, sep when thirsty."

The Indian woman, who had in her heart a general contempt for the white race, save those of our own household, drew her bright-colored shawl around her, and set off with her peculiar walk. Her walk was not ungraceful, because it was so purely natural; but it differed almost as much as the step of a quadruped from what we are taught. I, with heavy thoughts but careless steps, set off on my wanderings. I wanted to try to have no set purpose, course, or consideration, but to go wherever chance should lead me, without choice, as in my dream. And after many vague turns, and even closings of rebellious eyes, I found myself, perhaps by the force of habit, at the ruins of the mill.

I seemed to recognize some resemblance (which is as much as one can expect) to the scene which had been in my sleep before me. But sleeping I had seen roaring torrents; waking, I beheld a quiet stream. The little river, as blue as ever, and shrinking from all thoughts of wrath, showed nothing in its pure gaze now but a gladness to refresh and cool. In many nicely sheltered corners it was full of soft reflection as to the good it had to do; and then, in silver and golden runnels, on it went to do it. And the happy voice and many sweetly flashing little glances told that it knew of the lovely lives beside it, created and comforted by itself.

But I looked at the dark ruin it had wrought, and like a child I was angry with it for the sake of Uncle Sam. Only the foundations and the big heavy stones of the mill were left, and the clear bright water purled around, or made little eddies among them. All were touched with silvery sound, and soft caressing dimples. But I looked at the passionate mountains first, to be sure of no more violence; for if a burned child dreads the fire, one half drowned may be excused for little faith in water. The mountains in the sunshine looked as if nothing could move their grandeur, and so I stepped from stone to stone, in the bed of the placid brightness.

Presently I came to a place where one of the great black piles, driven in by order of the Sawyer, to serve as a back-stay for his walls, had been swept by the flood from its vertical sinking, but had not been swept away. The square tarred post of mountain pine reclined down stream, and gently nodded to the current's impact. But overthrown as it was, it could not make its exit and float away, as all its brethren had done. At this I had wondered before, and now I went to see what the reason was. By throwing a short piece of plank from one of the shattered foundations into a nick in the shoulder of the reclining pile, I managed to get there and sit upon it, and search for its obstruction.

The water was flowing smoothly toward me, and as clear as crystal, being scarcely more than a foot in depth. And there, on the upper verge of the hole, raised by the leverage of the butt from the granite sand of the river-bed, I saw a great bowlder of rich yellow light. I was so much amazed that I cried out at once, "Oh! what a beautiful great yellow fish!" And I shouted to Jowler, who had found where I was, and followed me, as usual. The great dog was famous for his love of fishing, and had often brought a fine salmon forth.

Jowler was always a zealous fellow, and he answered eagerly to my call by dashing at once into the water, and following the guidance of my hand. But when he saw what I pointed at, he was bitterly disappointed, and gave me to understand as much by looking at me foolishly. "Now don't be a stupid dog," I said; "do what I tell you immediately. Whatever it is, bring it out, Sir."

Jowler knew that I would be obeyed whenever I called him "Sir;" so he ducked his great head under the water, and tugged with his teeth at the object. His back corded up, and his tail grew rigid with the intensity of his labor, but the task was quite beyond him. He could not even stir the mighty mass at which he struggled, but he bit off a little projecting corner, and came to me with it in his mouth. Then he laid his dripping jaws on my lap, and his ears fell back, and his tail hung down with utter sense of failure.

I patted his broad intelligent forehead, and wiped his black eyes with his ears, and took from his lips what he offered to me. Then I saw that his grinders were framed with gold, as if he had been to a dentist regardless of expense, and into my hand he dropped a lump of solid glittering virgin ore. He had not the smallest idea of having done any thing worthy of human applause; and he put out his long red tongue and licked his teeth to get rid of uneatable dross, and gave me a quiet nudge to ask what more I wanted of him.

CHAPTER XI
ROVERS

From Jowler I wanted nothing more. Such matters were too grand for him. He had beaten the dog of Hercules, who had only brought the purple dye—a thing requiring skill and art and taste to give it value. But gold does well without all these, and better in their absence. From handling many little nuggets, and hearkening to Suan Isco's tales of treachery, theft, and murder done by white men for the sake of this, I knew that here I had found enough to cost the lives of fifty men.

At present, however, I was not possessed with dread so much as I was with joy, and even a secret exultation, at the power placed in my hands. For I was too young to moralize or attempt philosophy. Here I had a knowledge which the wisest of mankind might envy, much as they despise it when they have no chance of getting it. I looked at my father's grave, in the shadow of the quiet peach-trees, and I could not help crying as I thought that this was come too late for him. Then I called off Jowler, who wished (like a man) to have another tug at it; and home I ran to tell my news, but failing of breath, had time to think.

It was lucky enough that this was so, for there might have been the greatest mischief; and sadly excited as I was, the trouble I had seen so much of came back to my beating heart and told me to be careful. But surely there could be no harm in trusting Suan Isco. However, I looked at her several times, and was not quite so sure about it. She was wonderfully true and faithful, and scarcely seemed to concede to gold its paramount rank and influence. But that might only have been because she had never known the want of it, or had never seen a lump worth stealing, which I was sure that this must be; and the unregenerate state of all who have never been baptized had been impressed on me continually. How could I mistrust a Christian, and place confidence in an Indian? Therefore I tried to sleep without telling any one, but was unable.

But, as it happened, my good discovery did not keep me so very long awake, for on the following day our troop of horsemen returned from San Francisco. Of course I have done very foolish things once and again throughout my life, but perhaps I never did any thing more absurd than during the whole of that day. To begin with, I was up before the sun, and down at the mill, and along the plank, which I had removed overnight, but now replaced as my bridge to the pine-wood pile. Then I gazed with eager desire and fear—which was the stronger I scarcely knew—for the yellow under-gleam, to show the safety of my treasure. There it lay, as safe as could be, massive, grand, and beautiful, with tones of varying richness as the ripples varied over it. The pale light of the morning breathed a dewy lustre down the banks; the sun (although unrisen yet) drew furrows through the mountain gaps; the birds from every hanging tree addressed the day with melody; the crystal water, purer than religion's brightest dream, went by; and here among them lay, unmoved, unthought of, and inanimate, the thing which to a human being is worth all the rest put together.

This contemplation had upon me an effect so noble that here I resolved to spend my time, for fear of any robbery. I was afraid to gaze more than could be helped at this grand sight, lest other eyes should spy what was going on, and long to share it. And after hurrying home to breakfast and returning in like haste, I got a scare, such as I well deserved, for being so extremely foolish.

The carpentry of the mill-wheel had proved so very stanch and steadfast that even in that raging deluge the whole had held together. It had been bodily torn from its hold and swept away down the valley; but somewhere it grounded, as the flood ebbed out, and a strong team had tugged it back again. And the Sawyer had vowed that, come what would, his mill should work with the self-same wheel which he with younger hands had wrought. Now this wheel (to prevent any warp, and save the dry timber from the sun) was laid in a little shady cut, where water trickled under it. And here I had taken up my abode to watch my monster nugget.

I had pulled my shoes and stockings off, and was paddling in the runnel, sheltered by the deep rim of the wheel, and enjoying the water. Little fish darted by me, and lovely spotted lizards played about, and I was almost beginning even to forget my rock of gold. In self-defense it is right to say that for the gold, on my own account, I cared as much as I might have done for a fig worm-eaten. It was for Uncle Sam, and all his dear love, that I watched the gold, hoping in his sad disaster to restore his fortunes. But suddenly over the rim of the wheel (laid flat in the tributary brook) I descried across the main river a moving company of horsemen.

These men could have nothing to do with Uncle Sam and his party, for they were coming from the mountain-side, while he would return by the track across the plains. And they were already so near that I could see their dress quite plainly, and knew them to be Mexican rovers, mixed with loose Americans. There are few worse men on the face of the earth than these, when in the humor, and unluckily they seem almost always to be in that humor. Therefore, when I saw their battered sun-hats and baggy slouching boots, I feared that little ruth, or truth, or mercy dwelt between them.

On this account I shrank behind the shelter of the mill-wheel, and held my head in one trembling hand, and with the other drew my wind-tossed hair into small compass. For my blood ran cold at the many dreadful things that came into my mind. I was sure that they had not spied me yet, and my overwhelming desire was to decline all introduction.

I counted fourteen gentlemen, for so they always styled themselves, and would pistol any man who expressed a contrary opinion. Fourteen of them rode to the brink of the quiet blue river on the other side; and there they let their horses drink, and some dismounted and filled canteens, and some of longer reach stooped from the saddle and did likewise. But one, who seemed to be the captain, wanted no water for his rum.

"Cut it short, boys," I heard him say, with a fine South Californian twang (which, as well as his free swearing, I will freely omit). "If we mean to have fair play with the gal, now or never's the time for it: old Sam may come home almost any time."

What miserable cowards! Though there were so many of them, they really had no heart to face an old man known for courage. Frightened as I was, perhaps good indignation helped me to flutter no more, and not faint away, but watch those miscreants steadily.

The horses put down their sandy lips over and over again to drink, scarcely knowing when they ought to stop, and seemed to get thicker before my eyes. The dribbling of the water from their mouths prepared them to begin again, till the riders struck the savage unroweled spur into their refreshment. At this they jerked their noses up, and looked at one another to say that they expected it, and then they lifted their weary legs and began to plash through the river.

It is a pretty thing to see a skillful horse plod through a stream, probing with his eyes the depth, and stretching his head before his feet, and at every step he whisks his tail to tell himself that he is right. In my agony of observation all these things I heeded, but only knew that I had done so when I thought long afterward. At the moment I was in such a fright that my eyes worked better than my mind. However, even so, I thought of my golden millstone, and was aware that they crossed below, and could not see it.

They gained the bank upon our side within fifty yards of where I crouched; and it was not presence of mind, but abject fear, which kept me crouching. I counted them again as they leaped the bank and seemed to look at me. I could see the dark array of eyes, and could scarcely keep from shrieking. But my throat was dry and made no sound, and a frightened bird set up a scream, which drew off their attention.

In perils of later days I often thought of this fear, and almost felt that the hand of Heaven had been stretched forth on purpose to help my helplessness.

For the moment, however, I lay as close as if under the hand of the evil one; and the snorting of the horses passed me, and wicked laughter of the men. One was telling a horrible tale, and the rest rejoicing in it; and the bright sun, glowing on their withered skin, discovered perhaps no viler thing in all the world to shine upon. One of them even pointed at my mill-wheel with a witty gibe—at least, perhaps, it was wit to him—about the Sawyer's misfortune; but the sun was then in his eyes, and my dress was just of the color of the timber. So on they rode, and the pleasant turf (having lately received some rain) softly answered to the kneading of their hoofs as they galloped away to surround the house.

I was just at the very point of rising and running up into the dark of the valley, when a stroke of arithmetic stopped me. Fourteen men and fourteen horses I had counted on the other side; on this side I could not make any more than thirteen of them. I might have made a mistake; but still I thought I would stop just a minute to see. And in that minute I saw the other man walking slowly on the opposite bank. He had tethered his horse, and was left as outpost to watch and give warning of poor Uncle Sam's return.

At the thought of this, my frightened courage, in some extraordinary way, came back. I had played an ignoble part thus far, as almost any girl might have done. But now I resolved that, whatever might happen, my dear friend and guardian should not be entrapped and lose his life through my cowardice. We had been expecting him all the day; and if he should come and fall into an ambush, I only might survive to tell the tale. I ought to have hurried and warned the house, as my bitter conscience told me; but now it was much too late for that. The only amends that I could make was to try and warn our travelers.

Stooping as low as I could, and watching my time to cross the more open places when the sentry was looking away from me, I passed up the winding of the little watercourse, and sheltered in the swampy thicket which concealed its origin. Hence I could see for miles over the plain—broad reaches of corn land already turning pale, mazy river fringed with reed, hamlets scattered among clustering trees, and that which I chiefly cared to see, the dusty track from Sacramento.

Whether from ignorance of the country or of Mr. Gundry's plans, the sentinel had been posted badly. His beat commanded well enough the course from San Francisco; but that from Sacramento was not equally clear before him. For a jut of pine forest ran down from the mountains and cut off a part of his view of it. I had not the sense or the presence of mind to perceive this great advantage, but having a plain, quick path before me, forth I set upon it. Of course if the watchman had seen me, he would have leaped on his horse and soon caught me; but of that I scarcely even thought, I was in such confusion.

When I had run perhaps a mile (being at that time very slight, and of active figure), I saw a cloud of dust, about two miles off, rising through the bright blue haze. It was rich yellow dust of the fertile soil, which never seems to cake or clot. Sometimes you may walk for miles without the smallest fear of sinking, the earth is so elastic. And yet with a slight exertion you may push a walking-stick down through it until the handle stops it. My heart gave a jump: that cloud of dust was a sign of men on horseback. And who could it be but Uncle Sam and Firm and the foreman Martin?

As soon as it began to show itself, it proved to be these very three, carelessly lounging on their horses' backs, overcome with heat and dust and thirst. But when they saw me there all alone under the fury of the sun, they knew that something must have gone amiss, and were all wide awake in a moment.

"Well, now," said the Sawyer, when I had told my tale as well as short breath allowed, "put this thing over your head, my dear, or you may gain a sun-stroke. I call it too bad of them skunks to drive you in Californy noon, like this."

"Oh, Uncle Sam, never think of me; think of your house and your goods and Suan, and all at those bad men's mercy!"

"The old house ain't afire yet," he answered, looking calmly under his hand in that direction. "And as for Suan, no fear at all. She knows how to deal with such gallowses; and they will keep her to cook their dinner. Firm, my lad, let us go and embrace them. They wouldn't 'a made much bones of shooting us down if we hadn't known of it, and if they had got miss afore the saddle. But if they don't give bail, as soon as they see me ride up to my door, my name's not Sampson Gundry. Only you keep out of the way, Miss Remy. You go to sleep a bit, that's a dear, in the graywitch spinny yonder, and wait till you hear Firm sound the horn. And then come you in to dinner-time; for the Lord is always over you."

I hastened to the place which he pointed out—a beautiful covert of birch-trees—but to sleep was out of the question, worn out though I was with haste and heat, and (worst of all) with horror. In a soft mossy nest, where a breeze from the mountains played with the in and out ways of the wood, and the murmurous dream of genial insects now was beginning to drowse upon the air, and the heat of the sun could almost be seen thrilling through the alleys like a cicale's drum—here, in the middle of the languid peace, I waited for the terror of the rifle-crack.

For though Uncle Sam had spoken softly, and made so little of the peril he would meet, I had seen in his eyes some token of the deep wrath and strong indignation which had kept all his household and premises safe. And it seemed a most ominous sign that Firm had never said a word, but grasped his gun, and slowly got in front of his grandfather.

CHAPTER XII
GOLD AND GRIEF

It may have been an hour, but it seemed an age, ere the sound of the horn, in Firm's strong blast, released me from my hiding-place. I had heard no report of fire-arms, nor perceived any sign of conflict; and certainly the house was not on fire, or else I must have seen the smoke. For being still in great alarm, I had kept a very sharp lookout.

Ephraim Gundry came to meet me, which was very kind of him. He carried his bugle in his belt, that he might sound again for me, if needful. But I was already running toward the house, having made up my mind to be resolute. Nevertheless, I was highly pleased to have his company, and hear what had been done.

"Please to let me help you," he said, with a smile. "Why, miss, you are trembling dreadfully. I assure you there is no cause for that."

"But you might have been killed, and Uncle Sam, and Martin, and every body. Oh, those men did look so horrible!"

"Yes, they always do till you come to know them. But bigger cowards were never born. If they can take people by surprise, and shoot them without any danger, it is a splendid treat to them. But if any one like grandfather meets them face to face in the daylight, their respect for law and life returns. It is not the first visit they have paid us. Grandfather kept his temper well. It was lucky for them that he did."

Remembering that the Rovers must have numbered nearly three to one, even if all our men were stanch, I thought it lucky for ourselves that there had been no outbreak. But Firm seemed rather sorry that they had departed so easily. And knowing that he never bragged, I began to share his confidence.

"They must be shot, sooner or later," he said, "unless, indeed, they should be hanged. Their manner of going on is out of date in these days of settlement. It was all very well ten years ago. But now we are a civilized State, and the hand of law is over us. I think we were wrong to let them go.

But of course I yield to the governor. And I think he was afraid for your sake. And to tell the truth, I may have been the same."

Here he gave my arm a little squeeze, which appeared to me quite out of place; therefore I withdrew and hurried on. Before he could catch me I entered the door, and found the Sawyer sitting calmly with his own long pipe once more, and watching Suan cooking.

"They rogues have had all the best of our victuals," he said, as soon as he had kissed me. "Respectable visitors is my delight, and welcome to all of the larder; but at my time of life it goes agin the grain to lease out my dinner to galley-rakers. Suan, you are burning the fat again."

Suan Isco, being an excellent cook (although of quiet temper), never paid heed to criticism, but lifted her elbow and went on. Mr. Gundry knew that it was wise to offer no further meddling, although it is well to keep them up to their work by a little grumbling. But when I came to see what broken bits were left for Suan to deal with, I only wondered that he was not cross.

"Thank God for a better meal than I deserve," he said, when they all had finished. "Suan, you are a treasure, as I tell you every day a'most. Now if they have left us a bottle of wine, let us have it up. We be all in the dumps. But that will never do, my lad."

He patted Firm on the shoulder, as if he were the younger man of the two, and his grandson went down to the wreck of the cellar; while I, who had tried to wait upon them in an eager, clumsy way, perceived that something was gone amiss, something more serious and lasting than the mischief made by the robber troop. Was it that his long ride had failed, and not a friend could be found to help him?

When Martin and the rest were gone, after a single glass of wine, and Ephraim had made excuse of something to be seen to, the Sawyer leaned back in his chair, and his cheerful face was troubled. I filled his pipe and lit it for him, and waited for him to speak, well knowing his simple and outspoken heart. But he looked at me and thanked me kindly, and seemed to be turning some grief in his mind.

"It ain't for the money," he said at last, talking more to himself than to me; "the money might 'a been all very well and useful in a sort of way. But the feelin'—the feelin' is the thing I look at, and it ought to have been more hearty. Security! Charge on my land, indeed! And I can run away, but my land must stop behind! What security did I ask of them? 'Tis enough a'most to make a rogue of me."

"Nothing could ever do that, Uncle Sam," I exclaimed, as I came and sat close to him, while he looked at me bravely, and began to smile.

"Why, what was little missy thinking of?" he asked. "How solid she looks! Why, I never see the like!"

"Then you ought to have seen it, Uncle Sam. You ought to have seen it fifty times, with every body who loves you. And who can help loving you, Uncle Sam?"

"Well, they say that I charged too much for lumber, a-cuttin' on the cross, and the backstroke work. And it may 'a been so, when I took agin a man. But to bring up all that, with the mill strown down, is a cowardly thing, to my thinking. And to make no count of the beadin' I threw in, whenever it were a straightforrard job, and the turpsy knots, and the clogging of the teeth—'tis a bad bit to swallow, when the mill is strown."

"But the mill shall not be strown, Uncle Sam. The mill shall be built again. And I will find the money."

Mr. Gundry stared at me and shook his head. He could not bear to tell me how poor I was, while I thought myself almost made of money. "Five thousand dollars you have got put by for me," I continued, with great importance. "Five thousand dollars from the sale and the insurance fund. And five thousand dollars must be five-and-twenty thousand francs. Uncle Sam, you shall have every farthing of it. And if that won't build the mill again, I have got my mother's diamonds."

"Five thousand dollars!" cried the Sawyer, in amazement, opening his great gray eyes at me. And then he remembered the tale which he had told, to make me seem independent. "Oh yes, to be sure, my dear; now I recollect. To be sure—to be sure—your own five thousand dollars. But never will I touch one cent of your nice little fortune; no, not to save my life. After all, I am not so gone in years but what I can build the mill again myself. The Lord hath spared my hands and eyes, and gifted me still with machinery. And Firm is a very handy lad, and can carry out a job pretty fairly, with better brains to stand over him, although it has not pleased the Lord to gift him with sense of machinery, like me. But that is all for the best, no doubt. If Ephraim had too much of brains, he might have contradicted me. And that I could never abide, God knows, from any green young jackanapes."

"Oh, Uncle Sam, let me tell you something—something very important!"

"No, my dear, nothing more just now. It has done me good to have a little talk, and scared the blue somethings out of me. But just go and ask whatever is become of Firm. He was riled with them greasers. It was all I could do to keep the boy out of a difficulty with them. And if they camp any where nigh, it is like enough he may go hankerin' after them. The grand march of intellect hathn't managed yet to march old heads upon young shoulders. And Firm might happen to go outside the law."

The thought of this frightened me not a little; for Firm, though mild of speech, was very hot of spirit at any wrong, as I knew from tales of Suan Isco, who had brought him up and made a glorious idol of him. And now, when she could not say where he was, but only was sure that he must be quite safe (in virtue of a charm from a great medicine man which she had hung about him), it seemed to me, according to what I was used to, that in these regions human life was held a great deal too lightly.

It was not for one moment that I cared about Firm, any more than is the duty of a fellow-creature. He was a very good young man, and in his way good-looking, educated also quite enough, and polite, and a very good carver of a joint; and when I spoke, he nearly always listened. But of course he was not to be compared as yet to his grandfather, the true Sawyer.

When I ran back from Suan Isco, who was going on about her charm, and the impossibility of any one being scalped who wore it, I found Mr. Gundry in a genial mood. He never made himself uneasy about any trifles. He always had a very pure and lofty faith in the ways of Providence, and having lost his only son Elijah, he was sure that he never could lose Firm. He had taken his glass of hot whiskey and water, which always made him temperate; and if he felt any of his troubles deeply, he dwelt on them now from a high point of view.

"I may 'a said a little too much, my dear, about the badness of mankind," he observed, with his pipe lying comfortably on his breast; "all sayings of that sort is apt to go too far. I ought to have made more allowance for the times, which gets into a ticklish state, when a old man is put about with them. Never you pay no heed whatever to any harsh words I may have used. All that is a very bad thing for young folk."

"But if they treated you badly, Uncle Sam, how can you think that they treated you well?"

He took some time to consider this, because he was true in all his thoughts; and then he turned off to something else.

"Why, the smashing of the mill may have been a mercy, although in disguise to the present time of sight. It will send up the price of scantlings, and we was getting on too fast with them. By the time we have built up the mill again we shall have more orders than we know how to do with. When I come to reckon of it, to me it appears to be the reasonable thing to feel a lump of grief for the old mill, and then to set to and build a stronger one. Yes, that must be about the right thing to do. And we'll have all the neighbors in when we lay foundations."

"But what will be the good of it, Uncle Sam, when the new mill may at any time be washed away again?"

"Never, at any time," he answered, very firmly, gazing through the door as if he saw the vain endeavor. "That little game can easily be stopped, for about fifty dollars, by opening down the bank toward the old track of the river. The biggest waterspout that ever came down from the mountains could never come anigh the mill, but go right down the valley. It hath been in my mind to do it often, and now that I see the need, I will. Firm and I will begin tomorrow."

"But where is all the money to come from, Uncle Sam? You said that all your friends had refused to help you."

"Never mind, my dear. I will help myself. It won't be the first time, perhaps, in my life."

"But supposing that I could help you, just some little? Supposing that I had found the biggest lump of gold ever found in all California?"

Mr. Gundry ought to have looked surprised, and I was amazed that he did not; but he took it as quietly as if I had told him that I had just picked up a brass button of his; and I thought that he doubted my knowledge, very likely, even as to what gold was.

"It is gold, Uncle Sam, every bit of it gold—here is a piece of it; just look—and as large, I am sure, as this table. And it may be as deep as this room, for all that one can judge to the contrary. Why, it stopped the big pile from coming to the top, when even you went down the river."

"Well, now, that explains a thing or two," said the Sawyer, smiling peacefully, and beginning to think of another pipe, if preparation meant any thing. "Two things have puzzled me about that stump, and, indeed, I might say three things. Why did he take such a time to drive? and why would he never stand up like a man? and why wouldn't he go away when he ought to?"

"Because he had the best of all reasons, Uncle Sam. He was anchored on his gold, as I have read in French, and he had a good right to be crooked about it, and no power could get him away from it."

"Hush, my dear, hush! It is not at all good for young people to let their minds run on so. But this gold looks very good indeed. Are you sure that it is a fair sample, and that there is any more of it?"

"How can you be so dreadfully provoking, Uncle Sam, when I tell you that I saw it with my own eyes? And there must be at least half a ton of it."

"Well, half a hundred-weight will be enough for me. And you shall have all the rest, my dear—that is, if you will spare me a bit, Miss Remy. It all belongs to you by discovery, according to the diggers' law. And your eyes are so bright about it, miss, that the whole of your heart must be running upon it."

"Then you think me as bad as the rest of the world! How I wish that I had never seen it! It was only for you that I cared about it—for you, for you; and I will never touch a scrap of it."

Mr. Gundry had only been trying me, perhaps. But I did not see it in that light, and burst into a flood of childish tears, that he should misunderstand me so. Gold had its usual end, in grief. Uncle Sam rose up to soothe me and to beg my pardon, and to say that perhaps he was harsh because of the treatment he had received from his friends. He took me in his arms and kissed me; but before I could leave off sobbing, the crack of a rifle rang through the house, and Suan Isco, with a wail, rushed out.

CHAPTER XIII
THE SAWYER'S PRAYER

The darkness of young summer night was falling on earth and tree and stream. Every thing looked of a different form and color from those of an hour ago, and the rich bloom of shadow mixed with color, and cast by snowy mountains, which have stored the purple adieu of the sun, was filling the air with delicious calm. The Sawyer ran out with his shirt sleeves shining, so that any sneaking foe might shoot him; but, with the instinct of a settler, he had caught up his rifle. I stood beneath a carob-tree, which had been planted near the porch, and flung fantastic tassels down, like the ear-rings of a negress. And not having sense enough to do good, I was only able to be frightened.

Listening intently, I heard the sound of skirring steps on the other side of and some way down the river; and the peculiar tread, even thus far off, was plainly Suan Isco's. And then in the stillness a weary and heavy foot went toiling after it. Before I could follow, which I longed to do, to learn at once the worst of it, I saw the figure of a man much nearer, and even within twenty yards of me, gliding along without any sound. Faint as the light was, I felt sure that it was not one of our own men, and the barrel of a long gun upon his shoulder made a black line among silver leaves. I longed to run forth and stop him, but my courage was not prompt enough, and I shamefully shrank away behind the trunk of the carob-tree. Like a sleuth, compact, and calm-hearted villain, he went along without any breath of sound, stealing his escape with skill, till a white bower-tent made a background for him, and he leaped up and fell flat without a groan. The crack of a rifle came later than his leap, and a curl of white smoke shone against a black rock, and the Sawyer, in the distance, cried, "Well, now!" as he generally did when satisfied.

So scared was I that I caught hold of a cluster of pods to steady me; and then, without any more fear for myself, I ran to see whether it was possible to help. But the poor man lay beyond earthly help; he was too dead to palpitate. His life must have left him in the air, and he could not even have felt his fall.

In violent terror, I burst into tears, and lifted his heavy head, and strove to force his hot hands open, and did I know not what, without thinking, laboring only to recall his life.

"Are you grieving for the skulk who has shot my Firm?" said a stern voice quite unknown to me; and rising, I looked at the face of Mr. Gundry, unlike the countenance of Uncle Sam. I tried to speak to him, but was too frightened. The wrath of blood was in his face, and all his kind desires were gone.

"Yes, like a girl, you are sorry for a man who has stained this earth, till his only atonement is to stain it with his blood. Captain Pedro, there you lie, shot, like a coward, through the back. I wish you were alive to taste my boots. Murderer of men and filthy ravisher of women, miscreant of God, how can I keep from trampling on you?"

It never had been in my dream that a good man could so entirely forget himself. I wanted to think that it must be somebody else, and not our Uncle Sam. But he looked toward the west, as all men do when their spirits are full of death, and the wan light showed that his chin was triple.

Whether it may have been right or wrong, I made all haste to get away. The face of the dead man was quite a pleasant thing, compared with the face of the old man living. He may not have meant it, and I hope he never did, but beyond all controversy he looked barbarous for the moment.

As I slipped away, to know the worst, there I saw him standing still, longing to kick the vile man's corpse, but quieted by the great awe of death. If the man had stirred, or breathed, or even moaned, the living man would have lost all reverence in his fury. But the power of the other world was greater than even revenge could trample on. He let it lie there, and he stooped his head, and went away quite softly.

My little foolish heart was bitterly visited by a thing like this. The Sawyer, though not of great human rank, was gifted with the largest human nature that I had ever met with. And though it was impossible as yet to think, a hollow depression, as at the loss of some great ideal, came over me.

Returning wretchedly to the house, I met Suan Isco and two men bringing the body of poor Firm. His head and both his arms hung down, and they wanted somebody to lift them; and this I ran to do, although they called out to me not to meddle. The body was carried in, and laid upon three chairs, with a pillow at the head; and then a light was struck, and a candle brought by somebody or other. And Suan Isco sat upon the floor, and set up a miserable Indian dirge.

"Stow away that," cried Martin of the mill, for he was one of those two men; "wait till the lad is dead, and then pipe up to your liking. I felt him try to kick while we carried him along. He come forth on a arrand of that sort, and he seem to 'a been disappointed. A very fine young chap I call him, for to try to do it still, howsomever his mind might be wandering. Missy, keep his head up."

I did as I was told, and watched poor Firm as if my own life hung upon any sign of life in him. When I look back at these things, I think that fright and grief and pity must have turned an excitable girl almost into a real woman. But I had no sense of such things then.

"I tell you he ain't dead," cried Martin; "no more dead than I be. He feels the young gal's hand below him, and I see him try to turn up his eyes. He has taken a very bad knock, no doubt, and trouble about his breathing. I seed a fellow scalped once, and shot through the heart; but he came all round in about six months, and protected his head with a document. Firm, now, don't you be a fool. I have had worse things in my family."

Ephraim Gundry seemed to know that some one was upbraiding him. At any rate, his white lips trembled with a weak desire to breathe, and a little shadow of life appeared to flicker in his open eyes. And on my sleeve, beneath his back, some hot bright blood came trickling.

"Keep him to that," said Martin, with some carpenter sort of surgery; "less fear of the life when the blood begins to run. Don't move him, missy; never mind your arm. It will be the saving of him."

I was not strong enough to hold him up, but Suan ran to help me; and they told me afterward that I fell faint, and no doubt it must have been so. But when the rest were gone, and had taken poor Firm to his straw mattress, the cold night air must have flowed into the room, and that, perhaps, revived me. I went to the bottom of the stairs and listened, and then stole up to the landing, and heard Suan Isco, who had taken the command, speaking cheerfully in her worst English. Then I hoped for the best, and, without any knowledge, wandered forth into the open air.

Walking quite as in a dream this time (which I had vainly striven to do when seeking for my nugget), I came to the bank of the gleaming river, and saw the water just in time to stop from stepping into it. Careless about this and every other thing for the moment, I threw myself on the sod, and listened to the mournful melody of night. Sundry unknown creatures, which by day keep timid silence, were sending timid sounds into the darkness, holding quiet converse with themselves, or it, or one another. And the silvery murmur of the wavelets soothed the twinkling sleep of leaves.

I also, being worn and weary, and having a frock which improved with washing, and was spoiled already by nursing Firm, was well content to throw myself into a niche of river-bank and let all things flow past me. But before any thing had found time to flow far, or the lullaby of night had lulled me, there came to me a sadder sound than plaintive Nature can produce without her Master's aid, the saddest sound in all creation—a strong man's wail.

Child as I was—and, perhaps, all the more for that reason as knowing so little of mankind—I might have been more frightened, but I could not have been a bit more shocked, by the roaring of a lion. For I knew in a moment whose voice it was, and that made it pierce me tenfold. It was Uncle Sam, lamenting to himself, and to his God alone, the loss of his last hope on earth. He could not dream that any other than his Maker (and his Maker's works, if ever they have any sympathy) listened to the wild outpourings of an aged but still very natural heart, which had always been proud of controlling itself. I could see his great frame through a willow-tree, with the sere grass and withered reeds around, and the faint gleam of fugitive water beyond. He was kneeling toward his shattered mill, having rolled his shirt sleeves back to pray, and his white locks shone in the starlight; then, after trying several times, he managed to pray a little. First (perhaps partly from habit), he said the prayer of Our Lord pretty firmly, and then he went on to his own special case, with a doubting whether he should mention it. But as he went on he gathered courage, or received it from above, and was able to say what he wanted.

"Almighty Father of the living and the dead, I have lived long, and shall soon be dead, and my days have been full of trouble. But I never had such trouble as this here before, and I don't think I ever shall get over it. I have sinned every day of my life, and not thought of Thee, but of victuals, and money, and stuff; and nobody knows, but myself and Thou, all the little bad things inside of me. I cared a deal more to be respectable and get on with my business than to be prepared for kingdom come. And I have just been proud about the shooting of a villain, who might 'a gone free and repented. There is nobody left to me in my old age. Thou hast taken all of them. Wife, and son, and mill, and grandson, and my brother who robbed me—the whole of it may have been for my good, but I have got no good out of it. Show me the way for a little time, O Lord, to make the best of it; and teach me to bear it like a man, and not break down at this time of life. Thou knowest what is right. Please to do it. Amen."

CHAPTER XIV
NOT FAR TO SEEK

In the present state of controversies most profoundly religious, the Lord alone can decide (though thousands of men would hurry to pronounce) for or against the orthodoxy of the ancient Sawyer's prayer. But if sound doctrine can be established by success (as it always is), Uncle Sam's theology must have been unusually sound; for it pleased a gracious Power to know what he wanted, and to grant it.

Brave as Mr. Gundry was, and much-enduring and resigned, the latter years of his life on earth must have dragged on very heavily, with abstract resignation only, and none of his blood to care for him. Being so obstinate a man, he might have never admitted this, but proved against every one's voice, except his own, his special blessedness. But this must have been a trial to him, and happily he was spared from it.

For although Firm had been very badly shot, and kept us for weeks in anxiety about him, his strong young constitution and well-nourished frame got over it. A truly good and learned doctor came from Sacramento, and we hung upon his words, and found that there he left us hanging. And this was the wisest thing perhaps that he could do, because in America medical men are not absurdly expected, as they are in England, to do any good, but are valued chiefly upon their power of predicting what they can not help. And this man of science perceived that he might do harm to himself and his family by predicting amiss, whereas he could do no good to his patient by predicting rightly. And so he foretold both good and evil, to meet the intentions of Providence.

He had not been sent for in vain, however; and to give him his due, he saved Ephraim's life, for he drew from the wound a large bullet, which, if left, must have poisoned all his circulation, although it was made of pure silver. The Sawyer wished to keep this silver bullet as a token, but the doctor said that it belonged to him according to miners' law; and so it came to a moderate argument. Each was a thoroughly stubborn man, according to the bent of all good men, and reasoning increased their unreason. But the doctor won—as indeed he deserved, for the extraction had been delicate—because, when reason had been exhausted, he just said this:

"Colonel Gundry, let us have no more words. The true owner is your grandson. I will put it back where I took it from."

Upon this, the Sawyer being tickled, as men very often are in sad moments, took the doctor by the hand, and gave him the bullet heartily. And the medical man had a loop made to it, and wore it upon his watch chain. And he told the story so often (saying that another man perhaps might have got it out, but no other man could have kept it), that among a great race who judge by facts it doubled his practice immediately.

The leader of the robbers, known far and wide as "Captain Pedro," was buried where he fell; and the whole so raised Uncle Sam's reputation that his house was never attacked again; and if any bad characters were forced by circumstances to come near him, they never asked for any thing stronger than ginger-beer or lemonade, and departed very promptly. For as soon as Ephraim Gundry could give account of his disaster, it was clear that Don Pedro owed his fate to a bottle of the Sawyer's whiskey. Firm had only intended to give him a lesson for misbehavior, being fired by his grandfather's words about swinging me on the saddle. This idea had justly appeared to him to demand a protest; to deliver which he at once set forth with a valuable cowhide whip. Coming thus to the Rovers' camp, and finding their captain sitting in the shade to digest his dinner, Firm laid hold of him by the neck, and gave way to feelings of severity. Don Pedro regretted his misconduct, and being lifted up for the moment above his ordinary view, perceived that he might have done better, and shaped the pattern of his tongue to it. Firm, hearing this, had good hopes of him; yet knowing how volatile repentance is, he strove to form a well-marked track for it. And when the captain ceased to receive cowhide, he must have had it long enough to miss it.

Now this might have ended honorably and amicably for all concerned, if the captain had known when he was well off. Unluckily he had purloined a bottle of Mr. Gundry's whiskey, and he drew the cork now to rub his stripes, and the smell of it moved him to try it inside. And before very long his ideas of honor, which he had sense enough to drop when sober, began to come into his eyes again, and to stir him up to mischief. Hence it was that he followed Firm, who was riding home well satisfied, and appeased his honor by shooting in cold blood, and justice by being shot anyhow.

It was beautiful, through all this trying time, to watch Uncle Sam's proceedings: he appeared so delightfully calm and almost careless whenever he was looked at. And then he was ashamed of himself perpetually, if any one went on with it. Nobody tried to observe him, of course, or remark upon any of his doings, and for this he would become so grateful that he would long to tell all his thoughts, and then stop. This must have been a great worry to him, seeing how open his manner was; and whenever he wanted to hide any thing, he informed us of that intention. So that we exhorted Firm every day to come round and restore us to our usual state. This was the poor fellow's special desire; and often he was angry with himself, and made himself worse again by declaring that he must be a milksop to lie there so long. Whereas, it was much more near the truth that few other men, even in the Western States, would ever have got over such a wound. I am not learned enough to say exactly where the damage was, but the doctor called it, I think, the sternum, and pronounced that "a building-up process" was required, and must take a long time, if it ever could be done.

It was done at last, thanks to Suan Isco, who scarcely ever left him by day or night, and treated him skillfully with healing herbs. But he, without meaning it, vexed her often by calling for me—a mere ignorant child. Suan was dreadfully jealous of this, and perhaps I was proud of that sentiment of hers, and tried to justify it, instead of laboring to remove it, as would have been the more proper course. And Firm most ungratefully said that my hand was lighter than poor Suan's, and every thing I did was better done, according to him, which was shameful on his part, and as untrue as any thing could be. However, we yielded to him in all things while he was so delicate; and it often made us poor weak things cry to be the masters of a tall strong man.

Firm Gundry received that shot in May, about ten days before the twelvemonth was completed from my father's death. The brightness of summer and beauty of autumn went by without his feeling them, and while his system was working hard to fortify itself by walling up, as the learned man had called it. There had been some difficulties in this process, caused partly, perhaps, by our too lavish supply of the raw material; and before Firm's gap in his "sternum" was stopped, the mountains were coming down upon us, as we always used to say when the snow-line stooped. In some seasons this is a sharp time of hurry, broken with storms, and capricious, while men have to slur in the driving weather tasks that should have been matured long since. But in other years the long descent into the depth of winter is taken not with a jump like that, but gently and softly and windingly, with a great many glimpses back at the summer, and a good deal of leaning on the arm of the sun.

And so it was this time. The autumn and the winter for a fortnight stood looking quietly at each other. They had quite agreed to share the hours, to suit the arrangements of the sun. The nights were starry and fresh and brisk, without any touch of tartness; and the days were sunny and soft and gentle, without any sense of languor. It was a lovely scene—blue shadows gliding among golden light.

The Sawyer came forth, and cried, "What a shame! This makes me feel quite young again. And yet I have done not a stroke of work. No excuse; make no excuse. I can do that pretty well for myself. Praise God for all His mercies. I might do worse, perhaps, than have a pipe."

Then Firm came out to surprise him, and to please us all with the sight of himself. He steadied his steps with one great white hand upon his grandfather's Sunday staff, and his clear blue eyes were trembling with a sense of gratitude and a fear of tears. And I stepped behind a red strawberry-tree, for my sense of respect for him almost made me sob.

Then Jowler thought it high time to appear upon the scene, and convince us that he was not a dead dog yet. He had known tribulation, as his master had, and had found it a difficult thing to keep from the shadowy hunting ground of dogs who have lived a conscientious life. I had wondered at first what his reason could have been for not coming forward, according to his custom, to meet that troop of robbers. But his reason, alas! was too cogent to himself, though nobody else in that dreadful time could pay any attention to him. The Rovers, well knowing poor Jowler's repute, and declining the fair mode of testing it, had sent in advance a very crafty scout, a half-bred Indian, who knew as much about dogs as they could ever hope to know about themselves. This rogue approached faithful Jowler—so we were told long afterward—not in an upright way, but as if he had been a brother quadruped. And he took advantage of the dog's unfeigned surprise and interest to accost him with a piece of kidney containing a powerful poison. According to all sound analogy, this should have stopped the dear fellow's earthly tracks; but his spirit was such that he simply went away to nurse himself up in retirement. Neither man nor dog can tell what agonies he suffered; and doubtless his tortures of mind about duty unperformed were the worst of all. These things are out of human knowledge in its present unsympathetic state. Enough that poor Jowler came home at last, with his ribs all up and his tail very low.

Like friends who have come together again, almost from the jaws of death, we sat in the sunny noon, and thoroughly enjoyed ourselves. The trees above us looked proud and cheerful, laying aside the mere frippery of leaves with a good grace and contented arms, and a surety of having quite enough next spring. Much of the fruity wealth of autumn still was clustering in our sight, heavily fetching the arched bough down to lessen the fall, when fall they must. And against the golden leaves of maple behind the unpretending roof a special wreath of blue shone like a climbing Ipomaea. But coming to examine this, one found it to be nothing more nor less than the smoke of the kitchen chimney, busy with a quiet roasting job.

This shows how clear the air was; but a thousand times as much could never tell how clear our spirits were. Nobody made any "demonstration," or cut any frolicsome capers, or even said any thing exuberant. The steadfast brooding breed of England, which despises antics, was present in us all, and strengthened by a soil whose native growth is peril, chance, and marvel. And so we nodded at one another, and I ran over and courtesied to Uncle Sam, and he took me to him.

"You have been a dear good child," he said, as he rose, and looked over my head at Firm. "My own granddarter, if such there had been, could not have done more to comfort me, nor half so much, for aught I know. There is no picking and choosing among the females, as God gives them. But he has given you for a blessing and saving to my old age, my dearie."

"Oh, Uncle Sam, now the nugget!" I cried, desiring like a child to escape deep feeling, and fearing any strong words from Firm. "You have promised me ever so long that I should be the first to show Firm the nugget."

"And so you shall, my dear, and Firm shall see it before he is an hour older, and Jowler shall come down to show us where it is."

Firm, who had little faith in the nugget, but took it for a dream of mine, and had proved conclusively from his pillow that it could not exist in earnest, now with a gentle, satirical smile declared his anxiety to see it; and I led him along by his better arm, faster, perhaps, than he ought to have walked.

In a very few minutes we were at the place, and I ran eagerly to point it; but behold, where the nugget had been, there was nothing except the white bed of the river! The blue water flowed very softly on its way, without a gleam of gold to corrupt it.

"Oh, nobody will ever believe me again!" I exclaimed, in the saddest of sad dismay. "I dreamed about it first, but it never can have been a dream throughout. You know that I told you about it, Uncle Sam, even when you were very busy, and that shows that it never could have been a dream."

"You told me about it, I remember now," Mr. Gundry answered, dryly; "but it does not follow that there was such a thing. My dear, you may have imagined it; because it was the proper time for it to come, when my good friends had no money to lend. Your heart was so good that it got into your brain, and you must not be vexed, my dear child; it has done you good to dream of it."

"I said so all along," Firm observed. "Miss Rema felt that it ought to be, and so she believed that it must be, there. She is always so warm and trustful."

"Is that all you are good for?" I cried, with no gratitude for his compliment. "As sure as I stand here, I saw a great bowlder of gold, and so did Jowler, and I gave you the piece that he brought up. Did you take them all in a dream, Uncle Sam? Come, can you get over that?"

I assure you that for the moment I knew not whether I stood upon my feet or head, until I perceived an extraordinary grin on the Sawyer's ample countenance; but Firm was not in the secret yet, for he gazed at me with compassion, and Uncle Sam looked at us both as if he were balancing our abilities.

"Send your dog in, missy," at last he said. "He is more your dog than mine, I believe, and he obeys you like a Christian. Let him go and find it if he can."

At a sign from me, the great dog dashed in, and scratched with all four feet at once, and made the valley echo with the ring of mighty barkings; and in less than two minutes there shone the nugget, as yellow and as big as ever.

"Ha! ha! I never saw a finer thing," shouted Uncle Sam, like a schoolboy. "I were too many for you, missy dear; but the old dog wollops the whole of us. I just shot a barrow-load of gravel on your nugget, to keep it all snug till Firm should come round; and if the boy had never come round, there the gold might have waited the will of the Almighty. It is a big spot, anyhow."

It certainly was not a little spot, though they all seemed to make so light of it—which vexed me, because I had found it, and was as proud as if I had made it. Not by any means that the Sawyer was half as careless as he seemed to be; he put on much of this for my sake, having very lofty principles, especially concerning the duty of the young. Young people were never to have small ideas, so far as he could help it, particularly upon such matters as Mammon, or the world, or fashion; and not so very seldom he was obliged to catch himself up in his talking, when he chanced to be going on and forgetting that I, who required a higher vein of thought for my youth, was taking his words downright; and I think that all this had a great deal to do with his treating all that gold in such an exemplary manner; for if it had really mattered nothing, what made him go in the dark and shoot a great barrow-load of gravel over it?

CHAPTER XV
BROUGHT TO BANK

The sanity of a man is mainly tested among his neighbors and kindred by the amount of consideration which he has consistently given to cash. If money has been the chief object of his life, and he for its sake has spared nobody, no sooner is he known to be successful than admiration overpowers all the ill-will he has caused. He is shrewd, sagacious, long-headed, and great; he has earned his success, and few men grudge, while many seek to get a slice of it; but he, as a general rule, declines any premature distribution, and for this custody of his wealth he is admired all the more by those who have no hope of sharing it.

As soon as ever it was known that Uncle Sam had lodged at his banker's a tremendous lump of gold, which rumor declared to be worth at least a hundred thousand dollars, friends from every side poured in, all in hot haste, to lend him their last farthing. The Sawyer was pleased with their kindness, but thought that his second-best whiskey met the merits of the case. And he was more particular than usual with his words; for, according to an old saying of the diggers, a big nugget always has children, and, being too heavy to go very far, it is likely to keep all its little ones at home. Many people, therefore, were longing to seek for the frogs of this great toad; for so in their slang the miners called them, with a love of preternatural history. But Mr. Gundry allowed no search for the frogs, or even the tadpoles, of his patriarchal nugget. And much as he hated the idea of sowing the seeds of avarice in any one, he showed himself most consistent now in avoiding that imputation; for not only did he refuse to show the bed of his great treasure, after he had secured it, but he fenced the whole of it in, and tarred the fence, and put loopholes in it; and then he established Jowler where he could neither be shot nor poisoned, and kept a man with a double-barreled rifle in the ruin of the mill, handy to shoot, but not easy to be shot; and this was a resolute man, being Martin himself, who had now no business. Of course Martin grumbled; but the worse his temper was, the better for his duty, as seems to be the case with a great many men; and if any one had come to console him in his grumbling, never would he have gone away again.

It would have been reckless of me to pretend to say what any body ought to do; from the first to the last I left every thing to those who knew so much better; at the same time I felt that it might have done no harm if I had been more consulted, though I never dreamed of saying so, because the great gold had been found by me, and although I cared for it scarcely more than for the tag of a boot-lace, nobody seemed to me able to enter into it quite as I did; and as soon as Firm's danger and pain grew less, I began to get rather impatient, but Uncle Sam was not to be hurried.

Before ever he hoisted that rock of gold, he had made up his mind for me to be there, and he even put the business off, because I would not come one night, for I had a superstitious fear on account of its being my father's birthday. Uncle Sam had forgotten the date, and begged my pardon for proposing it; but he said that we must not put it off later than the following night, because the moonlight would be failing, and we durst not have any kind of lamp, and before the next moon the hard weather might begin. All this was before the liberal offers of his friends, of which I have spoken first, although they happened to come after it.

While the Sawyer had been keeping the treasure perdu, to abide the issue of his grandson's illness, he had taken good care both to watch it and to form some opinion of its shape and size; for, knowing the pile which I had described, he could not help finding it easily enough; and indeed the great fear was that others might find it, and come in great force to rob him; but nothing of that sort had happened, partly because he held his tongue rigidly, and partly, perhaps, because of the simple precaution which he had taken.

Now, however, it was needful to impart the secret to one man at least; for Firm, though recovering, was still so weak that it might have killed him to go into the water, or even to exert himself at all; and strong as Uncle Sam was, he knew that even with hoisting-tackle, he alone could never bring that piece of bullion to bank; so, after much consideration, he resolved to tell Martin of the mill, as being the most trusty man about the place, as well as the most surly; but he did not tell him until every thing was ready, and then he took him straightway to the place.

Here, in the moonlight, we stood waiting, Firm and myself and Suan Isco, who had more dread than love of gold, and might be useful to keep watch, or even to lend a hand, for she was as strong as an ordinary man. The night was sultry, and the fire-flies (though dull in the radiance of the moon) darted, like soft little shooting-stars, across the still face of shadow, and the flood of the light of the moon was at its height, submerging every thing.

While we were whispering and keeping in the shade for fear of attracting any wanderer's notice, we saw the broad figure of the Sawyer rising from a hollow of the bank, and behind him came Martin the foreman, and we soon saw that due preparation had been made, for they took from under some drift-wood (which had prevented us from observing it) a small movable crane, and fixed it on a platform of planks which they set up in the river-bed.

"Palefaces eat gold," Suan Isco said, reflectively, and as if to satisfy herself. "Dem eat, drink, die gold; dem pull gold out of one other's ears. Welly hope Mellican mans get enough gold now."

"Don't be sarcastic, now, Suan," I answered; "as if it were possible to have enough!"

"For my part," said Firm, who had been unusually silent all the evening, "I wish it had never been found at all. As sure as I stand here, mischief will come of it. It will break up our household. I hope it will turn out a lump of quartz, gilt on the face, as those big nuggets do, ninety-nine out of a hundred. I have had no faith in it all along."

"Because I found it, Mr. Firm, I suppose," I answered, rather pettishly, for I never had liked Firm's incessant bitterness about my nugget. "Perhaps if you had found it, Mr. Firm, you would have had great faith in it."

"Can't say, can't say," was all Firm's reply; and he fell into the silent vein again.

"Heave-ho! heave-ho! there, you sons of cooks!" cried the Sawyer, who was splashing for his life in the water. "I've tackled 'un now. Just tighten up the belt, to see if he biteth centre-like. You can't lift 'un! Lord bless 'ee, not you. It'll take all I know to do that, I guess; and Firm ain't to lay no hand to it. Don't you be in such a doggoned hurry. Hold hard, can't you?"

For Suan and Martin were hauling for their lives, and even I caught hold of a rope-end, but had no idea what to do with it, when the Sawyer swung himself up to bank, and in half a minute all was orderly. He showed us exactly where to throw our weight, and he used his own to such good effect that, after some creaking and groaning, the long horn of the crane rose steadily, and a mass of dripping sparkles shone in the moonlight over the water.

"Hurrah! what a whale! How the tough ash bends!" cried Uncle Sam, panting like a boy, and doing nearly all the work himself. "Martin, lay your chest to it. We'll grass him in two seconds. Californy never saw a sight like this, I reckon."

There was plenty of room for us all to stand round the monster and admire it. In shape it was just like a fat toad, squatting with his shoulders up and panting. Even a rough resemblance to the head and the haunches might be discovered, and a few spots of quartz shone here and there on the glistening and bossy surface. Some of us began to feel and handle it with vast admiration; but Firm, with his heavy boots, made a vicious kick at it, and a few bright scales, like sparks, flew off.

"Why, what ails the lad?" cried the Sawyer, in some wrath; "what harm hath the stone ever done to him? To my mind, this here lump is a proof of the whole creation of the world, and who hath lived long enough to gainsay? Here this lump hath lain, without changing color, since creation's day; here it is, as big and heavy as when the Lord laid hand to it. What good to argue agin such facts? Supposin' the world come out o' nothing, with nobody to fetch it, or to say a word of orders, how ever could it 'a managed to get a lump of gold like this in it? They clever fellers is too clever. Let 'em put all their heads together, and turn out a nugget, and I'll believe them."

Uncle Sam's reasoning was too deep for any but himself to follow. He was not long in perceiving this, though we were content to admire his words without asking him to explain them; so he only said, "Well, well," and began to try with both hands if he could heft this lump. He stirred it, and moved it, and raised it a little, as the glisten of the light upon its roundings showed; but lift it fairly from the ground he could not, however he might bow his sturdy legs and bend his mighty back to it; and, strange to say, he was pleased for once to acknowledge his own discomfiture.

"Five hundred and a half I used to lift to the height of my knee-cap easily; I may 'a fallen off now a hundred-weight with years, and strings in my back, and rheumatics; but this here little toad is a clear hundredweight out and beyond my heftage. If there's a pound here, there's not an ounce under six hundred-weight, I'll lay a thousand dollars. Miss Rema, give a name to him. All the thundering nuggets has thundering names."

"Then this shall be called 'Uncle Sam,'" I answered, "because he is the largest and the best of all."

"It shall stand, miss," cried Martin, who was in great spirits, and seemed to have bettered himself forever. "You could not have given it a finer name, miss, if you had considered for a century. Uncle Sam is the name of our glorious race, from the kindness of our natur'. Every body's uncle we are now, in vartue of superior knowledge, and freedom, and giving of general advice, and stickin' to all the world, or all the good of it. Darned if old Sam aren't the front of creation!"

"Well, well," said the Sawyer, "let us call it 'Uncle Sam,' if the dear young lady likes it; it would be bad luck to change the name; but, for all that, we must look uncommon sharp, or some of our glorious race will come and steal it afore we unbutton our eyes."

"Pooh!" cried Martin; but he knew very well that his master's words were common-sense; and we left him on guard with a double-barreled gun, and Jowler to keep watch with him. And the next day he told us that he had spent the night in such a frame of mind from continual thought that when our pet cow came to drink at daybreak, it was but the blowing of her breath that saved her from taking a bullet between her soft tame eyes.

Now it could not in any kind of way hold good that such things should continue; and the Sawyer, though loath to lose sight of the nugget, perceived that he must not sacrifice all the morals of the neighborhood to it, and he barely had time to dispatch it on its road at the bottom of a load of lumber, with Martin to drive, and Jowler to sit up, and Firm to ride behind, when a troop of mixed robbers came riding across, with a four-wheel cart and two sturdy mules—enough to drag off every thing. They had clearly heard of the golden toad, and desired to know more of him; but Uncle Sam, with his usual blandness, met these men at the gate of his yard, and upon the top rail, to ease his arm, he rested a rifle of heavy metal, with seven revolving chambers. The robbers found out that they had lost their way, and Mr. Gundry answered that so they had, and the sooner they found it in another direction, the better it would be for them. They thought that he had all his men inside, and they were mighty civil, though we had only two negroes to help us, and Suan Isco, with a great gun cocked. But their curiosity was such that they could not help asking about the gold; and, sooner than shoot them, Uncle Sam replied that, upon his honor, the nugget was gone. And the fame of his word was so well known that these fellows (none of whom could tell the truth, even at confession) believed him on the spot, and begged his pardon for trespassing on his premises. They hoped that he would not say a word to the Vigilance Committee, who hanged a poor fellow for losing his road; and he told them that if they made off at once, nobody should pursue them; and so they rode off very happily.

CHAPTER XVI
FIRM AND INFIRM

Strange as it may appear, our quiet little home was not yet disturbed by that great discovery of gold. The Sawyer went up to the summit of esteem in public opinion; but to himself and to us he was the same as ever. He worked with his own hard hands and busy head just as he used to do; for although the mill was still in ruins, there was plenty of the finer work to do, which always required hand-labor. And at night he would sit at the end of the table furthest from the fire-place, with his spectacles on, and his red cheeks glowing, while he designed the future mill, which was to be built in the spring, and transcend every mill ever heard, thought, or dreamed of.

We all looked forward to a quiet winter, snug with warmth and cheer indoors, and bright outside with sparkling trees, brisk air, and frosty appetite, when a foolish idea arose which spoiled the comfort at least of two of us. Ephraim Gundry found out, or fancied, that he was entirely filled with love of a very young maid, who never dreamed of such things, and hated even to hear of them; and the maid, unluckily, was myself.

During the time of his ailment I had been with him continually, being only too glad to assuage his pain, or turn his thoughts away from it. I partly suspected that he had incurred his bitter wound for my sake; though I never imputed his zeal to more than a young man's natural wrath at an outrage. But now he left me no longer in doubt, and made me most uncomfortable. Perhaps I was hard upon him, and afterward I often thought so, for he was very kind and gentle; but I was an orphan child, and had no one to advise me in such matters. I believe that he should have considered this, and allowed me to grow a little older; but perhaps he himself was too young as yet and too bashful to know how to manage things. It was the very evening after his return from Sacramento, and the beauty of the weather still abode in the soft warm depth around us. In every tint of rock and tree and playful glass of river a quiet clearness seemed to lie, and a rich content of color. The grandeur of the world was such that one could only rest among it, seeking neither voice nor thought.

Therefore I was more surprised than pleased to hear my name ring loudly through the echoing hollows, and then to see the bushes shaken, and an eager form leap out. I did not answer a word, but sat with a wreath of white bouvardia and small adiantum round my head, which I had plaited anyhow.

"What a lovely dear you are!" cried Firm, and then he seemed frightened at his own words.

"I had no idea that you would have finished your dinner so soon as this, Mr. Firm."

"And you did not want me. You are vexed to see me. Tell the truth, Miss Rema."

"I always tell the truth," I answered; "and I did not want to be disturbed just now. I have so many things to think of."

"And not me among them. Oh no, of course you never think of me, Erema."

"It is very unkind of you to say that," I answered, looking clearly at him, as a child looks at a man. "And it is not true, I assure you, Firm. Whenever I have thought of dear Uncle Sam, I very often go on to think of you, because he is so fond of you."

"But not for my own sake, Erema; you never think of me for my own sake."

"But yes, I do, I assure you, Mr. Firm; I do greatly. There is scarcely a day that I do not remember how hungry you are, and I think of you."

"Tush!" replied Firm, with a lofty gaze. "Even for a moment that does not in any way express my meaning. My mind is very much above all eating when it dwells upon you, Erema. I have always been fond of you, Erema."

"You have always been good to me, Firm," I said, as I managed to get a great branch between us. "After your grandfather, and Suan Isco, and Jowler, I think that I like you best of almost any body left to me. And you know that I never forget your slippers."

"Erema, you drive me almost wild by never understanding me. Now will you just listen to a little common-sense? You know that I am not romantic."

"Yes, Firm; yes, I know that you never did any thing wrong in any way."

"You would like me better if I did. What an extraordinary thing it is! Oh, Erema, I beg your pardon."

He had seen in a moment, as men seem to do, when they study the much quicker face of a girl, that his words had keenly wounded me—that I had applied them to my father, of whom I was always thinking, though I scarcely ever spoke of him. But I knew that Firm had meant no harm, and I gave him my hand, though I could not speak.

"My darling," he said, "you are very dear to me—dearer than all the world besides. I will not worry you any more. Only say that you do not hate me."

"How could I? How could any body? Now let us go in and attend to Uncle Sam. He thinks of every body before himself."

"And I think of every body after myself. Is that what you mean, Erema?"

"To be sure! if you like. You may put any meaning on my words that you think proper. I am accustomed to things of that sort, and I pay no attention whatever, when I am perfectly certain that I am right."

"I see," replied Firm, applying one finger to the side of his nose in deep contemplation, which, of all his manners, annoyed me most. "I see how it is; Miss Rema is always perfectly certain that she is right, and the whole of the rest of the world quite wrong. Well, after all, there is nothing like holding a first-rate opinion of one's self."

"You are not what I thought of you," I cried, being vexed beyond bearance by such words, and feeling their gross injustice. "If you wish to say any thing more, please to leave it until you recover your temper. I am not quite accustomed to rudeness."

With these words, I drew away and walked off, partly in earnest and partly in joke, not wishing to hear another word; and when I looked back, being well out of sight, there he sat still, with his head on his hands, and my heart had a little ache for him.

However, I determined to say no more, and to be extremely careful. I could not in justice blame Ephraim Gundry for looking at me very often. But I took good care not to look at him again unless he said something that made me laugh, and then I could scarcely help it. He was sharp enough very soon to find out this; and then he did a thing which was most unfair, as I found out long afterward. He bought an American jest-book, full of ideas wholly new to me, and these he committed to heart, and brought them out as his own productions. If I had only known it, I must have been exceedingly sorry for him. But Uncle Sam used to laugh and rub his hands, perhaps for old acquaintance' sake; and when Uncle Sam laughed, there was nobody near who could help laughing with him. And so I began to think Firm the most witty and pleasant of men, though I tried to look away.

But perhaps the most careful and delicate of things was to see how Uncle Sam went on. I could not understand him at all just then, and thought him quite changed from my old Uncle Sam; but afterward, when I came to know, his behavior was as clear and shallow as the water of his own river. He had very strange ideas about what he generally called "the female kind." According to his ideas (and perhaps they were not so unusual among mankind, especially settlers), all "females" were of a good but weak and consistently inconsistent sort. The surest way to make them do whatever their betters wanted, was to make them think that it was not wanted, but was hedged with obstacles beyond their power to overcome, and so to provoke and tantalize them to set their hearts upon doing it. In accordance with this idea (than which there can be none more mistaken), he took the greatest pains to keep me from having a word to say to Firm; and even went so far as to hint, with winks and nods of pleasantry, that his grandson's heart was set upon the pretty Miss Sylvester, the daughter of a man who owned a herd of pigs, much too near our saw-mills, and herself a young woman of outrageous dress, and in a larger light contemptible. But when Mr. Gundry, without any words, conveyed this piece of news to me, I immediately felt quite a liking for gaudy but harmless Pennsylvania—for so her parents had named her when she was too young to help it; and I heartily hoped that she might suit Firm, which she seemed all the more likely to do as his conduct could not be called noble. Upon that point, however, I said not a word, leaving him purely to judge for himself, and feeling it a great relief that now he could not say any thing more to me. I was glad that his taste was so easily pleased, and I told Suan Isco how glad I was.

This I had better have left unsaid, for it led to a great explosion, and drove me away from the place altogether before the new mill was finished, and before I should otherwise have gone from friends who were so good to me; not that I could have staid there much longer, even if this had never come to pass; for week by week and month by month I was growing more uneasy: uneasy not at my obligations or dependence upon mere friends (for they managed that so kindly that I seemed to confer the favor), but from my own sense of lagging far behind my duty.

For now the bright air, and the wholesome food, and the pleasure of goodness around me, were making me grow, without knowledge or notice, into a tall and not altogether to be overlooked young woman. I was exceedingly shy about this, and blushed if any one spoke of it; but yet in my heart I felt it was so; and how could I help it? And when people said, as rough people will, and even Uncle Sam sometimes, "Handsome is as handsome does," or "Beauty is only skin-deep," and so on, I made it my duty not to be put out, but to bear it in mind and be thankful. And though I

CHAPTER XVII
HARD AND SOFT

Before very long it was manifest enough that Mr. Gundry looked down upon Miss Sylvester with a large contempt. But while this raised my opinion of his judgment, it almost deprived me of a great relief—the relief of supposing that he wished his grandson to marry this Pennsylvania. For although her father, with his pigs and cattle, and a low sort of hostelry which he kept, could settle "a good pile of dollars" upon her, and had kept her at the "learnedest ladies' college" even in San Francisco till he himself trembled at her erudition, still it was scarcely to be believed that a man of the Sawyer's strong common-sense and disregard of finery would ever accept for his grandchild a girl made of affectation, vulgarity, and conceit. And one day, quite in the early spring, he was so much vexed with the fine lady's airs that he left no doubt about his meaning.

Miss Sylvester was very proud of the figure she made on horseback; and having been brought up, perhaps as a child, to ride after pigs and so on, she must have had fine opportunities of acquiring a graceful style of horsemanship. And now she dashed through thick and thin in a most commanding manner, caring no more for a snow-drift than ladies do for a scraping of the road. No one with the least observation could doubt that this young woman was extremely anxious to attract Firm Gundry's notice; and therefore, on the day above spoken of, once more she rode over, with her poor father in waiting upon her as usual.

Now I know very well how many faults I have, and to deny them has never been my practice; but this is the honest and earnest truth, that no smallness of mind, or narrowness of feeling, or want of large or fine sentiments made me bolt my door when that girl was in the house. I simply refused, after seeing her once, to have any thing more to say to her; by no means because of my birth and breeding (which are things that can be most easily waived when the difference is acknowledged), nor yet on account of my being brought up in the company of ladies, nor even by reason of any dislike which her bold brown eyes put into me. My cause was sufficient and just and wise. I felt myself here as a very young girl, in safe and pure and honest hands, yet thrown on my own discretion, without any feminine guidance whatever. And I had learned enough from the wise French sisters to know at a glance that Miss Sylvester was not a young woman who would do me good.

Even Uncle Sam, who was full of thought and delicate care about me, so far as a man can understand, and so far as his simple shrewdness went, in spite of all his hospitable ways and open universal welcome, though he said not a word (as on such a point he was quite right in doing)—even he, as I knew by his manner, was quite content with my decision. But Firm, being young and in many ways stupid, made a little grievance of it. And, of course, Miss Sylvester made a great one.

"Oh, I do declare, I am going away," through my open window I heard her exclaim in her sweetly affected tone, at the end of that long visit, "without even having the honor of saying a kind word to your young visitor. Do not wait for me, papa; I must pay my devoirs. Such a distinguished and travelled person can hardly be afflicted with mauvaise honte. Why does she not rush to embrace me? All the French people do; and she is so French! Let me see her, for the sake of my accent."

"We don't want no French here, ma'am," replied Uncle Sam, as Sylvester rode off, "and the young lady wants no Doctor Hunt. Her health is as good as your own, and you never catch no French actions from her. If she wanted to see you, she would 'a come down."

"Oh, now, this is too barbarous! Colonel Gundry, you are the most tyrannous man; in your own dominions an autocrat. Every body says so, but I never would believe it. Oh, don't let me go away with that impression. And you do look so good-natured!"

"And so I mean to look, Miss Penny, until you are out of sight."

The voice of the Sawyer was more dry than that of his oldest and rustiest saw. The fashionable and highly finished girl had no idea what to make of him; but gave her young horse a sharp cut, to show her figure as she reined him; and then galloping off, she kissed her tan gauntlet with crimson network down it, and left Uncle Sam to revolve his rudeness, with the dash of the wet road scattered in the air.

"I wouldn't 'a spoke to her so course," he said to Firm, who now returned from opening the gate and delivering his farewell, "if she wasn't herself so extra particular, gild me, and sky-blue my mouldings fine. How my mother would 'a stared at the sight of such a gal! Keep free of her, my lad, keep free of her. But no harm to put her on, to keep our missy alive and awake, my boy."

had no idea of any such influence at the moment, I hope that the grandeur of nature around and the lofty style of every thing may have saved me from dwelling too much on myself, as Pennsylvania Sylvester did.

Now the more I felt my grown-up age and health and buoyant vigor, the surer I knew that the time was come for me to do some good with them; not to benefit the world in general, in a large and scattery way (as many young people set out to do, and never get any further), but to right the wrong of my own house, and bring home justice to my own heart. This may be thought a partial and paltry object to set out with; and it is not for me to say otherwise. At the time, it occurred to me in no other light except as my due business, and I never took any large view at all. But even now I do believe (though not yet in pickle of wisdom) that if every body, in its own little space and among its own little movements, will only do and take nothing without pure taste of the salt of justice, no reeking atrocity of national crimes could ever taint the heaven.

Such questions, however, become me not. I have only to deal with very little things, sometimes too slim to handle well, and too hazy to be woven; and if they seem below my sense and dignity to treat of, I can only say that they seemed very big at the time when I had to encounter them.

For instance, what could be more important, in a little world of life, than for Uncle Sam to be put out, and dare even to think ill of me? Yet this he did; and it shows how shallow are all those theories of the other sex which men are so pleased to indulge in. Scarcely any thing could be more ridiculous from first to last, when calmly and truly considered, than the firm belief which no power of reason could for the time root out of him.

Uncle Sam, the dearest of all mankind to me, and the very kindest, was positively low-enough to believe, in his sad opinion of the female race, that my young head was turned because of the wealth to which I had no claim, except through his own justice. He had insisted at first that the whole of that great nugget belonged to me by right of sole discovery. I asked him whether, if any stranger had found it, it would have been considered his, and whether he would have allowed a "greaser," upon finding, to make off with it. At the thought of this, Mr. Gundry gave a little grunt, and could not go so far as to maintain that view of it. But he said that my reasoning did not fit; that I was not a greaser, but a settled inhabitant of the place, and entitled to all a settler's rights; that the bed of the river would have been his grave but for the risk of my life, and therefore whatever I found in the bed of the river belonged to me, and me only.

In argument he was so much stronger than I could ever attempt to be that I gave it up, and could only say that if he argued forever it could never make any difference. He did not argue forever, but only grew obstinate and unpleasant, so that I yielded at last to own the half share of the bullion.

Very well. Every body would have thought, who has not studied the nature of men or been dragged through it heavily, that now there could be no more trouble between two people entirely trusting each other, and only anxious that the other should have the best of it. Yet, instead of that being the case, the mischief, the myriad mischief, of money set in, until I heartily wished sometimes that my miserable self was down in the hole which the pelf had left behind it.

For what did Uncle Sam take into his head (which was full of generosity and large ideas, so loosely packed that little ones grew between them, especially about womankind)—what else did he really seem to think, with the downright stubbornness of all his thoughts, but that I, his poor debtor and pensioner and penniless dependent, was so set up and elated by this sudden access of fortune that henceforth none of the sawing race was high enough for me to think of? It took me a long time to believe that so fair and just a man ever could set such interpretation upon me. And when it became too plain that he did so, truly I know not whether grief or anger was uppermost in my troubled heart.

Immediately I withdrew from ear-shot, more deeply mortified than I can tell, and perhaps doing Firm an injustice by not waiting for his answer. I knew not then how lightly men will speak of such delicate subjects; and it set me more against all thoughts of Firm than a month's reflection could have done. When I came to know more of the world, I saw that I had been very foolish. At the time, however, I was firmly set in a strong resolve to do that which alone seemed right, or even possible—to quit with all speed a place which could no longer be suited for me.

For several days I feared to say a single word about it, while equally I condemned myself for having so little courage. But it was not as if there were any body to help me, or tell me what to do; sometimes I was bold with a surety of right, and then again I shook with the fear of being wrong. Because, through the whole of it, I felt how wonderfully well I had been treated, and what a great debt I owed of kindness; and it seemed to be only a nasty little pride which made me so particular. And being so unable to settle for myself, I waited for something to settle it.

Something came, in a way which I had not by any means expected. I had told Suan Isco how glad I was that Firm had fixed his liking steadily upon Miss Sylvester. If any woman on earth could be trusted not to say a thing again, that one was this good Indian. Not only because of her provident habits, but also in right of the difficulty which encompassed her in our language. But she managed to get over both of these, and to let Mr. Ephraim know, as cleverly as if she had lived in drawing-rooms, whatever I had said about him. She did it for the best; but it put him in a rage, which he came at once to have out with me.

"And so, Miss Erema," he said, throwing down his hat upon the table of the little parlor, where I sat with an old book of Norman ballads, "I have your best wishes, then, have I, for a happy marriage with Miss Sylvester?"

I was greatly surprised at the tone of his voice, while the flush on his cheeks and the flash of his eyes, and even his quick heavy tread, showed plainly that his mind was a little out of balance. He deserved it, however, and I could not grieve.

"You have my best wishes," I replied, demurely, "for any state of life to which you may be called. You could scarcely expect any less of me than that."

"How kind you are! But do you really wish that I should marry old Sylvester's girl?"

Firm, as he asked this question, looked so bitterly reproachful (as if he were saying, "Do you wish to see me hanged?"), while his eyes took a form which reminded me so of the Sawyer in a furious puzzle, that it was impossible for me to answer as lightly as I meant to do.

"No, I can not say, Firm, that I wish it at all; unless your heart is set on it—"

"Don't you know, then, where my heart is set?" he asked me, in a deep voice, coming nearer, and taking the ballad-book from my hands. "Why will you feign not to know, Erema, who is the only one I can ever think of twice? Above me, I know, in every possible way—birth and education and mind and appearance, and now far above me in money as well. But what are all these things? Try to think if only you could like me. Liking gets over every thing, and without it nothing is any thing. Why do I like you so, Erema? Is it because of your birth, and teaching, and manners, and sweet looks, and all that, or even because of your troubles?"

"How can I tell, Firm—how can I tell? Perhaps it is just because of myself. And why do you do it at all, Firm?"

"Ah, why do I do it? How I wish I knew! Perhaps then I might cure it. To begin with, what is there, after all, so very wonderful about you?"

"Oh, nothing, I should hope. Most surely nothing. It would grieve me to be at all wonderful. That I leave for American ladies."

"Now you don't understand me. I mean, of course, that you are wonderfully good and kind and clever; and your eyes, I am sure, and your lips and smile, and all your other features—there is nothing about them that can be called any thing else but wonderful."

"Now, Firm, how exceedingly foolish you are! I did hope that you knew better."

"Erema, I never shall know better. I never can swerve or change, if I live to be a hundred and fifty. You think me presumptuous, no doubt, from what you are brought up to. And you are so young that to seek to bind you, even if you loved me, would be an unmanly thing. But now you are old enough, and you know your own mind surely well enough, just to say whether you feel as if you could ever love me as I love you."

He turned away, as if he felt that he had no right to press me so, and blamed himself for selfishness; and I liked him better for doing that than for any thing he had done before. Yet I knew that I ought to speak clearly, and though my voice was full of tears, I tried.

"Dear Firm," I said, as I took his hand and strove to look at him steadily, "I like and admire you very much; and by-and-by—by-and-by, I might, that is, if you did not hurry me. Of all the obstacles you have mentioned, none is worth considering. I am nothing but a poor castaway, owing my life to Uncle Sam and you. But one thing there is which could never be got over, even if I felt as you feel toward me. Never can I think of little matters, or of turning my thoughts to—to any such things as you speak of, as long as a vile reproach and wicked imputation lies on me. And before even that, I have to think of my father, who gave his life for me. Firm, I have been here too long delaying, and wasting my time in trifles. I ought to have been in Europe long ago. If I am old enough for what you talk of, I am old enough to do my duty. If I am old enough for love, as it is called, I am old enough for hate. I have more to do with hate than love, I think."

"Erema," cried Firm, "what a puzzle you are! I never even dreamed that you could be so fierce. You are enough to frighten Uncle Sam himself."

"If I frighten you, Firm, that is quite enough. You see now how vain it is to say another word."

"I do not see any thing of the sort. Come back, and look at me quite calmly."

Being frightened at the way in which I had spoken, and having passed the prime of it, I obeyed him in a moment, and came up gently and let him look at me to his liking. For little as I thought of such things till now, I seemed already to know more about them, or at least to wonder—which is the stir of the curtain of knowledge. I did not say any thing, but labored to think nothing and to look up with unconscious eyes. But Firm put me out altogether by his warmth, and made me flutter like a stupid little bird.

"My darling," he said, smoothing back my hair with a kindness such as I could not resent, and quieting me with his clear blue eyes, "you are not fit for the stormy life to which your high spirit is devoting you. You have not the hardness and bitterness of mind, the cold self-possession and contempt of others, the power of dissembling and the iron will—in a word, the fundamental nastiness, without which you never could get through such a job. Why, you can not be contemptuous even to me!"

"I should hope not. I should earn your contempt, if I could."

"There, you are ready to cry at the thought. Erema, do not mistake yourself. Remember that your father would never have wished it—would have given his life ten thousand times over to prevent it. Why did he bring you to this remote, inaccessible part of the world except to save you from further thought of evil? He knew that we listen to no rumors here, no social scandals, or malignant lies; but we value people as we find them. He meant this to be a haven for you; and so it shall be if you will only rest; and you shall be the queen of it. Instead of redressing his memory now, you would only distress his spirit. What does he care for the world's gossip now? But he does care for your happiness. I am not old enough to tell you things as I should like to tell them. I wish I could—how I wish I could! It would make all the difference to me."

"It would make no difference, Firm, to me; because I should know it was selfishness. Not selfishness of yours, I mean, for you never could be selfish; but the vilest selfishness of mine, the same as starved my father. You can not see things as I see them, or else you would not talk so. When you know that a thing is right, you do it. Can you tell me otherwise? If you did, I should despise you."

"If you put it so, I can say no more. You will leave us forever, Erema?"

"No, not forever. If the good God wills it, I will come back when my work is done. Forgive me, dear Firm, and forget me."

"There is nothing to forgive, Erema; but a great deal I never can hope to forgot."

CHAPTER XVIII
OUT OF THE GOLDEN GATE

Little things, or what we call little, always will come in among great ones, or at least among those which we call great. Before I passed the Golden Gate in the clipper ship Bridal Veil (so called from one of the Yosemite cascades) I found out what I had long wished to know—why Firm had a crooked nose. At least, it could hardly be called crooked if any body looked aright at it; but still it departed from the bold straight line which nature must have meant for it, every thing else about him being as straight as could be required. This subject had troubled me more than once, though of course it had nothing whatever to do with the point of view whence I regarded him.

Suan Isco could not tell me, neither could Martin of the mill; I certainly could not ask Firm himself, as the Sawyer told me to do when once I put the question, in despair, to him. But now, as we stood on the wharf exchanging farewells, perhaps forever, and tears of anguish were in my eyes, and my heart was both full and empty, ample and unexpected light was thrown on the curvature of Firm's nose.

For a beautiful girl, of about my own age, and very nicely dressed, came up and spoke to the Sawyer (who stood at my side), and then, with a blush, took his grandson's hand. Firm took off his hat to her very politely, but allowed her to see perhaps by his manner that he was particularly engaged just now; and the young lady, with a quick glance at me, walked off to rejoin her party. But a garrulous old negro servant, who seemed to be in attendance upon her, ran up and caught Firm by his coat, and peered up curiously at his face.

"How young massa's poor nose dis long time? How him feel, spose now again?" he inquired, with a deferential grin. "Young massa ebber able take a pinch of good snuff? He! he! missy berry heavy den? Missy no learn to dance de nose polka den?"

"What on earth does he mean?" I could not help asking, in spite of our sorrowful farewell, as the negro went on with sundry other jokes and cackles at his own facetiousness. And then Uncle Sam, to divert my thoughts, while

I waited for signal to say good-by, told me how Firm got a slight twist to his nose.

Ephraim Gundry had been well taught, in all the common things a man should learn, at a good quiet school at Frisco, which distinguished itself from all other schools by not calling itself a college. And when he was leaving to begin home life, with as much put into him as he could manage—for his nature was not bookish—when he was just seventeen years old, and tall and straight and upright, but not set into great bodily strength, which could not yet be expected, a terrible fire broke out in a great block of houses newly occupied, over against the school-house front. Without waiting for master's leave or matron's, the boys, in the Californian style, jumped over the fencing and went to help. And they found a great crowd collected, and flames flaring out of the top of the house. At the top of the house, according to a stupid and therefore general practice, was the nursery, made of more nurses than children, as often happens with rich people. The nurses had run away for their lives, taking two of the children with them; but the third, a fine little girl of ten, had been left behind, and now ran to the window with red hot flames behind her. The window was open, and barbs of fire, like serpents' tongues, played over it.

"Jump, child, jump! for God's sake, jump!" cried half a hundred people, while the poor scared creature quivered on the ledge, and shrank from the frightful depth below. At last, stung by a scorching volley, she gathered her night-gown tight, and leaped, trusting to the many faces and many arms raised toward her. But though many gallant men were there, only one stood fast just where she fell, and that one was the youth, Firm Gundry. Upon him she fell, like a stone from heaven, and though he held up his arms in the smoky glare, she came down badly: badly, at least, for him, but, as her father said, providentially; for one of her soles, or heels, alighted on the bridge of Ephraim's young nose. He caught her on his chest, and forgetful of himself, he bore her to her friends triumphantly, unharmed, and almost smiling. But the symmetry of an important part of his face was spoiled forever.

When I heard of this noble affair, and thought of my own pusillanimous rendering—for verily I had been low enough, from rumors of Firm's pugnacity, to attribute these little defects of line to some fisticuffs with some miner—I looked at Firm's nose through the tears in my eyes, and had a great mind not to go away at all. For what is the noblest of all things in man—as I bitterly learned thereafter, and already had some guesses? Not the power of moving multitudes with eloquence or by orders; not the elevation of one tribe through the lowering of others, nor even the imaginary lift of all by sentiments as yet above them: there may be glory in all of these, but the greatness is not with them. It remains with those who behave like Firm, and get their noses broken.

However, I did not know those things at that time of life, though I thought it right for every man to be brave and good; and I could not help asking who the young lady was, as if that were part of the heroism. The Sawyer, who never was unready for a joke, of however ancient quality, gave a great wink at Firm (which I failed to understand), and asked him how much the young lady was worth. He expected that Firm would say, "Five hundred thousand dollars"—which was about her value, I believe—and Uncle Sam wanted me to hear it; not that he cared a single cent himself, but to let me know what Firm could do.

Firm, however, was not to be led into any trap of that sort. He knew me better than the old man did, and that nothing would stir me to jealousy, and he quite disappointed the Sawyer.

"I have never asked what she is worth," he said, with a glance of contempt at money; "but she scarcely seems worth looking at, compared—compared with certain others."

In the distance I saw the young lady again, attempting no attraction, but walking along quite harmlessly, with the talkative negro after her. It would have been below me to pursue the subject, and I waited for others to re-open it; but I heard no more about her until I had been for more than a week at sea, and was able again to feel interest. Then I heard that her name was Annie Banks, of the firm of Heniker, Banks, and Co., who owned the ship I sailed in.

But now it was nothing to me who she was, or how beautiful, or how wealthy, when I clung for the last time to Uncle Sam, and implored him not to forget me. Over and over again he promised to be full of thoughts of me, even when the new mill was started, which would be a most trying time. He bowed his tall white head into my sheveled hair, and blessed and kissed me, although I never deserved it, and a number of people were looking on. Then I laid my hand in Firm's, and he did not lift it to his lips, or sigh, but pressed it long and softly, and looked into my eyes without a word. And I knew that there would be none to love like them, wherever I might go.

But the last of all to say "good-by" was my beloved Jowler. He jumped into the boat after me (for we were obliged to have a boat, the ship having laden further down), and he put his fore-paws on my shoulders, and whined and drooped his under-jaw. And when he looked at me as he used, to know whether I was in fun or earnest, with more expression in his bright brown eyes than any human being has, I fell back under his weight and sobbed, and could not look at any one.

We had beautiful weather, and the view was glorious, as we passed the Golden Gate, the entrance to what will one day be the capital of the world, perhaps. For, as our captain said, all power and human energy and strength are always going westward, and when they come here they must stop, or else they would be going eastward again, which they never yet have done. His argument may have been right or wrong—and, indeed, it must have been one or the other—but who could think of such things now, with a grander thing than human power—human love fading away behind? I could not even bear to see the glorious mountains sinking, but ran below and cried for hours, until all was dark and calm.

The reason for my sailing by this particular ship, and, indeed, rather suddenly, was that an old friend and Cornish cousin of Mr. Gundry, who had spent some years in California, was now returning to England by the Bridal Veil. This was Major Hockin, an officer of the British army, now on half-pay, and getting on in years. His wife was going home with him; for their children were married and settled in England, all but one, now in San Francisco. And that one being well placed in the firm of Heniker, Banks, and Co., had obtained for his father and mother passage upon favorable terms, which was, as we say, "an object to them."

For the Major, though admirably connected (as his kinship to Colonel Gundry showed), and having a baronet not far off (if the twists of the world were set aside), also having served his country, and received a furrow on the top of his head, which made him brush his hair up, nevertheless, or all the more for that, was as poor as a British officer must be without official sesame. How he managed to feed and teach a large and not clever family, and train them all to fight their way in a battle worse than any of his own, and make gentlemen and ladies of them, whatever they did or wherever they went, he only knew, and his faithful wife, and the Lord who helps brave poverty. Of such things he never spoke, unless his temper was aroused by luxury and self-indulgence and laziness.

But now he was a little better off, through having his children off his hands, and by means of a little property left him by a distant relative. He was on his way home to see to this; and a better man never returned to England, after always standing up for her.

Being a child in the ways of the world, and accustomed to large people, I could not make out Major Hockin at first, and thought him no more than a little man with many peculiarities. For he was not so tall as myself, until he put his high-heeled boots on, and he made such a stir about trifles at which Uncle Sam would have only grunted, that I took him to be nothing more than a fidgety old campaigner. He wore a black-rimmed double eyeglass with blue side-lights at his temples, and his hat, from the shape of his forehead, hung back; he had narrow white wiry whiskers, and a Roman nose, and most prominent chin, and keen gray eyes with gingery brows, which contracted, like sharp little gables over them, whenever any thing displeased him. Rosy cheeks, tight-drawn, close-shaven, and gleaming with friction of yellow soap, added vigor to the general expression of his face, which was firm and quick and straightforward. The weather being warm, and the tropics close at hand, Major Hockin was dressed in a fine suit of Nankin, spruce and trim, and beautifully made, setting off his spare and active figure, which, though he was sixty-two years of age, seemed always to be ready for a game of leap-frog.

We were three days out of the Golden Gate, and the hills of the coast ridge were faint and small, and the spires of the lower Nevada could only be caught when the hot haze lifted; and every body lay about in our ship where it seemed to afford the least smell and heat, and nobody for a moment dreamed—for we really all were dreaming—of any body with energy enough to be disturbed about any thing, when Major Hockin burst in upon us all (who were trying not to be red-hot in the feeble shade of poop awnings), leading by the hand an ancient woman, scarcely dressed with decency, and howling in a tone very sad to hear.

"This lady has been robbed!" cried the Major; "robbed, not fifteen feet below us. Robbed, ladies and gentlemen, of the most cherished treasures of her life, the portrait of her only son, the savings of a life of honest toil, her poor dead husband's tobacco-box, and a fine cut of Colorado cheese."

"Ten pounds and a quarter, gospel true!" cried the poor woman, wringing her hands, and searching for any kind face among us.

"Go to the captain," muttered one sleepy gentleman. "Go to the devil," said another sleepy man: "what have we to do with it?"

"I will neither go to the captain," replied the Major, very distinctly, "nor yet to the devil, as a fellow who is not a man has dared to suggest to me—"

"All tied in my own pocket-handkerchief!" the poor old woman began to scream; "the one with the three-cornered spots upon 'un. Only two have I ever owned in all my life, and this was the very best of 'em. Oh dear! oh dear! that ever I should come to this exposing of my things!"

"Madam, you shall have justice done, as sure as my name is Hockin. Gentlemen and ladies, if you are not all asleep, how would you like to be treated so? Because the weather is a trifle warm, there you lie like a parcel of Mexicans. If any body picked your pockets, would you have life enough to roll over?"

"I don't think I should," said a fat young Briton, with a very good-natured face; "but for a poor woman I can stand upright. Major Hockin, here is a guinea for her. Perhaps more of us will give a trifle."

"Well done!" cried the Major; "but not so much as that. Let us first ascertain all the rights of the case. Perhaps half a crown apiece would reach it."

Half a crown apiece would have gone beyond it, as we discovered afterward, for the old lady's handkerchief was in her box, lost under some more of her property; and the tide of sleepy charity taking this direction under such vehement impulse, several other steerage passengers lost their goods, but found themselves too late in doing so. But the Major was satisfied, and the rude man who had told him to go amiss, begged his pardon, and thus we sailed on slowly and peaceably.

CHAPTER XIX
INSIDE THE CHANNEL

That little incident threw some light upon Major Hockin's character. It was not for himself alone that he was so particular, or, as many would call it, fidgety, to have every thing done properly; for if any thing came to his knowledge which he thought unfair to any one, it concerned him almost as much as if the wrong had been done to his own home self. Through this he had fallen into many troubles, for his impressions were not always accurate; but they taught him nothing, or rather, as his wife said, "the Major could not help it." The leading journals of the various places in which Major Hockin sojourned had published his letters of grievances sometimes, in the absence of the chief editor, and had suffered in purse by doing so. But the Major always said, "Ventilate it, ventilate the subject, my dear Sir; bring public opinion to bear on it." And Mrs. Hockin always said that it was her husband to whom belonged the whole credit of this new and spirited use of the fine word "ventilation."

As betwixt this faithful pair, it is scarcely needful perhaps to say that the Major was the master. His sense of justice dictated that, as well as his general briskness. Though he was not at all like Mr. Gundry in undervaluing female mind, his larger experience and more frequent intercourse with our sex had taught him to do justice to us; and it was pleasant to hear him often defer to the judgment of ladies. But this he did more, perhaps, in theory than in practice; yet it made all the ladies declare to one another that he was a perfect gentleman. And so he was, though he had his faults; but his faults were such as we approve of.

But Mrs. Hockin had no fault in any way worth speaking of. And whatever she had was her husband's doing, through her desire to keep up with him. She was pretty, even now in her sixtieth year, and a great deal prettier because she never tried to look younger. Silver hair, and gentle eyes, and a forehead in which all the cares of eight children had scarcely imprinted a wrinkle, also a kind expression of interest in whatever was spoken of, with a quiet voice and smile, and a power of not saying too much at a time, combined to make this lady pleasant.

Without any fuss or declaration, she took me immediately under her care; and I doubt not that, after two years passed in the society of Suan Isco and the gentle Sawyer, she found many things in me to amend, which she did by example and without reproof. She shielded me also in the cleverest way from the curiosity of the saloon, which at first was very trying. For the Bridal Veil being a well-known ship both for swift passages and for equipment, almost every berth was taken, and when the weather was calm, quite a large assembly sat down to dinner. Among these, of course, were some ill-bred people, and my youth and reserve and self-consciousness, and so on, made my reluctant face the mark for many a long and searching gaze. My own wish had been not to dine thus in public; but hearing that my absence would only afford fresh grounds for curiosity, I took my seat between the Major and his wife, the former having pledged himself to the latter to leave every thing to her management. His temper was tried more than once to its utmost—which was not a very great distance—but he kept his word, and did not interfere; and I having had some experience with Firm, eschewed all perception of glances. And as for all words, Mrs. Hockin met them with an obtuse obliqueness; so that after a day or two it was settled that nothing could be done about "Miss Wood."

It had been a very sore point to come to, and cost an unparalleled shed of pride, that I should be shorn of two-thirds of my name, and called "Miss Wood," like almost anybody else. I refused to entertain such a very poor idea, and clung to the name which had always been mine—for my father would never depart from it—and I even burst into tears, which would, I suppose, be called "sentimental;" but still the stern fact stared me in the face—I must go as "Miss Wood," or not go at all. Upon this Major Hockin had insisted; and even Colonel Gundry could not move him from his resolution.

Uncle Sam had done his utmost, as was said before, to stop me from wishing to go at all; but when he found my whole heart bent upon it, and even my soul imperiled by the sense of neglecting life's chief duty, his own stern sense of right came in and sided with my prayers to him. And so it was that he let me go, with pity for my youth and sex, but a knowledge that I was in good hands, and an inborn, perhaps "Puritanical" faith, that the Lord of all right would see to me.

The Major, on the other hand, had none of this. He differed from Uncle Sam as much as a trim-cut and highly cultured garden tree differs from a great spreading king of the woods. He was not without a strict sense of religion, especially when he had to march men to church; and he never even used a bad word, except when wicked facts compelled him. When properly let alone, and allowed to nurse his own opinions, he had a respectable idea that all things were certain to be ordered for the best; but nothing enraged him so much as to tell him that when things went against him, or even against his predictions.

It was lucky for me, then, that Major Hockin had taken a most adverse view of my case. He formed his opinions with the greatest haste, and with the greatest perseverance stuck to them; for he was the most generous of mankind, if generous means one quite full of his genus. And in my little case he had made up his mind that the whole of the facts were against me. "Fact" was his favorite word, and one which he always used with great effect, for nobody knows very well what it means, as it does not belong to our language. And so when he said that the facts were against me, who was there to answer that facts are not truth?

This fast-set conclusion of his was known to me not through himself, but through his wife. For I could not yet bring myself to speak of the things that lay close at my heart to him, though I knew that he must be aware of them. And he, like a gentleman, left me to begin. I could often see that he was ready and quite eager to give me the benefit of his opinion, which would only have turned me against him, and irritated him, perhaps, with me. And having no home in England, or, indeed, I might say, any where, I was to live with the Major and his wife, supposing that they could arrange it so, until I should discover relatives.

We had a long and stormy voyage, although we set sail so fairly; and I thought that we never should round Cape Horn in the teeth of the furious northeast winds; and after that we lay becalmed, I have no idea in what latitude, though the passengers now talked quite like seamen, at least till the sea got up again. However, at last we made the English Channel, in the dreary days of November, and after more peril there than any where else, we were safely docked at Southampton. Here the Major was met by two dutiful daughters, bringing their husbands and children, and I saw more of family life (at a distance) than had fallen to my lot to observe before; and although there were many little jars and brawls and cuts at one another, I was sadly inclined to wish sometimes for some brothers and sisters to quarrel with.

But having none to quarrel with, and none to love, except good Mrs. Hockin, who went away by train immediately, I spent such a wretched time in that town that I longed to be back in the Bridal Veil in the very worst of weather. The ooze of the shore and the reek of the water, and the dreary flatness of the land around (after the glorious heaven-clad heights, which made me ashamed of littleness), also the rough, stupid stare of the men, when I went about as an American lady may freely do in America, and the sharpness of every body's voice (instead of the genial tones which those who can not produce them call "nasal," but which from a higher view are cordial)—taken one after other, or all together, these things made me think, in the first flush of thought, that England was not a nice country. After a little while I found that I had been a great deal too quick, as foreigners are with things which require quiet comprehension. For instance, I was annoyed at having a stupid woman put over me, as if I could not mind myself—a cook, or a nurse, or housekeeper, or something very useful in the Hockin family, but to me a mere incumbrance, and (as I thought in my wrath sometimes) a spy. What was I likely to do, or what was any one likely to do to me, in a thoroughly civilized country, that I could not even stay in private lodgings, where I had a great deal to think of, without this dull creature being forced upon me? But the Major so ordered it, and I gave in.

There I must have staid for the slowest three mouths ever passed without slow starvation finishing my growth, but not knowing how to "form my mind," as I was told to do. Major Hockin came down once or twice to see me, and though I did not like him, yet it was almost enough to make me do so to see a little liveliness. But I could not and would not put up with a frightful German baron of music, with a polished card like a toast-rack, whom the Major tried to impress on me. As if I could stop to take music lessons!

"Miss Wood," said Major Hockin, in his strongest manner, the last time he came to see me, "I stand to you in loco parentis. That means, with the duties, relationships, responsibilities, and what not, of the unfortunate—I should say rather of the beloved—parent deceased. I wish to be more careful of you than of a daughter of my own—a great deal more careful, ten times, Miss Wood; I may say a thousand times more careful, because you have not had the discipline which a daughter of mine would have enjoyed. And you are so impulsive when you take an idea! You judge every body by your likings. That leads to error, error, error."

"My name is not Miss Wood," I answered; "my name is 'Erema Castlewood.' Whatever need may have been on board ship for nobody knowing who I am, surely I may have my own name now."

When any body says "surely," at once up springs a question; nothing being sure, and the word itself at heart quite interrogative. The Major knew all those little things which manage women so manfully. So he took me by the hand and led me to the light and looked at me.

I had not one atom of Russian twist or dyed China grass in my hair, nor even the ubiquitous aid of horse and cow; neither in my face or figure was I conscious of false presentment. The Major was welcome to lead me to the light and to throw up all his spectacles and gaze with all his eyes. My only vexation was with myself, because I could not keep the weakness—which a stranger should not see—out of my eyes, upon sudden remembrance who it was that used to have the right to do such things to me. This it was, and nothing else, that made me drop my eyes, perhaps.

"There, there, my dear!" said Major Hockin, in a softer voice than usual. "Pretty fit you are to combat with the world, and defy the world, and brave the world, and abolish the world—or at least the world's opinion! 'Bo to a goose,' you can say, my dear; but no 'bo' to a gander. No, no; do quietly what I advise—by-the-bye, you have never asked my advice."

I can not have been hypocritical, for of all things I detest that most; but in good faith I said, being conquered by the Major's relaxation of his eyes,

"Oh, why have you never offered it to me? You knew that I never could ask for it."

For the moment he looked surprised, as if our ideas had gone crosswise; and then he remembered many little symptoms of my faith in his opinions; which was now growing inevitable, with his wife and daughters, and many grandchildren—all certain that he was a Solomon.

"Erema," he said, "you are a dear good girl, though sadly, sadly romantic. I had no idea that you had so much sense. I will talk with you, Erema, when we both have leisure."

"I am quite at leisure, Major Hockin," I replied, "and only too happy to listen to you."

"Yes, yes, I dare say. You are in lodgings. You can do exactly as you please. But I have a basin of ox-tail soup, a cutlet, and a woodcock waiting for me at the Cosmopolitan Hotel. Bless me! I am five minutes late already. I will come and have a talk with you afterward."

"Thank you," I said; "we had better leave it. It seems of no importance, compared—compared with—"

"My dinner!" said the Major; but he was offended, and so was I a little, though neither of us meant to vex the other.

CHAPTER XX
BRUNTSEA

It would be unfair to Major Hockin to take him for an extravagant man or a self-indulgent one because of the good dinner he had ordered, and his eagerness to sit down to it. Through all the best years of his life he had been most frugal, abstemious, and self-denying, grudging every penny of his own expense, but sparing none for his family. And now, when he found himself so much better off, with more income and less outlay, he could not be blamed for enjoying good things with the wholesome zest of abstinence.

For, coming to the point, and going well into the matter, the Major had discovered that the "little property" left to him, and which he was come to see to, really was quite a fine estate for any one who knew how to manage it, and would not spare courage and diligence. And of these two qualities he had such abundance that, without any outlet, they might have turned him sour.

The property lately devised to him by his cousin, Sir Rufus Hockin, had long been far more plague than profit to that idle baronet. Sir Rufus hated all exertion, yet could not comfortably put up with the only alternative—extortion. Having no knowledge of his cousin Nick (except that he was indefatigable), and knowing his own son to be lazier even than himself had been, longing also to inflict even posthumous justice upon the land agent, with the glad consent of his heir he left this distant, fretful, and naked spur of land to his beloved cousin Major Nicholas Hockin.

The Major first heard of this unexpected increase of his belongings while he was hovering, in the land of gold, between his desire to speculate and his dread of speculation. At once he consulted our Colonel Gundry, who met him by appointment at Sacramento; and Uncle Sam having a vast idea of the value of land in England, which the Major naturally made the most of, now being an English land-owner, they spent a most pleasant evening, and agreed upon the line marked out by Providence.

Thus it was that he came home, bringing (by kind arrangement) me, who was much more trouble than comfort to him, and at first disposed to be cold and curt. And thus it was that I was left so long in that wretched

Southampton, under the care of a very kind person who never could understand me. And all this while (as I ought to have known, without any one to tell me) Major Hockin was testing the value and beating the bounds of his new estate, and prolonging his dinner from one to two courses, or three if he had been travelling. His property was large enough to afford him many dinners, and rich enough (when rightly treated) to insure their quality.

Bruntsea is a quiet little village on the southeast coast of England, in Kent or in Sussex, I am not sure which, for it has a constitution of its own, and says that it belongs to neither. It used to be a place of size and valor, furnishing ships, and finding money for patriotic purposes. And great people both embarked and landed, one doing this and the other that, though nobody seems to have ever done both, if history is to be relied upon. The glory of the place is still preserved in a seal and an immemorial stick, each of which is blessed with marks as incomprehensible as could be wished, though both are to be seen for sixpence. The name of the place is written in more than forty different ways, they say; and the oldest inhabitant is less positive than the youngest how to spell it.

This village lies in the mouth, or rather at the eastern end of the mouth, of a long and wide depression among the hills, through which a sluggish river wins its muddy consummation. This river once went far along the sea-brink, without entering (like a child who is afraid to bathe), as the Adur does at Shoreham, and as many other rivers do. And in those days the mouth and harbor were under the cliff at Bruntsea, whence its seal and corporation, stick, and other blessings. But three or four centuries ago the river was drawn by a violent storm, like a badger from his barrel, and forced to come straight out and face the sea, without any three miles of dalliance. The time-serving water made the best of this, forsook its ancient bed (as classic nymphs and fountains used to do), and left poor Bruntsea with a dry bank, and no haven for a cockle-shell. A new port, such as it is, incrusted the fickle jaw of the river; piles were driven and earth-works formed, lest the water should return to its old love; and Bruntsea, as concerned her traffic, became but a mark of memory. Her noble corporation never demanded their old channel, but regarded the whole as the will of the Lord, and had the good sense to insist upon nothing except their time-honored ceremonies.

In spite of all these and their importance, land became of no value there. The owner of the Eastern Manor and of many ancient rights, having no means of getting at them, sold them for an "old song," which they were; and the buyer was one of the Hockin race, a shipwrecked mariner from Cornwall, who had been kindly treated there, and took a fancy accordingly. He sold his share in some mine to pay for it, settled here, and died here; and his son, getting on in the world, built a house, and took to serious smuggling. In the chalk cliff's eastward he found holes of honest value to him, capable of cheap enlargement (which the Cornish holes were not), and much more accessible from France. Becoming a magistrate and deputy-lieutenant, he had the duty and privilege of inquiring into his own deeds, which enabled him to check those few who otherwise might have competed with him. He flourished, and bought more secure estates; and his son, for activity against smugglers, was made a gentle baronet.

These things now had passed away, and the first fee-simple of the Hockin family became a mere load and incumbrance. Sir George and Sir Robert and Sir Rufus, one after another, did not like the hints about contraband dealings which met them whenever they deigned to come down there, till at last the estate (being left to an agent) cost a great deal more than he ever paid in. And thus—as should have been more briefly told—the owner was our Major Hockin.

No wonder that this gentleman, with so many cares to attend to, had no time at first to send for me. And no wonder that when he came down to see me, he was obliged to have good dinners. For the work done by him in those three months surprised every body except himself, and made in old Bruntsea a stir unknown since the time of the Spanish Armada. For he owned the house under the eastern cliff, and the warren, and the dairy-farm inland, and the slope of the ground where the sea used to come, and fields where the people grew potatoes gratis, and all the eastern village, where the tenants paid their rents whenever they found it rational.

A hot young man, in a place like this, would have done a great deal of mischief. Either he would have accepted large views, and applauded this fine communism (if he could afford it, and had no wife), or else he would have rushed at every body headlong, and batted them back to their abutments. Neither course would have created half the excitement which the Major's did. At least, there might have been more talk at first, but not a quarter so much in sum total. Of those things, however, there is time enough to speak, if I dare to say any thing about them.

The things more to my mind (and therefore more likely to be made plain to another mind) are not the petty flickering phantoms of the shadow we call human, and which alone we realize, and dwell inside it and upon it, as if it were all creation; but the infinitely nobler things of ever-changing but perpetual beauty, and no selfishness. These, without deigning to us even sense to be aware of them, shape our little minds and bodies and our large self-importance, and fail to know when the lord or king who owns is buried under them. To have perception of such mighty truths is good for all of us:

and I never had keener perception of them than when I sat down on the Major's camp-stool, and saw all his land around me, and even the sea—where all the fish were his, as soon as he could catch them—and largely reflected that not a square foot of the whole world would ever belong to me.

"Bruntlands," as the house was called, perhaps from standing well above the sea, was sheltered by the curve of the eastern cliff, which looked down over Bruntsea. The cliff was of chalk, very steep toward the sea, and showing a prominent headland toward the south, but prettily rising in grassy curves from the inland and from the westward. And then, where it suddenly chined away from land-slope into sea-front, a long bar of shingle began at right angles to it, and, as level as a railroad, went to the river's mouth, a league or so now to the westward. And beyond that another line of white cliffs rose, and looked well till they came to their headland. Inside this bank of shingle, from end to end, might be traced the old course of the river, and to landward of that trough at the hither end stood, or lay, the calm old village.

Forsaken as it was by the river, this village stuck to its ancient site and home, and instead of migrating, contracted itself, and cast off needless members. Shrunken Bruntsea clung about the oldest of its churches, while the four others fell to rack and ruin, and settled into cow-yards and barns, and places where old men might sit and sigh. But Bruntsea distinctly and trenchantly kept the old town's division into east and west.

East Bruntsea was wholly in the Major's manor, which had a special charter; and most of the houses belonged to him. This ownership hitherto had meant only that the landlord should do all the tumble-down repairs (when the agent reported that they must be done), but never must enter the door for his rent. The borough had been disfranchised, though the snuggest of the snug for generations; and the freemen, thus being robbed of their rights, had no power to discharge their duties. And to complicate matters yet further, for the few who wished to simplify them, the custom of "borough-English" prevailed, and governed the descent of dilapidations, making nice niceties for clever men of law.

"You see a fine property here, Miss Wood," Major Hockin said to me, as we sat, on the day after I was allowed to come, enjoying the fresh breeze from the sea and the newness of the February air, and looking abroad very generally: "a very fine property, but neglected—shamefully, horribly, atrociously neglected—but capable of noble things, of grand things, of magnificent, with a trifle of judicious outlay."

"Oh, please not to talk of outlay, my dear," said good Mrs. Hockin, gently; "it is such an odious word; and where in the world is it to come from?"

"Leave that to me. When I was a boy my favorite copy in my copy-book was, 'Where there's a will there's a way.' Miss Wood, what is your opinion? But wait, you must have time to understand the subject. First we bring a railway—always the first step; why, the line is already made for it by the course of the old river, and the distance from Newport three miles and a half. It ought not to cost quite 200 pounds a mile—the mere outlay for rails and sleepers. The land is all mine, and—and of course other landed proprietors'. Very well: these would all unite, of course; so that not a farthing need be paid for land, which is the best half of the battle. We have the station here—not too near my house; that would never do; I could not bear the noise—but in a fine central place where nobody on earth could object to it—lively, and close at hand for all of them. Unluckily I was just too late. We have lost a Parliamentary year through that execrable calm—you remember all about it. Otherwise we would have had Billy Puff stabled at Bruntsea by the first of May. But never mind; we shall do it all the better and cheaper by taking our time about it. Very well: we have the railway opened and the trade of the place developed. We build a fine terrace of elegant villas, a crescent also, and a large hotel replete with every luxury; and we form the finest sea-parade in England by simply assisting nature. Half London comes down here to bathe, to catch shrimps, to flirt, and to do the rest of it. We become a select, salubrious, influential, and yet economical place; and then what do we do, Mrs. Hockin?"

"My dear, how can I tell? But I hope that we should rest and be thankful."

"Not a bit of it. I should hope not, indeed. Erema, what do we do then?"

"It is useless to ask me. Well, then, perhaps you set up a handsome saw-mill!"

"A saw-mill! What a notion of Paradise! No; this is what we do—but remember that I speak in the strictest confidence; dishonest antagonism might arise, if we ventilated our ideas too soon—Mrs. Hockin and Miss Wood, we demand the restoration of our river!—the return of our river to its ancient course."

"I see," said his wife; "oh, how grand that would be! and how beautiful from our windows! That really, now, is a noble thought!"

"A just one—simply a just one. Justice ought not to be noble, my dear, however rare it may be. Generosity, magnanimity, heroism, and so on—those are the things we call noble, my dear."

"And the founding of cities. Oh, my dear, I remember, when I was at school, it was always said, in what we called our histories, that the founders of cities had honors paid them, and altars built, and divinities done, and holidays held in their honor."

"To that I object," cried the Major, sternly. "If I founded fifty cities, I would never allow one holiday. The Sabbath is enough; one day in seven—fifteen per cent, of one's whole time; and twenty per cent, of your Sunday goes in church. Very right, of course, and loyal, and truly edifying—Mrs. Hockin's father was a clergyman, Miss Wood; and the last thing I would ever allow on my manor would be a Dissenting chapel; but still I will have no new churches here, and a man who might go against me. They all want to pick their own religious views, instead of reflecting who supports them! It never used to be so; and such things shall never occur on my manor. A good hotel, attendance included, and a sound and moderate table d'hote; but no church, with a popish bag sent round, and money to pay, 'without anything to eat.'"

"My dear! my dear!" cried Mrs. Hockin, "I never like you to talk like that. You quite forget who my father was, and your own second son such a very sound priest!"

"A priest! Don't let him come here," cried the Major, "or I'll let him know what tonsure is, and read him the order of Melchisedec. A priest! After going round the world three times, to come home and be hailed as the father of a priest! Don't let him come near me, or I'll sacrifice him."

"Now, Major, you are very proud of him," his good wife answered, as he shook his stick. "How could he help taking orders when he was under orders to do so? And his views are sound to the last degree, most strictly correct and practical—at least except as to celibacy."

"He holds that his own mother ought never to have been born! Miss Wood, do you call that practical?"

"I have no acquaintance with such things," I replied; "we had none of them in California. But is it practical, Major Hockin—of course you know best in your engineering—I mean, would it not require something like a tunnel for the river and the railway to run on the same ground?"

"Why, bless me! That seems to have escaped my notice. You have not been with old Uncle Sam for nothing. We shall have to appoint you our chief engineer."

CHAPTER XXI
LISTLESS

It seemed an unfortunate thing for me, and unfavorable to my purpose, that my host, and even my hostess too, should be so engrossed with their new estate, its beauties and capabilities. Mrs. Hockin devoted herself at once to fowls and pigs and the like extravagant economies, having bought, at some ill-starred moment, a book which proved that hens ought to lay eggs in a manner to support themselves, their families, and the family they belonged to, at the price of one penny a dozen. Eggs being two shillings a dozen in Bruntsea, here was a margin for profit—no less than two thousand per cent, to be made, allowing for all accidents. The lady also found another book, divulging for a shilling the author's purely invaluable secret—how to work an acre of ground, pay house rent, supply the house grandly, and give away a barrow-load of vegetables every day to the poor of the parish, by keeping a pig—if that pig were kept properly. And after that, pork and ham and bacon came of him, while another golden pig went on.

Mrs. Hockin was very soft-hearted, and said that she never could make bacon of a pig like that; and I answered that if she ever got him it would be unwise to do so. However, the law was laid down in both books that golden fowls and diamondic pigs must die the death before they begin to overeat production; and the Major said, "To be sure. Yes, yes. Let them come to good meat, and then off with their heads." And his wife said that she was sure she could do it. When it comes to a question of tare and tret, false sentiment must be excluded.

At the moment, these things went by me as trifles, yet made me more impatient. Being older now, and beholding what happens with tolerance and complacence, I am only surprised that my good friends were so tolerant of me and so complacent. For I must have been a great annoyance to them, with my hurry and my one idea. Happily they made allowance for me, which I was not old enough to make for them.

"Go to London, indeed! Go to London by yourself!" cried the Major, with a red face, and his glasses up, when I told him one morning that I could stop no longer without doing something. "Mary, my dear, when you have done out there, will you come in and reason—if you can—with Miss Wood. She vows that she is going to London, all alone."

"Oh, Major Hockin—oh, Nicholas dear, such a thing has happened!" Mrs. Hockin had scarcely any breath to tell us, as she came in through the window. "You know that they have only had three bushels, or, at any rate, not more than five, almost ever since they came. Erema, you know as well as I do."

"Seven and three-quarter bushels of barley, at five and ninepence a bushel, Mary," said the Major, pulling out a pocket-book; "besides Indian corn, chopped meat, and potatoes."

"And fourteen pounds of paddy," I said—which was a paltry thing of me; "not to mention a cake of graves, three sacks of brewers' grains, and then—I forget what next."

"You are too bad, all of you. Erema, I never thought you would turn against me so. And you made me get nearly all of it. But please to look here. What do you call this? Is this no reward? Is this not enough? Major, if you please, what do you call this? What a pity you have had your breakfast!"

"A blessing—if this was to be my breakfast. I call that, my dear, the very smallest egg I have seen since I took sparrows' nests. No wonder they sell them at twelve a penny. I congratulate you upon your first egg, my dear Mary."

"Well, I don't care," replied Mrs. Hockin, who had the sweetest temper in the world. "Small beginnings make large endings; and an egg must be always small at one end. You scorn my first egg, and Erema should have had it if she had been good. But she was very wicked, and I know not what to do with it."

"Blow it!" cried the Major. "I mean no harm, ladies. I never use low language. What I mean is, make a pinhole at each end, give a puff, and away goes two pennyworth, and you have a cabinet specimen, which your egg is quite fitted by its cost to be. But now, Mary, talk to Miss Wood, if you please. It is useless for me to say any thing, and I have three appointments in the town"—he always called it "the town" now—"three appointments, if not four; yes, I may certainly say four. Talk to Miss Wood, my dear, if you please. She wants to go to London, which would be absurd. Ladies seem to enter into ladies' logic. They seem to be able to appreciate it better, to see all the turns, and the ins and outs, which no man has intellect enough to see, or at least to make head or tail of. Good-by for the present; I had better be off."

"I should think you had," exclaimed Mrs. Hockin, as her husband marched off, with his side-lights on, and his short, quick step, and well-satisfied glance at the hill which belonged to him, and the beach, over which he had rights of plunder—or, at least, Uncle Sam would have called them so, strictly as he stood up for his own.

"Now come and talk quietly to me, my dear," Mrs. Hockin began, most kindly, forgetting all the marvel of her first-born egg. "I have noticed how restless you are, and devoid of all healthy interest in any thing. 'Listless' is the word. 'Listless' is exactly what I mean, Erema. When I was at your time of life, I could never have gone about caring for nothing. I wonder that you knew that I even had a fowl; much more how much they had eaten!"

"I really do try to do all I can, and that is a proof of it," I said. "I am not quite so listless as you think. But those things do seem so little to me."

"My dear, if you were happy, they would seem quite large, as, after all the anxieties of my life, I am able now to think them. It is a power to be thankful for, or, at least, I often think so. Look at my husband! He has outlived and outlasted more trouble than any one but myself could reckon up to him; and yet he is as brisk, as full of life, as ready to begin a new thing to-morrow—when, at our age, there may be no to-morrow, except in that better world, my dear, of which it is high time for him and me to think, as I truly hope we may spare the time to do."

"Oh, don't talk like that," I cried. "Please, Mrs. Hockin, to talk of your hens and chicks—at least there will be chicks by-and-by. I am almost sure there will, if you only persevere. It seems unfair to set our minds on any other world till justice has been done in this."

"You are very young, my child, or you would know that in that case we never should think of it at all. But I don't want to preach you a sermon, Erema, even if I could do so. I only just want you to tell me what you think, what good you imagine that you can do."

"It is no imagination. I am sure that I can right my father's wrongs. And I never shall rest till I do so."

"Are you sure that there is any wrong to right?" she asked, in the warmth of the moment; and then, seeing perhaps how my color changed, she looked at me sadly, and kissed my forehead.

"Oh, if you had only once seen him," I said; "without any exaggeration, you would have been satisfied at once. That he could ever have done any harm was impossible—utterly impossible. I am not as I was. I can listen to almost any thing now quite calmly. But never let me hear such a wicked thing again."

"You must not go on like that, Erema, unless you wish to lose all your friends. No one can help being sorry for you. Very few girls have been placed as you are. I am sure when I think of my own daughters I can never be too thankful. But the very first thing you have to learn, above all things, is to control yourself."

"I know it—I know it, of course," I said; "and I keep on trying my very best. I am thoroughly ashamed of what I said, and I hope you will try to forgive me."

"A very slight exertion is enough for that. But now, my dear, what I want to know is this—and you will excuse me if I ask too much—what good do you expect to get by going thus to London? Have you any friend there, any body to trust, any thing settled as to what you are to do?"

"Yes, every thing is settled in my own mind," I answered, very bravely: "I have the address of a very good woman, found among my father's papers, who nursed his children and understood his nature, and always kept her faith in him. There must be a great many more who do the same, and she will be sure to know them and introduce me to them; and I shall be guided by their advice."

"But suppose that this excellent woman is dead, or not to be found, or has changed her opinion?"

"Her opinion she never could change. But if she is not to be found, I shall find her husband, or her children, or somebody; and besides that, I have a hundred things to do. I have the address of the agent through whom my father drew his income, though Uncle Sam let me know as little as he could. And I know who his bankers were (when he had a bank), and he may have left important papers there."

"Come, that looks a little more sensible, my dear; bankers may always be relied upon. And there may be some valuable plate, Erema. But why not let the Major go with you? His advice is so invaluable."

"I know that it is, in all ordinary things. But I can not have him now, for a very simple reason. He has made up his mind about my dear father—horribly, horribly; I can't speak of it. And he never changes his mind; and sometimes when I look at him I hate him."

"Erema, you are quite a violent girl, although you so seldom show it. Is the whole world divided, then, into two camps—those who think as you wish and those who are led by their judgment to think otherwise? And are you to hate all who do not think as you wish?"

"No, because I do not hate you," I said; "I love you, though you do not think as I wish. But that is only because you think your husband must be right of course. But I can not like those who have made up their minds according to their own coldness."

"Major Hockin is not cold at all. On the contrary, he is a warm-hearted man—I might almost say hot-hearted."

"Yes, I know he is. And that makes it ten times worse. He takes up every body's case—but mine."

"Sad as it is, you almost make me smile," my hostess answered, gravely; "and yet it must be very bitter for you, knowing how just and kind my husband is. I am sure that you will give him credit for at least desiring to take your part. And doing so, at least you might let him go with you, if only as a good protection."

"I have no fear of any one; and I might take him into society that he would not like. In a good cause he would go any where, I know. But in my cause, of course he would be scrupulous. Your kindness I always can rely upon, and I hope in the end to earn his as well."

"My dear, he has never been unkind to you. I am certain that you never can say that of him. Major Hockin unkind to a poor girl like you!"

"The last thing I wish to claim is any body's pity," I answered, less humbly than I should have spoken, though the pride was only in my tone, perhaps. "If people choose to pity me, they are very good, and I am not at all offended, because—because they can not help it, perhaps, from not knowing any thing about me. I have nothing whatever to be pitied for, except that I have lost my father, and have nobody left to care for me, except Uncle Sam in America."

"Your Uncle Sam, as you call him, seems to be a very wonderful man, Erema," said Mrs. Hockin, craftily, so far as there could be any craft in her; "I never saw him—a great loss on my part. But the Major went up to meet him somewhere, and came home with the stock of his best tie broken, and two buttons gone from his waistcoat. Does Uncle Sam make people laugh so much? or is it that he has some extraordinary gift of inducing people to taste whiskey? My husband is a very—most abstemious man, as you must be well aware, Miss Wood, or we never should have been as we are, I am sure. But, for the first time in all my life, I doubted his discretion on the following day, when he had—what shall I say?—when he had been exchanging sentiments with Uncle Sam."

"Uncle Sam never takes too much in any way," I replied to this new attack; "he knows what he ought to take, and then he stops. Do you think that it may have been his 'sentiments,' perhaps, that were too strong and large for the Major?"

"Erema!" cried Mrs. Hockin, with amazement, as if I had no right to think or express my thoughts on life so early; "if you can talk politics at eighteen, you are quite fit to go any where. I have heard a great deal of American ladies, and seen not a little of them, as you know. But I thought that you called yourself an English girl, and insisted particularly upon it."

"Yes, that I do; and I have good reason. I am born of an old English family, and I hope to be no disgrace to it. But being brought up in a number of ways, as I have been without thinking of it, and being quite different from the fashionable girls Major Hockin likes to walk with—"

"My dear, he never walks with any body but myself!"

"Oh yes, I remember! I was thinking of the deck. There are no fashionable girls here yet. Till the terrace is built, and the esplanade—"

"There shall be neither terrace nor esplanade if the Major is to do such things upon them."

"I am sure that he never would," I replied; "it was only their dresses that he liked at all, and that very, to my mind, extraordinary style, as well as unbecoming. You know what I mean, Mrs. Hockin, that wonderful—what shall I call it?—way of looping up."

"Call me 'Aunt Mary,' my dear, as you did when the waves were so dreadful. You mean that hideous Mexican poncho, as they called it, stuck up here, and going down there. Erema, what observation you have! Nothing ever seems to escape you. Did you ever see any thing so indecorous?"

"It made me feel just as if I ought not to look at them," I answered, with perfect truth, for so it did; "I have never been accustomed to such things. But seeing how the Major approved of them, and liked to be walking up and down between them, I knew that they must be not only decorous, but attractive. There is no appeal from his judgment, is there?"

"I agree with him upon every point, my dear child; but I have always longed to say a few words about that. For I can not help thinking that he went too far."

CHAPTER XXII
BETSY BOWEN

So far, then, there was nobody found to go into my case, and to think with me, and to give me friendly countenance, with the exception of Firm Gundry. And I feared that he tried to think with me because of his faithful and manly love, more than from balance of evidence. The Sawyer, of course, held my father guiltless, through his own fidelity and simple ways; but he could not enter into my set thought of a stern duty laid upon me, because to his mind the opinion of the world mattered nothing so long as a man did aright. For wisdom like this, if wisdom it is, I was a great deal too young and ardent; and to me fair fame was of almost equal value with clear conscience. And therefore, wise or foolish, rich or poor, beloved or unloved, I must be listless about other things, and restless in all, until I should establish truth and justice.

However, I did my best to be neither ungrateful nor stupidly obstinate, and, beginning more and more to allow for honest though hateful opinions, I yielded to dear Mrs. Hockin's wish that I should not do any thing out of keeping with English ideas and habits. In a word, I accepted the Major's kind offer to see me quite safe in good hands in London, or else bring me straightway back again. And I took only just things enough for a day or two, meaning to come back by the end of the week. And I kissed Mrs. Hockin just enough for that.

It would not be a new thing for me to say that "we never know what is going to happen;" but, new or stale, it was true enough, as old common sayings of common-sense (though spurned when not wanted) show themselves. At first, indeed, it seemed as if I were come for nothing, at least as concerned what I thought the chief business of my journey. The Major had wished to go first to the bank, and appeared to think nothing of any thing else; but I, on the other hand, did not want him there, preferring to keep him out of my money matters, and so he was obliged to let me have my way.

I always am sorry when I have been perverse, and it seemed to serve me right for willfulness when no Betsy Bowen could be discovered either at the place which we tried first, or that to which we were sent thence. Major Hockin looked at me till I could have cried, as much as to hint that the whole of my story was all of a piece, all a wild-goose chase. And being more curious than ever now to go to the bank and ransack, he actually called out to the cabman to drive without delay to Messrs. Shovelin, Wayte, and Shovelin. But I begged him to allow me just one minute while I spoke to the servant-maid alone. Then I showed her a sovereign, at which she opened her mouth in more ways than one, for she told me that "though she had faithfully promised to say nothing about it, because of a dreadful quarrel between her mistress and Mrs. Strouss that was now, and a jealousy between them that was quite beyond belief, she could not refuse such a nice young lady, if I would promise faithfully not to tell." This promise I gave with fidelity, and returning to the cabman, directed him to drive not to Messrs. Shovelin, Wayte, and Shovelin just yet, but to No. 17 European Square, St. Katharine's.

From a maze of streets and rugged corners, and ins and outs nearly as crooked as those of a narrow human nature, we turned at last into European Square, which was no square at all, but an oblong opening pitched with rough granite, and distinguished with a pump. There were great thoroughfares within a hundred yards, but the place itself seemed unnaturally quiet upon turning suddenly into it, only murmurous with distant London din, as the spires of a shell hold the heavings of the sea. After driving three or four times round the pump, for the houses were numbered anyhow, we found No. 17, and I jumped out.

"Now don't be in such a fierce hurry, Miss Wood," cried the Major, who was now a little crusty; "English ladies allow themselves to be handed out, without hurrying the gentlemen who have the honor."

"But I wanted to save you the honor," I said. "I will come back immediately, if you will kindly wait." And with this I ran up the old steps, and rang and knocked, while several bearded faces came and gazed through dingy windows.

"Can I see Mrs. Strouss?" I asked, when a queer old man in faded brown livery came to the door with a candle in his hand, though the sun was shining.

"I am the Meesther Strouss; when you see me, you behold the good Meeses Strouss also."

"Thank you, but that will not do," I replied; "my business is with Mrs. Strouss alone."

He did not seem to like this at first sight, but politely put the chain-bolt on the door while he retired to take advice; and the Major looked out of the cab and laughed.

"You had better come back while you can," he said, "though they seem in no hurry to swallow you."

This was intended to vex me, and I did not even turn my head to him. The house looked very respectable, and there were railings to the area.

"The house is very respectable," continued Major Hockin, who always seemed to know what I was thinking of, and now in his quick manner ran up the steps; "just look, the scraper is clean. You never see that, or at least not often, except with respectable people, Erema."

"Pray what would my scraper be? and who is Erema?" cried a strong, clear voice, as the chain of the door was set free, and a stout, tall woman with a flush in her cheeks confronted us. "I never knew more than one Erema—Good mercy!"

My eyes met hers, and she turned as pale as death, and fell back into a lobby chair. She knew me by my likeness to my father, falling on the memories started by my name; and strong as she was, the surprise overcame her, at the sound of which up rushed the small Herr Strouss.

"Vhat are you doing dere, all of you? vhat have you enterprised with my frau? Explain, Vilhelmina, or I call de policemans, vhat I should say de peelers."

"Stop!" cried the Major, and he stopped at once, not for the word, which would have had no power, although I knew nothing about it then, but because he had received a sign which assured him that here was a brother Mason. In a moment the infuriated husband vanished into the rational and docile brother.

"Ladies and gentlemans, valk in, if you please," he said, to my great astonishment; "Vilhelmina and my good self make you velcome to our poor house. Vilhelmina, arise and say so."

"Go to the back kitchen, Hans," replied Wilhelmina, whose name was "Betsy," "and don't come out until I tell you. You will find work to do there, and remember to pump up. I wish to hear things that you are not to hear, mind you. Shut yourself in, and if you soap the door to deceive me, I shall know it."

"Vere goot, vere goot," said the philosophical German; "I never meddle with nothing, Vilhelmina, no more than vhat I do for de money and de house."

Betsy, however, was not quite so sure of that. With no more ceremony she locked him in, and then came back to us, who could not make things out.

"My husband is the bravest of the brave," she told us, while she put down his key on the table; "and a nobler man never lived; I am sure of that. But every one of them foreigners—excuse me, Sir, you are an Englishman?"

"I am," replied the Major, pulling up his little whiskers; "I am so, madam, and nothing you can say will in any way hurt my feelings. I am above nationalities."

"Just so, Sir. Then you will feel with me when I say that they foreigners is dreadful. Oh, the day that I ever married one of 'em—but there, I ought to be ashamed of myself, and my lord's daughter facing me."

"Do you know me?" I asked, with hot color in my face, and my eyes, I dare say, glistening. "Are you sure that you know me? And then please to tell me how."

As I spoke I was taking off the close silk bonnet which I had worn for travelling, and my hair, having caught in a pin, fell round me, and before I could put it up, or even think of it, I lay in the great arms of Betsy Bowen, as I used to lie when I was a little baby, and when my father was in his own land, with a home and wife and seven little ones. And to think of this made me keep her company in crying, and it was some time before we did any thing else.

"Well, well," replied the Major, who detested scenes, except when he had made them; "I shall be off. You are in good hands; and the cabman pulled out his watch when we stopped. So did I. But he is sure to beat me. They draw the minute hand on with a magnet, I am told, while the watch hangs on their badge, and they can swear they never opened it. Wonderful age, very wonderful age, since the time when you and I were young, ma'am."

"Yes, Sir; to be sure, Sir!" Mrs. Strouss replied, as she wiped her eyes to speak of things; "but the most wonderfulest of all things, don't you think, is the going of the time, Sir? No cabby can make it go faster while he waits, or slower while he is a-driving, than the minds inside of us manage it. Why, Sir, it wore only like yesterday that this here tall, elegant, royal young lady was a-lying on my breast, and what a hand she was to kick! And I said that her hair was sure to grow like this. If I was to tell you only half what comes across me—"

"If you did, ma'am, the cabman would make his fortune, and I should lose mine, which is more than I can afford. Erema, after dinner I shall look you up. I know a good woman when I see her, Mrs. Strouss, which does not happen every day. I can trust Miss Castlewood with you. Good-by, good-by for the present."

It was the first time he had ever called me by my proper name, and that made me all the more pleased with it.

"You see, Sir, why I were obliged to lock him in," cried the "good woman," following to the door, to clear every blur from her virtues; "for his own sake I done it, for I felt my cry a-coming, and to see me cry—Lord bless you, the effect upon him is to call out for a walking-stick and a pint of beer."

"All right, ma'am, all right!" the Major answered, in a tone which appeared to me unfeeling. "Cabman, are you asleep there? Bring the lady's bag this moment."

As the cab disappeared without my even knowing where to find that good protector again in this vast maze of millions, I could not help letting a little cold fear encroach on the warmth of my outburst. I had heard so much in America of the dark, subtle places of London, and the wicked things that happen all along the Thames, discovered or invented by great writers of their own, that the neighborhood of the docks and the thought of rats (to which I could never grow accustomed) made me look with a flash perhaps of doubt at my new old friend.

"You are not sure of me, Miss Erema," said Mrs. Strouss, without taking offense. "After all that has happened, who can blame it on you? But your father was not so suspicious, miss. It might have been better for him if he had—according, leastways, to my belief, which a team of wild horses will never drag out."

"Oh, only let me hear you talk of that!" I exclaimed, forgetting all other things. "You know more about it than any body I have ever met with, except my own father, who would never tell a word."

"And quite right he was, miss, according to his views. But come to my little room, unless you are afraid. I can tell you some things that your father never knew."

"Afraid! do you think I am a baby still? But I can not bear that Mr. Strouss should be locked up on my account."

"Then he shall come out," said Mrs. Strouss, looking at me very pleasantly. "That was just like your father, Miss Erema. But I fall into the foreign ways, being so much with the foreigners." Whether she thought it the custom among "foreigners" for wives to lock their husbands in back kitchens was more than she ever took the trouble to explain. But she walked away, in her stout, firm manner, and presently returned with Mr. Strouss, who seemed to be quite contented, and made me a bow with a very placid smile.

"He is harmless; his ideas are most grand and good," his wife explained to me, with a nod at him. "But I could not have you in with the gentleman, Hans. He always makes mistakes with the gentlemen, miss, but with the ladies he behaves quite well."

"Yes, yes, with the ladies I am nearly always goot," Herr Strouss replied, with diffidence. "The ladies comprehend me right, all right, because I am so habitual with my wife. But the gentlemans in London have no comprehension of me."

"Then the loss is on their side," I answered, with a smile; and he said, "Yes, yes, they lose vere much by me."

CHAPTER XXIII
BETSY'S TALE

Now I scarcely know whether it would be more clear to put into narrative what I heard from Betsy Bowen, now Wilhelmina Strouss, or to let her tell the whole in her own words, exactly as she herself told it then to me. The story was so dark and sad—or at least to myself it so appeared—that even the little breaks and turns of lighter thought or livelier manner, which could scarcely fail to vary now and then the speaker's voice, seemed almost to grate and jar upon its sombre monotone. On the other hand, by omitting these, and departing from her homely style, I might do more of harm than good through failing to convey impressions, or even facts, so accurately. Whereas the gist and core and pivot of my father's life and fate are so involved (though not evolved) that I would not miss a single point for want of time or diligence. Therefore let me not deny Mrs. Strouss, my nurse, the right to put her words in her own way. And before she began to do this she took the trouble to have every thing cleared away and the trays brought down, that her boarders (chiefly German) might leave their plates and be driven to their pipes.

"If you please, Miss Castlewood," Mrs. Strouss said, grandly, "do you or do you not approve of the presence of 'my man,' as he calls himself?—an improper expression, in my opinion; such, however, is their nature. He can hold his tongue as well as any man, though none of them are very sure at that. And he knows pretty nigh as much as I do, so far as his English can put things together, being better accustomed in German. For when we were courting I was fain to tell him all, not to join him under any false pretenses, miss, which might give him grounds against me."

"Yes, yes, it is all vere goot and true—so goot and true as can be."

"And you might find him come very handy, my dear, to run of any kind of messages. He can do that very well, I assure you, miss—better than any Englishman."

Seeing that he wished to stay, and that she desired it, I begged him to stop, though it would have been more to my liking to hear the tale alone.

"Then sit by the door, Hans, and keep off the draught," said his Wilhelmina, kindly. "He is not very tall, miss, but he has good shoulders; I scarcely know what I should do without him. Well, now, to begin at the very beginning: I am a Welshwoman, as you may have heard. My father was a farmer near Abergavenny, holding land under Sir Watkin Williams, an old friend of your family. My father had too many girls, and my mother scarcely knew what to do with the lot of us. So some of us went out to service, while the boys staid at home to work the land. One of my sisters was lady's-maid to Lady Williams, Sir Watkin's wife, at the time when your father came visiting there for the shooting of the moor-fowl, soon after his marriage with your mother. What a sweet good lady your mother was! I never saw the like before or since. No sooner did I set eyes upon her but she so took my fancy that I would have gone round the world with her. We Welsh are a very hot people, they say—not cold-blooded, as the English are. So, wise or foolish, right, wrong, or what might be, nothing would do for me but to take service, if I could, under Mrs. Castlewood. Your father was called Captain Castlewood then—as fine a young man as ever clinked a spur, but without any boast or conceit about him; and they said that your grandfather, the old lord, kept him very close and spare, although he was the only son. Now this must have been—let me see, how long ago?—about five-and-twenty years, I think. How old are you now, Miss Erema? I can keep the weeks better than the years, miss."

"I was eighteen on my last birthday. But never mind about the time—go on."

"But the time makes all the difference, miss, although at the time we may never think so. Well, then, it must have been better than six-and-twenty year agone; for though you came pretty fast, in the Lord's will, there was eight years between you and the first-born babe, who was only just a-thinking of when I begin to tell. But to come back to myself, as was—mother had got too many of us still, and she was glad enough to let me go, however much she might cry over it, as soon as Lady Williams got me the place. My place was to wait upon the lady first, and make myself generally useful, as they say. But it was not very long before I was wanted in other more important ways, and having been brought up among so many children, they found me very handy with the little ones; and being in a poor way, as they were then—for people, I mean, of their birth and place—they were glad enough soon to make head nurse of me, although I was under-two-and-twenty.

"We did not live at the old lord's place, which is under the hills looking on the river Thames, but we had a quiet little house in Hampshire; for the Captain was still with his regiment, and only came to and fro to us. But a happier little place there could not be, with the flowers, and the cow, and the birds all day, and the children running gradually according to their age, and the pretty brook shining in the valley. And as to the paying of their way, it is true that neither of them was a great manager. The Captain could not bear to keep his pretty wife close; and she, poor thing, was trying always to surprise him with other presents besides all the beautiful babies. But they never were in debt all round, as the liars said when the trouble burst; and if they owed two or three hundred pounds, who could justly blame them?

"For the old lord, instead of going on as he should, and widening his purse to the number of the mouths, was niggling at them always for offense or excuse, to take away what little he allowed them. The Captain had his pay, which would go in one hand, and the lady had a little money of her own; but still it was cruel for brought-up people to have nothing better to go on with. Not that the old lord was a miser neither; but it was said, and how far true I know not, that he never would forgive your father for marrying the daughter of a man he hated. And some went so far as to say that if he could have done it, he would have cut your father out of all the old family estates. But such a thing never could I believe of a nobleman having his own flesh and blood.

"But, money or no money, rich or poor, your father and mother, I assure you, my dear, were as happy as the day was long. For they loved one another and their children dearly, and they did not care for any mixing with the world. The Captain had enough of that when put away in quarters; likewise his wife could do without it better and better at every birth, though once she had been the very gayest of the gay, which you never will be, Miss Erema.

"Now, my dear, you look so sad and so 'solid,' as we used to say, that if I can go on at all, I must have something ready. I am quite an old nurse now, remember. Hans, go across the square, and turn on the left hand round the corner, and then three more streets toward the right, and you see one going toward the left, and you go about seven doors down it, and then you see a corner with a lamp-post."

"Vilhelmina, I do see de lamp-post at de every corner."

"That will teach you to look more bright, Hans. Then you find a shop window with three blue bottles, and a green one in the middle."

"How can be any middle to three, without it is one of them?"

"Then let it be two of them. How you contradict me! Take this little bottle, and the man with a gold braid round a cap, and a tassel with a tail to it, will fill it for four-pence when you tell him who you are."

"Yes, yes; I do now comprehend. You send me vhere I never find de vay, because I am in de vay, Vilhelmina!"

I was most thankful to Mrs. Strouss for sending her husband (however good and kind-hearted he might be) to wander among many shops of chemists, rather than to keep his eyes on me, while I listened to things that were almost sure to make me want my eyes my own. My nurse had seen, as any good nurse must, that, grown and formed as I might be, the nature of the little child that cries for its mother was in me still.

"It is very sad now," Mrs. Strouss began again, without replying to my grateful glance; "Miss Erema, it is so sad that I wish I had never begun with it. But I see by your eyes—so like your father's, but softer, my dear, and less troublesome—that you will have the whole of it out, as he would with me once when I told him a story for the sake of another servant. It was just about a month before you were born, when the trouble began to break on us. And when once it began, it never stopped until all that were left ran away from it. I have read in the newspapers many and many sad things coming over whole families, such as they call 'shocking tragedies;' but none of them, to my mind, could be more galling than what I had to see with my very own eyes.

"It must have been close upon the middle of September when old Lord Castlewood came himself to see his son's house and family at Shoxford. We heard that he came down a little on the sudden to see to the truth of some rumors which had reached him about our style of living. It was the first time he had ever been there; for although he had very often been invited, he could not bear to be under the roof of the daughter, as he said, of his enemy. The Captain, just happening to come home on leave for his autumn holiday, met his father quite at his own door—the very last place to expect him. He afterward acknowledged that he was not pleased for his father to come 'like a thief in the night.' However, they took him in and made him welcome, and covered up their feelings nicely, as high-bred people do.

"What passed among them was unknown to any but themselves, except so far as now I tell you. A better dinner than usual for two was ready, to celebrate the master's return and the beginning of his holiday; and the old lord, having travelled far that day, was persuaded to sit down with them. The five eldest children (making all except the baby, for you was not born, miss, if you please) they were to have sat up at table, as pretty as could be— three with their high cushioned stools, and two in their arm-chairs screwed on mahogany, stuffed with horsehair, and with rods in front, that the little dears might not tumble out in feeding, which they did—it was a sight to see them! And how they would give to one another, with their fingers wet and shining, and saying, 'Oo, dat for oo.' Oh dear, Miss Erema, you were never born to see it! What a blessing for you! All those six dear darlings laid in their little graves within six weeks, with their mother planted under them; and the only wonder is that you yourself was not upon her breast.

"Pay you no heed to me, Miss Erema, when you see me a-whimpering in and out while I am about it. It makes my chest go easy, miss, I do assure you, though not at the time of life to understand it. All they children was to have sat up for the sake of their dear father, as I said just now; but because of their grandfather all was ordered back. And back they come, as good as gold, with Master George at the head of them, and asked me what milk-teeth was. Grandpa had said that 'a dinner was no dinner if milk-teeth were allowed at it.' The hard old man, with his own teeth false! He deserved to sit down to no other dinner—and he never did, miss.

"You may be sure that I had enough to do to manage all the little ones and answer all their questions; but never having seen a live lord before, and wanting to know if the children would be like him before so very long, I went quietly down stairs, and the biggest of my dears peeped after me. And then, by favor of the parlor-maid—for they kept neither butler nor footman now—I saw the Lord Castlewood, sitting at his ease, with a glass of port-wine before him, and my sweet mistress (the Captain's wife, and your mother, if you understand, miss) doing her very best, thinking of her children, to please him and make the polite to him. To me he seemed very much to be thawing to her—if you can understand, miss, what my meaning is—and the Captain was looking at them with a smile, as if it were just what he had hoped for. From my own eyesight I can contradict the lies put about by nobody knows who, that the father and the son were at hot words even then.

"And I even heard my master, when they went out at the door, vainly persuading his father to take such a bed as they could offer him. And good enough it would have been for ten lords; for I saw nothing wonderful in him, nor fit to compare any way with the Captain. But he would not have it, for no other reason of ill-will or temper, but only because he had ordered his bed at the Moonstock Inn, where his coach and four were resting.

"'I expect you to call me in the morning, George,' I heard him say, as clear as could be, while his son was helping his coat on. 'I am glad I have seen you. There are worse than you. And when the times get better, I will see what I can do.'

"With him this meant more than it might have done; for he was not a man of much promises, as you might tell by his face almost, with his nose so stern, and his mouth screwed down, and the wrinkles the wrong way for smiling. I could not tell what the Captain answered, for the door banged on them, and it woke the baby, who was dreaming, perhaps, about his lordship's face, and his little teeth gave him the wind on his chest, and his lungs was like bellows—bless him!

"Well, that stopped me, Miss Erema, from being truly accurate in my testimony. What with walking the floor, and thumping his back, and rattling of the rings to please him—when they put me on the Testament, cruel as they did, with the lawyers' eyes eating into me, and both my ears buzzing with sorrow and fright, I may have gone too far, with my heart in my mouth, for my mind to keep out of contradiction, wishful as I was to tell the whole truth in a manner to hurt nobody. And without any single lie or glaze of mine, I do assure you, miss, that I did more harm than good; every body in the room—a court they called it, and no bigger than my best parlor—one and all they were convinced that I would swear black was white to save my master and mistress! And certainly I would have done so, and the Lord in heaven thought the better of me, for the sake of all they children, if I could have made it stick together, as they do with practice."

At thought of the little good she had done, and perhaps the great mischief, through excess of zeal, Mrs. Strouss was obliged to stop, and put her hand to her side, and sigh. And eager as I was for every word of this miserable tale, no selfish eagerness could deny her need of refreshment, and even of rest; for her round cheeks were white, and her full breast trembled. And now she was beginning to make snatches at my hand, as if she saw things she could only tell thus.

CHAPTER XXIV
BETSY'S TALE—(Continued)

"I am only astonished, my dear," said my nurse, as soon as she had had some tea and toast, and scarcely the soft roe of a red herring, "that you can put up so well, and abide with my instincts in the way you do. None of your family could have done it, to my knowledge of their dispositions, much less the baby that was next above you. But it often comes about to go in turns like that; 'one, three, five, and seven is sweet, while two, four, and six is a-squalling with their feet.' But the Lord forgive me for an ill word of them, with their precious little bodies washed, and laying in their patterns till the judgment-day.

"But putting by the words I said in the dirty little room they pleased to call a 'court,' and the Testament so filthy that no lips could have a hold of it, my meaning is to tell you, miss, the very things that happened, so that you may fairly judge of them. The Captain came back from going with his father, I am sure, in less than twenty minutes, and smoking a cigar in his elegant way, quite happy and contented, for I saw him down the staircase. As for sign of any haste about him, or wiping of his forehead, or fumbling with his handkerchief, or being in a stew in any sort of way—as the stupid cook who let him in declared, by reason of her own having been at the beer-barrel—solemnly, miss, as I hope to go to heaven, there was nothing of the sort about him.

"He went into the dining-room, and mistress, who had been up stairs to see about the baby, went down to him; and there I heard them talking as pleasant and as natural as they always were together. Not one of them had the smallest sense of trouble hanging over them; and they put away both the decanters and cruets, and came up to bed in their proper order, the master stopping down just to finish his cigar and see to the doors and the bringing up the silver, because there was no man-servant now. And I heard him laughing at some little joke he made as he went into the bedroom. A happier household never went to bed, nor one with better hopes of a happy time to come. And the baby slept beside his parents in his little cot, as his mother liked to have him, with his blessed mouth wide open.

"Now we three (cook and Susan and myself) were accustomed to have a good time of it whenever the master first came home and the mistress was taken up with him. We used to count half an hour more in bed, without any of that wicked bell-clack, and then go on to things according to their order, without any body to say any thing. Accordingly we were all snug in bed, and turning over for another tuck of sleep, when there came a most vicious ringing of the outer bell. 'You get up, Susan,' I heard the cook say, for there only was a door between us; and Susan said, 'Blest if I will! Only Tuesday you put me down about it when the baker came.' Not a peg would either of them stir, no more than to call names on one another; so I slipped on my things, with the bell going clatter all the while, like the day of judgment. I felt it to be hard upon me, and I went down cross a little—just enough to give it well to a body I were not afraid of.

"But the Lord in His mercy remember me, miss! When I opened the door, I had no blood left. There stood two men, with a hurdle on their shoulders, and on the hurdle a body, with the head hanging down, and the front of it slouching, like a sack that has been stolen from; and behind it there was an authority with two buttons on his back, and he waited for me to say something; but to do so was beyond me. Not a bit of caution or of fear about my sham dress-up, as the bad folk put it afterward; the whole of such thoughts was beyond me outright, and no thought of any thing came inside me, only to wait and wonder.

"'This corpse belongeth here, as I am informed,' said the man, who seemed to be the master of it, and was proud to be so. 'Young woman, don't you please to stand like that, or every duffer in the parish will be here, and the boys that come hankering after it. You be off!' he cried out to a boy who was calling some more round the corner. 'Now, young woman, we must come in if you please, and the least said the soonest mended.'

"'Oh, but my mistress, my mistress!' I cried; 'and her time up, as nigh as may be, any day or night before new moon. 'Oh, Mr. Constable, Mr. Rural Polishman, take it to the tool shed, if you ever had a wife, Sir.' Now even this was turned against us as if I had expected it. They said that I must have known who it was, and to a certain length so I did, miss, but only by the dress and the manner of the corpse, and lying with an attitude there was no contradicting.

"I can not tell you now, my dear, exactly how things followed. My mind was gone all hollow with the sudden shock upon it. However, I had thought enough to make no noise immediate, nor tell the other foolish girls, who would have set up bellowing. Having years to deal with little ones brings knowledge of the rest to us. I think that I must have gone to master's door, where Susan's orders were to put his shaving water in a tin, and fetched him out, with no disturbance, only in his dressing-gown. And when I told him what it was, his rosy color turned like sheets, and he just said, 'Hush!' and nothing more. And guessing what he meant, I ran and put my things on properly.

"But having time to think, the shock began to work upon me, and I was fit for nothing when I saw the children smiling up with their tongues out for their bread and milk, as they used to begin the day with. And I do assure you, Miss Erema, my bitterest thought was of your coming, though unknown whether male or female, but both most inconvenient then, with things in such a state of things. You have much to answer for, miss, about it; but how was you to help it, though?

"The tool-shed door was too narrow to let the hurdle and the body in, and finding some large sea-kale pots standing out of use against the door, the two men (who were tired with the weight and fright, I dare say) set down their burden upon these, under a row of hollyhocks, at the end of the row of bee-hives. And here they wiped their foreheads with some rags they had for handkerchiefs, or one of them with his own sleeve, I should say, and, gaining their breath, they began to talk with the boldness of the sunrise over them. But Mr. Rural Polishman, as he was called in those parts, was walking up and down on guard, and despising of their foolish words.

"My master, the Captain, your father, miss, came out of a window and down the cross-walk, while I was at the green door peeping, for I thought that I might be wanted, if only to take orders what was to be done inside. The constable stiffly touched his hat, and marched to the head of the hurdle, and said,

"'Do you know this gentleman?'

"Your father took no more notice of him than if he had been a stiff hollyhock, which he might have resembled if he had been good-looking. The Captain thought highly of discipline always, and no kinder gentleman could there be to those who gave his dues to him. But that man's voice had a low and dirty impertinent sort of a twang with it. Nothing could have been more unlucky. Every thing depended on that fellow in an ignorant neighborhood like that; and his lordship, for such he was now, of course, would not even deign to answer him. He stood over his head in his upright way by a good foot, and ordered him here and there, as the fellow had been expecting, I do believe, to order his lordship. And that made the bitterest enemy of him, being newly sent into these parts, and puffed up with authority. And the two miller's men could not help grinning, for he had waved them about like a pair of dogs.

"But to suppose that my master 'was unmoved, and took it brutally' (as that wretch of a fellow swore afterward), only shows what a stuck-up dolt he was. For when my master had examined his father, and made his poor body be brought in and spread on the couch in the dining-room, and sent me hot-foot for old Dr. Diggory down at the bottom of Shoxford, Susan peeped in through the crack of the door, with the cook to hold her hand behind, and there she saw the Captain on his knees at the side of his father's corpse, not saying a word, only with his head down. And when the doctor came back with me, with his night-gown positive under his coat, the first thing he said was, 'My dear Sir—my lord, I mean—don't take on so; such things will always happen in this world;' which shows that my master was no brute.

"Then the Captain stood up in his strength and height, without any pride and without any shame, only in the power of a simple heart, and he said words fit to hang him:

"'This is my doing! There is no one else to blame. If my father is dead, I have killed him!'

"Several of us now were looking in, and the news going out like a winnowing woman with no one to shut the door after her; our passage was crowding with people that should have had a tar-brush in their faces. And of course a good score of them ran away to tell that the Captain had murdered his father. The milk-man stood there with his yoke and cans, and his naily boots on our new oil-cloth, and, not being able to hide himself plainly, he pulled out his slate and began to make his bill.

"'Away with you all!' your father said, coming suddenly out of the dining-room, while the doctor was unbuttoning my lord, who was dead with all his day clothes on; and every body brushed away like flies at the depth of his voice and his stature. Then he bolted the door, with only our own people and the doctor and the constable inside. Your mother was sleeping like a lamb, as I could swear, having had a very tiring day the day before, and being well away from the noise of the passage, as well as at a time when they must sleep whenever sleep will come, miss. Bless her gentle heart, what a blessing to be out of all that scare of it!

"All this time, you must understand, there was no sign yet what had happened to his lordship, over and above his being dead. All of us thought, if our minds made bold to think, that it must have pleased the Lord to take his lordship either with an appleplexy or a sudden heart-stroke, or, at any rate, some other gracious way not having any flow of blood in it. But now, while your father was gone up stairs—for he knew that his father was dead enough—to be sure that your mother was quiet, and perhaps to smooth her down for trouble, and while I was run away to stop the ranting of the children, old Dr. Diggory and that rural officer were handling poor Lord Castlewood. They set him to their liking, and they cut his clothes off—so Susan told me afterward—and then they found why they were forced to do so, which I need not try to tell you, miss. Only they found that he was not dead from any wise visitation, but because he had been shot with a bullet through his heart.

"Old Dr. Diggory came out shaking, and without any wholesome sense to meet what had arisen, after all his practice with dead men, and he called out 'Murder!' with a long thing in his hand, till my master leaped down the stairs, twelve at a time, and laid his strong hand on the old fool's mouth.

"'Would you kill my wife?' he said; 'you shall not kill my wife.'

"'Captain Castlewood,' the constable answered, pulling out his staff importantly, 'consider yourself my prisoner.'

"The Captain could have throttled him with one hand, and Susan thought he would have done it. But, instead of that, he said, 'Very well; do your duty. But let me see what you mean by it.' Then he walked back again to the body of his father, and saw that he had been murdered.

"But, oh, Miss Erema, you are so pale! Not a bit of food have you had for hours. I ought not to have told you such a deal of it to once. Let me undo all your things, my dear, and give you something cordial; and then lie down and sleep a bit."

"No, thank you, nurse," I answered, calling all my little courage back. "No sleep for me until I know every word. And to think of all my father had to see and bear! I am not fit to be his daughter."

CHAPTER XXV
BETSY'S TALE—(Concluded)

"Well, now," continued Mrs. Strouss, as soon as I could persuade her to go on, "if I were to tell you every little thing that went on among them, miss, I should go on from this to this day week, or I might say this day fortnight, and then not half be done with it. And the worst of it is that those little things make all the odds in a case of that sort, showing what the great things were. But only a counselor at the Old Bailey could make head or tail of the goings on that followed.

"For some reason of his own, unknown to any living being but himself, whether it were pride (as I always said) or something deeper (as other people thought), he refused to have any one on earth to help him, when he ought to have had the deepest lawyer to be found. The constable cautioned him to say nothing, as it seems is laid down in their orders, for fear of crimination. And he smiled at this, with a high contempt, very fine to see, but not bodily wise. But even that jack-in-office could perceive that the poor Captain thought of his sick wife up stairs, and his little children, ten times for one thought he ever gave to his own position. And yet I must tell you that he would have no denial, but to know what it was that had killed his parent. When old Dr. Diggory's hands were shaking so that his instrument would not bite on the thing lodged in his lordship's back, after passing through and through him, and he was calling for somebody to run for his assistant, who do you think did it for him, Miss Erema? As sure as I sit here, the Captain! His face was like a rock, and his hands no less; and he said, 'Allow me, doctor. I have been in action.' And he fetched out the bullet—which showed awful nerve, according to my way of thinking—as if he had been a man with three rows of teeth.

"'This bullet is just like those of my own pistol!' he cried, and he sat down hard with amazement. You may suppose how this went against him, when all he desired was to know and tell the truth; and people said that of course he got it out, after a bottleful of doctors failed, because he knew best how it was put in.'

"'I shall now go and see the place, if you please, or whether you please or not,' my master said. 'Constable, you may come and point it out, unless you prefer going to your breakfast. My word is enough that I shall not run away. Otherwise, as you have acted on your own authority, I shall act on mine, and tie you until you have obtained a warrant. Take your choice, my man; and make it quickly, while I offer it.'

"The rural polishman stared at this, being used on the other hand to be made much of. But seeing how capable the Captain was of acting up to any thing, he made a sulky scrape, and said, 'Sir, as you please for the present,' weighting his voice on those last three words, as much as to say, 'Pretty soon you will be handcuffed.' 'Then,' said my master, 'I shall also insist on the presence of two persons, simply to use their eyes without any fear or favor. One is my gardener, a very honest man, but apt to be late in the morning. The other is a faithful servant, who has been with us for several years. Their names are Jacob Rigg and Betsy Bowen. You may also bring two witnesses, if you choose. And the miller's men, of course, will come. But order back all others.'

"'That is perfectly fair and straightforward, my lord,' the constable answered, falling naturally into abeyance to orders. 'I am sure that all of us wishes your lordship kindly out of this rum scrape. But my duty is my duty.'

"With a few more words we all set forth, six in number, and no more; for the constable said that the miller's men, who had first found the late Lord Castlewood, were witnesses enough for him. And Jacob Rigg, whose legs were far apart (as he said) from trenching celery, took us through the kitchen-garden, and out at a gap, which saved every body knowing.

"Then we passed through a copse or two, and across a meadow, and then along the turnpike-road, as far as now I can remember. And along that we went to a stile on the right, without any house for a long way off. And from that stile a foot-path led down a slope of grass land to the little river, and over a hand-bridge, and up another meadow full of trees and bushes, to a gate which came out into the road again a little to this side of the Moonstock Inn, saving a quarter of a mile of road, which ran straight up the valley and turned square at the stone bridge to get to the same inn.

"I can not expect to be clear to you, miss, though I see it all now as I saw it then, every tree, and hump, and hedge of it; only about the distances from this to that, and that to the other, they would be beyond me. You must be on the place itself; and I never could carry distances—no, nor even clever men, I have heard my master say. But when he came to that stile he stopped and turned upon all of us clearly, and as straight as any man of men could be. 'Here I saw my father last, at a quarter past ten o'clock last night, or within a few minutes of that time.' I wished to see him to his inn, but he would not let me do so, and he never bore contradiction. He said that he knew the way well, having fished more than thirty years ago up and down this stream. He crossed this stile, and we shook hands over it, and the moon being bright, I looked into his face, and he said, 'My boy, God bless you!' Knowing his short ways, I did not even look after him, but turned away, and went straight home along this road. Upon my word as an Englishman, and as an officer of her Majesty, that is all I know of it. Now let us go on to the—to the other place.

"We all of us knew in our hearts, I am sure, that the Captain spoke the simple truth, and his face was grand as he looked at us. But the constable thought it his duty to ask,

"'Did you hear no sound of a shot, my lord? For he fell within a hundred yards of this.'

"'I heard no sound of any shot whatever. I heard an owl hooting as I went home, and then the rattle of a heavy wagon, and the bells of horses. I have said enough. Let us go forward.'

"We obeyed him at once; and even the constable looked right and left, as if he had been wrong. He signed to the miller's man to lead the way, and my lord walked proudly after him. The path was only a little narrow track, with the grass, like a front of hair, falling over it on the upper side and on the under, dropping away like side curls; such a little path that I was wondering how a great lord could walk over it. Then we came down a steep place to a narrow bridge across a shallow river—a bridge made of only two planks and a rail, with a prop or two to carry them. And one end of the handrail was fastened into a hollow and stubby old hawthorn-tree, overhanging the bridge and the water a good way. And just above this tree, and under its shadow, there came a dry cut into the little river, not more than a yard or two above the wooden bridge, a water-trough such as we have in Wales, miss, for the water to run in, when the farmer pleases; but now there was no water in it, only gravel.

"The cleverest of the miller's men, though, neither of them had much intellect, stepped down at a beck from the constable, right beneath the old ancient tree, and showed us the marks on the grass and the gravel made by his lordship where he fell and lay. And it seemed that he must have fallen off the bridge, yet not into the water, but so as to have room for his body, if you see, miss, partly on the bank, and partly in the hollow of the meadow trough.

"'Have you searched the place well?' the Captain asked. 'Have you found any weapon or implement?'

"'We have found nothing but the corpse, so far,' the constable answered, in a surly voice, not liking to be taught his business. 'My first duty was to save life, if I could. These men, upon finding the body, ran for me, and knowing who it was, I came with it to your house.'

"'You acted for the best, my man. Now search the place carefully, while I stand here. I am on my parole, I shall not run away. Jacob, go down and help them.'

"Whether from being in the army, or what, your father always spoke in such a way that the most stiff-neckedest people began without thinking to obey him. So the constable and the rest went down, while the Captain and I stood upon the plank, looking at the four of them.

"For a long time they looked about, according to their attitudes, without finding any thing more than the signs of the manner in which the poor lord fell, and of these the constable pulled out a book and made a pencil memorial. But presently Jacob, a spry sort of man, cried, 'Hulloa! whatever have I got hold of here? Many a good craw-fish have I pulled out from this bank when the water comes down the gully, but never one exactly like this here afore.'

"'Name of the Lord!' cried the constable, jumping behind the hawthorn stump; 'don't point it at me, you looby! It's loaded, loaded one barrel, don't you see? Put it down, with the muzzle away from me.'

"'Hand it to me, Jacob,' the Captain said. 'You understand a gun, and this goes off just the same.' Constable Jobbins have no fear. 'Yes, it is exactly as I thought. This pistol is one of the double-barreled pair which I bought to take to India. The barrels are rifled; it shoots as true as any rifle, and almost as hard up to fifty yards. The right barrel has been fired, the other is still loaded. The bullet I took from my father's body most certainly came from this pistol.'

"'Can 'e say, can 'e say then, who done it, master?' asked Jacob, a man very sparing of speech, but ready at a beck to jump at constable and miller's men, if only law was with him. 'Can 'e give a clear account, and let me chuck 'un in the river?'

"'No, Jacob, I can do nothing of the kind,' your father answered; while the rural man came up and faced things, not being afraid of a fight half so much as he was of an accident; by reason of his own mother having been blown up by a gunpowder start at Dartford, yet came down all right, miss, and had him three months afterward, according to his own confession;

nevertheless, he came up now as if he had always been upright, in the world, and he said, 'My lord, can you explain all this?'

"Your father looked at him with one of his strange gazes, as if he were measuring the man while trying his own inward doing of his own mind. Proud as your father was, as proud as ever can be without cruelty, it is my firm belief, Miss Erema, going on a woman's judgment, that if the man's eyes had come up to my master's sense of what was virtuous, my master would have up and told him the depth and contents of his mind and heart, although totally gone beyond him.

"But Jobbins looked back at my lord with a grin, and his little eyes, hard to put up with. 'Have you nothing to say, my lord? Then I am afeared I must ask you just to come along of me.' And my master went with him, miss, as quiet as a lamb; which Jobbins said, and even Jacob fancied, was a conscience sign of guilt.

"Now after I have told you all this, Miss Erema, you know very nearly as much as I do. To tell how the grief was broken to your mother, and what her state of mind was, and how she sat up on the pillows and cried, while things went on from bad to worse, and a verdict of 'willful murder' was brought against your father by the crowner's men, and you come headlong, without so much as the birds in the ivy to chirp about you, right into the thick of the worst of it. I do assure you, Miss Erema, when I look at your bright eyes and clear figure, the Lord in heaven, who has made many cripples, must have looked down special to have brought you as you are. For trouble upon trouble fell in heaps, faster than I can wipe my eyes to think. To begin with, all the servants but myself and gardener Jacob ran away. They said that the old lord haunted the house, and walked with his hand in the middle of his heart, pulling out a bullet if he met any body, and sighing 'murder' three times, till every hair was crawling. I took it on myself to fetch the Vicar of the parish to lay the evil spirit, as they do in Wales. A nice kind gentleman he was as you could see, and wore a velvet skull-cap, and waited with his legs up. But whether he felt that the power was not in him, or whether his old lordship was frightened of the Church, they never made any opportunity between them to meet and have it out, miss.

"Then it seemed as if Heaven, to avenge his lordship, rained down pestilence upon that house. A horrible disease, the worst I ever met, broke out upon the little harmless dears, the pride of my heart and of every body's eyes, for lovelier or better ones never came from heaven. They was all gone to heaven in a fortnight and three days, and laid in the church-yard at one another's side, with little beds of mould to the measure of their stature, and their little carts and drums, as they made me promise, ready for the judgment-day. Oh, my heart was broken, miss, my heart was broken! I cried so, I thought I could never cry more.

"But when your dear mother, who knew nothing of all this (for we put all their illness, by the doctor's orders, away at the further end of the house), when she was a little better of grievous pain and misery (for being so upset her time was hard), when she sat up on the pillow, looking like a bride almost, except that she had what brides hasn't—a little red thing in white flannel at her side—then she says to me, 'I am ready, Betsy; it is high time for all of them to see their little sister. They always love the baby so, whenever there is a new one. And they are such men and women to it. They have been so good this time that I have never heard them once. And I am sure that I can trust them, Betsy, not to make the baby cry. I do so long to see the darlings. Now do not even whisper to them not to make a noise. They are too good to require it; and it would hurt their little feelings.'

"I had better have been shot, my dear, according as the old lord was, than have the pain that went through all my heart, to see the mother so. She sat up, leaning on one arm, with the hand of the other round your little head, and her beautiful hair was come out of its loops, and the color in her cheeks was like a shell. Past the fringe of the curtain, and behind it too, her soft bright eyes were a-looking here and there for the first to come in of her children. The Lord only knows what lies I told her, so as to be satisfied without them. First I said they were all gone for a walk; and then that the doctor had ordered them away; and then that they had got the measles. That last she believed, because it was worse than what I had said before of them; and she begged to see Dr. Diggory about it, and I promised that she should as soon as he had done his dinner. And then, with a little sigh, being very weak, she went down into her nest again, with only you to keep her company.

"Well, that was bad enough, as any mortal sufferer might have said; enough for one day at any rate. But there was almost worse to come. For when I was having a little sit down stairs, with my supper and half pint of ale (that comes like drawing a long breath to us when spared out of sickrooms, miss), and having no nursery now on my mind, was thinking of all the sad business, with only a little girl in the back kitchen come in to muck up the dishes, there appeared a good knock at the garden door, and I knew it for the thumb of the Captain. I locked the young girl up, by knowing what their tongues are, and then I let your father in, and the candle-sight of him made my heart go low.

"He had come out of prison; and although not being tried, his clothes were still in decency, they had great holes in them, and the gloss all gone to a smell of mere hedges and ditches. The hat on his head was quite out of the fashion, even if it could be called a hat at all, and his beautiful beard had no sign of a comb, and he looked as old again as he had looked a month ago.

"'I know all about it. You need not be afraid,' he said, as I took him to the breakfast-room, where no one up stairs could hear us. 'I know that my children are all dead and buried, except the one that was not born yet. Ill news flies quick. I know all about it. George, Henrietta, Jack, Alf, little Vi, and Tiny. I have seen their graves and counted them, while the fool of a policeman beat his gloves through the hedge within a rod of me. Oh yes, I have much to be thankful for. My life is in my own hand now.'

"'Oh, master; oh, Captain; oh, my lord!' I cried; 'for the sake of God in heaven, don't talk like that. Think of your sweet wife, your dear lady.'

"'Betsy,' he answered, with his eyes full upon me, noble, yet frightful to look at, 'I am come to see my wife. Go and let her know it, according to your own discretion.'

"My discretion would have been not to let him see her, but go on and write to her from foreign countries, with the salt sea between them; but I give you my word that I had no discretion, but from pity and majesty obeyed him. I knew that he must have broken prison, and by good rights ought to be starving. But I could no more offer him the cold ham and pullet than take him by his beard and shake him.

"'Is he come, at last, at last?' my poor mistress said, whose wits were wandering after her children. 'At last, at last! Then he will find them all.'

"'Yes, ma'am, at last, at the last he will,' I answered, while I thought of the burial service, which I had heard three times in a week—for the little ones went to their graves in pairs to save ceremony; likewise of the Epistle of Saint Paul, which is not like our Lord's way of talking at all, but arguing instead of comforting. And not to catch her up in that weak state, I said, 'He will find every one of them, ma'am.'

"'Oh, but I want him for himself, for himself, as much as all the rest put together,' my dear lady said, without listening to me, but putting her hand to her ear to hearken for even so much as a mouse on the stairs. 'Do bring him, Betsy; only bring him, Betsy, and then let me go where my children are.'

"I was surprised at her manner of speaking, which I would not have allowed to her, but more than all about her children, which she could only have been dreaming yet, for nobody else came nigh her except only me, miss, and you, miss, and for you to breathe words was impossible. All you did was to lie very quiet, tucked up into your mother's side; and as regular as the time-piece went, wide came your eyes and your mouth to be fed. If your nature had been cross or squally, 'baby's coffin No. 7' would have come after all the other six, which the thief of a carpenter put down on his bill as if it was so many shavings.

"Well, now, to tell you the downright truth, I have a lot of work to do to-morrow, miss, with three basketfuls of washing coming home, and a man about a tap that leaks and floods the inside of the fender; and if I were to try to put before you the way that those two for the last time of their lives went on to one another—the one like a man and the other like a woman, full of sobs and choking—my eyes would be in such a state to-morrow that the whole of them would pity and cheat me. And I ought to think of you as well, miss, who has been sadly harrowed listening when you was not born yet. And to hear what went on, full of weeping, when yourself was in the world, and able to cry for yourself, and all done over your own little self, would leave you red eyes and no spirit for the night, and no appetite in the morning; and so I will pass it all over, if you please, and let him go out of the backdoor again.

"This he was obliged to do quick, and no mistake, glad as he might have been to say more words, because the fellows who call themselves officers, without any commission, were after him. False it was to say, as was said, that he got out of Winchester jail through money. That story was quite of a piece with the rest. His own strength and skill it was that brought him out triumphantly, as the scratches on his hands and cheeks might show. He did it for the sake of his wife, no doubt. When he heard that the children were all in their graves, and their mother in the way to follow them, madness was better than his state of mind, as the officers told me when they could not catch him—and sorry they would have been to do it, I believe.

"To overhear my betters is the thing of all things most against my nature; and my poor lady being unfit to get up, there was nothing said on the landing, which is the weakest part of gentlefolks. They must have said 'Good-by' to one another quite in silence, and the Captain, as firm a man as ever lived, had lines on his face that were waiting for tears, if nature should overcome bringing up. Then I heard the words, 'for my sake,' and the other said, 'for your sake,' a pledge that passed between them, making breath more long than life is. But when your poor father was by the back-door, going out toward the woods and coppices, he turned sharp round, and he said, 'Betsy Bowen!' and I answered, 'Yes, at your service, Sir.' 'You have been the best woman in the world,' he said—'the bravest, best, and kindest.

I leave my wife and my last child to you. The Lord has been hard on me, but He will spare me those two. I do hope and believe He will.'

"We heard a noise of horses in the valley, and the clank of swords—no doubt the mounted police from Winchester a-crossing of the Moonstock Bridge to search our house for the runaway. And the Captain took my hand, and said, 'I trust them to you. Hide the clothes I took off, that they may not know I have been here. I trust my wife and little babe to you, and may God bless you, Betsy!'

"He had changed all his clothes, and he looked very nice, but a sadder face was never seen. As he slipped through the hollyhocks I said to myself, 'There goes a broken-hearted man, and he leaves a broken heart behind.' And your dear mother died on the Saturday night. Oh my! oh my! how sad it was!"

CHAPTER XXVI
AT THE BANK

In telling that sad tale my faithful and soft-hearted nurse had often proved her own mistake in saying, as she did, that tears can ever be exhausted. And I, for my part, though I could scarcely cry for eager listening, was worse off perhaps than if I had wetted each sad fact as it went by. At any rate, be it this way or that, a heavy and sore heart was left me, too distracted for asking questions, and almost too depressed to grieve.

In the morning Mrs. Strouss was bustling here and there and every where, and to look at her nice Welsh cheeks and aprons, and to hear how she scolded the butcher's boy, nobody would for a moment believe that her heart was deeper than her skin, as the saying of the west country is. Major Hockin had been to see me last night, for he never forgot a promise, and had left me in good hands, and now he came again in the morning. According to his usual way of taking up an opinion, he would not see how distracted I was, and full of what I had heard overnight, but insisted on dragging me off to the bank, that being in his opinion of more importance than old stories. I longed to ask Betsy some questions which had been crowding into my mind as she spoke, and while I lay awake at night; however, I was obliged to yield to the business of the morning, and the good Major's zeal and keen knowledge of the world; and he really gave me no time to think.

"Yes, I understand all that as well as if I had heard every word of it," he said, when he had led me helpless into the Hansom cab he came in, and had slammed down the flood-gates in front of us. "You must never think twice of what old women say" (Mrs. Strouss was some twenty years younger than himself); "they always go prating and finding mares'-nests, and then they always cry. Now did she cry, Erema?"

I would have given a hundred dollars to be able to say, "No, not one drop;" but the truth was against me, and I said, "How could she help it?"

"Exactly!" the Major exclaimed, so loudly that the cabman thought he was ordered to stop. "No, go on, cabby, if your horse can do it. My dear, I beg your pardon, but you are so very simple! You have not been among the eye-openers of the west. This comes of the obsolete Uncle Sam."

"I would rather be simple than 'cute!'" I replied; "and my own Uncle Sam will be never obsolete."

Silly as I was, I could never speak of the true Uncle Sam in this far country without the bright shame of a glimmer in my eyes; and with this, which I cared not to hide, I took my companion's hand and stood upon the footway of a narrow and crowded lane.

"Move on! move on!" cried a man with a high-crowned hat japanned at intervals, and, wondering at his rudeness to a lady, I looked at him. But he only said, "Now move on, will you?" without any wrath, and as if he were vexed at our littleness of mind in standing still. Nobody heeded him any more than if he had said, "I am starving," but it seemed a rude thing among ladies. Before I had time to think more about this—for I always like to think of things—I was led through a pair of narrow swinging doors, and down a close alley between two counters full of people paying and receiving money. The Major, who always knew how to get on, found a white-haired gentleman in a very dingy corner, and whispered to him in a confidential way, though neither had ever seen the other before, and the white-haired gentleman gazed at me as sternly as if I were a bank-note for at least a thousand pounds; and then he said, "Step this way, young lady. Major Hockin, step this way, Sir."

The young lady "stepped that way" in wonder as to what English English is, and then we were shown into a sacred little room, where the daylight had glass reflectors for it, if it ever came to use them. But as it cared very little to do this, from angular disabilities, three bright gas-lights were burning in soft covers, and fed the little room with a rich, sweet glow. And here shone one of the partners of the bank, a very pleasant-looking gentleman, and very nicely dressed.

"Major Hockin," he said, after looking at the card, "will you kindly sit down, while I make one memorandum? I had the pleasure of knowing your uncle well—at least I believe that the late Sir Rufus was your uncle."

"Not so," replied the Major, well pleased, however. "I fear that I am too old to have had any uncle lately. Sir Rufus Hockin was my first cousin."

"Oh, indeed! To be sure, I should have known it, but Sir Rufus being much your senior, the mistake was only natural. Now what can I do to serve you, or perhaps this young lady—Miss Hockin, I presume?"

"No," said his visitor, "not Miss Hockin. I ought to have introduced her, but for having to make my own introduction. Mr. Shovelin, this lady is Miss Erema Castlewood, the only surviving child of the late Captain George Castlewood, properly speaking, Lord Castlewood."

Mr. Shovelin had been looking at me with as much curiosity as good manners and his own particular courtesy allowed. And I fancied that he felt that I could not be a Hockin.

"Oh, dear, dear me!" was all he said, though he wanted to say, "God bless me!" or something more sudden and stronger. "Lord Castlewood's daughter—poor George Castlewood! My dear young lady, is it possible?"

"Yes, I am my father's child," I said; "and I am proud to hear that I am like him."

"That you well may be," he answered, putting on his spectacles. "You are astonished at my freedom, perhaps; you will allow for it, or at least, you will not be angry with me, when you know that your father was my dearest friend at Harrow; and that when his great trouble fell upon him—"

Here Mr. Shovelin stopped, as behooves a man who begins to outrun himself. He could not tell me that it was himself who had found all the money for my father's escape, which cost much cash as well as much good feeling. Neither did I, at the time, suspect it, being all in the dark upon such points. Not knowing what to say, I looked from the banker to the Major, and back again.

"Can you tell me the exact time?" the latter asked. "I am due in the Temple at 12.30, and I never am a minute late, whatever happens."

"You will want a swift horse," Mr. Shovelin answered, "or else this will be an exception to your rule. It is twenty-one minutes past twelve now."

"May I leave my charge to you, then, for a while? She will be very quiet; she is always so. Erema, will you wait for me?"

I was not quick enough then to see that this was arranged between them. Major Hockin perceived that Mr. Shovelin wished to have a talk with me about dearer matters than money, having children of his own, and being (as his eyes and forehead showed) a man of peculiar views, perhaps, but clearly of general good-will.

"In an hour, in an hour, in less than an hour"—the Major intensified his intentions always—"in three-quarters of an hour I shall be back. Meanwhile, my dear, you will sit upon a stool, and not say a word, nor make any attempt to do any thing every body is not used to."

This vexed me, as if I were a savage here; and I only replied with a very gentle bow, being glad to see his departure; for Major Hockin was one of those people, so often to be met with, whom any one likes or dislikes according to the changes of their behavior. But Mr. Shovelin was different from that.

"Miss Castlewood, take this chair," he said; "a hard one, but better than a stool, perhaps. Now how am I to talk to you—as an inquirer upon business matters, or as the daughter of my old friend? Your smile is enough. Well, and you must talk to me in the same unreasonable manner. That being clearly established between us, let us proceed to the next point. Your father, my old friend, wandered from the track, and unfortunately lost his life in a desolate part of America."

"No; oh no. It was nothing like that. He might have been alive, and here at this moment, if I had not drunk and eaten every bit and drop of his."

"Now don't, my dear child, don't be so romantic—I mean, look at things more soberly. You did as you were ordered, I have no doubt; George Castlewood always would have that. He was a most commanding man. You do not quite resemble him in that respect, I think."

"Oh, but did he do it, did he do it?" I cried out. "You were at school with him, and knew his nature. Was it possible for him to do it, Sir?"

"As possible as it is for me to go down to Sevenoaks and shoot my dear old father, who is spending a green and agreeable old age there. Not that your grandfather, if I may say it without causing pain to you, was either green or agreeable. He was an uncommonly sharp old man; I might even say a hard one. As you never saw him, you will not think me rude in saying that much. Your love, of course, is for your father; and if your father had had a father of larger spirit about money, he might have been talking to me pleasantly now, instead of—instead of all these sad things."

"Please not to slip away from me," I said, bluntly, having so often met with that. "You believe, as every good person does, that my father was wholly innocent. But do tell me who could have done it instead. Somebody must have done it; that seems clear."

"Yes," replied Mr. Shovelin, with a look of calm consideration; "somebody did it, undoubtedly; and that makes the difficulty of the whole affair. 'Cui bono,' as the lawyers say. Two persons only could have had any motive, so far as wealth and fortune go. The first and most prominent, your father, who, of course, would come into every thing (which made the suspicion so hot and strong); and the other, a very nice gentleman, whom it is wholly impossible to suspect."

"Are you sure of that? People have more than suspected—they have condemned—my father. After that, I can suspect any body. Who is it? Please to tell me."

"It is the present Lord Castlewood, as he is beginning to be called. He would not claim the title, or even put forward his right in any way, until he had proof of your dear father's death; and even then he behaved so well—"

"He did it! he did it!" I cried, in hot triumph. "My father's name shall be clear of it. Can there be any doubt that he did it? How very simple the whole of it becomes! Nothing astonishes me, except the stupidity of people. He had every thing to gain, and nothing to lose—a bad man, no doubt—though I never heard of him. And putting it all on my father, of course, to come in himself, and abide his time, till the misery killed my father. How simple, how horribly simple, it becomes!"

"You are much too quick, too hot, too sudden. Excuse me a minute"—as a silver bell struck—"I am wanted in the next room. But before I go, let me give you a glass of cold water, and beg you to dismiss that new idea from your mind."

I could see, as I took with a trembling hand the water he poured out for me, that Mr. Shovelin was displeased. His kind and handsome face grew hard. He had taken me for a nice young lady, never much above the freezing-point, and he had found me boil over in a moment. I was sorry to have grieved him; but if he had heard Betsy Bowen's story, and seen her tell it, perhaps he would have allowed for me. I sat down again, having risen in my warmth, and tried to quiet and command myself by thinking of the sad points only. Of these there were plenty to make pictures of, the like of which had kept me awake all night; and I knew by this time, from finding so much more of pity than real sympathy, that men think a woman may well be all tears, but has no right to even the shadow of a frown. That is their own prerogative.

And so, when Mr. Shovelin returned, with a bundle of papers which had also vexed him—to judge by the way in which he threw them down—I spoke very mildly, and said that I was very sorry for my display of violence, but that if he knew all, he would pardon me; and he pardoned me in a moment.

"I was going to tell you, my dear Miss Castlewood," he continued, gently, "that your sudden idea must be dismissed, for reasons which I think will content you. In the first place, the present Lord Castlewood is, and always has been, an exemplary man, of great piety and true gentleness; in the next place, he is an invalid, who can not walk a mile with a crutch to help him, and so he has been for a great many years; and lastly, if you have no faith in the rest, he was in Italy at the time, and remained there for some years afterward. There he received and sheltered your poor father after his sad calamity, and was better than a brother to him, as your father, in a letter to me, declared. So you see that you must acquit him."

"That is not enough. I would beg his pardon on my knees, since he helped my father, for he must have thought him innocent. Now, Mr. Shovelin, you were my father's friend, and you are such a clever man—"

"How do you know that, young lady? What a hurry you are always in!"

"Oh, there can be no doubt about it. But you must not ask reasons, if I am so quick. Now please to tell me what your own conclusion is. I can talk of it calmly now; yes, quite calmly, because I never think of any thing else. Only tell me what you really believe, and I will keep it most strictly to myself."

"I am sure you will do that," he answered, smiling, "not only from the power of your will, my dear, but also because I have nothing to say. At first I was strongly inclined to believe (knowing, from my certainty of your father, that the universal opinion must be wrong) that the old lord had done it himself; for he always had been of a headstrong and violent nature, which I am sure will never re-appear in you. But the whole of the evidence went against this, and little as I think of evidence, especially at an inquest, your father's behavior confirmed what was sworn to. Your father knew that his father had not made away with himself in a moment of passion, otherwise he was not the man to break prison and fly trial. He would have said, boldly, 'I am guiltless; there are many things that I can not explain; I can not help that; I will face it out. Condemn me, if you like, and I will suffer.' From your own remembrance of your father's nature, is not that certainly the course he would have taken?"

"I have not an atom of doubt about it. His flight and persistent dread of trial puzzle me beyond imagination. Of his life he was perfectly reckless, except, at least, for my sake."

"I know that he was," Mr. Shovelin replied; "as a boy he was wonderfully fearless. As a man, with a sweet wife and a lot of children, he might have begun to be otherwise. But when all those were gone, and only a poor little baby left—"

"Yes, I suppose I was all that."

"Forgive me. I am looking back at you. Who could dream that you would ever even live, without kith or kin to care for you? Your life was saved by some good woman who took you away to Wales. But when you were such a poor little relic, and your father could scarcely have seen you, to have such a mite left must have been almost a mockery of happiness.

That motive could not have been strong enough to prevent a man of proud honor from doing what honor at once demanded. Your father would have returned and surrendered as soon as he heard of his dear wife's death, if in the balance there had been only you."

"Yes, Mr. Shovelin, perhaps he would. I was never very much as a counter-balance. Yet my father loved me." I could have told him of the pledge exchanged—"For my sake," and, "Yes, for your sake," with love and wedded honor set to fight cold desolate repute—but I did not say a word about it.

"He loved you afterward, of course. But a man who has had seven children is not enthusiastic about a baby. There must have been a larger motive."

"But when I was the only one left alive. Surely I became valuable then. I can not have been such a cipher."

"Yes, for a long time you would have been," replied the Saturnian banker. "I do not wish to disparage your attractions when you were a fortnight old. They may have begun already to be irresistible. Excuse me; you have led me into the light vein, when speaking of a most sad matter. You must blame your self-assertion for it. All I wish to convey to you is my belief that something wholly unknown to us, some dark mystery of which we have no inkling, lies at the bottom of this terrible affair. Some strange motive there must have been, strong enough even to overcome all ordinary sense of honor, and an Englishman's pride in submitting to the law, whatever may be the consequence. Consider that his 'flight from justice,' as it was called, of course, by every one, condemned his case and ruined his repute. Even for that he would not have cared so much as for his own sense of right. And though he was a very lively fellow, as I first remember him, full of tricks and jokes, and so on, which in this busy age are out of date, I am certain that he always had a stern sense of right. One never knows how love affairs and weakness about children may alter almost any man; but my firm conviction is that my dear old school-fellow, George Castlewood, even with a wife and lovely children hanging altogether upon his life, not only would not have broken jail, but would calmly have given up his body to be hanged—pardon me, my dear, for putting it so coarsely—if there had not been something paramount to override even apparent honor. What it can have been I have no idea, and I presume you have none."

"None whatever," I said at once, in answer to his inquiring gaze. "I am quite taken by surprise; I never even thought of such a thing. It has always seemed to me so natural that my dear father, being shamefully condemned, because appearances were against him, and nobody could enter into him, should, for the sake of his wife and children, or even of one child like me, depart or banish himself, or emigrate, or, as they might call it, run away. Knowing that he never could have a fair trial, it was the only straightforward and good and affectionate thing for him to do."

"You can not see things as men see them. We must not expect it of you," Mr. Shovelin answered, with a kind but rather too superior smile, which reminded me a little of dear Uncle Sam when he listened to what, in his opinion, was only female reason; "but, dear me, here is Major Hockin come! Punctuality is the soul of business."

"So I always declare," cried the Major, who was more than three-quarters of an hour late, for which in my heart I thanked him. "My watch keeps time to a minute, Sir, and its master to a second. Well, I hope you have settled all questions of finance, and endowed my young maid with a fortune."

"So far from that," Mr. Shovelin replied, in a tone very different from that he used to me, "we have not even said one word of business; all that has been left for your return. Am I to understand that you are by appointment or relationship the guardian of this young lady?"

"God forbid!" cried Major Hockin, shortly. I thought it very rude of him, yet I could not help smiling to see how he threw his glasses up and lifted his wiry crest of hair. "Not that she is bad, I mean, but good, very good; indeed, I may say the very best girl ever known outside of my own family. My cousin, Colonel Gundry, who owns an immense estate in the most auriferous district of all California, but will not spoil his splendid property by mining, he will—he will tell you the very same thing, Sir."

"I am very glad to hear it," said the banker, smiling at me, while I wondered what it was, but hoped that it meant my praises. "Now I really fear that I must be very brief, though the daughter of my oldest friend may well be preferred to business. But now we will turn at once to business, if you please."

CHAPTER XXVII
COUSIN MONTAGUE

Mr. Shovelin went to a corner of the room, which might be called his signal-box, having a little row of port-holes like a toy frigate or accordion, and there he made sounds which brought steps very promptly, one clerk carrying a mighty ledger, and the other a small strong-box.

"No plate," Major Hockin whispered to me, shaking his gray crest with sorrow; "but there may be diamonds, you know, Erema. One ounce of diamonds is worth a ton of plate."

"No," said Mr. Shovelin, whose ears were very keen, "I fear that you will find nothing of mercantile value. Thank you, Mr. Robinson; by-and-by perhaps we shall trouble you. Strictly speaking, perhaps I should require the presence of your father's lawyer, or of some one producing probate, ere I open this box, Miss Castlewood. But having you here, and Major Hockin, and knowing what I do about the matter (which is one of personal confidence), I will dispense with formalities. We have given your father's solicitor notice of this deposit, and requested his attention, but he never has deigned to attend to it; so now we will dispense with him. You see that the seal is unbroken; you know your father's favorite seal, no doubt. The key is nothing; it was left to my charge. You wish that I should open this?"

Certainly I did, and the banker split the seal with an ebony-handled paper-knife, and very soon unlocked the steel-ribbed box, whose weight was chiefly of itself. Some cotton-wool lay on the top to keep the all-penetrative dust away, and then a sheet of blue foolscap paper, partly covered with clear but crooked writing, and under that some little twists of silver paper, screwed as if there had been no time to tie them, and a packet of letters held together by a glittering bracelet.

"Poor fellow!" Mr. Shovelin said, softly, while I held my breath, and the Major had the courtesy to be silent. "This is his will; of no value, I fear, in a pecuniary point of view, but of interest to you his daughter. Shall I open it, Miss Castlewood, or send it to his lawyers?"

"Open it, and never think of them," said I. "Like the rest, they have forsaken him. Please to read it to yourself, and then tell us."

"Oh, I wish I had known this before!" cried the banker, after a rapid glance or two. "Very kind, very flattering, I am sure! Yes, I will do my duty by him; I wish there was more to be done in the case. He has left me sole executor, and trustee of all his property, for the benefit of his surviving child. Yet he never gave me the smallest idea of expecting me to do this for him. Otherwise, of course, I should have had this old box opened years ago."

"We must look at things as they are," said Major Hockin, for I could say nothing. "The question is, what do you mean to do now?"

"Nothing whatever," said the banker, crisply, being displeased at the other's tone; and then, seeing my surprise, he addressed himself to me: "Nothing at present, but congratulate myself upon my old friend's confidence, and, as Abernethy said, 'take advice.' A banker must never encroach upon the province of the lawyer. But so far as a layman may judge, Major Hockin, I think you will have to transfer to me the care of this young lady."

"I shall be only too happy, I assure you," the Major answered, truthfully. "My wife has a great regard for her, and so have I—the very greatest, the strongest regard, and warm parental feelings; as you know, Erema. But—but, I am not so young as I was; and I have to develop my property."

"Of which she no longer forms a part," Mr. Shovelin answered, with a smile at me, which turned into pleasure my momentary pain at the other's calm abandonment. "You will find me prompt and proud to claim her, as soon as I am advised that this will is valid; and that I shall learn to-morrow."

In spite of pride, or by its aid, my foolish eyes were full of tears, and I gave him a look of gratitude which reminded him of my father, as he said in so many words.

"Oh, I hope it is valid! How I hope it is!" I exclaimed, turning round to the Major, who smiled rather grimly, and said he hoped so too.

"But surely," he continued, "as we are all here, we should not neglect the opportunity of inspecting the other contents of this box. To me it appears that we are bound to do so; that it is our plain duty to ascertain—Why, there might even be a later will. Erema, my dear, you must be most anxious to get to the bottom of it."

So I was, but desired even more that his curiosity should be foiled. "We must leave that to Mr. Shovelin," I said.

"Then for the present we will seal it down again," the banker answered, quietly; "we can see that there is no other will, and a later one would scarcely be put under this. The other little packets, whatever they may be, are objects of curiosity, perhaps, rather than of importance. They will keep till we have more leisure."

"We have taken up a great deal of your time, Sir, I am sure," said the Major, finding that he could take no more. "We ought to be, and we are, most grateful."

"Well," the banker answered, as we began to move, "such things do not happen every day. But there is no friend like an old friend, Erema, as I mean to call you now. I was to have been your godfather; but I fear that you never have been baptized."

"What!" cried the Major, staring at us both. "Is such a thing possible in a Christian land? Oh, how I have neglected my duty to the Church! Come back with me to Bruntsea, and my son shall do it. The church there is under my orders, I should hope; and we will have a dinner party afterward. What a horrible neglect of duty!"

"But how could I help it?" I exclaimed, with some terror at Major Hockin's bristling hair. "I can not remember—I am sure I can not say. It may have been done in France, or somewhere, if there was no time in England. At any rate, my father is not to be blamed."

"Papistical baptism is worse than none," the Major said, impressively. "Never mind, my dear, we will make that all right. You shall not be a savage always. We will take the opportunity to change your name. Erema is popish and outlandish; one scarcely knows how to pronounce it. You shall have a good English Christian name—Jemima, Jane, or Sophy. Trust me to know a good name. Trust me."

"Jemima!" I cried. "Oh, Mr. Shovelin, save me from ever being called Jemima! Rather would I never be baptized at all."

"I am no judge of names," he answered, smiling, as he shook hands with us; "but, unless I am a very bad judge of faces, you will be called just what you please."

"And I please to be called what my father called me. It may be unlucky, as a gentleman told me, who did not know how to pronounce it. However, it will do very well for me. You wish to see me, then, to-morrow, Mr. Shovelin?"

"If you please; but later in the day, when I am more at leisure. I do not run away very early. Come at half past four to this door, and knock. I hear every sound at this door in my room; and the place will be growing quiet then."

He showed us out into a narrow alley through a heavy door sheathed with iron, and soon we recovered the fair light of day, and the brawl and roar of a London street.

"Now where shall we go?" the Major asked, as soon as he had found a cab again; for he was very polite in that way. "You kept early hours with your 'uncle Sam,' as you call Colonel Gundry, a slow-witted man, but most amusing when he likes, as slow-witted men very often are. Now will you come and dine with me? I can generally dine, as you, with virtuous indignation, found out at Southampton. But we are better friends now, Miss Heathen."

"Yes, I have more than I can ever thank you for," I answered, very gravely, for I never could become jocose to order, and sadness still was uppermost. "I will go where you like. I am quite at your orders, because Betsy Bowen is busy now. She will not have done her work till six o'clock."

"Well done!" he cried. "Bravo, Young America! Frankness is the finest of all good manners. And what a lot of clumsy deception it saves! Then let us go and dine. I will imitate your truthfulness. It was two words for myself, and one for you. The air of London always makes me hungry after too much country air. It is wrong altogether, but I can not help it. And going along, I smell hungry smells coming out of deep holes with a plate at the top. Hungry I mean to a man who has known what absolute starvation is—when a man would thank God for a blue-bottle fly who had taken his own nip any where. When I see the young fellows at the clubs pick this, and poke that, and push away the other, may I be d——d—my dear, I beg your pardon. Cabby, to the 'Grilled Bone and Scolloped Cockle,' at the bottom of St. Ventricle Lane, you know."

This place seemed, from what the Major said, to have earned repute for something special, something esteemed by the very clever people, and only to be found in true virtue here. And he told me that luxury and self-indulgence were the greatest sins of the present age, and how he admired a man who came here to protest against Epicureans, by dining (liquors not included) for the sum of three and sixpence.

All this, no doubt, was wise and right; but I could not attend to it properly now, and he might take me where he would, and have all the talking to himself, according to his practice. And I might not even have been able to say what this temple of bones and cockles was like, except for a little thing which happened there. The room, at the head of a twisting staircase, was low and dark, and furnished almost like a farmhouse kitchen. It had no carpet, nor even a mat, but a floor of black timber, and a ceiling colored blue, with stars and comets, and a full moon near the fire-place. On either side of the room stood narrow tables endwise to the walls, inclosed with high-backed seats like settles, forming thus a double set of little stalls or boxes, with scarcely space enough between for waiters, more urgent than New York firemen, to push their steaming and breathless way.

"Square or round, miss?" said one of them to me as soon as the Major had set me on a bench, and before my mind had time to rally toward criticism of the knives and forks, which deprecated any such ordeal; and he cleverly whipped a stand for something dirty, over something still dirtier, on the cloth.

"I don't understand what you mean," I replied to his highly zealous aspect, while the Major sat smiling dryly at my ignorance, which vexed me. "I have never received such a question before. Major Hockin, will you kindly answer him?"

"Square," said the Major; "square for both." And the waiter, with a glance of pity at me, hurried off to carry out his order.

"Erema, your mind is all up in the sky," my companion began to remonstrate. "You ought to know better after all your travels."

"Then the sky should not fall and confuse me so," I said, pointing to the Milky Way, not more than a yard above me; "but do tell me what he meant, if you can. Is it about the formation of the soup?"

"Hush, my dear. Soup is high treason here until night, when they make it of the leavings. His honest desire was to know whether you would have a grilled bone of mutton, which is naturally round, you know, or of beef, which, by the same law of nature, seems always to be square, you know."

"Oh, I see," I replied, with some confusion, not at his osteology, but at the gaze of a pair of living and lively eyes fastened upon me. A gentleman, waiting for his bill, had risen in the next low box, and stood calmly (as if he had done all his duty to himself) gazing over the wooden back at me, who thus sat facing him. And Major Hockin, following my glance, stood up and turned round to see to it.

"What! Cousin Montague! Bless my heart, who could have dreamed of lighting on you here? Come in, my dear follow; there is plenty of room. Let me introduce you to my new ward, Miss Erema Castlewood. Miss Castlewood, this is Sir Montague Hockin, the son of my lamented first cousin Sir Rufus, of whom you have heard so much. Well, to be sure! I have not seen you for an age. My dear fellow, now how are you?"

"Miss Castlewood, please not to move; I sit any where. Major, I am most delighted to see you. Over and over again I have been at the point of starting for Bruntsea Island—it is an island now, isn't it? My father would never believe that it was till I proved it from the number of rabbits that came up. However, not a desolate island now, if it contains you and all your energies, and Miss Castlewood, as well as Mrs. Hockin."

"It is not an island, and it never shall be," the Major cried, knocking a blue plate over, and spilling the salt inauspiciously. "It never was an island, and it never shall be. My intention is to reclaim it altogether. Oh, here come the squares. Well done! well done! I quite forget the proper thing to have to drink. Are the cockles in the pan, Mr. Waiter? Quite right, then; ten minutes is the proper time; but they know that better than I do. I am very sorry, Montague, that you have dined."

"Surely you would not call this a dinner; I take my true luncheon afterward. But lately my appetite has been so bad that it must be fed up at short intervals. You can understand that, perhaps, Miss Castlewood. It makes the confectioners' fortunes, you know. The ladies once came only twice to feed, but now they come three times, I am assured by a young man who knows all about it. And cherry brandy is the mildest form of tipple."

"Shocking scandal! abominable talk!" cried the Major, who took every thing at its word. "I have heard all that sort of stuff ever since I was as high as this table. Waiter, show me this gentleman's bill. Oh well, oh well! you have not done so very badly. Two squares and a round, with a jug of Steinberg, and a pint of British stout with your Stilton. If this is your antelunch, what will you do when you come to your real luncheon? But I must not talk now; you may have it as you please."

"The truth of it is, Miss Castlewood," said the young man, while I looked with some curiosity at my frizzling bone, with the cover just whisked off, and drops of its juice (like the rays of a lustre) shaking with soft inner wealth—"the truth of it is just this, and no more: we fix our minds and our thoughts, and all the rest of our higher intelligence, a great deal too much upon our mere food."

"No doubt we do," I was obliged to answer. "It is very sad to think of, as soon as one has dined. But does that reflection occur, as it should, at the proper time to be useful—I mean when we are hungry?"

"I fear not; I fear that it is rather praeterite than practical."

"No big words now, my dear fellow," cried the Major. "You have had your turn; let us have ours. But, Erema, you are eating nothing. Take a knife and fork, Montague, and help her. The beauty of these things consists entirely, absolutely, essentially, I may say, in their having the smoke rushing out of them. A gush of steam like this should follow every turn of the knife. But there! I am spoiling every bit by talking so."

"Is that any fault of mine?" asked Sir Montague, in a tone which made me look at him. The voice was not harsh, nor rough, nor unpleasant, yet it gave me the idea that it could be all three, and worse than all three, upon occasion. So I looked at him, which I had refrained from doing, to see whether his face confirmed that idea. To the best of my perception, it did not. Sir Montague Hockin was rather good-looking, so far as form and color go, having regular features, and clear blue eyes, very beautiful teeth, and a golden beard. His appearance was grave, but not morose, as if he were always examining things and people without condemning them. It was evident that he expected to take the upper hand in general, to play the first fiddle, to hold the top saw, to "be helped to all the stuffing of the pumpkin," as dear Uncle Sam was fond of saying. Of moderate stature, almost of middle age, and dressed nicely, without any gewgaws, which look so common upon a gentleman's front, he was likely to please more people than he displeased at first on-sight.

The Major was now in the flush of goodwill, having found his dinner genial; and being a good man, he yielded to a little sympathetic anger with those who had done less justice to themselves. And in this state of mind he begged us to take note of one thing—that his ward should be christened in Bruntsea Church, as sure as all the bells were his, according to their inscriptions, no later than next Thursday week, that being the day for a good sirloin; and if Sir Montague failed to come to see how they could manage things under proper administration, he might be sure of one thing, if no more—that Major Hockin would never speak to him again.

CHAPTER XXVIII
A CHECK

So many things now began to open upon me, to do and to think of, that I scarcely knew which to begin with. I used to be told how much wiser it was not to interfere with any thing—to let by-gones be by-gones, and consider my own self only. But this advice never came home to my case, and it always seemed an unworthy thing even to be listening to it. And now I saw reason to be glad for thanking people who advised me, and letting them go on to advise themselves. For if I had listened to Major Hockin, or even Uncle Sam for that part, where must I have been now? Why, simply knowing no more than as a child I knew, and feeling miserable about it. Whereas I had now at least something to go upon, and enough for a long time to occupy my mind. The difficulty was to know what to do first, and what to resolve to leave undone, or at least to put off for the present. One of my special desires had been to discover that man, that Mr. Goad, who had frightened me so about two years back, and was said to be lost in the snow-drifts. But nobody like him had ever been found, to the sorrow of the neighborhood; and Sylvester himself had been disappointed, not even to know what to do with his clothes.

His card, however, before he went off, had been left to the care of Uncle Sam for security of the 15,000 dollars; and on it was printed, with a glazing and much flourish, "Vypan, Goad, and Terryer: Private Inquiry Office, Little England Polygon, W.C." Uncle Sam, with a grunt and a rise of his foot, had sent this low card flying to the fire, after I had kissed him so for all his truth and loveliness; but I had caught it and made him give it to me, as was only natural. And having this now, I had been quite prepared to go and present it at its mean address, and ask what they wanted me for in America, and what they would like to do with me now, taking care to have either the Major close at hand, or else a policeman well recommended.

But now I determined to wait a little while (if Betsy Bowen's opinion should be at all the same as mine was), and to ask Mr. Shovelin what he thought about it, before doing any thing that might arouse a set of ideas quite opposite to mine, and so cause trouble afterward. And being unable to think any better for the time than to wait and be talked to, I got Major Hockin to take me back again to the right number in European Square.

Here I found Mrs. Strouss (born Betsy Bowen) ready and eager to hear a great deal more than I myself had heard that day. On the other hand, I had many questions, arising from things said to me, to which I required clear answers; and it never would do for her to suppose that because she had known me come into this world, she must govern the whole of my course therein. But it cost many words and a great deal of demeanor to teach her that, good and faithful as she was, I could not be always under her. Yet I promised to take her advice whenever it agreed with my own opinions.

This pleased her, and she promised to offer it always, knowing how well it would be received, and she told all her lodgers that they might ring and ring, for she did not mean to answer any of their bells; but if they wanted any thing, they must go and fetch it. Being Germans, who are the most docile of men in England, whatever they may be at home, they made no complaint, but retired to their pipes in a pleasant condition of surprise at London habits.

Mrs. Strouss, being from her earliest years of a thrifty and reputable turn of mind, had managed, in a large yet honest way, to put by many things which must prove useful in the long-run, if kept long enough. And I did hear—most careful as I am to pay no attention to petty rumors—that the first thing that moved the heart of Herr Strouss, and called forth his finest feelings, was a winding-up chair, which came out to make legs, with a pocket for tobacco, and a flat place for a glass.

This was certainly a paltry thought; and to think of such low things grieved me. And now, when I looked at Mr. Strouss himself, having heard of none of these things yet, I felt that my nurse might not have done her best, yet might have done worse, when she married him. For he seemed to have taken a liking toward me, and an interest in my affairs, which redounded to his credit, if he would not be too inquisitive. And now I gladly allowed him to be present, and to rest in the chair which had captivated him, although last night I could scarcely have borne to have heard in his presence what I had to hear. To-night there was nothing distressful to be said, compared, at least, with last night's tale; whereas there were several questions to be put, in some of which (while scouting altogether Uncle Sam's low estimate) two females might, with advantage perhaps, obtain an opinion from the stronger sex.

And now, as soon as I had told my two friends as well as I could what had happened at the bank (with which they were pleased, as I had been), those questions arose, and were, I believe, chiefly to the following purport—setting aside the main puzzle of all.

Why did my father say, on that dreadful morning, that if his father was dead, he himself had killed or murdered him? Betsy believed, when she came to think, that he had even used the worse word of these two.

How could the fatal shot have been discharged from his pistol—as clearly it had been—a pistol, moreover, which, by his own account, as Betsy now remembered, he had left in his quarters near Chichester?

What was that horrible disease which had carried off all my poor little brothers and sisters, and frightened kind neighbors and servants away? Betsy said it was called "Differeria," as differing so much from all other complaints. I had never yet heard of this, but discovered, without asking further than of Mr. Strouss, that she meant that urgent mandate for a levy of small angels which is called on earth "diphtheria."

Who had directed those private inquirers, Vypan, Goad, and Terryer, to send to the far West a member of their firm to get legal proof of my dear father's death, and to bring me back, if possible? The present Lord Castlewood never would have done so, according to what Mr. Shovelin said; it was far more likely that (but for weak health) he would have come forth himself to seek me, upon any probable tidings. At once a religious and chivalrous man, he would never employ mean agency. And while thinking of that, another thought occurred—What had induced that low man Goad to give Uncle Sam a date wrong altogether for the crime which began all our misery? He had put it at ten, now twelve, years back, and dated it in November, whereas it had happened in September month, six years and two months before the date he gave. This question was out of all answer to me, and also to Mrs. Strouss herself; but Herr Strouss, being of a legal turn, believed that the law was to blame for it. He thought that proceedings might be bound to begin, under the Extradition Act, within ten years of the date of the crime; or there might be some other stipulation compelling Mr. Goad to add one to all his falsehoods; and not knowing any thing about it, both of us thought it very likely.

Again, what could have been that last pledge which passed between my father and mother, when they said "good-by" to one another, and perhaps knew that it was forever, so far as this bodily world is concerned? Was it any thing about a poor little sleeping and whimpering creature like myself, who could not yet make any difference to any living being except the mother? Or was it concerning far more important things, justice, clear honor, good-will, and duty, such as in the crush of time come upward with high natures? And if so, was it not a promise from my mother, knowing every thing, to say nothing, even at the quivering moment of lying beneath the point of death?

This was a new idea for Betsy, who had concluded from the very first that the pledge must be on my father's part—to wit, that he had vowed not to surrender, or hurt himself in any way, for the sake of his dear wife. And to my suggestion she could only say that she never had seen it in that light; but the landings were so narrow and the walls so soft that, with all her duty staring in her face, neither she, nor the best servant ever in an apron, could be held responsible to repeat their very words. And her husband said that this was good—very good—so good as ever could be; and what was to show now from the mouth of any one, after fifteen, sixteen, eighteen, the years?

After this I had no other word to say, being still too young to contradict people duly married and of one accord. No other word, I mean, upon that point; though still I had to ask, upon matters more immediate, what was the next thing for me, perhaps, to do. And first of all it was settled among us that for me to present myself at the head-quarters of Vypau, Goad, and Terryer would be a very clumsy and stupid proceeding, and perhaps even dangerous. Of course they would not reveal to me the author of those kind inquiries about myself, which perhaps had cost the firm a very valuable life, the life of Mr. Goad himself. And while I should learn less than nothing from them, they would most easily extract from me, or at any rate find out afterward, where I was living, and what I was doing, and how I could most quietly be met and baffled, and perhaps even made away with, so as to save all further trouble.

Neither was that the only point upon which I resolved to do nothing. Herr Strouss was a very simple-minded man, yet full of true sagacity, and he warmly advised, in his very worst English, that none but my few trusty friends should be told of my visit to this country.

"Why for make to know your enemies?" he asked, with one finger on his forehead, which was his mode of indicating caution. "Enemies find out vere soon, too soon, soon enough. Begin to plot—no, no, young lady begin first. Vilhelmina, your man say the right. Is it good, or is it bad?"

It appeared to us both to be good, so far as might be judged for the present; and therefore I made up my mind to abstain from calling even on my father's agent, unless Mr. Shovelin should think it needful. In that and other matters I would act by his advice; and so with better spirits than I long had owned, at finding so much kindness, and with good hopes of the morrow, I went to the snug little bedroom which my good nurse had provided.

Alas! What was my little grief on the morrow, compared to the deep and abiding loss of many by a good man's death? When I went to the door at which I had been told to knock, it was long before I got an answer. And even when somebody came at last, so far from being my guardian, it was only a poor old clerk, who said, "Hush, miss!" and then prayed that the will of the Lord might be done. "Couldn't you see the half-shutters up?" he continued, rather roughly. "'Tis a bad job for many a poor man to-day. And it seems no more than yesterday I was carrying him about!"

"Do you mean Mr. Shovelin?" I asked. "Is he poorly? Has any thing happened? I can wait, or come again."

"The Lord has taken him to the mansions of the just, from his private address at Sydenham Hill. A burning and a shining light! May we like him be found watching in that day, with our lamps trimmed and our loins girded!"

For the moment I was too surprised to speak, and the kind old man led me into the passage, seeing how pale and faint I was. He belonged, like his master, and a great part of their business, to a simple religious persuasion, or faith, which now is very seldom heard of.

"It was just in this way," he said, as soon as tears had enabled me to speak—for even at the first sight I had felt affection toward my new guardian. "Our master is a very punctual man, for five-and-thirty years never late—never late once till this morning. Excuse me, miss, I ought to be ashamed. The Lord knoweth what is best for us. Well, you threw him out a good bit yesterday, and there was other troubles. And he had to work late last night, I hear; for through his work he would go, be it anyhow—diligent in business, husbanding the time—and when he came down to breakfast this morning, he prayed with his household as usual, but they noticed his voice rather weak and queer; and the mistress looked at him when he got up from his knees; but he drank his cup of tea and he ate his bit of toast, which was all he ever took for breakfast. But presently when his cob came up to the door—for he always rode in to business, miss, no matter what the weather was—he went to kiss his wife and his daughters all round, according to their ages; and he got through them all, when away he fell down, with the riding-whip in one hand, and expired on a piece of Indian matting."

"How terrible!" I exclaimed, with a sob. And the poor old man, in spite of all his piety, was sobbing.

"No, miss; not a bit of terror about it, to a man prepared as he was. He had had some warning just a year ago; and the doctors all told him he must leave off work. He could no more do without his proper work than he could without air or victuals. What this old established concern will do without him, our Divine Master only knows. And a pinch coming on in Threadneedle Street, I hear—but I scarcely know what I am saying, miss; I was thinking of the camel and the needle."

"I will not repeat what you have not meant to tell," I answered, seeing his confusion, and the clumsy turn he had made of it. "Only tell me what dear Mr. Shovelin died of."

"Heart-disease, miss. You might know in a moment. Nothing kills like that. His poor father died of it, thirty years agone. And the better people are, the more they get it."

CHAPTER XXIX
AT THE PUMP

This blow was so sharp and heavy that I lost for the moment all power to go on. The sense of ill fortune fell upon me, as it falls upon stronger people, when a sudden gleam of hope, breaking through long troubles, mysteriously fades away.

Even the pleasure of indulging in the gloom of evil luck was a thing to be ashamed of now, when I thought of that good man's family thus, without a moment's warning, robbed of love and hope and happiness. But Mrs. Strouss, who often brooded on predestination, imbittered all my thoughts by saying, or rather conveying without words, that my poor fathers taint of some Divine ill-will had re-appeared, and even killed his banker.

Betsy held most Low-Church views, by nature being a Dissenter. She called herself a Baptist, and in some strange way had stopped me thus from ever having been baptized. I do not understand these things, and the battles fought about them; but knowing that my father was a member of the English Church, I resolved to be the same, and told Betsy that she ought not to set up against her master's doctrine. Then she herself became ashamed of trying to convert me, not only because of my ignorance (which made argument like shooting into the sea), but chiefly because she could mention no one of title with such theology.

This settled the question at once; and remembering (to my shame) what opinions I had held even of Suan Isco, while being in the very same predicament myself, reflecting also what Uncle Sam and Firm would have thought of me, had they known it, I anticipated the Major and his dinner party by going to a quiet ancient clergyman, who examined me, and being satisfied with little, took me to an old City church of deep and damp retirement. And here, with a great din of traffic outside, and a mildewy depth of repose within, I was presented by certain sponsors (the clerk and his wife and his wife's sister), and heard good words, and hope to keep the impression, both outward and inward, gently made upon me.

I need not say that I kept, and now received with authority, my old name; though the clerk prefixed an aspirate to it, and indulged in two syllables only. But the ancient parson knew its meaning, and looked at me with curiosity; yet, being a gentleman of the old school, put never a question about it.

Now this being done, and full tidings thereof sent off to Mrs. Hockin, to save trouble to the butcher, or other disappointment, I scarcely knew how to be moving next, though move I must before very long. For it cost me a great deal of money to stay in European Square like this, albeit Herr Strouss was of all men the most generous, by his own avowal, and his wife (by the same test) noble-hearted among women. Yet each of them spoke of the other's pecuniary views in such a desponding tone (when the other was out of the way), and so lamented to have any thing at all to say about cash—by compulsion of the other—also both, when met together, were so large and reckless, and not to be insulted by a thought of payment, that it came to pass that my money did nothing but run away between them.

This was not their fault at all, but all my own, for being unable to keep my secret about the great nugget. The Major had told me not to speak of this, according to wise experience; and I had not the smallest intention of doing an atom of mischief in that way; but somehow or other it came out one night when I was being pitied for my desolation. And all the charges against me began to be doubled from that moment.

If this had been all, I should not have cared so much, being quite content that my money should go as fast as it came in to me. But there was another thing here which cost me as much as my board and lodgings and all the rest of my expenses. And that was the iron pump in European Square. For this pump stood in the very centre of a huddled district of famine, filth, and fever. When once I had seen from the leads of our house the quag of reeking life around, the stubs and snags of chimney-pots, the gashes among them entitled streets, and the broken blains called houses, I was quite ashamed of paying any thing to become a Christian.

Betsy, who stood by me, said that it was better than it used to be, and that all these people lived in comfort of their own ideas, fiercely resented all interference, and were good to one another in their own rough way. It was more than three years since there had been a single murder among them, and even then the man who was killed confessed that he deserved it. She told me, also, that in some mining district of Wales, well known to her, things were a great deal worse than here, although the people were not half so poor. And finally, looking at a ruby ring which I had begged her to wear always, for the sake of her truth to me, she begged me to be wiser than to fret about things that I could not change. "All these people, whose hovels I saw, had the means of grace before them, and if they would not stretch forth their hands, it was only because they were vessels of wrath. Her pity was rather for our poor black brethren who had never enjoyed no opportunities, and therefore must be castaways."

Being a stranger, and so young, and accustomed to receive my doctrine (since first I went to America), I dropped all intention of attempting any good in places where I might be murdered. But I could not help looking at the pump which was in front, and the poor things who came there for water, and, most of all, the children. With these it was almost the joy of the day, and perhaps the only joy, to come into this little open space and stand, and put their backs up stiffly, and stare about, ready for some good luck to turn up—such as a horse to hold, or a man coming out of the docks with a half-penny to spare—and then, in failure of such golden hope, to dash about, in and out, after one another, splashing, and kicking over their own cans, kettles, jars, or buckets, and stretching their dirty little naked legs, and showing very often fine white chests, and bright teeth wet with laughter. And then, when this chivy was done, and their quick little hearts beat aloud with glory, it was pretty to see them all rally round the pump, as crafty as their betters, and watching with sly humor each other's readiness to begin again.

Then suddenly a sense of neglected duty would seize some little body with a hand to its side, nine times out of ten a girl, whose mother, perhaps, lay sick at home, and a stern idea of responsibility began to make the buckets clank. Then might you see, if you cared to do so, orderly management have its turn—a demand for pins and a tucking up of skirts (which scarcely seemed worthy of the great young fuss), large children scolding little ones not a bit more muddy than themselves, the while the very least child of all, too young as yet for chivying, and only come for company, would smooth her comparatively clean frock down, and look up at her sisters with condemnatory eyes.

Trivial as they were, these things amused me much, and made a little checker of reflected light upon the cloud of selfish gloom, especially when the real work began, and the children, vying with one another, set to at the iron handle. This was too large for their little hands to grasp, and by means of some grievance inside, or perhaps through a cruel trick of the plumber, up went the long handle every time small fingers were too confiding, and there it stood up like the tail of a rampant cow, or a branch inaccessible, until an old shawl or the cord of a peg-top could be cast up on high to reduce it. But some engineering boy, "highly gifted," like Uncle Sam's self, "with machinery," had discovered an ingenious cure for this. With the help of the girls he used to fasten a fat little thing, about twelve months old, in the bend at the middle of the handle, and there (like a ham on the steelyard) hung this baby and enjoyed seesaw, and laughed at its own utility.

I never saw this, and the splashing and dribbling and play and bright revelry of water, without forgetting all sad counsel and discretion, and rushing out as if the dingy pump were my own delicious Blue River. People used to look at me from the windows with pity and astonishment, supposing me to be crazed or frantic, especially the Germans. For to run out like this, without a pocket full of money, would have been insanity; and to run out with it, to their minds, was even clearer proof of that condition. For the money went as quickly as the water of the pump; on this side and on that it flew, each child in succession making deeper drain upon it, in virtue of still deeper woes. They were dreadful little story-tellers, I am very much afraid; and the long faces pulled, as soon as I came out, in contrast with all the recent glee and frolic, suggested to even the youngest charity suspicions of some inconsistency. However, they were so ingenious and clever that they worked my pockets like the pump itself, only with this unhappy difference, that the former had no inexhaustible spring of silver, or even of copper.

And thus, by a reason (as cogent as any of more exalted nature), was I driven back to my head-quarters, there to abide till a fresh supply should come. For Uncle Sam, generous and noble as he was, did not mean to let me melt all away at once my share of the great Blue River nugget, any more than to make ducks and drakes of his own. Indeed, that rock of gold was still untouched, and healthily reposing in a banker's cellar in the good town of Sacramento. People were allowed to go in and see it upon payment of a dollar, and they came out so thirsty from feasting upon it that a bar was set up, and a pile of money made—all the gentlemen, and ladies even worse than they, taking a reckless turn about small money after seeing that. But dear Uncle Sam refused every cent of the profit of all this excitable work. It was wholly against his wish that any thing so artificial should be done at all, and his sense of religion condemned it. He said, in his very first letter to me, that even a heathen must acknowledge this champion nugget as the grandest work of the Lord yet discovered in America—a country more full of all works of the Lord than the rest of the world put together. And to keep it in a cellar, without any air or sun, grated harshly upon his ideas of right.

However, he did not expect every body to think exactly as he did, and if they could turn a few dollars upon it, they were welcome, as having large families. And the balance might go to his credit against the interest on any cash advanced to him. Not that he meant to be very fast with this, never having run into debt in all his life.

This, put shortly, was the reason why I could not run to the pump any longer. I had come into England with money enough to last me (according to the Sawyer's calculations) for a year and a half of every needful work; whereas, in less than half that time, I was arriving at my last penny. This reminded me of my dear father, who was nearly always in trouble about money (although so strictly upright); and at first I was proud to be like him about this, till I came to find the disadvantages.

It must not even for a moment be imagined that this made any difference in the behavior of any one toward me. Mrs. Strouss, Herr Strouss, the lady on the stairs, and a very clever woman who had got no rooms, but was kindly accommodated every where, as well as the baron on the first floor front, and the gentleman from a hotel at Hanover, who looked out the other way, and even the children at the pump—not one made any difference toward me (as an enemy might, perhaps, suppose) because my last half crown was gone. It was admitted upon every side that I ought to be forgiven for my random cast of money, because I knew no better, and was sure to have more in a very little time. And the children of the pump came to see me go away, through streets of a mile and a half, I should think; and they carried my things, looking after one another, so that none could run away. And being forbidden at the platform gate, for want of respectability, they set up a cheer, and I waved my hat, and promised, amidst great applause, to come back with it full of sixpences.

CHAPTER XXX
COCKS AND COXCOMBS

Major Hockin brought the only fly as yet to be found in Bruntsea, to meet me at Newport, where the railway ended at present, for want of further encouragement.

"Very soon you go," he cried out to the bulkheads, or buffers, or whatever are the things that close the career of a land-engine. "Station-master, you are very wise in putting in your very best cabbage plants there. You understand your own company. Well done! If I were to offer you a shilling apiece for those young early Yorks, what would you say, now?"

"Weel, a think I should say nah, Sir," the Scotch station-master made answer, with a grin, while he pulled off his cap of office and put on a dissolute Glengary. "They are a veery fine young kail, that always pays for planting."

"The villain!" said the Major, as I jumped into the fly. "However, I suppose he does quite right. Set a thief to watch a thief. The company are big rogues, and he tries to be a bigger. We shall cut through his garden in about three months, just when his cabbages are getting firm, and their value will exceed that of pine-apples. The surveyor will come down and certify, and the 'damage to crops' will be at least five pounds, when they have no right to sow even mustard and cress, and a saucepan would hold all the victuals on the land."

From this I perceived that my host was as full of his speculative schemes as ever; and soon he made the driver of the one-horse fly turn aside from the unfenced road and take the turf. "Coachman," he cried, "just drive along the railway; you won't have the chance much longer."

There was no sod turned yet and no rod set up; but the driver seemed to know what was meant, and took us over the springy turf where once had run the river. And the salt breath of the sea came over the pebble ridge, full of appetite and briskness, after so much London.

"It is one of the saddest things I ever heard of," Major Hockin began to say to me. "Poor Shovelin! poor Shovelin! A man of large capital—the very thing we want. It might have been the making of this place. I have very little doubt that I must have brought him to see our great natural advantages—the beauty of the situation, the salubrity of the air, the absence of all clay, or marsh, or noxious deposit, the bright crisp turf, and the noble underlay of chalk, which (if you perceive my meaning) can not retain any damp, but transmits it into sweet natural wells. Why, driver, where the devil are you driving us?"

"No fear, your honor. I know every trick of it. It won't come over the wheels, I do believe, and it does all the good in the world to his sand-cracks. Whoa-ho, my boy, then! And the young lady's feet might go up upon the cushion, if her boots is thin, Sir; and Mr. Rasper will excuse of it."

"What the"—something hot—"do you mean, Sir?" the Major roared over the water, which seemed to be deepening as we went on. "Pull out this instant; pull out, I tell you, or you shall have three months' hard labor. May I be d——d now—my dear, I beg your pardon for speaking with such sincerity—I simply mean, may I go straightway to the devil, if I don't put this fellow on the tread-mill. Oh, you can pull out now, then, can you?"

"If your honor pleases, I never did pull in," the poor driver answered, being frightened at the excitement of the lord of the manor. "My orders was, miss, to drive along the line coming on now just to Bruntsea, and keep in the middle of that same I did, and this here little wet is a haxident—a haxident of the full moon, I do assure you, and the wind coming over the sea, as you might say. These pebbles is too round, miss, to stick to one another; you couldn't expect it of them; and sometimes the water here and there comes a-leaking like through the bottom. I have seed it so, ever since I can remember."

"I don't believe a word of it," the Major said, as we waited a little for the vehicle to drain, and I made a nosegay of the bright sea flowers. "Tell me no lies, Sir; you belong to the West Bruntseyans, and you have driven us into a vile bog to scare me. They have bribed you. I see the whole of it. Tell me the truth, and you shall have five shillings."

The driver looked over the marshes as if he had never received such an offer before. Five shillings for a falsehood would have seemed the proper thing, and have called for a balance of considerations, and made a demand upon his energies. But to earn five shillings by the truth had never fallen to his luck before; and he turned to me, because I smiled, and he said, "Will you taste the water, miss?"

"Bless me!" cried the Major, "now I never thought of that. Common people have such ways about things they are used to! I might have stood here for a month, and never have thought of that way to settle it. Ridiculously simple. Give me a taste, Erema. Ah, that is the real beauty of our coast, my dear! The strongest proportion of the saline element—I should know the taste of it any where. No sea-weed, no fishy particles, no sludge, no beards of oysters. The pure, uncontaminated, perfect brine, that sets every male and female on his legs, varicose, orthopedic—I forget their scientifics, but I know the smack of it."

"Certainly," I said, "it is beautifully salt. It will give you an appetite for dinner, Major Hockin. I could drink a pint of it, after all that smoke. But don't you think it is a serious thing for the sea itself to come pouring through the bottom of this pebble bank in this way?"

"Not at all. No, I rather like it. It opens up many strictly practical ideas. It adds very much to the value of the land. For instance, a 'salt-lick,' as your sweet Yankees call it—and set up an infirmary for foot and mouth disease. And better still, the baths, the baths, my dear. No expense for piping, or pumping, or any thing. Only place your marble at the proper level, and twice a day you have the grand salubrious sparkling influx of ocean's self, self-filtered, and by its own operation permeated with a fine siliceous element. What foreign mud could compete with such a bath?"

"But supposing there should come too much of it," I said, "and wash both the baths and the bathers away?"

"Such an idea is ridiculous. It can be adjusted to a nicety. I am very glad I happened to observe this thing, this—this noble phenomenon. I shall speak to Montague about it at once, before I am half an hour older. My dear, you have made a conquest; I quite forgot to tell you; but never mind that for the present. Driver, here is half a crown for you. Your master will put down the fly to my account. He owes me a heriot. I shall claim his best beast, the moment he gets one without a broken wind."

As the Major spoke, he got out at his own door with all his wonted alacrity; but instead of offering me his hand, as he always had done in London, he skipped up his nine steps, on purpose (as I saw) that somebody else might come down for me. And this was Sir Montague Hockin, as I feared was only too likely from what had been said. If I had even suspected that this gentleman was at Bruntlands, I would have done my utmost to stay where I was, in spite of all absence of money. Betsy would gladly have allowed me to remain, without paying even a farthing, until it should become convenient. Pride had forbidden me to speak of this; but I would have got over that pride much rather than meet this Sir Montague Hockin thus. Some instinct told me to avoid him altogether; and having so little now of any other guidance, I attached, perhaps, foolish importance to that.

However, it was not the part of a lady to be rude to any one through instinct; and I knew already that in England young women are not quite such masters of their own behavior as in the far West they are allowed to be. And so I did my best that, even in my eyes, he should not see how vexed I was at meeting him. And soon it appeared that this behavior, however painful to me, was no less wise than good, because both with my host and hostess this new visitor was already at the summit of all good graces. He had conquered the Major by admiration of all his schemes and upshots, and even offering glimmers of the needful money in the distance; and Mrs. Hockin lay quite at his feet ever since he had opened a hamper and produced a pair of frizzled fowls, creatures of an extraordinary aspect, toothed all over like a dandelion plant, with every feather sticking inside out. When I saw them, I tried for my life not to laugh, and biting my lips very hard, quite succeeded, until the cock opened up a pair of sleepy eyes, covered with comb and very sad inversions, and glancing with complacency at his wife (who stood beneath him, even more turned inside out), capered with his twiggy legs, and gave a long, sad crow. Mrs. Hockin looked at him with intense delight.

"Erema, is it possible that you laugh? I thought that you never laughed, Erema. At any rate, if you ever do indulge, you might choose a fitter opportunity, I think. You have spoiled his demonstration altogether—see, he does not understand such unkindness—and it is the very first he has uttered since he came. Oh, poor Fluffsky!"

"I am very, very sorry. But how was I to help it? I would not, on any account, have stopped him if I had known he was so sensitive. Fluffsky, do please to begin again."

"These beggars are nothing at all, I can assure you," said Sir Montague, coming to my aid, when Fluffsky spurned all our prayers for one more crow. "Mrs. Hockin, if you really would like to have a fowl that even Lady Clara Crowcombe has not got, you shall have it in a week, or a fortnight, or, at any rate, a month, if I can manage it. They are not to be had except through certain channels, and the fellows who write the poultry books have never even heard of them."

"Oh, how delighted I shall be! Lady Clara despises all her neighbors so. But do they lay eggs? Half the use of keeping poultry, when you never kill them, is to get an egg for breakfast; and Major Hockin looks round and says, 'Now is this our own?' and I can not say that it is; and I am vexed with the books, and he begins to laugh at me. People said it was for want of chalk, but they walk upon nothing but chalk, as you can see."

"And their food, Mrs. Hockin. They are walking upon that. Starve them for a week, and forty eggs at least will reward you for stern discipline."

But all this little talk I only tell to show how good and soft Mrs. Hockin was; and her husband, in spite of all his self-opinion, and resolute talk about money and manorial dues, in his way, perhaps, was even less to be trusted to get his cash out of any poor and honest man.

On the very day after my return from London I received a letter from "Colonel Gundry" (as we always called the Sawyer now, through his kinship to the Major), and, as it can not easily be put into less compass, I may as well give his very words:

"DEAR MISS REMA,—Your last favor to hand, with thanks. Every thing is going on all right with us. The mill is built up, and goes better than ever; more orders on hand than we can get through. We have not cracked the big nugget yet. Expect the government to take him at a trifle below value, for Washington Museum. Must have your consent; but, for my part, would rather let him go there than break him. Am ready to lose a few dollars upon him, particularly as he might crack up all quartzy in the middle. They offer to take him by weight at three dollars and a half per pound below standard. Please say if agreeable.

"I fear, my dear, that there are bad times coming for all of us here in this part. Not about money, but a long sight worse; bad will, and contention, and rebellion, perhaps. What we hear concerning it is not much here; but even here thoughts are very much divided. Ephraim takes a different view from mine; which is not a right thing for a grandson to do; and neighbor Sylvester goes with him. The Lord send agreement and concord among us; but, if He doeth so, He must change his mind first, for every man is borrowing his neighbor's gun.

"If there is any thing that you can do to turn Ephraim back to his duty, my dear, I am sure that, for love of us, you will do it. If Firm was to run away from me now, and go fighting on behalf of slavery, I never should care more for naught upon this side of Jordan; and the new mill might go to Jericho; though it does look uncommon handsome now, I can assure you, and tears through its work like a tiger.

"Noting symptoms in your last of the price of things in England, and having carried over some to your account, inclosed please to find a bill for five hundred dollars, though not likely to be wanted yet. Save a care of your money, my dear; but pay your way handsome, as a Castlewood should do. Jowler goes his rounds twice a day looking for you; and somebody else never hangs his hat up without casting one eye at the corner you know. Sylvester's girl was over here last week, dashing about as usual. If Firm goes South, he may have her, for aught I care, and never see saw-mill again. But I hope that the Lord will spare my old days such disgrace and tribulation.

"About you know what, my dear, be not overanxious. I have been young, and now am old, as the holy Psalmist says; and the more I see of the ways of men, the less I verily think of them. Their good esteem, their cap in hand, their fair fame, as they call it, goes by accident, and fortune, the whim of the moment, and the way the clever ones have of tickling them. A great man laughs at the flimsy of it, and a good one goes to his conscience. Your father saw these things at their value. I have often grieved that you can not see them so; but perhaps I have liked you none the worse, my dear.

"Don't forget about going South. A word from you may stop him. It is almost the only hope I have, and even that may be too late. Suan Isco and Martin send messages. The flowers are on your father's grave. I have got a large order for pine cradles in great haste, but have time to be,

"Truly yours,

"SAMPSON GUNDRY."

That letter, while it relieved me in one way, from the want of money, cost me more than ten times five hundred dollars' worth of anxiety. The Sawyer had written to me twice ere this—kind, simple letters, but of no importance, except for their goodness and affection. But now it was clear that when he wrote this letter he must have been sadly put out and upset. His advice to me was beyond all value; but he seemed to have kept none at home for himself. He was carried quite out of his large, staid ways when he wrote those bitter words about poor Firm—the very apple of his eye, as the holy Psalmist says. And, knowing the obstinacy of them both, I dreaded clash between them.

CHAPTER XXXI
ADRIFT

Having got money enough to last long with one brought up to simplicity, and resolved to have nothing to do for a while with charity or furnished lodgings (what though kept by one's own nurse), I cast about now for good reason to be off from all the busy works at Bruntsea. So soon after such a tremendous blow, it was impossible for me to push my own little troubles and concerns upon good Mr. Shovelin's family, much as I longed to know what was to become of my father's will, if any thing. But my desire to be doing something, or, at least, to get away for a time from Bruntsea, was largely increased by Sir Montague Hockin's strange behavior toward me.

That young man, if still he could be called young—which, at my age, scarcely seemed to be his right, for he must have been ten years older than poor Firm—began more and more every day to come after me, just when I wanted to be quite alone. There was nothing more soothing to my thoughts and mind (the latter getting quiet from the former, I suppose) than for the whole of me to rest a while in such a little scollop of the shingle as a new-moon tide, in little crescents, leaves just below high-water mark. And now it was new-moon tide again, a fortnight after the flooding of our fly by the activity of the full moon; and, feeling how I longed to understand these things—which seem to be denied to all who are of the same sex as the moon herself—I sat in a very nice nick, where no wind could make me look worse than nature willed. But of my own looks I never did think twice, unless there was any one to speak of such a subject.

Here I was sitting in the afternoon of a gentle July day, wondering by what energy of nature all these countless pebbles were produced, and not even a couple to be found among them fit to lie side by side and purely tally with each other. Right and left, for miles and miles, millions multiplied into millions; yet I might hold any one in my palm and be sure that it never had been there before. And of the quiet wavelets even, taking their own time and manner, in default of will of wind, all to come and call attention to their doom by arching over, and endeavoring to make froth, were any two in sound and size, much more in shape and shade, alike? Every one had its own little business, of floating pop-weed or foam bubbles or of blistered light, to do; and every one, having done it, died and subsided into its successor.

"A trifle sentimental, are we?" cried a lively voice behind me, and the waves of my soft reflections fell, and instead of them stood Sir Montague Hockin, with a hideous parasol.

I never received him with worse grace, often as I had repulsed him; but he was one of those people who think that women are all whims and ways.

"I grieve to intrude upon large ideas," he said, as I rose and looked at him, "but I act under positive orders now. A lady knows what is best for a lady. Mrs. Hockin has been looking from the window, and she thinks that you ought not to be sitting in the sun like this. There has been a case of sunstroke at Southbourne—a young lady meditating under the cliff—and she begs you to accept this palm leaf."

I thought of the many miles I had wandered under the fierce Californian sun; but I would not speak to him of that. "Thank you," I said; "it was very kind of her to think of it, and of you to do it. But will it be safe for you to go back without it?"

"Oh, why should I do so?" he answered, with a tone of mock pathos which provoked me always, though I never could believe it to be meant in ridicule of me, for that would have been too low a thing; and, besides, I never spoke so. "Could you bear to see me slain by the shafts of the sun? Miss Castlewood, this parasol is amply large for both of us."

I would not answer him in his own vein, because I never liked his vein at all; though I was not so entirely possessed as to want every body to be like myself.

"Thank you; I mean to stay here," I said; "you may either leave the parasol or take it, whichever will be less troublesome. At any rate, I shall not use it."

A gentleman, according to my ideas, would have bowed and gone upon his way; but Sir Montague Hockin would have no rebuff. He seemed to look upon me as a child, such as average English girls, fresh from little schools, would be. Nothing more annoyed me, after all my thoughts and dream of some power in myself, than this.

"Perhaps I might tell you a thing or two," he said, while I kept gazing at some fishing-boats, and sat down again, as a sign for him to go—"a little thing or two of which you have no idea, even in your most lonely musings, which might have a very deep interest for you. Do you think that I came to this hole to see the sea? Or that fussy old muff of a Major's doings?"

"Perhaps you would like me to tell him your opinion of his intellect and great plans," I answered. "And after all his kindness to you!"

"You never will do that," he said; "because you are a lady, and will not repeat what is said in confidence. I could help you materially in your great object, if you would only make a friend of me."

"And what would your own object be? The pure anxiety to do right?"

"Partly, and I might say mainly, that; also an ambition for your good opinion, which seems so inaccessible. But you will think me selfish if I even hint at any condition of any kind. Every body I have ever met with likes me, except Miss Castlewood."

As he spoke he glanced down his fine amber-colored beard, shining in the sun, and even in the sun showing no gray hair (for a reason which Mrs. Hockin told me afterward), and he seemed to think it hard that a man with such a beard should be valued lightly.

"I do not see why we should talk," I said, "about either likes or dislikes. Only, if you have any thing to tell, I shall be very much obliged to you."

This gentleman looked at me in a way which I have often observed in England. A general idea there prevails that the free and enlightened natives of the West are in front of those here in intelligence, and to some extent, therefore, in dishonesty. But there must be many cases where the two are not the same.

"No," I replied, while he was looking at his buttons, which had every British animal upon them; "I mean nothing more than the simple thing I say. If you ought to tell me any thing, tell it. I am accustomed to straightforward people. But they disappoint one by their never knowing any thing."

"But I know something," he answered, with a nod of grave, mysterious import; "and perhaps I will tell you some day, when admitted, if ever I have such an honor, to some little degree of friendship."

"Oh, please not to think of yourself," I exclaimed, in a manner which must have amused him. "In such a case, the last thing that you should do is that. Think only of what is right and honorable, and your duty toward a lady. Also your duty to the laws of your country. I am not at all sure that you ought not to be arrested. But perhaps it is nothing at all, after all; only something invented to provoke me."

"In that case, I can only drop the subject," he answered, with that stern gleam of the eyes which I had observed before, and detested. "I was also to tell you that we dine to-day an hour before the usual time, that my cousin may go out in the boat for whiting. The sea will be as smooth as glass. Perhaps you will come with us."

With these words, he lifted his hat and went off, leaving me in a most uncomfortable state, as he must have known if he had even tried to think. For I could not get the smallest idea what he meant; and, much as I tried to believe that he must be only pretending, for reasons of his own, to have something important to tell me, scarcely was it possible to be contented so. A thousand absurd imaginations began to torment me as to what he meant. He lived in London so much, for instance, that he had much quicker chance of knowing whatever there was to know; again, he was a man of the world, full of short, sharp sagacity, and able to penetrate what I could not; then, again, he kept a large account with Shovelin, Wayte, and Shovelin, as Major Hockin chanced to say; and I knew not that a banker's reserve is much deeper than his deposit; moreover—which, to my mind, was almost stronger proof than any thing—Sir Montague Hockin was of smuggling pedigree, and likely to be skillful in illicit runs of knowledge.

However, in spite of all this uneasiness, not another word would I say to him about it, waiting rather for him to begin again upon it. But, though I waited and waited, as, perhaps, with any other person I scarcely could have done, he would not condescend to give me even another look about it.

Disliking that gentleman more and more for his supercilious conduct and certainty of subduing me, I naturally turned again to my good host and hostess. But here there was very little help or support to be obtained at present. Major Hockin was laying the foundations of "The Bruntsea Assembly-Rooms, Literary Institute, Mutual Improvement Association, Lyceum, and Baths, from sixpence upward;" while Mrs. Hockin had a hatch of "White Sultans," or, rather, a prolonged sitting of eggs, fondly hoped to hatch at last, from having cost so much, like a chicken-hearted Conference. Much as I sorrowed at her disappointment—for the sitting cost twelve guineas—I could not feel quite guiltless of a petty and ignoble smile, when, after hoping against hope, upon the thirtieth day she placed her beautifully sound eggs in a large bowl of warm water, in which they floated as calmly as if their price was a penny a dozen. The poor lady tried to believe that they were spinning with vitality; but at last she allowed me to break one, and lo! it had been half boiled by the advertiser. "This is very sad," cried Mrs. Hockin; and the patient old hen, who was come in a basket of hay to see the end of it, echoed with a cluck that sentiment.

These things being so, I was left once more to follow my own guidance, which had seemed, in the main, to be my fortune ever since my father died. For one day Mr. Shovelin had appeared, to my great joy and comfort, as a guide and guardian; but, alas! for one day only. And, except for his good advice and kind paternal conduct to me, it seemed at present an unlucky thing that I had ever discovered him. Not only through deep sense of loss and real sorrow for him, but also because Major Hockin, however good and great and generous, took it unreasonably into his head that I threw him over, and threw myself (as with want of fine taste he expressed it) into the arms of the banker. This hurt me very much, and I felt that Major Hockin could never have spoken so hastily unless his hair had been originally red; and so it might be detected, even now, where it survived itself, though blanched where he brushed it into that pretentious ridge. Sometimes I liked that man, when his thoughts were large and liberal; but no sooner had he said a fine brave thing than he seemed to have an after-thought not to go too far with it; just as he had done about the poor robbed woman from the steerage and the young man who pulled out his guinea. I paid him for my board and lodging, upon a scale settled by Uncle Sam himself, at California prices; therefore I am under no obligation to conceal his foibles. But, take him altogether, he was good and brave and just, though unable, from absence of inner light, to be to me what Uncle Sam had been.

When I perceived that the Major condemned my simple behavior in London, and (if I may speak it, as I said it to myself) "blew hot and cold" in half a minute—hot when I thought of any good things to be done, and cold as soon as he became the man to do them—also, when I remembered what a chronic plague was now at Bruntsea, in the shape of Sir Montague, who went to and fro, but could never be trusted to be far off, I resolved to do what I had long been thinking of, and believed that my guardian, if he had lived another day, would have recommended. I resolved to go and see Lord Castlewood, my father's first cousin and friend in need.

When I asked my host and hostess what they thought of this, they both declared that it was the very thing they were at the point of advising, which, however, they had forborne from doing because I never took advice. At this, as being such a great exaggeration, I could not help smiling seriously; but I could not accept their sage opinion that, before I went to see my kinsman, I ought to write and ask his leave to do so. For that would have made it quite a rude thing to call, as I must still have done, if he should decline beforehand to receive me. Moreover, it would look as if I sought an invitation, while only wanting an interview. Therefore, being now full of money again, I hired the flyman who had made us taste the water, and taking train at Newport, and changing at two or three places as ordered, crossed many little streams, and came to a fair river, which proved to be the Thames itself, a few miles above Reading.

In spite of all the larger lessons of travel, adventure, and tribulation, my heart was throbbing with some rather small feelings, as for the first time I drew near to the home of my forefathers. I should have been sorry to find it ugly or mean, or lying in a hole, or even modern or insignificant; and when none of these charges could be brought against it, I was filled with highly discreditable pain that Providence had not seen fit to issue me into this world in the masculine form; in which case this fine property would, according to the rules of mankind, have been mine. However, I was very soon ashamed of such ideas, and sat down on a bank to dispel them with the free and fair view around me.

The builder of that house knew well both where to place and how to shape it, so as not to spoil the site. It stood near the brow of a bosoming hill, which sheltered it, both with wood and clevice, from the rigor and fury of the north and east; while in front the sloping foreground widened its soft lap of green. In bays and waves of rolling grass, promontoried, here and there, by jutting copse or massive tree, and jotted now and then with cattle as calm as boats at anchor, the range of sunny upland fell to the reedy fringe and clustered silence of deep river meadows. Here the Thames, in pleasant bends of gentleness and courtesy, yet with will of its own ways, being now a plenteous river, spreads low music, and holds mirror to the woods and hills and fields, casting afar a broad still gleam, and on the banks presenting tremulous infinitude of flash.

Now these things touched me all the more because none of them belonged to me; and, after thus trying to enlarge my views, I got up with much better heart, and hurried on to have it over, whatever it might be. A girl brought up in the real English way would have spent her last shilling to drive up to the door in the fly at the station—a most sad machine—but I thought it no disgrace to go in a more becoming manner.

One scarcely ever acts up to the force of situation; and I went as quietly into that house as if it were Betsy Bowen's. If any body had been rude to me, or asked who I was, or a little thing of that sort, my spirit might have been up at once, and found, as usually happens then, good reason to go down afterward. But happily there was nothing of the kind. An elderly man, without any gaudy badges, opened the door very quietly, and begged my pardon, before I spoke, for asking me to speak softly. It was one of his lordship's very worst days, and when he was so, every sound seemed to reach him. I took the hint, and did not speak at all, but followed him over deep matting into a little room to which he showed me. And then I gave him a little note, written before I left Bruntsea, and asked him whether he thought that his master was well enough to attend to it.

He looked at me in a peculiar manner, for he had known my father well, having served from his youth in the family; but he only asked whether my message was important. I answered that it was, but that I would wait for another time rather than do any harm. But he said that, however ill his master was, nothing provoked him more than to find that any thing was neglected through it. And before I could speak again he was gone with my letter to Lord Castlewood.

CHAPTER XXXII
AT HOME

Some of the miserable, and I might say strange, things which had befallen me from time to time unseasonably, now began to force their remembrance upon me. Such dark figures always seem to make the most of a nervous moment, when solid reason yields to fluttering fear and small misgivings. There any body seems to lie, as a stranded sailor lies, at the foot of perpendicular cliffs of most inhuman humanity, with all the world frowning down over the crest, and no one to throw a rope down. Often and often had I felt this want of any one to help me, but the only way out of it seemed to be to do my best to help myself.

Even, now I had little hope, having been so often dashed, and knowing that my father's cousin possessed no share of my father's strength. He might, at the utmost, give good advice, and help me with kind feeling; but if he wanted to do more, surely he might have tried ere now. But my thoughts about this were cut short by a message that he would be glad to see me, and I followed the servant to the library.

Here I found Lord Castlewood sitting in a high-backed chair, uncushioned and uncomfortable. When he saw me near him he got up and took my hand, and looked at me, and I was pleased to find his face well-meaning, brave, and generous. But even to rise from his chair was plainly no small effort to him, and he leaned upon a staff or crutch as he offered me a small white hand.

"Miss Castlewood," he said, with a very weak yet clear and silvery voice, "for many years I have longed in vain and sought in vain to hear of you. I have not escaped all self-reproach through my sense of want of energy; yet, such as I am, I have done my best, or I do my best to think so."

"I am sure you have," I replied, without thinking, knowing his kindness to my father, and feeling the shame of my own hot words to Mr. Shovelin about him. "I owe you more gratitude than I can tell, for your goodness to my dear father. I am not come now to trouble you, but because it was my duty."

While I was speaking he managed to lead me, feebly as himself could walk, to a deep chair for reading, or some such use, whereof I have had few chances. And in every step and word and gesture I recognized that foreign grace which true-born Britons are proud to despise on both sides of the Atlantic. And, being in the light, I watched him well, because I am not a foreigner.

In the clear summer light of the westering sun (which is better for accurate uses than the radiance of the morning) I saw a firm, calm face, which might in good health have been powerful—a face which might be called the moonlight image of my father's. I could not help turning away to cry, and suspicion fled forever.

"My dear young cousin," he said, as soon as I was fit to speak to, "your father trusted me, and so must you. You may think that I have forgotten you, or done very little to find you out. It was no indifference, no forgetfulness: I have not been able to work myself, and I have had very deep trouble of my own."

He leaned on his staff, and looked down at me, for I had sat down when thus overcome, and I knew that the forehead and eyes were those of a learned and intellectual man. How I knew this it is impossible to say, for I never had met with such a character as this, unless it were the Abbe of Flechon, when I was only fourteen years old, and valued his great skill in spinning a top tenfold more than all his deep learning. Lord Castlewood had long, silky hair, falling in curls of silver gray upon either side of his beautiful forehead, and the gaze of his soft dark eyes was sad, gentle, yet penetrating. Weak health and almost constant pain had chastened his delicate features to an expression almost feminine, though firm thin lips and rigid lines showed masculine will and fortitude. And when he spoke of his own trouble (which, perhaps, he would not have done except for consolation's sake), I knew that he meant something even more grievous than bodily anguish.

"It is hard," he said, "that you, so young and healthy and full of high spirit as you are (unless your face belies you), should begin the best years of your life, as common opinion puts such things, in such a cloud of gloom and shame."

"There is no shame at all," I answered; "and if there is gloom, I am used to that; and so was my father for years and years. What is my trouble compared with his?"

"Your trouble is nothing when compared with his, so far as regards the mere weight of it; but he was a strong man to carry his load; you are a young and a sensitive woman. The burden may even be worse for you. Now tell me all about yourself, and what has brought you to me."

His voice was so quiet and soothing that I seemed to rest beneath it. He had not spoken once of religion or the will of God, nor plied me at all with those pious allusions, which even to the reverent mind are like illusions when so urged. Lord Castlewood had too deep a sense of the will of God to know what it is; and he looked at me wistfully as at one who might have worse experience of it.

Falling happily under his influence, as his clear, kind eyes met mine, I told him every thing I could think of about my father and myself, and all I wanted to do next, and how my heart and soul were set upon getting to the bottom of every thing. And while I spoke with spirit, or softness, or, I fear, sometimes with hate, I could not help seeing that he was surprised, but not wholly displeased, with my energy. And then, when all was exhausted, came the old question I had heard so often, and found so hard to answer—

"And what do you propose to do next, Erema?"

"To go to the very place itself," I said, speaking strongly under challenge, though quite unresolved about such a thing before; "to live in the house where my father lived, and my mother and all of the family died; and from day to day to search every corner and fish up every bit of evidence, until I get hold of the true man at last, of the villain who did it—who did it, and left my father and all the rest of us to be condemned and die for it."

"Erema," replied my cousin, as he had told me now to call him, "you are too impetuous for such work, and it is wholly unfit for you. For such a task, persons of trained sagacity and keen observation are needed. And after all these eighteen years, or nearly nineteen now it must be, there can not be any thing to discover there."

"But if I like, may I go there, cousin, if only to satisfy my own mind? I am miserable now at Bruntsea, and Sir Montague Hockin wears me out."

"Sir Montague Hockin!" Lord Castlewood exclaimed; "why, you did not tell me that he was there. Wherever he is, you should not be."

"I forgot to speak of him. He does not live there, but is continually to and fro for bathing, or fishing, or rabbit-shooting, or any other pretext. And he makes the place very unpleasant to me, kind as the Major and Mrs. Hockin are, because I can never make him out at all."

"Do not try to do so," my cousin answered, looking at me earnestly; "be content to know nothing of him, my dear. If you can put up with a very dull house, and a host who is even duller, come here and live with me, as your father would have wished, and as I, your nearest relative, now ask and beg of you."

This was wonderfully kind, and for a moment I felt tempted. Lord Castlewood being an elderly man, and, as the head of our family, my natural protector, there could be nothing wrong, and there might be much that was good, in such an easy arrangement. But, on the other hand, it seemed to me that after this my work would languish. Living in comfort and prosperity under the roof of my forefathers, beyond any doubt I should begin to fall into habits of luxury, to take to the love of literature, which I knew to be latent within me, to lose the clear, strong, practical sense of the duty for which I, the last of seven, was spared, and in some measure, perhaps, by wanderings and by hardships, fitted. And then I thought of my host's weak health, continual pain (the signs of which were hardly repressed even while he was speaking), and probably also his secluded life. Was it fair to force him, by virtue of his inborn kindness and courtesy, to come out of his privileges and deal with me, who could not altogether be in any place a mere nobody? And so I refused his offer.

"I am very much obliged to you indeed," I said, "but I think you might be sorry for it. I will come and stop with you every now and then, when your health is better, and you ask me. But to live here altogether would not do; I should like it too well, and do nothing else."

"Perhaps you are right," he replied, with the air of one who cares little for any thing, which is to me the most melancholy thing, and worse than any distress almost; "you are very young, my dear, and years should be allowed to pass before you know what full-grown sorrow is. You have had enough, for your age, of it. You had better not live in this house; it is not a house for cheerfulness."

"Then if I must neither live here nor at Bruntsea," I asked, with sudden remonstrance, feeling as if every body desired to be quit of me or to worry me, "to what place in all the world am I to go, unless it is back to America? I will go at once to Shoxford, and take lodgings of my own."

"Perhaps you had better wait a little while," Lord Castlewood answered, gently, "although I would much rather have you at Shoxford than where you are at present. But please to remember, my good Erema, that you can not go to Shoxford all alone. I have a most faithful and trusty man—the one who opened the door to you. He has been here before his remembrance. He disdains me still as compared with your father. Will you have him to superintend you? I scarcely see how you can do any good, but if you do go, you must go openly, and as your father's daughter."

"I have no intention whatever of going in any other way, Lord Castlewood; but perhaps," I continued, "it would be as well to make as little stir as possible. Of an English village I know nothing but the little I have seen at Bruntsea, but there they make a very great fuss about any one who comes down with a man-servant."

"To be sure," replied my cousin, with a smile; "they would not be true Britons otherwise. Perhaps you would do better without Stixon; but of course you must not go alone. Could you by any means persuade your old nurse Betsy to go with you?"

"How good of you to think of it!—how wise you are!" I really could not help saying, as I gazed at his delicate and noble face. "I am sure that if Betsy can come, she will; though of course she must be compensated well for the waste all her lodgers will make of it. They are very wicked, and eat most dreadfully if she even takes one day's holiday. What do you think they even do? She has told me with tears in her eyes of it. They are all allowed a pat of butter, a penny roll, and two sardines for breakfast. No sooner do they know that her back is turned—"

"Erema!" cried my cousin, with some surprise; and being so recalled, I was ashamed. But I never could help taking interest in very little things indeed, until my own common-sense, or somebody else, came to tell me what a child I was. However, I do believe that Uncle Sam liked me all the better for this fault.

"My dear, I did not mean to blame you," Lord Castlewood said, most kindly; "it must be a great relief for you to look on at other people. But tell me—or rather, since you have told me almost every thing you know—let me, if only in one way I can help you, help you at least in that way."

Knowing that he must mean money, I declined, from no false pride, but a set resolve to work out my work, if possible, through my own resources. But I promised to apply to him at once if scarcity should again befall me, as had happened lately. And then I longed to ask him why he seemed to have so low an opinion of Sir Montague Hockin. That question, however, I feared to put, because it might not be a proper one, and also because my cousin had spoken in a very strange tone, as if of some private dislike or reserve on that subject. Moreover, it was too evident that I had tried his courtesy long enough. From time to time pale shades of bodily pain, and then hot flushes, had flitted across his face, like clouds on a windy summer evening. And more than once he had glanced at the time-piece, not to hurry me, but as if he dreaded its announcements. It was a beautiful clock, and struck with a silvery sound every quarter of an hour. And now, as I rose to say good-by, to catch my evening train, it struck a quarter to five, and my cousin stood up, with his weight upon his staff, and looked at me with an inexpressible depth of weary misery.

"I have only a few minutes left," he said, "during which I can say any thing. My time is divided into two sad parts: the time when I am capable of very little, and the time when I am capable of nothing; and the latter part is twice the length of the other. For sixteen hours of every day, far better had I be dead than living, so far as our own little insolence may judge. But I speak of it only to excuse bad manners, and perhaps I show worse by doing so. I shall not be able to see you again until to-morrow morning. Do not go; they will arrange all that. Send a note to Major Hockin by Stixon's boy. Stixon and Mrs. Price will see to your comfort, if those who are free from pain require any other comfort. Forgive me; I did not mean to be rude. Sometimes I can not help giving way."

Less enviable than the poorest slave, Lord Castlewood sank upon his hard stiff chair, and straightened his long narrow hands upon his knees, and set his thin lips in straight blue lines. Each hand was as rigid as the ivory handle of an umbrella or walking-stick, and his lips were like clamped wire. This was his regular way of preparing for the onset of the night, so that no grimace, no cry, no moan, or other token of fierce agony should be wrung from him.

"My lord will catch it stiff to-night," said Mr. Stixon, who came as I rang, and then led me away to the drawing-room; "he always have it ten times worse after any talking or any thing to upset him like. And so, then, miss—excuse a humble servant—did I understand from him that you was the Captain's own daughter?"

"Yes; but surely your master wants you—he is in such dreadful pain. Do please to go to him, and do something."

"There is nothing to be done, miss," Stixon answered, with calm resignation; "he is bound to stay so for sixteen hours, and then he eases off again. But bless my heart, miss—excuse me in your presence—his lordship is thoroughly used to it. It is my certain knowledge that for seven years now he has never had seven minutes free from pain—seven minutes all of a heap, I mean. Some do say, miss, as the Lord doeth every thing according to His righteousness, that the reason is not very far to seek."

I asked him what he meant, though I ought, perhaps, to have put a stop to his loquacity; and he pretended not to hear, which made me ask him all the more.

"A better man never lived than my lord," he answered, with a little shock at my misprision; "but it has been said among censoorous persons that nobody ever had no luck as came in suddenly to a property and a high state of life on the top of the heads of a family of seven."

"What a poor superstition!" I cried, though I was not quite sure of its being a wicked one. "But what is your master's malady, Stixon? Surely there might be something done to relieve his violent pain, even if there is no real cure for it?"

"No, miss, nothing can be done. The doctors have exorced themselves. They tried this, that, and the other, but nature only flew worse against them. 'Tis a thing as was never heard of till the Constitooshon was knocked on the head and to pieces by the Reform Bill. And though they couldn't cure it, they done what they could do, miss. They discovered a very good name for it—they christened it the 'New-rager!'"

CHAPTER XXXIII
LORD CASTLEWOOD

In the morning, when I was called again to see my afflicted cousin—Stixon junior having gladly gone to explain things for me at Bruntsea—little as I knew of any bodily pain (except hunger, or thirst, or weariness, and once in my life a headache), I stood before Lord Castlewood with a deference and humility such as I had never felt before toward any human being. Not only because he bore perpetual pain in the two degrees of night and day—the day being dark and the night jet-black—without a murmur or an evil word; not only because through the whole of this he had kept his mind clear and his love of knowledge bright; not even because he had managed, like Job, to love God through the whole of it. All these were good reasons for very great and very high respect of any man; and when there was no claim whatever on his part to any such feeling, it needs must come. But when I learned another thing, high respect at once became what might be called deep reverence. And this came to pass in a simple and, as any one must confess, quite inevitable way.

It was not to be supposed that I could sit the whole of my first evening in that house without a soul to speak to. So far as my dignity and sense of right permitted, I wore out Mr. Stixon, so far as he would go, not asking him any thing that the very worst-minded person could call "inquisitive," but allowing him to talk, as he seemed to like to do, while he waited upon me, and alternately lamented my hapless history and my hopeless want of taste.

"Ah, your father, the Captain, now, he would have knowed what this is! You've no right to his eyes, Miss Erma, without his tongue and palate. No more of this, miss! and done for you a-purpose! Well, cook will be put out, and no mistake! I better not let her see it go down, anyhow." And the worthy man tearfully put some dainty by, perhaps without any view to his own supper.

"Lord Castlewood spoke to me about a Mrs. Price—the housekeeper, is she not?" I asked at last, being so accustomed to like what I could get, that the number of dishes wearied me.

"Oh yes, miss," said Stixon, very shortly, as if that description exhausted Mrs. Price.

"If she is not too busy, I should like to see her as soon as these things are all taken away. I mean if she is not a stranger, and if she would like to see me."

"No new-comers here," Mr. Stixon replied; "we all works our way up regular, the same as my lad is beginning for to do. New-fangled ways is not accepted here. We puts the reforming spirits scrubbing of the steps till their knuckles is cracked and their knees like a bean. The old lord was the man for discipline—your grandfather, if you please, miss. He catched me when I were about that high—"

"Excuse me, Mr. Stixon; but would he have encouraged you to talk as you so very kindly talk to me, instead of answering a question?"

I thought that poor Stixon would have been upset by this, and was angry with myself for saying it; but instead of being hurt, he only smiled and touched his forehead.

"Well, now, you did remind me uncommon of him then, miss. I could have heard the old lord speak almost, though he were always harsh and distant. And as I was going for to say, he catched me fifty years agone next Lammas-tide; a pear-tree of an early sort it was; you may see the very tree if you please to stand here, miss, though the pears is quite altered now, and scarcely fit to eat. Well, I was running off with my cap chock-full, miss—"

"Please to keep that story for another time," I said; "I shall be most happy to hear it then. But I have a particular wish, if you please, to see Mrs. Price before dark, unless there is any good reason why I should not."

"Oh no, Miss Erma, no reason at all. Only please to bear in mind, miss, that she is a coorous woman. She is that jealous, and I might say forward—"

"Then she is capable of speaking for herself."

"You are right, miss, there, and no mistake. She can speak for herself and for fifty others—words enough, I mean, for all of them. But I would not have her know for all the world that I said it."

"Then if you do not send her to me at once, the first thing I shall do will be to tell her."

"Oh no, miss, none of your family would do that; that never has been done anonymous."

I assured him that my threat was not in earnest, but of pure impatience. And having no motive but downright jealousy for keeping Mrs. Price from me, he made up his mind at last to let her come. But he told me to be careful what I said; I must not expect it to be at all like talking to himself, for instance.

The housekeeper came up at last, by dint of my persistence, and she stopped in the doorway and made me a courtesy, which put me out of countenance, for nobody ever does that in America, and scarcely any one in England now, except in country-dancing. Instead of being as described by Stixon, Mrs. Price was of a very quiet, sensible, and respectful kind. She was rather short, but looked rather tall, from her even walk and way of carrying her head. Her figure was neat, and her face clear-spoken, with straight pretty eyebrows, and calm bright eyes. I felt that I could tell her almost any thing, and she would think before she talked of it. And in my strong want of some woman to advise with—Betsy Bowen being very good but very narrow, and Mrs. Hockin a mere echo of the Major until he contradicted her, and Suan Isco, with her fine, large views, five thousand miles out of sight just now—this was a state of things to enhance the value of any good countenance feminine.

At any rate, I was so glad to see her that, being still ungraduated in the steps of rank (though beginning to like a good footing there), I ran up and took her by both hands, and fetched her out of her grand courtesy and into a low chair. At this she was surprised, as one quick glance showed; and she thought me, perhaps, what is called in England "an impulsive creature." This put me again upon my dignity, for I never have been in any way like that, and I clearly perceived that she ought to understand a little more distinctly my character.

It is easy to begin with this intention, but very hard indeed to keep it up when any body of nice ways and looks is sitting with a proper deferential power of listening, and liking one's young ideas, which multiply and magnify themselves at each demand. So after some general talk about the weather, the country, the house, and so on, we came to the people of the house, or at any rate the chief person. And I asked her a few quiet questions about Lord Castlewood's health and habits, and any thing else she might like to tell me. For many things had seemed to me a little strange and out of the usual course, and on that account worthy to be spoken of without common curiosity. Mrs. Price told me that there were many things generally divulged and credited, which therefore lay in her power to communicate without any derogation from her office. Being pleased with these larger words (which I always have trouble in pronouncing), I asked her whether there was any thing else. And she answered yes, but unhappily of a nature to which it was scarcely desirable to allude in my presence. I told her that this was not satisfactory, and I might say quite the opposite; that having "alluded" to whatever it might be, she was bound to tell me all about it. That

I had lived in very many countries, in all of which wrong things continually went on, of which I continually heard just in that sort of way and no more. Enough to make one uncomfortable, but not enough to keep one instructed and vigilant as to things that ought to be avoided. Upon this she yielded either to my arguments or to her own dislike of unreasonable silence, and gave me the following account of the misfortunes of Lord Castlewood:

Herbert William Castlewood was the third son of Dean Castlewood, a younger brother of my grandfather, and was born in the year 1806. He was older, therefore, than my father, but still (even before my father's birth, which provided a direct heir) there were many lives betwixt him and the family estates. And his father, having as yet no promotion in the Church, found it hard to bring up his children. The eldest son got a commission in the army, and the second entered the navy, while Herbert was placed in a bank at Bristol—not at all the sort of life which he would have chosen. But being of a gentle, unselfish nature, as well as a weak constitution, he put up with his state in life, and did his best to give satisfaction.

This calm courage generally has its reward, and in the year 1842, not very long before the death of my grandfather at Shoxford, Mr. Herbert Castlewood, being well-connected, well-behaved, diligent, and pleasing, obtained a partnership in the firm, which was, perhaps, the foremost in the west of England. His two elder brothers happened then to be at home, Major and Commander Castlewood, each of whom had seen very hard service, and found it still harder slavery to make both ends meet, although bachelors. But, returning full of glory, they found one thing harder still, and that was to extract any cash from their father, the highly venerated Dean, who in that respect, if in no other, very closely resembled the head of the family. Therefore these brave men resolved to go and see their Bristol brother, to whom they were tenderly attached, and who now must have money enough and to spare. So they wrote to their brother to meet them on the platform, scarcely believing that they could be there in so short a time from London; for they never had travelled by rail before; and they set forth in wonderful spirits, and laughed at the strange, giddy rush of the travelling, and made bets with each other about punctual time (for trains kept much better time while new), and, as long as they could time it, they kept time to a second. But, sad to relate, they wanted no chronometers when they arrived at Bristol, both being killed at a blow, with their watches still going, and a smile on their faces. For the train had run into a wall of Bath stone, and several of the passengers were killed.

The sight of his two brothers carried out like this, after so many years of not seeing them, was too much for Mr. Herbert Castlewood's nerves, which always had been delicate. And he shivered all the more from reproach of conscience, having made up his mind not to lend them any money, as a practical banker was compelled to do. And from that very moment he began to feel great pain.

Mrs. Price assured me that the doctors all agreed that nothing but change of climate could restore Mr. Castlewood's tone and system, and being full of art (though so simple, as she said, which she could not entirely reconcile), he set off for Italy, and there he stopped, with the good leave of his partners, being now valued highly as heir to the Dean, who was known to have put a good trifle together. And in Italy my father must have found him, as related by Mr. Shovelin, and there received kindness and comfort in his trouble, if trouble so deep could be comforted.

Now I wondered and eagerly yearned to know whether my father, at such a time, and in such a state of loneliness, might not have been led to impart to his cousin and host and protector the dark mystery which lay at the bottom of his own conduct. Knowing how resolute and stern he was, and doubtless then imbittered by the wreck of love and life, I thought it more probable that he had kept silence even toward so near a relative, especially as he had seen very little of his cousin Herbert till he had found him thus. Moreover, my grandfather and the Dean had spent little brotherly love on each other, having had a life-long feud about a copy-hold furze brake of nearly three-quarters of an acre, as Betsy remembered to have heard her master say.

To go on, however, with what Mrs. Price was saying. She knew scarcely any thing about my father, because she was too young at that time to be called into the counsels of the servants' hall, for she scarcely was thirty-five yet, as she declared, and she certainly did not look forty. But all about the present Lord Castlewood she knew better than any body else, perhaps, because she had been in the service of his wife, and, indeed, her chief attendant. Then, having spoken of her master's wife, Mrs. Price caught herself up, and thenceforth called her only his "lady."

Mr. Herbert Castlewood, who had minded his business for so many years, and kept himself aloof from ladies, spending all his leisure in good literature, at this time of life and in this state of health (for the shock he had received struck inward), fell into an accident tenfold worse—the fatal accident of love. And this malady raged the more powerfully with him on account of breaking out so late in life. In one of the picture-galleries at Florence, or some such place, Mrs. Price declared, he met with a lady who made all the pictures look cold and dull and dead to him. A lovely young creature she must have been (as even Mrs. Price, who detested her, acknowledged), and to the eyes of a learned but not keen man as good as lovely. My father was gone to look after me, and fetch me out of England, but even if he had been there, perhaps he scarcely could have stopped it; for this Mr. Castlewood, although so quiet, had the family fault of tenacity.

Mrs. Price, being a very steady person, with a limited income, and enough to do, was inclined to look down upon the state of mind in which Mr. Castlewood became involved. She was not there at the moment, of course, but suddenly sent for when all was settled; nevertheless, she found out afterward how it began from her master's man, through what he had for dinner. And in the kitchen-garden at Castlewood no rampion would she allow while she lived. I asked her whether she had no pity, no sympathy, no fine feeling, and how she could have become Mrs. Price if she never had known such sentiments. But she said that they only called her "Mistress" on account of her authority, and she never had been drawn to the opposite sex, though many times asked in marriage. And what she had seen of matrimony led her far away from it. I was sorry to hear her say this, and felt damped, till I thought that the world was not all alike.

Then she told me, just as if it were no more than a bargain for a pound of tallow candles, how Mr. Herbert Castlewood, patient and persistent, was kept off and on for at least two years by the mother of his sweet idol. How the old lady held a balance in her mind as to the likelihood of his succession, trying, through English friends, to find the value and the course of property. Of what nation she was, Mrs. Price could not say, and only knew that it must be a bad one. She called herself the Countess of Ixorism, as truly pronounced in English; and she really was of good family too, so far as any foreigner can be. And her daughter's name was Flittamore, not according to the right spelling, perhaps, but pronounced with the proper accent.

Flittamore herself did not seem to care, according to what Mrs. Price had been told, but left herself wholly in her mother's hands, being sure of her beauty still growing upon her, and desiring to have it admired and praised. And the number of foreigners she always had about her sometimes made her real lover nearly give her up. But, alas! he was not quite wise enough for this, with all that he had read and learned and seen. Therefore, when it was reported from Spain that my father had been killed by bandits—the truth being that he was then in Greece—the Countess at last consented to the marriage of her daughter with Herbert Castlewood, and even seemed to press it forward for some reasons of her own. And the happy couple set forth upon their travels, and Mrs. Price was sent abroad to wait upon the lady.

For a few months they seemed to get on very well, Flittamore showing much affection for her husband, whose age was a trifle more than her own doubled, while he was entirely wrapped up in her, and labored that the graces of her mind might be worthy to compare with those more visible. But her spiritual face and most sweet poetic eyes were vivid with bodily brilliance alone. She had neither mind enough to learn, nor heart enough to pretend to learn.

It is out of my power to describe such things, even if it were my duty to do so, which, happily, it has never been; moreover, Mrs. Price, in what she told me, exercised a just and strict reserve. Enough that Mr. Castlewood's wedded life was done with in six months and three days. Lady Castlewood, as she would be called, though my father still was living and his cousin disclaimed the title—away she ran from some dull German place, after a very stiff lesson in poetry, and with her ran off a young Englishman, the present Sir Montague Hockin. He was Mr. Hockin then, and had not a halfpenny of his own; but Flittamore met that difficulty by robbing her husband to his last farthing.

This had happened about twelve years back, soon after I was placed at the school in Languedoc, to which I was taken so early in life that I almost forget all about it. But it might have been better for poor Flittamore if she had been brought up at a steady place like that, with sisters and ladies of retreat, to teach her the proper description of her duties to mankind. I seemed now in my own mind to condemn her quite enough, feeling how superior her husband must have been; but Mrs. Price went even further, and became quite indignant that any one should pity her.

"A hussy! a hussy! a poppet of a hussy!" she exclaimed, with greater power than her quiet face could indicate; "never would I look at her. Speak never so, Miss Castlewood. My lord is the very best of all men, and she has made him what he is. The pity she deserves is to be trodden under foot, as I saw them do in Naples."

After all the passion I had seen among rough people, I scarcely could help trembling at the depth of wrath dissembled and firmly controlled in calm clear eyes under very steadfast eyebrows. It was plain that Lord Castlewood had, at any rate, the gift of being loved by his dependents.

"I hope that he took it aright!" I cried, catching some of her indignation; "I hope that he cast her to the winds, without even a sigh for such a cruel creature!"

"He was not strong enough," she answered, sadly; "his bodily health was not equal to it. From childhood he had been partly crippled and spoiled in his nerves by an accident. And the shock of that sight at Bristol flew to his weakness, and was too much for him. And now this third and worst disaster, coming upon him where his best hope lay, and at such a time of life, took him altogether off his legs. And off his head too, I might almost say, miss; for, instead of blaming her, he put the fault entirely upon himself. At his time of life, and in such poor health, he should not have married a bright young girl: how could he ever hope to make her happy? That was how he looked at it, when he should have sent constables after her."

"And what became of her—the mindless animal, to forsake so good and great a man! I do hope she was punished, and that vile man too."

"She was, Miss Castlewood; but he was not; at least he has not received justice yet. But he will, he will, he will, miss. The treacherous thief! And my lord received him as a young fellow-countryman under a cloud, and lent him money, and saved him from starving; for he had broken with his father and was running from his creditors."

"Tell me no more," I said; "not another word. It is my fate to meet that—well, that gentleman—almost every day. And he, and he—oh, how thankful I am to have found out all this about him!"

The above will show why, when I met my father's cousin on the following morning—with his grand, calm face, as benevolent as if he had passed a night of luxurious rest instead of sleepless agony—I knew myself to be of a lower order in mind and soul and heart than his; a small, narrow, passionate girl, in the presence of a large, broad-sighted, and compassionate man.

I threw myself altogether on his will; for, when I trust, I trust wholly. And, under his advice, I did not return with any rash haste to Bruntsea, but wrote in discharge of all duty there; while Mrs. Price, a clear and steadfast woman, was sent to London to see Wilhelmina Strouss. These two must have had very great talks together, and, both being zealous and faithful, they came to many misunderstandings. However, on the whole, they became very honest friends, and sworn allies at last, discovering more, the more they talked, people against whom they felt a common and just enmity.

CHAPTER XXXIV
SHOXFORD

Are there people who have never, in the course of anxious life, felt desire to be away, to fly away, from every thing, however good and dear to them, and rest a little, and think new thought, or let new thought flow into them, from the gentle air of some new place, where nobody has heard of them—a place whose cares, being felt by proxy, almost seem romantic, and where the eyes spare brain and heart with a critic's self-complacence? If any such place yet remains, the happy soul may seek it in an inland English village.

A village where no billows are to stun or to confound it, no crag or precipice to trouble it with giddiness, and where no hurry of restless tide makes time, its own father, uneasy. But in the quiet, at the bottom of the valley, a beautiful rivulet, belonging to the place, hastens or lingers, according to its mood; hankering here and there, not to be away yet; and then, by the doing of its own work, led to a swift perplexity of ripples. Here along its side, and there softly leaning over it, fresh green meadows lie reposing in the settled meaning of the summer day. For this is a safer time of year than the flourish of the spring-tide, when the impulse of young warmth awaking was suddenly smitten by the bleak east wind, and cowslip and cuckoo-flower and speedwell got their bright lips browned with cold. Then, moreover, must the meads have felt the worry of scarcely knowing yet what would be demanded of them; whether to carry an exacting load of hay, or only to feed a few sauntering cows.

But now every trouble has been settled for the best; the long grass is mown, and the short grass browsed, and capers of the fairies and caprices of the cows have dappled worn texture with a deeper green. Therefore let eyes that are satisfied here—as any but a very bad eye must be, with so many changes of softness—follow the sweet lead of the valley; and there, in a bend of the gently brawling river, stands the never-brawling church.

A church less troubled with the gift of tongues is not to be found in England: a church of gray stone that crumbles just enough to entice frail mortal sympathy, and confesses to the storms it has undergone in a tone that conciliates the human sigh. The tower is large, and high enough to tell what the way of the wind is without any potato-bury on the top, and the simple roof is not cruciated with tiles of misguided fancy. But gray rest, and peace of ages, and content of lying calmly six feet deeper than the bustle of the quick; memory also, and oblivion, following each other slowly, like the shadows of the church-yard trees—for all of these no better place can be, nor softer comfort.

For the village of Shoxford runs up on the rise, and straggles away from its burial-place, as a child from his school goes mitching. There are some few little ups and downs in the manner of its building, as well as in other particulars about it; but still it keeps as parallel with the crooked river as the far more crooked ways of men permit. But the whole of the little road of houses runs down the valley from the church-yard gate; and above the church, looking up the pretty valley, stands nothing but the mill and the plank bridge below it; and a furlong above that again the stone bridge, where the main road crosses the stream, and is consoled by leading to a big house—the Moonstock Inn.

The house in which my father lived so long—or rather, I should say, my mother, while he was away with his regiment—and where we unfortunate seven saw the light, stands about half-way down the little village, being on the right-hand side of the road as you come down the valley from the Moonstock bridge. Therefore it is on the further and upper side of the street—if it can be called a street—from the valley and the river and the meads below the mill, inasmuch as every bit of Shoxford, and every particle of the parish also, has existence—of no mean sort, as compared with other parishes, in its own esteem—on the right side of the river Moon.

My father's house, in this good village, standing endwise to the street, was higher at one end than at the other. That is to say, the ground came sloping, or even falling, as fairly might be said, from one end to the other of it, so that it looked like a Noah's ark tilted by Behemoth under the stern-post. And a little lane, from a finely wooded hill, here fell steeply into the "High Street" (as the grocer and the butcher loved to call it), and made my father's house most distinct, by obeying a good deal of its outline, and discharging in heavy rain a free supply of water under the weather-board of our front-door. This front-door opened on the little steep triangle formed by the meeting of lane and road, while the back-door led into a long but narrow garden running along the road, but raised some feet above it; the bank was kept up by a rough stone wall crested with stuck-up snap-dragon and valerian, and faced with rosettes and disks and dills of houseleek, pennywort, and hart's-tongue.

Betsy and I were only just in time to see the old house as it used to be; for the owner had died about half a year ago, and his grandson, having proved his will, was resolved to make short work with it. The poor house was blamed for the sorrows it had sheltered, and had the repute of two spectres, as well as the pale shadow of misfortune. For my dear father was now believed by the superstitious villagers to haunt the old home of his happiness and love, and roam from room to room in search of his wife and all his children. But his phantom was most careful not to face that of his father, which stalked along haughtily, as behooved a lord, and pointed forever to a red wound in its breast. No wonder, therefore, that the house would never let; and it would have been pulled down long ago if the owner had not felt a liking for it, through memories tender and peculiar to himself. His grandson, having none of these to contend with, resolved to make a mere stable of it, and build a public-house at the bottom of the garden, and turn the space between them into skittle-ground, and so forth.

To me this seemed such a very low idea, and such a desecration of a sacred spot, that if I had owned any money to be sure of, I would have offered hundreds to prevent it. But I found myself now in a delicate state of mind concerning money, having little of my own, and doubting how much other people might intend for me. So that I durst not offer to buy land and a house without any means to pay.

And it was not for that reason only that Betsy and I kept ourselves quiet. We knew that any stir in this little place about us—such as my name might at once set going—would once for all destroy all hope of doing good by coming. Betsy knew more of such matters than I did, besides all her knowledge of the place itself, and her great superiority of age; therefore I left to her all little management, as was in every way fair and wise. For Mrs. Strouss had forsaken a large and good company of lodgers, with only Herr Strouss to look after them—and who was he among them? If she trod on one side of her foot, or felt a tingling in her hand, or a buzzing in her ear, she knew in a moment what it was—of pounds and pounds was she being cheated, a hundred miles off, by foreigners!

For this reason it had cost much persuasion and many appeals to her faithfulness, as well as considerable weekly payment, ere ever my good nurse could be brought away from London; and perhaps even so she never would have come if I had not written myself to Mrs. Price, then visiting Betsy in European Square, that if the landlady was too busy to be spared by her lodgers, I must try to get Lord Castlewood to spare me his housekeeper. Upon this Mrs. Strouss at once declared that Mrs. Price would ruin every thing; and rather than that—no matter what she lost—she herself would go with me. And so she did, and she managed very well, keeping my name out of sight (for, happen what might, I would have no false one); and she got quiet lodgings in her present name, which sounded nicely foreign; and the village being more agitated now about my father's material house, and the work they were promised in pulling it down, than about his shattered household, we had a very favorable time for coming in, and were pronounced to be foreigners who must not be allowed to run up bills.

This rustic conclusion suited us quite well, and we soon confirmed it unwittingly, Betsy offering a German thaler and I an American dollar at the shop of the village chandler and baker, so that we were looked upon with some pity, and yet a kind desire for our custom. Thus, without any attempt of ours at either delusion or mystery, Mrs. Strouss was hailed throughout the place as "Madam Straw," while I, through the sagacity of a deeply read shoe-maker, obtained a foreign name, as will by-and-by appear.

We lodged at the post-office, not through any wisdom or even any thought on our part, but simply because we happened there to find the cleanest and prettiest rooms in the place. For the sun being now in the height of August, and having much harvest to ripen, at middle day came ramping down the little street of Shoxford like the chairman of the guild of bakers. Every house having lately brightened up its whitewash—which they always do there when the frosts are over, soon after the feast of St. Barnabas—and the weeds of the way having fared amiss in the absence of any water-cart, it was not in the strong, sharp character of the sun to miss such an opportunity. After the red Californian glare, I had no fear of any English sun; but Betsy was frightened, and both of us were glad to get into a little place sheltered by green blinds. This chanced to be the post-office, and there we found nice lodgings.

By an equal chance this proved to be the wisest thing we could possibly have done, if we had set about it carefully. For why, that nobody ever would impute any desire of secrecy to people who straightway unpacked their boxes at the very head-quarters of all the village news. And the mistress of the post was a sharp-tongued woman, pleased to speak freely of her neighbors' doings, and prompt with good advice that they should heed their own business, if any of them durst say a word about her own. She kept a tidy little shop, showing something of almost every thing; but we had a side door, quite of our own, where Betsy met the baker's wife and the veritable milkman; and neither of them knew her, which was just what she had hoped; and yet it made her speak amiss of them.

But if all things must be brought to the harsh test of dry reason, I myself might be hard pushed to say what good I hoped to do by coming thus to Shoxford. I knew of a great many things, for certain, that never had been thoroughly examined here; also I naturally wished to see, being a native, what the natives were; and, much more than that, it was always on my mind that here lay my mother and the other six of us.

Therefore it was an impatient thing for me to hear Betsy working out the afternoon with perpetual chatter and challenge of prices, combating now as a lodger all those points which as a landlady she never would allow even to be moot questions. If any applicant in European Square had dared so much as hint at any of all the requirements which she now expected gratis, she would simply have whisked her duster, and said that the lodgings for such people must be looked for down the alley. However, Mrs. Busk, our new landlady, although she had a temper of her own (as any one keeping a post-office must have) was forced by the rarity of lodgers here to yield many points, which Mrs. Strouss, on her own boards, would not even have allowed to be debated. All this was entirely against my wish; for when I have money, I spend it, finding really no other good in it; but Betsy told me that the purest principle of all was—not to be cheated.

So I left her to have these little matters out, and took that occasion for stealing away (as the hours grew on toward evening) to a place where I wished to be quite alone. And the shadow of the western hills shed peace upon the valley, when I crossed a little stile leading into Shoxford churchyard.

For a minute or two I was quite afraid, seeing nobody any where about, nor even hearing any sound in the distance to keep me company. For the church lay apart from the village, and was thickly planted out from it, the living folk being full of superstition, and deeply believing in the dead people's ghosts. And even if this were a wife to a husband, or even a husband reappearing to his wife, there was not a man or a woman in the village that would not run away from it.

This I did not know at present, not having been there long enough; neither had I any terror of that sort, not being quite such a coward, I should hope. But still, as the mantles of the cold trees darkened, and the stony remembrance of the dead grew pale, and of the living there was not even the whistle of a grave-digger—my heart got the better of my mind for a moment, and made me long to be across that stile again. Because (as I said to myself) if there had been a hill to go up, that would be so different and so easy; but going down into a place like this, whence the only escape must be by steps, and where any flight must be along channels that run in and out of graves and tombstones, I tried not to be afraid, yet could not altogether help it.

But lo! when I came to the north side of the tower, scarcely thinking what to look for, I found myself in the middle of a place which made me stop and wonder. Here were six little grassy tuffets, according to the length of children, all laid east and west, without any stint of room, harmoniously.

From the eldest to the youngest, one could almost tell the age at which their lowly stature stopped, and took its final measurement.

And in the middle was a larger grave, to comfort and encourage them, as a hen lies down among her chicks and waits for them to shelter. Without a name to any of them, all these seven graves lay together, as in a fairy ring of rest, and kind compassion had prevented any stranger from coming to be buried there.

I would not sit on my mother's grave for fear of crushing the pretty grass, which some one tended carefully; but I stood at its foot, and bent my head, and counted all the little ones. Then I thought of my father in the grove of peaches, more than six thousand miles away, on the banks of the soft Blue River. And a sense of desolate sorrow and of the blessing of death overwhelmed me.

CHAPTER XXXV
THE SEXTON

With such things in my mind, it took me long to come back to my work again. It even seemed a wicked thing, so near to all these proofs of God's great visitation over us, to walk about and say, "I will do this," or even to think, "I will try to do that." My own poor helplessness, and loss of living love to guide me, laid upon my heart a weight from which it scarcely cared to move. All was buried, all was done with, all had passed from out the world, and left no mark but graves behind. What good to stir anew such sadness, even if a poor weak thing like me could move its mystery?

Time, however, and my nurse Betsy, and Jacob Rigg the gardener, brought me back to a better state of mind, and renewed the right courage within me. But, first of all, Jacob Rigg aroused my terror and interest vividly. It may be remembered that this good man had been my father's gardener at the time of our great calamity, and almost alone of the Shoxford people had shown himself true and faithful. Not that the natives had turned against us, or been at all unfriendly; so far from this was the case, that every one felt for our troubles, and pitied us, my father being of a cheerful and affable turn, until misery hardened him; but what I mean is that only one or two had the courage to go against the popular conclusion and the convictions of authority.

But Jacob was a very upright man, and had a strong liking for his master, who many and many a time—as he told me—had taken a spade and dug along with him, just as if he were a jobbing gardener born, instead of a fine young nobleman; "and nobody gifted with that turn of mind, likewise very clever in white-spine cowcumbers, could ever be relied upon to go and shoot his father." Thus reasoned old Jacob, and he always had done so, and meant evermore to abide by it; and the graves which he had tended now for nigh a score of years, and meant to tend till he called for his own, were—as sure as he stood there in Shoxford church-yard a-talking to me, who was the very image of my father, God bless me, though not of course so big like—the graves of slaughtered innocents, and a mother who was always an angel. And the parson might preach forever to him about the resurrection, and the right coming uppermost when you got to heaven, but to his mind that was scarcely any count at all; and if you came to that, we ought to hang Jack Ketch, as might come to pass in the Revelations. But while a man had got his own bread to earn, till his honor would let him go to the work-house, and his duty to the rate-payers, there was nothing that vexed him more than to be told any texts of Holy Scripture. Whatever God Almighty had put down there was meant for ancient people, the Jews being long the most ancient people, though none the more for that did he like them; and so it was mainly the ancient folk, who could not do a day's work worth eighteenpence, that could enter into Bible promises. Not that he was at all behindhand about interpretation; but as long as he could fetch and earn, at planting box and doing borders, two shillings and ninepence a day and his beer, he was not going to be on for kingdom come.

I told him that I scarcely thought his view of our condition here would be approved by wise men who had found time to study the subject. But he answered that whatever their words might be, their doings showed that they knew what was the first thing to attend to. And if it ever happened him to come across a parson who was as full of heaven outside as he was inside his surplice, he would keep his garden in order for nothing better than his blessing.

I knew of no answer to be made to this. And indeed he seemed to be aware that his conversation was too deep for me; so he leaned upon his spade, and rubbed his long blue chin in the shadow of the church tower, holding as he did the position of sexton, and preparing even now to dig a grave.

"I keeps them well away from you," he said, as he began to chop out a new oblong in the turf; "many a shilling have I been offered by mothers about their little ones, to put 'em inside of the 'holy ring,' as we calls this little cluster; but not for five golden guineas would I do it, and have to face the Captain, dead or alive, about it. We heard that he was dead, because it was put in all the papers; and a pleasant place I keeps for him, to come home alongside of his family. A nicer gravelly bit of ground there couldn't be in all the county; and if no chance of him occupying it, I can drive down a peg with your mark, miss."

"Thank you," I answered; "you are certainly most kind; but, Mr. Rigg, I would rather wait a little. I have had a very troublesome life thus far, and nothing to bind me to it much; but still I would rather not have my peg driven down just—just at present."

"Ah, you be like all the young folk that think the tree for their coffins ain't come to the size of this spade handle yet. Lord bless you for not knowing what He hath in hand! Now this one you see me a-raising of the turf for, stood as upright as you do, a fortnight back, and as good about the chest and shoulders, and three times the color in her cheeks, and her eyes a'most as bright as yourn be. Not aristocratic, you must understand me, miss, being only the miller's daughter, nor instructed to throw her voice the same as you do, which is better than gallery music; but setting these haxidents to one side, a farmer would have said she was more preferable, because more come-at-able, though not in my opinion to be compared—excuse me for making so free, miss, but when it comes to death we has a kind of right to do it—and many a young farmer, coming to the mill, was disturbed in his heart about her, and far and wide she was known, being proud, as the Beauty of the Moonshine, from the name of our little river. She used to call me 'Jacob Diggs,' because of my porochial office, with a meaning of a joke on my parenshal name. Ah, what a merry one she were! And now this is what I has to do for her! And sooner would I 'a doed it a'most for my own old ooman!"

"Oh, Jacob!" I cried, being horrified at the way in which he tore up the ground, as if his wife was waiting, "the things you say are quite wrong, I am sure, for a man in your position. You are connected with this church almost as much as the clerk is."

"More, miss, ten times more! He don't do nothing but lounge on the front of his desk, and be too lazy to keep up 'Amen,' while I at my time of life go about, from Absolution to the fifth Lord's prayer, with a stick that makes my rheumatics worse, for the sake of the boys with their pocket full of nuts. When I was a boy there was no nuts, except at the proper time of year, a month or two on from this time of speaking; and we used to crack they in the husk, and make no noise to disturb the congregation; but now it is nuts, nuts, round nuts, flat nuts, nuts with three corners to them—all the year round nuts to crack, and me to find out who did it!"

"But, Mr. Rigg," I replied, as he stopped, looking hotter in mind than in body, "is it not Mrs. Rigg, your good wife, who sells all the nuts on a Saturday for the boys to crack on a Sunday?"

"My missus do sell some, to be sure; yes, just a few. But not of a Saturday more than any other day."

"Then surely, Mr. Rigg, you might stop it, by not permitting any sale of nuts except to good boys of high principles. And has it not happened sometimes, Mr. Rigg, that boys have made marks on their nuts, and bought them again at your shop on a Monday? I mean, of course, when your duty has compelled you to empty the pockets of a boy in church."

Now this was a particle of shamefully small gossip, picked up naturally by my Betsy, but pledged to go no further; and as soon as I had spoken I became a little nervous, having it suddenly brought to my mind that I had promised not even to whisper it; and now I had told it to the man of all men! But Jacob appeared to have been quite deaf, and diligently went on digging. And I said "good-evening," for the grave was for the morrow; and he let me go nearly to the stile before he stuck his spade into the ground and followed.

"Excoose of my making use," he said, "of a kind of a personal reference, miss; but you be that pat with your answers, it maketh me believe you must be sharp inside—more than your father, the poor Captain, were, as all them little grass buttons argueth. Now, miss, if I thought you had head-piece enough to keep good counsel and ensue it, maybe I could tell you a thing as would make your hair creep out of them coorous hitch-ups, and your heart a'most bust them there braids of fallallies."

"Why, what in the world do you mean?" I asked, being startled by the old man's voice and face.

"Nothing, miss, nothing. I was only a-joking. If you bain't come to no more discretion than that—to turn as white as the clerk's smock-frock of a Easter-Sunday—why, the more of a joke one has, the better, to bring your purty color back to you. Ah! Polly of the mill was the maid for color—as good for the eyesight as a chaney-rose in April. Well, well, I must get on with her grave; they're a-coming to speak the good word over un on sundown."

He might have known how this would vex and perplex me. I could not bear to hinder him in his work—as important as any to be done by man for man—and yet it was beyond my power to go home and leave him there, and wonder what it was that he had been so afraid to tell. So I quietly said, "Then I will wish you a very good evening again, Mr. Rigg, as you are too busy to be spoken with." And I walked off a little way, having met with men who, having begun a thing, needs must have it out, and fully expecting him to call me back. But Jacob only touched his hat, and said, "A pleasant evening to you, ma'am."

Nothing could have made me feel more resolute than this did. I did not hesitate one moment in running back over the stile again, and demanding of Jacob Rigg that he should tell me whether he meant any thing or nothing; for I was not to be played with about important matters, like the boys in the church who were cracking nuts.

"Lord! Lord, now!" he said, with his treddled heel scraping the shoulder of his shining spade; "the longer I live in this world, the fitter I grow to get into the ways of the Lord. His ways are past finding out, saith King David: but a man of war, from his youth upward, hath no chance such as a gardening man hath. What a many of them have I found out!"

"What has that got to do with it!" I cried. "Just tell me what it was you were speaking of just now."

"I was just a-thinking, when I looked at you, miss," he answered, in the prime of leisure, and wiping his forehead from habit only, not because he wanted it, "how little us knows of the times and seasons and the generations of the sons of men. There you stand, miss, and here stand I, as haven't seen your father for a score of years a'most; and yet there comes out of your eyes into mine the very same look as the Captain used to send, when snakes in the grass had been telling lies about me coming late, or having my half pint or so on. Not that the Captain was a hard man, miss—far otherwise, and capable of allowance, more than any of the women be. But only the Lord, who doeth all things aright, could 'a made you come, with a score of years atween, and the twinkle in your eyes like—Selah!"

"You know what you mean, perhaps, but I do not," I answered, quite gently, being troubled by his words and the fear of having tried to hurry him; "but you should not say what you have said, Jacob Rigg, to me, your master's daughter, if you only meant to be joking. Is this the place to joke with me?"

I pointed to all that lay around me, where I could not plant a foot without stepping over my brothers or sisters; and the old man, callous as he might be, could not help feeling for—a pinch of snuff. This he found in the right-hand pocket of his waistcoat, and took it very carefully, and made a little noise of comfort; and thus, being fully self-assured again, he stood, with his feet far apart and his head on one side, regarding me warily. And I took good care not to say another word.

"You be young," he said at last; "and in these latter days no wisdom is ordained in the mouths of babes and sucklings, nor always in the mouths of them as is themselves ordained. But you have a way of keeping your chin up, miss, as if you was gifted with a stiff tongue likewise. And whatever may hap, I has as good mind to tell 'e."

"That you are absolutely bound to do," I answered, as forcibly as I could. "Duty to your former master and to me, his only child—and to yourself, and your Maker too—compel you, Jacob Rigg, to tell me every thing you know."

"Then, miss," he answered, coming nearer to me, and speaking in a low, hoarse voice, "as sure as I stand here in God's churchyard, by all this murdered family, I knows the man who done it!"

He looked at me, with a trembling finger upon his hard-set lips, and the spade in his other hand quivered like a wind vane; but I became as firm as the monument beside me, and my heart, instead of fluttering, grew as steadfast as a glacier. Then, for the first time, I knew that God had not kept me living, when all the others died, without fitting me also for the work there was to do.

"Come here to the corner of the tower, miss," old Jacob went on, in his excitement catching hold of the sleeve of my black silk jacket. "Where we stand is a queer sort of echo, which goeth in and out of them big tombstones. And for aught I can say to contrairy, he may be a-watching of us while here we stand."

I glanced around, as if he were most welcome to be watching me, if only I could see him once. But the place was as silent as its graves; and I followed the sexton to the shadow of a buttress. Here he went into a deep gray corner, lichened and mossed by a drip from the roof; and being, both in his clothes and self, pretty much of that same color, he was not very easy to discern from stone when the light of day was declining.

"This is where I catches all the boys," he whispered; "and this is where I caught him, one evening when I were tired, and gone to nurse my knees a bit. Let me see—why, let me see! Don't you speak till I do, miss. Were it the last but one I dug? Or could un 'a been the last but two? Never mind; I can't call to mind quite justly. We puts down about one a month in this parish, without any distemper or haxident. Well, it must 'a been the one afore last—to be sure, no call to scratch my head about un. Old Sally Mock, as sure as I stand here—done handsome by the rate-payers. Over there, miss, if you please to look—about two land-yard and a half away. Can you see un with the grass peeking up a'ready?"

"Never mind that, Jacob. Do please to go on."

"So I be, miss. So I be doing to the best of the power granted me. Well, I were in this little knuckle of a squat, where old Sally used to say as I went to sleep, and charged the parish for it—a spiteful old ooman, and I done her grave with pleasure, only wishing her had to pay for it; and to prove to her mind that I never goed asleep here, I was just making ready to set fire to my pipe, having cocked my shovel in to ease my legs, like this, when from round you corner of the chancel-foot, and over again that there old tree, I seed a something movin' along—movin' along, without any noise or declarance of solid feet walking. You may see the track burnt in the sod, if you let your eyes go along this here finger."

"Oh, Jacob, how could you have waited to see it?"

"I did, miss, I did; being used to a-many antics in this dead-yard, such as a man who hadn't buried them might up foot to run away from. But they no right, after the service of the Church, to come up for more than one change of the moon, unless they been great malefactors. And then they be ashamed of it; and I reminds them of it. 'Amen,' I say, in the very same voice as I used at the tail of their funerals; and then they knows well that I covered them up, and the most uneasy goes back again. Lor' bless you, miss, I no fear of the dead. At both ends of life us be harmless. It is in the life, and mostways in the middle of it, we makes all the death for one another."

This was true enough; and I only nodded to him, fearing to interject any new ideas from which he might go rambling.

"Well, that there figure were no joke, mind you," the old man continued, as soon as he had freshened his narrative powers with another pinch of snuff, "being tall and grim, and white in the face, and very onpleasant for to look at, and its eyes seemed a'most to burn holes in the air. No sooner did I see that it were not a ghostie, but a living man the same as I be, than my knees begins to shake and my stumps of teeth to chatter. And what do you think it was stopped me, miss, from slipping round this corner, and away by belfry? Nort but the hoddest idea you ever heared on. For all of a suddint it was borne unto my mind that the Lord had been pleased to send us back the Captain; not so handsome as he used to be, but in the living flesh, however, in spite of they newspapers. And I were just at the pint of coming forrard, out of this here dark corndor, knowing as I had done my duty by them graves that his honor, to my mind, must 'a come looking after, when, lucky for me, I see summat in his walk, and then in his countenance, and then in all his features, unnateral on the Captain's part, whatever his time of life might be. And sure enough, miss, it were no Captain more nor I myself be."

"Of course not. How could it be? But who was it, Jacob?"

"You bide a bit, miss, and you shall hear the whole. Well, by that time 'twas too late for me to slip away, and I was bound to scrooge up into the elbow of this nick here, and try not to breathe, as nigh as might be, and keep my Lammas cough down; for I never see a face more full of malice and uncharity. However, he come on as straight as a arrow, holding his long chin out, like this, as if he gotten crutches under it, as the folk does with bad water. A tall man, as tall as the Captain a'most, but not gifted with any kind aspect. He trampsed over the general graves, like the devil come to fetch their souls out; but when he come here to the 'holy ring,' he stopped short, and stood with his back to me. I could hear him count the seven graves, as pat as the shells of oysters to pay for, and then he said all their names, as true, from the biggest to the leastest one, as Betsy Bowen could 'a done it, though none of 'em got no mark to 'em. Oh, the poor little hearts, it was cruel hard upon them! And then my lady in the middle, making seven. So far as I could catch over his shoulder, he seemed to be quite a-talking with her—not as you and I be, miss, but a sort of a manner of a way, like."

"And what did he seem to say? Oh, Jacob, how long you do take over it!"

"Well, he did not, miss; that you may say for sartain. And glad I was to have him quick about it; for he might have redooced me to such a condition—ay, and I believe a' would, too, if onst a' had caught sight of me—as the parish might 'a had to fight over the appintment of another sexton. And so at last a' went away. And I were that stiff with scrooging in this cornder—"

"Is that all? Oh, that comes to nothing. Surely you must have more to tell me? It may have been some one who knew our names. It may have been some old friend of the family."

"No, miss, no! No familiar friend; or if he was, he were like King David's. He bore a tyrannous hate against 'e, and the poison of asps were under his lips. In this here hattitude he stood, with his back toward me, and his reins more upright than I be capable of putting it. And this was how he held up his elbow and his head. Look 'e see, miss, and then 'e know as much as I do."

Mr. Rigg marched with a long smooth step—a most difficult strain for his short bowed legs—as far as the place he had been pointing out; and there he stood with his back to me, painfully doing what the tall man had done, so far as the difference of size allowed.

It was not possible for me to laugh in a matter of such sadness; and yet Jacob stood, with his back to me, spreading and stretching himself in such a way, to be up to the dimensions of the stranger, that—low as it was—I was compelled to cough, for fear of fatally offending him.

"That warn't quite right, miss. Now you look again," he exclaimed, with a little readjustment. "Only he had a thing over one shoulder, the like of what the Scotchmen wear; and his features was beyond me, because of the back of his head, like. For God's sake keep out of his way, miss."

The sexton stood in a musing and yet a stern and defiant attitude, with the right elbow clasped in the left-hand palm, the right hand resting half-clinched upon the forehead, and the shoulders thrown back, as if ready for a blow.

"What a very odd way to stand!" I said.

"Yes, miss. And what he said was odder. 'Six, and the mother!' I heared un say; 'no cure for it, till I have all seven.' But stop, miss. Not a breath to any one! Here comes the poor father and mother to speak the blessing across their daughter's grave—and the grave not two foot down yet!"

CHAPTER XXXVI
A SIMPLE QUESTION

Now this account of what Jacob Rigg had seen and heard threw me into a state of mind extremely unsatisfactory. To be in eager search of some unknown person who had injured me inexpressibly, without any longing for revenge on my part, but simply with a view to justice—this was a very different thing from feeling that an unknown person was in quest of me, with the horrible purpose of destroying me to insure his own wicked safety.

At first I almost thought that he was welcome to do this; that such a life as mine (if looked at from an outer point of view) was better to be died than lived out. Also that there was nobody left to get any good out of all that I could do; and even if I ever should succeed, truth would come out of her tomb too late. And this began to make me cry, which I had long given over doing, with no one to feel for the heart of it.

But a thing of this kind could not long endure; and as soon as the sun of the morrow arose (or at least as soon as I was fit to see him), my view of the world was quite different. Here was the merry brook, playing with the morning, spread around with ample depth and rich retreat of meadows, and often, after maze of leisure, hastening with a tinkle into shadowy delight of trees. Here, as well, were happy lanes, and footpaths of a soft content, unworn with any pressure of the price of time or business. None of them knew (in spite, at flurried spots, of their own direction posts) whence they were coming or whither going—only that here they lay, between the fields or through them, like idle veins of earth, with sometimes company of a man or boy, whistling to his footfall, or a singing maid with a milking pail. And how ungrateful it would be to forget the pleasant copses, in waves of deep green leafage flowing down and up the channeled hills, waving at the wind to tints and tones of new refreshment, and tempting idle folk to come and hear the hush, and see the twinkled texture of pellucid gloom.

Much, however, as I loved to sit in places of this kind alone, for some little time I feared to do so, after hearing the sexton's tale; for Jacob's terror was so unfeigned (though his own life had not been threatened) that, knowing as I did from Betsy's account, as well as his own appearance, that he was not at all a nervous man, I could not help sharing his vague alarm. It seemed so terrible that any one should come to the graves of my sweet mother and her six harmless children, and, instead of showing pity, as even a monster might have tried to do, should stand, if not with threatening gestures, yet with a most hostile mien, and thirst for the life of the only survivor—my poor self.

But terrible or not, the truth was so; and neither Betsy nor myself could shake Mr. Rigg's conclusion. Indeed, he became more and more emphatic, in reply to our doubts and mild suggestions, perhaps that his eyes had deceived him, or perhaps that, taking a nap in the corner of the buttress, he had dreamed at least a part of it. And Betsy, on the score of ancient friendship and kind remembrance of his likings, put it to him in a gentle way whether his knowledge of what Sally Mock had been, and the calumnies she might have spoken of his beer (when herself, in the work-house, deprived of it), might not have induced him to take a little more than usual in going down so deep for her. But he answered, "No; it was nothing of the sort. Deep he had gone, to the tiptoe of his fling; not from any feeling of a wish to keep her down, but just because the parish paid, and the parish would have measurement. And when that was on, he never brought down more than the quart tin from the public; and never had none down afterward. Otherwise the ground was so ticklish, that a man, working too free, might stay down there. No, no! That idea was like one of Sally's own. He just had his quart of Persfield ale—short measure, of course, with a woman at the bar—and if that were enough to make a man dream dreams, the sooner he dug his own grave, the better for all connected with him."

We saw that we had gone too far in thinking of such a possibility; and if Mr. Rigg had not been large-minded, as well as notoriously sober, Betsy might have lost me all the benefit of his evidence by her London-bred clumsiness with him. For it takes quite a different handling, and a different mode of outset, to get on with the London working class and the laboring kind of the country; or at least it seemed to me so.

Now my knowledge of Jacob Rigg was owing, as might be supposed, to Betsy Strouss, who had taken the lead of me in almost every thing ever since I brought her down from London. And now I was glad that, in one point at least, her judgment had overruled mine—to wit, that my name and parentage were as yet not generally known in the village. Indeed, only Betsy herself and Jacob and a faithful old washer-woman, with no roof to her mouth, were aware of me as Miss Castlewood. Not that I had taken any other name—to that I would not stoop—but because the public, of its own accord, paying attention to Betsy's style of addressing me, followed her lead (with some little improvement), and was pleased to entitle me "Miss Raumur."

Some question had been raised as to spelling me aright, till a man of advanced intelligence proved to many eyes, and even several pairs of spectacles (assembled in front of the blacksmith's shop), that no other way could be right except that. For there it was in print, as any one able might see, on the side of an instrument whose name and qualities were even more mysterious than those in debate. Therefore I became "Miss Raumur;" and a protest would have gone for nothing unless printed also. But it did not behoove me to go to that expense, while it suited me very well to be considered and pitied as a harmless foreigner—a being who on English land may find some cause to doubt whether, even in his own country, a prophet could be less thought of. And this large pity for me, as an outlandish person, in the very spot where I was born, endowed me with tenfold the privilege of the proudest native. For the natives of this valley are declared to be of a different stock from those around them, not of the common Wessex strain, but of Jutish or Danish origin. How that may be I do not know; at any rate, they think well of themselves, and no doubt they have cause to do so.

Moreover, they all were very kind to me, and their primitive ways amused me, as soon as they had settled that I was a foreigner, equally beyond and below inquiry. They told me that I was kindly welcome to stay there as long as it pleased me; and knowing how fond I was of making pictures, after beholding my drawing-book, every farmer among them gave me leave to come into his fields, though he never had heard there was any thing there worth painting.

When once there has been a deposit of idea in the calm deep eocene of British rural mind, the impression will outlast any shallow deluge of the noblest education. Shoxford had settled two points forever, without troubling reason to come out of her way—first, that I was a foreign young lady of good birth, manners, and money; second, and far more important, I was here to write and paint a book about Shoxford. Not for the money, of that I had no need (according to the congress at the "Silver-edged Holly"), but for the praise and the knowledge of it, like, and to make a talk among high people. But the elders shook their heads—as I heard from Mr. Rigg, who hugged his knowledge proudly, and uttered dim sayings of wisdom let forth at large usury: he did not mind telling me that the old men shook their heads, for fear of my being a deal too young, and a long sight too well favored (as any man might tell without his specs on), for to write any book upon any subject yet, leave alone an old, ancient town like theirs. However, there might be no harm in my trying, and perhaps the school-master would cross out the bad language.

Thus for once fortune now was giving me good help, enabling me to go about freely, and preventing (so far as I could see, at least) all danger of discovery by my unknown foe. So here I resolved to keep my head-quarters, dispensing, if it must be so, with Betsy's presence, and not even having Mrs. Price to succeed her, unless my cousin should insist upon it. And partly to dissuade him from that, and partly to hear his opinion of the sexton's tale, I paid a flying visit to Lord Castlewood; while "Madam Straw," as Betsy now was called throughout the village, remained behind at Shoxford. For I long had desired to know a thing which I had not ventured to ask my cousin—though I did ask Mr. Shovelin—whether my father had intrusted him with the key of his own mysterious acts. I scarcely knew whether it was proper even now to put this question to Lord Castlewood; but even without doing so, I might get at the answer by watching him closely while I told my tale. Not a letter had reached me since I came to Shoxford, neither had I written any, except one to Uncle Sam; and keeping to this excellent rule, I arrived at Castlewood without notice.

In doing this I took no liberty, because full permission had been given me about it; and indeed I had been expected there, as Stixon told me, some days before. He added that his master was about as usual, but had shown some uneasiness on my account, though the butler was all in the dark about it, and felt it very hard after all these years, "particular, when he could hardly help thinking that Mrs. Price—a new hand compared to himself, not to speak of being a female—knowed all about it, and were very aggravating. But there, he would say no more; he knew his place, and he always had been valued in it, long afore Mrs. Price come up to the bottom of his waistcoat."

My cousin received me with kindly warmth, and kissed me gently on the forehead. "My dear, how very well you look!" he said. "Your native air has agreed with you. I was getting, in my quiet way, rather sedulous and self-reproachful about you. But you would have your own way, like a young American; and it seems that you were right."

"It was quite right," I answered, with a hearty kiss, for I never could be cold-natured; and this was my only one of near kin, so far, at least, as my knowledge went. "I was quite right in going; and I have done good. At any rate, I have found out something—something that may not be of any kind of use; but still it makes me hope things."

With that, in as few words as ever I could use, I told Lord Castlewood the whole of Jacob's tale, particularly looking at him all the while I spoke, to settle in my own mind whether the idea of such a thing was new to him. Concerning that, however, I could make out nothing. My cousin, at his time of life, and after so much travelling, had much too large a share of mind and long skill of experience for me to make any thing out of his face beyond his own intention. And whether he had suspicion or not of any thing at all like what I was describing, or any body having to do with it, was more than I ever might have known, if I had not gathered up my courage and put the question outright to him. I told him that if I was wrong in asking, he was not to answer; but, right or wrong, ask him I must.

"The question is natural, and not at all improper," replied Lord Castlewood, standing a moment for change of pain, which was all his relief. "Indeed, I expected you to ask me that before. But, Erema, I have also had to ask myself about it, whether I have any right to answer you. And I have decided not to do so, unless you will pledge yourself to one thing."

"I will pledge myself to any thing," I answered, rashly; "I do not care what it is, if only to get at the bottom of this mystery."

"I scarcely think you will hold good to your words when you hear what you have to promise. The condition upon which I tell you what I believe to be the cause of all is, that you let things remain as they are, and keep silence forever about them."

"Oh, you can not be so cruel, so atrocious!" I cried, in my bitter disappointment. "What good would it be for me to know things thus, and let the vile wrong continue? Surely you are not bound to lay on me a condition so impossible?"

"After much consideration and strong wish to have it otherwise, I have concluded that I am so bound."

"In duty to my father, or the family, or what? Forgive me for asking, but it does seem so hard."

"It seems hard, my dear, and it is hard as well," he answered, very gently, yet showing in his eyes and lips no chance of any yielding. "But remember that I do not know, I only guess, the secret; and if you give the pledge I speak of, you merely follow in your father's steps."

"Never," I replied, with as firm a face as his. "It may have been my father's duty, or no doubt he thought it so; but it can not be mine, unless I make it so by laying it on my honor. And I will not do that."

"Perhaps you are right; but, at any rate, remember that I have not tried to persuade you. I wish to do what is for your happiness, Erema. And I think that, on the whole, with your vigor and high spirit, you are better as you are than if you had a knowledge which you could only brood over and not use."

"I will find out the whole of it myself," I cried, for I could not repress all excitement; "and then I need not brood over it, but may have it out and get justice. In the wildest parts of America justice comes with perseverance:

am I to abjure it in the heart of England? Lord Castlewood, which is first—justice or honor?"

"My cousin, you are fond of asking questions difficult to answer. Justice and honor nearly always go together. When they do otherwise, honor stands foremost, with people of good birth, at least."

"Then I will be a person of very bad birth. If they come into conflict in my life, as almost every thing seems to do, my first thought shall be of justice; and honor shall come in as its ornament afterward."

"Erema," said my cousin, "your meaning is good, and at your time of life you can scarcely be expected to take a dispassionate view of things."

At first I felt almost as if I could hate a "dispassionate view of things." Things are made to arouse our passion, so long as meanness and villainy prevail; and if old men, knowing the balance of the world, can contemplate them all "dispassionately," more clearly than any thing else, to my mind, that proves the beauty of being young. I am sure that I never was hot or violent—qualities which I especially dislike—but still I would rather almost have those than be too philosophical. And now, while I revered my father's cousin for his gentleness, wisdom, and long-suffering, I almost longed to fly back to the Major, prejudiced, peppery, and red-hot for justice, at any rate in all things that concerned himself.

CHAPTER XXXVII
SOME ANSWER TO IT

Hasty indignation did not drive me to hot action. A quiet talk with Mrs. Price, as soon as my cousin's bad hour arrived, was quite enough to bring me back to a sense of my own misgovernment. Moreover, the evening clouds were darkening for a night of thunder, while the silver Thames looked nothing more than a leaden pipe down the valleys. Calm words fall at such times on quick temper like the drip of trees on people who have been dancing. I shivered, as my spirit fell, to think of my weak excitement, and poor petulance to a kind, wise friend, a man of many sorrows and perpetual affliction. And then I recalled what I had observed, but in my haste forgotten — Lord Castlewood was greatly changed even in the short time since I had left his house for Shoxford. Pale he had always been, and his features (calm as they were, and finely cut) seemed almost bleached by in-door life and continual endurance. But now they showed worse sign than this — a delicate transparence of faint color, and a waxen surface, such as I had seen at a time I can not bear to think of. Also he had tottered forward, while he tried for steadfast footing, quite as if his worried members were almost worn out at last.

Mrs. Price took me up quite sharply — at least for one of her well-trained style — when I ventured to ask if she had noticed this, which made me feel uneasy. "Oh dear, no!" she said, looking up from the lace-frilled pockets of her silk apron, which appeared to my mind perhaps a little too smart, and almost of a vulgar tincture; and I think that she saw in my eyes that much, and was vexed with herself for not changing it — "oh dear, no, Miss Castlewood! We who know and watch him should detect any difference of that nature at the moment of its occurrence. His lordship's health goes vacillating; a little up now, and then a little down, like a needle that is mounted to show the dip of compass; and it varies according to the electricity, as well as the magnetic influence."

"What doctor told you that?" I asked, seeing in a moment that this housekeeper was dealing in quotation.

"You are very"—she was going to say "rude," but knew better when she saw me waiting for it—"well, you are rather brusque, as we used to call it abroad, Miss Castlewood; but am I incapable of observing for myself?"

"I never implied that," was my answer. "I believe that you are most intelligent, and fit to nurse my cousin, as you are to keep his house. And what you have said shows the clearness of your memory and expression."

"You are very good to speak so," she answered, recovering her temper beautifully, but, like a true woman, resolved not to let me know any thing more about it. "Oh, what a clap of thunder! Are you timid? This house has been struck three times, they say. It stands so prominently. It is this that has made my lord look so."

"Let us hope, then to see him much better to-morrow," I said, very bravely, though frightened at heart, being always a coward of thunder. "What are these storms you get in England compared to the tropical outbursts? Let us open the window, if you please, and watch it."

"I hear myself called," Mrs. Price exclaimed. "I am sorry to leave you, miss. You know best. But please not to sit by an open window; nothing is more dangerous."

"Except a great bunch of steel keys," I replied; and gazing at her nice retreating figure, saw it quickened, as a flash of lightning passed, with the effort of both hands to be quit of something.

The storm was dreadful; and I kept the window shut, but could not help watching, with a fearful joy, the many-fingered hazy pale vibrations, the reflections of the levin in the hollow of the land. And sadly I began to think of Uncle Sam and all his goodness; and how in a storm, a thousandfold of this, he went down his valley in the torrent of the waves, and must have been drowned, and perhaps never found again, if he had not been wearing his leathern apron.

This made me humble, as all great thoughts do, and the sidelong drizzle in among the heavy rain (from the big drops jostling each other in the air, and dashing out splashes of difference) gave me an idea of the sort of thing I was—and how very little more. And feeling rather lonely in the turn that things had taken, I rang the bell for somebody; and up came Stixon.

"Lor', miss! Lor', what a burning shame of Prick!—'Prick' we call her, in our genial moments, hearing as the 'k' is hard in Celtic language; and all abroad about her husband. My very first saying to you was, not to be too much okkipied with her. Look at the pinafore on her! Lord be with me! If his lordship, as caught me, that day of this very same month fifty years, in the gooseberry bush—"

"To be sure!" I said, knowing that story by heart, together with all its embellishments; "but things are altered since that day. Nothing can be more to your credit, I am sure, than to be able to tell such a tale in the very place where it happened."

"But, Miss—Miss Erma, I ain't begun to tell it."

"Because you remember that I am acquainted with it. A thing so remarkable is not to be forgotten. Now let me ask you a question of importance; and I beg you, as an old servant of this family, to answer it carefully and truly. Do you remember any one, either here or elsewhere, so like my father, Captain Castlewood, as to be taken for him at first sight, until a difference of expression and of walk was noticed?"

Mr. Stixon looked at me with some surprise, and then began to think profoundly, and in doing so he supported his chin with one hand.

"Let me see—like the Captain?" He reflected slowly: "Did I ever see a gentleman like poor Master George, as was? A gentleman, of course, it must have been—and a very tall, handsome, straight gentleman, to be taken anyhow for young Master George. And he must have been very like him, too, to be taken for him by resemblance. Well then, miss, to the best of my judgment, I never did see such a gentleman."

"I don't know whether it was a gentleman or not," I answered, with some impatience at his tantalizing slowness; "but he carried his chin stretched forth—like this."

For Stixon's own attitude had reminded me of a little point in Jacob Rigg's description, which otherwise might have escaped me.

"Lor', now, and he carried his chin like that!" resumed the butler, with an increase of intelligence by no means superfluous. "Why, let me see, now, let me see. Something do come across my mind when you puts out your purty chin, miss; but there, it must have been a score of years agone, or more—perhaps five-and-twenty. What a daft old codger I be getting, surely! No wonder them new lights puts a bushel over me."

"No," I replied; "you are simply showing great power of memory, Stixon. And now please to tell me, as soon as you can, who it was—a tall man, remember, and a handsome one, with dark hair, perhaps, or at any rate dark eyes—who resembled (perhaps not very closely, but still enough to mislead at a distance) my dear father—Master George, as you call him, for whose sake you are bound to tell me every thing you know. Now try to think—do please try your very best, for my sake."

"That I will, miss; that I will, with all my heart, with all my mind, with all my soul, and with all my strength, as I used to have to say with my hands behind my back, afore education were invented. Only please you to stand with your chin put out, miss, and your profield towards me. That is what brings it up, and nothing else at all, miss. Only, not to say a word of any sort to hurry me. A tracherous and a deep thing is the memory and the remembrance."

Mr. Stixon's memory was so deep that there seemed to be no bottom to it, or, at any rate, what lay there took a very long time to get at. And I waited, with more impatience than hope, the utterance of his researches.

"I got it now; I got it all, miss, clear as any pictur'!" the old man cried out, at the very moment when I was about to say, "Please to leave off; I am sure it is too much for you." "Not a pictur' in all of our gallery, miss, two-and-fifty of 'em, so clear as I see that there man, dark as it was, and a heavy wind a-blowing. What you call them things, miss, if you please, as comes with the sun, like a face upon the water? Wicked things done again the will of the Lord, and He makes them fade out afterwards."

"Perhaps you mean photographs. Is that the word?"

"The very word, and no mistake. A sinful trespass on the works of God, to tickle the vanity of gals. But he never spread himself abroad like them. They shows all their ear-rings, and their necks, and smiles. But he never would have shown his nose, if he could help it, that stormy night when I come to do my duty. He come into this house without so much as a 'by your leave' to nobody, and vexed me terrible accordingly. It was in the old lord's time, you know, miss, a one of the true sort, as would have things respectful, and knock down any man as soon as look. And it put me quite upon the touch-and-go, being responsible for all the footman's works, and a young boy promoted in the face of my opinion, having my own son worth a dozen of him. This made me look at the nature of things, miss, and find it on my conscience to be after every body."

"Yes, Stixon, yes! Now do go on. You must always have been, not only after, but a very long way after, every body."

"Miss Erma, if you throw me out, every word goes promiscuous. In a heffort of the mind like this it is every word, or no word. Now, did I see him come along the big passage?—a 'currydoor' they call it now, though no more curry in it than there is door. No, I never seed him come along the passage, and that made it more reproachful. He come out of a green-baize door—the very place I can point out to you, and the selfsame door, miss, though false to the accuracy of the mind that knows it, by reason of having been covered up red, and all the brass buttons lost to it in them new-fangled upholsteries. Not that I see him come through, if you please, but the sway of the door, being double-jointed, was enough to show legs, had been there. And knowing that my lord's private room was there, made me put out my legs quite wonderful."

"Oh, do please to put out your words half as quickly."

"No, miss, no. I were lissome in those days, though not so very stiff at this time of speaking, and bound to be guarded in the guidance of the tongue. And now, miss, I think if you please to hear the rest to-morrow, I could tell it better."

A more outrageous idea than this was never presented to me. Even if I could have tried to wait, this dreadful old man might have made up his mind not to open his lips in the morning, or, if he would speak, there might be nothing left to say. His memory was nursed up now, and my only chance was to keep it so. Therefore I begged him to please to go on, and no more would I interrupt him. And I longed to be ten years older, so as not to speak when needless.

"So then, Miss Erma, if I must go on," resumed the well-coaxed Stixon, "if my duty to the family driveth me to an 'arrowing subjeck, no words can more justly tell what come to pass than my language to my wife. She were alive then, the poor dear hangel, and the mother of seven children, which made me, by your leave comparing humble roofs with grandeur, a little stiff to him up stairs, as come in on the top of seven. For I said to my wife when I went home—sleeping out of the house, you see, miss, till the Lord was pleased to dissolve matrimony—'Polly,' I said, when I took home my supper, 'you may take my word for it there is something queer.' Not another word did I mean to tell her, as behooved my dooty. Howsoever, no peace was my lot till I made a clean bosom of it, only putting her first on the Testament, and even that not safe with most of them. And from that night not a soul has heard a word till it comes to you, miss. He come striding along, with his face muffled up, for all the world like a bugglar, and no more heed did he pay to me than if I was one of the pedestals. But I were in front of him at the door, and to slip out so was against all orders. So in front of him I stands, with my hand upon the handles, and meaning to have a word with him, to know who he was, and such like, and how he comes there, and what he had been seeking, with the spoons and the forks and the gravies on my mind. And right I would have been in a court of law (if the lawyers was put out of it) for my hefforts in that situation. And then, what do you think he done, miss? So far from entering into any conversation with me, or hitting at me, like a man—which would have done good to think of—he send out one hand to the bottom of my vest—as they call it now in all the best livery tailors—and afore I could reason on it, there I was a-lying on a star in six colors of marble. When I come to think on it, it was but a push directed to a part of my system, and not a hit under the belt, the like of which no Briton would think of delivering. Nevertheless, there was no differ in what came to me, miss, and my spirit was roused, as if I had been hit foul by one of the prizemen. No time to get up, but I let out one foot at his long legs as a' was slipping through the door, and so nearly did I fetch him over that he let go his muffle to balance himself with the jamb, and same moment a strong rush of wind laid bare the whole of his wicked face to me. For a bad wicked face it was, as ever I did see; whether by reason of the kick I gave, and a splinter in the shin, or by habit of the mind, a proud and 'aughty and owdacious face, and, as I said to my poor wife, reminded me a little of our Master George; not in his ordinary aspect, to be sure, but as Master George might look if he was going to the devil. Pray excoose me, miss, for bad words, but no good ones will do justice. And so off he goes, after one look at me on the ground, not worth considering, with his chin stuck up, as if the air was not good enough to be breathed perpendiklar like."

"And of course you followed him," I exclaimed, perceiving that Stixon would allow me now to speak. "Without any delay you went after him."

"Miss Erma, you forget what my dooty was. My dooty was to stay by the door and make it fast, as custodian of all this mansion. No little coorosity, or private resentment, could 'a borne me out in doing so. As an outraged man I was up for rushing out, but as a trusted official, and responsible head footman, miss—for I were not butler till nine months after that—my dooty was to put the big bolt in."

"And you did it, without even looking out to see if he tried to set the house on fire! Oh, Stixon, I fear that you were frightened."

"Now, Miss Erma, I calls it ungrateful, after all my hefforts to obleege you, to put a bad construction upon me. You hurts me, miss, in my tenderest parts, as I never thought Master George's darter would 'a doed. But there, they be none of them as they used to be! Master George would 'a said, if he ever had heard it. 'Stixon, my man, you have acted for the best, and showed a sound discretion. Stixon,' he would have said, 'here's a George and Dragon in reward of your gallant conduck.' Ah, that sort of manliness is died out now."

This grated at first upon my feelings, because it seemed tainted with selfishness, and it did not entirely agree with my own recollections of my father. But still Mr. Stixon must have suffered severely in that conflict, and to blame him for not showing rashness was to misunderstand his position. And so, before putting any other questions to him, I felt in my pocket for a new half sovereign, which I hoped would answer.

Mr. Stixon received it in an absent manner, as if he were still in the struggle of his story, and too full of duty to be thankful. Yet I saw that he did not quite realize the truth of a nobly philosophic proverb—"the half is more than the whole." Nevertheless, he stowed away his half, in harmony with a good old English saying.

"Now, when you were able to get up at last," I inquired, with tender interest, "what did you see, and what did you do, and what conclusion did you come to?"

"I came to the conclusion, miss, that I were hurt considerable. Coorosity on my part were quenched by the way as I had to rub myself. But a man is a man, and the last thing to complain of is the exercise of his functions. And when I come round I went off to his lordship, as if I had heared his bell ring. All of us knew better than to speak till him beginning, for he were not what they now call 'halfable,' but very much to the contrary. So he says, 'You door-skulker, what do you want there?' And I see that he got his hot leg up, certain to fly to bad language. According, I asked, with my breath in my hand, if he pleased to see any young man there just now, by reason that such likes had been observated going out in some direction. But his lordship roared to me to go in another direction, not fit for young ladies. My old lord was up to every word of English; but his present lordship is the hopposite extreme."

"Is that all you have to tell me, Stixon? Did you never see that fearful man again? Did you never even hear of him?"

"Never, miss, never! And to nobody but you have I ever told all as I told now. But you seems to be born to hear it all."

CHAPTER XXXVIII
A WITCH

It was true enough that Stixon now had nothing more to tell, but what he had told already seemed of very great importance, confirming strongly, as it did, the description given me by Jacob Rigg. And even the butler's concluding words—that I seemed born to hear it all—comforted me like some good omen, and cheered me forward to make them true. Not that I could, in my sad and dangerous enterprise, always be confident. Some little spirit I must have had, and some resolve to be faithful, according to the power of a very common mind, admiring but never claiming courage. For I never did feel in any kind of way any gift of inspiration, or even the fitness of a quick, strong mind for working out deeds of justice. There were many good ladies in America then, and now there are some in England, perceiving so clearly their own superiority as to run about largely proclaiming it. How often I longed to be a little more like these, equal to men in achievements of the body, and very far beyond them in questions of the mind!

However, it was useless to regret my lacks, and foolish, perhaps, to think of them. To do my very best with what little gifts I had was more to the purpose and more sensible. Taking in lonely perplexity now this dim yet exciting view of things, I resolved, right or wrong, to abide at the place where the only chance was of pursuing my search. I was pledged, as perhaps has been said before, to keep from every one excepting faithful Betsy, and above all from Lord Castlewood, the unexpected little tale wrung out of Mr. Stixon. That promise had been given without any thought, in my eagerness to hear every thing, and probably some people would have thought of it no more. But the trusty butler was so scared when I asked him to release me from it, so penitent also at his own indiscretion, which never would have overcome him (as he said in the morning) only for the thunderstorm, that instead of getting off, I was quite obliged to renew and confirm my assurances.

Therefore, in truth, I had no chance left but to go back to Shoxford and do my best, meeting all dark perils with the shield of right spread over me. And a great thing now in my favor was to feel some confidence again in the guidance of kind Wisdom. The sense of this never had abandoned me so much as to make me miserable about it; but still I had never tried to shelter under it, and stay there faithfully, as the best of people do. And even now I was not brought to such a happy attitude, although delivered by these little gleams of light from the dark void of fatalism, into which so many bitter blows had once been driving me.

However, before setting off again, I made one more attempt upon Lord Castlewood, longing to know whether his suspicions would help me at all to identify the figure which had frightened both the sexton and the butler. That the person was one and the same, I did not for a moment call in question, any more than I doubted that he was the man upon whose head rested the blood of us. But why he should be allowed to go scot-free while another bore his brand, and many others died for him, and why all my most just and righteous efforts to discover him should receive, if not discouragement, at any rate most lukewarm aid—these and several other questions were as dark as ever.

"You must not return to Shoxford, my cousin," Lord Castlewood said to me that day, after a plain though courteous refusal to enlighten me even with a mere surmise, except upon the condition before rejected. "I can not allow you to be there without strict supervision and protection. You will not, perhaps, be aware of it, as perhaps you have not been before; but a careful watch will be kept on you. I merely tell you this that you may not make mistakes, and confound friendly vigilance with the spying of an enemy. Erema, you will be looked after."

I could not help being grateful for his kindness, and really, try as I might to be fearless, it would be a great comfort to have some one to protect me. On the other hand, how would this bear upon my own freedom of looking about, my desire to make my own occasions, and the need of going every where? Could these be kept to my liking at all while an unknown power lay in kind regard of me? Considering these things, I begged my cousin to leave me to my own devices, for that I was afraid of nobody on earth, while only seeking justice, and that England must be worse than the worst parts of America if any harm to me could be apprehended at quiet times and in such a quiet place.

My cousin said no more upon that point, though I felt that he was not in any way convinced; but he told me that he thought I should pay a little visit, if only for a day, such as I treated him with, to my good friends at Bruntsea, before I returned to Shoxford. There was no one now at Bruntsea whom I might not wish to meet, as he knew by a trifling accident; and after all the kind services rendered by Major and Mrs. Hockin, it was hardly right to let them begin to feel themselves neglected. Now the very same thing had occurred to me, and I was going to propose it; and many things which I found it hard to do without were left in my little chest of locked-up drawers there. But of that, to my knowledge, I scarcely thought twice; whereas I longed to see and have a talk with dear "Aunt Mary." Now, since my affairs had been growing so strange, and Lord Castlewood had come forward—not strongly, but still quite enough to speak of—there had been a kind-hearted and genuine wish at Bruntsea to recover me. And this desire had unreasonably grown while starved with disappointment. The less they heard of me, the more they imagined in their rich good-will, and the surer they became that, after all, there was something in my ideas.

But how could I know this, without any letters from them, since letters were a luxury forbidden me at Shoxford? I knew it through one of the simplest and commonest of all nature's arrangements. Stixon's boy, as every body called him (though he must have been close upon five-and-twenty, and carried a cane out of sight of the windows), being so considered, and treated boyishly by the maids of Castlewood, asserted his dignity, and rose above his value as much as he had lain below it, by showing that he owned a tender heart, and them that did not despise it. For he chanced to be walking with his cane upon the beach (the very morning after he first went to Bruntsea, too late for any train back again), and casting glances of interior wonder over the unaccustomed sea—when from the sea itself out-leaped a wondrous rosy deity.

"You there, Mr. Stixon! Oh my! How long?" exclaimed Mrs. Hockin's new parlormaid, ready to drop, though in full print now, on the landward steps of the bathing-machine set up by the reckless Major.

"Come this very hinstant, miss, honor bright!" replied the junior Stixon, who had moved in good society; "and just in the hackmy of time, miss, if I may offer you my 'umble hand."

The fair nymph fixed him with a penetrating gaze through tresses full of salt curliness, while her cheeks were conscious of an unclad dip. But William Stixon's eyes were firm with pure truth, gently toning into shy reproach and tenderness. He had met her at supper last night, and done his best; but (as he said to the Castlewood maids) it was only feeling then, whereas now it was emoshun.

"Then you are a gentleman!" Polly Hopkins cried; "and indeed, Mr. Stixon, these are slippery things." She was speaking of the steps, as she came down them, and they had no hand-rails; and the young man felt himself to be no more Stixon's boy, but a gentleman under sweet refining pressure.

From that hour forth it was pronounced, and they left the world to its own opinion, that they were keeping company; and although they were sixty miles apart by air, and eighty-two by railway, at every post their hearts were one, with considerable benefit to the United Kingdom's revenue. Also they met by the sad sea waves, when the bathing-machines had been hauled up—for the Major now had three of them—as often as Stixon senior smiled—which he did whenever he was not put out—on the bygone ways of these children. For Polly Hopkins had a hundred pounds, as well as being the only child of the man who kept the only shop for pickled pork in Bruntsea. And my Mr. Stixon could always contrive to get orders from his lordship to send the boy away, with his carriage paid, when his health demanded bathing. Hence it is manifest that the deeds and thoughts of Bruntsea House, otherwise called "Bruntlands," were known quite as well, and discussed even better—because dispassionately—at Castlewood than and as they were at home.

Now I won forever the heart of Stixon's boy, and that of Polly Hopkins, by recoiling with horror from the thought of going to Bruntsea unattended. After all my solitary journeys, this might have been called hypocrisy, if it had been inconvenient; but coming as it did, it was pronounced, by all who desired either news or love, to be another proof of the goodness of my heart.

Escorted thus by William Stixon (armed with a brilliant cane bought for this occasion), and knowing that Sir Montague Hockin was not there, I arrived at Bruntlands in the afternoon, and received a kindly welcome from my dear friend Mrs. Hockin. Her husband was from home, and she grieved to say that now he was generally doing this; but nobody else could have any idea what his avocations were! Then she paid me some compliments on my appearance—a thing that I never thought of, except when I came to a question of likeness, or chanced to be thinking of things, coming up as they will, at a looking-glass.

That the Major was out was a truth established in my mind some time ago; because I had seen him, as our fly crawled by, expressly and emphatically at work on a rampart of his own designing. The work was quite new to me, but not so his figure. Though I could not see people three miles off, as Firm Gundry was said to do, I had pretty clear sight, and could not mistake the Major within a furlong. And there he was, going about in a row of square notches against the sea-line, with his coat off, and brandishing some tool, vehemently carrying on to spirits less active than his own. I burned with desire to go and join him, for I love to see activity; but Mrs. Hockin thought that I had better stay away, because it was impossible to get on there without language too strong for young ladies.

This closed the question, and I stopped with her, and found the best comfort that I ever could have dreamed of. "Aunt Mary" was so steadfast, and so built up with, or rather built of, the very faith itself, that to talk with her was as good as reading the noblest chapter of the Bible. She put by all possibility of doubt as to the modern interference of the Lord, with such a sweet pity and the seasoned smile of age, and so much feeling (which would have been contempt if she had not been softened by her own escapes), that really I, who had come expecting to set her beautiful white hair on end, became like a little child put into the corner, but too young yet for any other punishment at school, except to be looked at. Nevertheless, though I did look small, it made me all the happier. I seemed to become less an individual, and more a member of a large kind race under paternal management. From a practical point of view this may have been amiss, but it helped to support me afterward. And before I began to get weary or rebel against her gentle teaching, in came her husband; and she stopped at once, because he had never any time for it.

"My geological hammer!" cried the Major, being in a rush as usual. "Oh, Miss Castlewood! I did not see you. Pardon me! It is the want of practice only; so wholly have you deserted us. Fallen into better hands, of course. Well, how are you? But I need not ask. If ever there was a young lady who looked well—don't tell me of troubles, or worries, or nerves—I put up my glasses, and simply say, 'Pretty young ladies are above all pity!' My hammer, dear Mary; my hammer I must have. The geological one, you know; we have come on a bit of old Roman work; the bricklayer's hammers go flat, like lead. I have just one minute and a half to spare. What fine fellows those Romans were! I will build like a Roman. See to every bit of it myself, Erema. No contractor's jobs for me. Mary, you know where to find it."

"Well, dear, I think that you had it last, to get the bung out of the beer barrel, when the stool broke down in the corner, you know, because you would—"

"Never mind about that. The drayman made a fool of himself. I proceeded upon true principles. That fellow knew nothing of leverage."

"Well, dear, of course you understand it best. But he told cook that it was quite a mercy that you got off without a broken leg; and compared with that, two gallons of spilled ale—" Mrs. Hockin made off, without finishing her sentence.

"What a woman she is!" cried the Major; "she takes such a lofty view of things, and she can always find my tools. Erema, after dinner I must have a talk with you. There is something going on here—on my manor—which I can not at all get a clew to, except by connecting you with it, the Lord knows how. Of course you have nothing to do with it; but still my life has been so free from mystery that, that—you know what I mean—"

"That you naturally think I must be at the bottom of every thing mysterious. Now is there any thing dark about me? Do I not labor to get at the light? Have I kept from your knowledge any single thing? But you never cared to go into them."

"It is hardly fair of you to say that. The fact is that you, of your own accord, have chosen other counselors. Have you heard any more of your late guardian, Mr. Shovelin? I suppose that his executor, or some one appointed by him, is now your legal guardian."

"I have not even asked what the law is," I replied. "Lord Castlewood is my proper guardian, according to all common-sense, and I mean to have him so. He has inquired through his solicitors as to Mr. Shovelin, and I am quite free there. My father's will is quite good, they say; but it never has been proved, and none of them care to do it. My cousin thinks that I could compel them to prove it, or to renounce in proper form; but Mr. Shovelin's sons are not nice people—as different from him as night from day, careless and wild and dashing."

"Then do you mean to do nothing about it? What a time she is finding that hammer!"

"I leave it entirely to my cousin, and he is waiting for legal advice. I wish to have the will, of course, for the sake of my dear father; but with or without any will, my mother's little property comes to me. And if my dear father had nothing to leave, why should we run up a great lawyer's bill?"

"To be sure not! I see. That makes all the difference. I admire your common-sense," said the Major—"but there! Come and look, and just exercise it here. There is that very strange woman again, just at the end of my new road. She stands quite still, and then stares about, sometimes for an hour together. Nobody knows who she is, or why she came. She has taken a tumble-down house on my manor, from a wretch of a fellow who denies my title; and what she lives on is more than any one can tell, for she never spends sixpence in Bruntsea. Some think that she walks in the dark to Newport, and gets all her food at some ship stores there. And one of our fishermen vows that he met her walking on the sea, as he rowed home one night, and she had a long red bag on her shoulder. She is a witch, that is certain; for she won't answer me, however politely I accost her. But the oddest thing of all is the name she gave to the fellow she took the house from. What do you think she called herself? Of all things in the world—'Mrs. Castlewood!' I congratulate you on your relative."

"How very strange!" I answered. "Oh, now I see why you connect me with it; and I beg your pardon for having been vexed. But let me go and see her. Oh, may I go at once, if you please, and speak to her?"

"The very thing I wish—if you are not afraid. I will come with you, when I get my hammer. Oh, here it is! Mary, how clever you are! Now look out of the window, and you shall see Erema make up to her grandmamma."

CHAPTER XXXIX
NOT AT HOME

Mrs. Hockin, however, had not the pleasure promised her by the facetious Major of seeing me "make up to my grandmamma." For although we set off at once to catch the strange woman who had roused so much curiosity, and though, as we passed the door of Bruntlands, we saw her still at her post in the valley, like Major Hockin's new letter-box, for some reason best known to herself we could not see any more of her. For, hurry as he might upon other occasions, nothing would make the Major cut a corner of his winding "drive" when descending it with a visitor. He enjoyed every yard of its length, because it was his own at every step, and he counted his paces in an under-tone, to be sure of the length, for perhaps the thousandth time. It was long enough in a straight line, one would have thought, but he was not the one who thought so; and therefore he had doubled it by judicious windings, as if for the purpose of breaking the descent.

"Three hundred and twenty-one," he said, as he came to a post, where he meant to have a lodge as soon as his wife would let him; "now the old woman stands fifty-five yards on, at a spot where I mean to have an ornamental bridge, because our fine saline element runs up there when the new moon is perigee. My dear, I am a little out of breath, which affects my sight for the moment. Doubtless that is why I do not see her."

"If I may offer an opinion," I said, "in my ignorance of all the changes you have made, the reason why we do not see her may be that she is gone out of sight."

"Impossible!" Major Hockin cried—"simply impossible, Erema! She never moves for an hour and a half. And she was not come, was she, when you came by?"

"I will not be certain," I answered; "but I think that I must have seen her if she had been there, because I was looking about particularly at all your works as we came by."

"Then she must be there still; let us tackle her."

This was easier said than done, for we found no sign of any body at the place where she certainly had been standing less than five minutes ago. We stood at the very end and last corner of the ancient river trough, where a little seam went inland from it, as if some trifle of a brook had stolen down while it found a good river to welcome it. But now there was only a little oozy gloss from the gleam of the sun upon some lees of marshy brine left among the rushes by the last high tide.

"You see my new road and the key to my intentions?" said the Major, forgetting all about his witch, and flourishing his geological hammer, while standing thus at his "nucleus." "To understand all, you have only to stand here. You see those leveling posts, adjusted with scientific accuracy. You see all those angles, calculated with micrometric precision. You see how the curves are radiated—"

"It is very beautiful, I have no doubt; but you can not have Uncle Sam's gift of machinery. And do you understand every bit of it yourself?"

"Erema, not a jot of it. I like to talk about it freely when I can, because I see all its beauties. But as to understanding it, my dear, you might set to, if you were an educated female, and deliver me a lecture upon my own plan. Intellect is, in such matters, a bubble. I know good bricks, good mortar, and good foundations."

"With your great ability, you must do that," I answered, very gently, being touched with his humility and allowance of my opinion; "you will make a noble town of it. But when is the railway coming?"

"Not yet. We have first to get our Act; and a miserable-minded wretch, who owns nothing but a rabbit-warren, means to oppose it. Don't let us talk of him. It puts one out of patience when a man can not see his own interest. But come and see our assembly-rooms, literary institute, baths, etc., etc.— that is what we are urging forward now."

"But may I not go first and look for my strange namesake? Would it be wrong of me to call upon her?"

"No harm whatever," replied my companion; "likewise no good. Call fifty times, but you will get no answer. However, it is not a very great round, and you will understand my plans more clearly. Step out, my dear, as if you had got a troop of Mexicans after you. Ah, what a fine turn for that lot now!" He was thinking of the war which had broken out, and the battle of Bull's Run.

Without any such headlong speed, we soon came to the dwelling-place of the stranger, and really for once the good Major had not much overdone his description. Truly it was almost tumbling down, though massively built, and a good house long ago; and it looked the more miserable now from being placed in a hollow of the ground, whose slopes were tufted with rushes and thistles and ragwort. The lower windows were blocked up from within, the upper were shattered and crumbling and dangerous, with blocks of cracked stone jutting over them; and the last surviving chimney gave less smoke than a workman's homeward whiff of his pipe to comfort and relieve the air.

The only door that we could see was of heavy black oak, without any knocker; but I clinched my hand, having thick gloves on, and made what I thought a very creditable knock, while the Major stood by, with his blue-lights up, and keenly gazed and gently smiled.

"Knock again, my dear," he said; "you don't knock half hard enough."

I knocked again with all my might, and got a bruised hand for a fortnight, but there was not even the momentary content produced by an active echo. The door was as dead as every thing else.

"Now for my hammer," my companion cried. "This house, in all sound law, is my own. I will have a 'John Doe and Richard Roe'—a fine action of ejectment. Shall I be barred out upon my own manor?"

With hot indignation he swung his hammer, but nothing came of it except more noise. Then the Major grew warm and angry.

"My charter contains the right of burning witches or drowning them, according to their color. The execution is specially imposed upon the bailiff of this ancient town, and he is my own pickled-pork man. His name is Hopkins, and I will have him out with his seal and stick and all the rest. Am I to be laughed at in this way?"

For we thought we heard a little screech of laughter from the loneliness of the deep dark place, but no other answer came, and perhaps it was only our own imagining.

"Is there no other door—perhaps one at the back?" I asked, as the lord of the manor stamped.

"No, that has been walled up long ago. The villain has defied me from the very first. Well, we shall see. This is all very fine. You witness that they deny the owner entrance?"

"Undoubtedly I can depose to that. But we must not waste your valuable time."

"After all, the poor ruin is worthless," he went on, calming down as we retired. "It must be leveled, and that hole filled up. It is quite an eye-sore to our new parade. And no doubt it belongs to me—no doubt it does. The fellow who claims it was turned out of the law. Fancy any man turned out of the law! Erema, in all your far West experience, did you ever see a man bad enough to be turned out of the law?"

"Major Hockin, how can I tell? But I fear that their practice was very, very sad—they very nearly always used to hang them."

"The best use—the best use a rogue can be put to. Some big thief has put it the opposite way, because he was afraid of his own turn. The constitution must be upheld, and, by the Lord! it shall be—at any rate, in East Bruntsea. West Bruntsea is all a small-pox warren out of my control, and a skewer in my flesh. And some of my tenants have gone across the line to snap their dirty hands at me."

Being once in this cue, Major Hockin went on, not talking to me much, but rather to himself, though expecting me now and then to say "yes;" and this I did when necessary, for his principles of action were beyond all challenge, and the only question was how he carried them out.

He took me to his rampart, which was sure to stop the sea, and at the same time to afford the finest place in all Great Britain for a view of it. Even an invalid might sit here in perfect shelter from the heaviest gale, and watch such billows as were not to be seen except upon the Major's property.

"The reason of that is quite simple," he said, "and a child may see the force of it. In no other part of the kingdom can you find so steep a beach fronting the southwest winds, which are ten to one of all other winds, without any break of sand or rock outside. Hence we have what you can not have on a shallow shore—grand rollers: straight from the very Atlantic, Erema; you and I have seen them. You may see by the map that they all end here, with the wind in the proper quarter."

"Oh, please not to talk of such horrors," I said. "Why, your ramparts would go like pie crust."

The Major smiled a superior smile, and after more talk we went home to dinner.

From something more than mere curiosity, I waited at Bruntsea for a day or two, hoping to see that strange namesake of mine who had shown so much inhospitality. For she must have been at home when we made that pressing call, inasmuch as there was no other place to hide her within the needful distance of the spot where she had stood. But the longer I waited, the less would she come out—to borrow the good Irishman's expression—and the Major's pillar-box, her favorite resort, was left in conspicuous solitude. And when a letter came from Sir Montague Hockin, asking leave to be at

Bruntlands on the following evening, I packed up my goods with all haste, and set off, not an hour too soon, for Shoxford.

But before taking leave of these kind friends, I begged them to do for me one little thing, without asking me to explain my reason, which, indeed, was more than I could do. I begged them, not of course to watch Sir Montague, for that they could not well do to a guest, but simply to keep their eyes open and prepared for any sign of intercourse, if such there were, between this gentleman and that strange interloper. Major Hockin stared, and his wife looked at me as if my poor mind must have gone astray, and even to myself my own thought appeared absurd. Remembering, however, what Sir Montague had said, and other little things as well, I did not laugh as they did. But perhaps one part of my conduct was not right, though the wrong (if any) had been done before that—to wit, I had faithfully promised Mrs. Price not to say a word at Bruntlands about their visitor's low and sinful treachery toward my cousin. To give such a promise had perhaps been wrong, but still without it I should have heard nothing of matters that concerned me nearly. And now it seemed almost worse to keep than to break such a pledge, when I thought of a pious, pure-minded, and holy-hearted woman, like my dear "Aunt Mary," unwittingly brought into friendly contact with a man of the lowest nature. And as for the Major, instead of sitting down with such a man to dinner, what would he have done but drive him straightway from the door, and chase him to the utmost verge of his manor with the peak end of his "geological hammer?"

However, away I went without a word against that contemptible and base man, toward whom—though he never had injured me—I cherished, for my poor cousin's sake, the implacable hatred of virtuous youth. And a wild idea had occurred to me (as many wild ideas did now in the crowd of things gathering round me) that this strange woman, concealed from the world, yet keenly watching some members of it, might be that fallen and miserable creature who had fled from a good man with a bad one, because he was more like herself—Flittamore, Lady Castlewood. Not that she could be an "old woman" yet, but she might look old, either by disguise, or through her own wickedness; and every body knows how suddenly those southern beauties fall off, alike in face and figure. Mrs. Price had not told me what became of her, or even whether she was dead or alive, but merely said, with a meaning look, that she was "punished" for her sin, and I had not ventured to inquire how, the subject being so distasteful.

To my great surprise, and uneasiness as well, I had found at Bruntlands no letter whatever, either to the Major or myself, from Uncle Sam or any other person at the saw-mills. There had not been time for any answer to my letter of some two months back, yet being alarmed by the Sawyer's last tidings,

I longed, with some terror, for later news. And all the United Kingdom was now watching with tender interest the dismemberment, as it almost appeared, of the other mighty Union. Not with malice, or snug satisfaction, as the men of the North in their agony said, but certainly without any proper anguish yet, and rather as a genial and sprightly spectator, whose love of fair play perhaps kindles his applause of the spirit and skill of the weaker side. "'Tis a good fight—let them fight it out!" seemed to be the general sentiment; but in spite of some American vaunt and menace (which of late years had been galling) every true Englishman deeply would have mourned the humiliation of his kindred.

In this anxiety for news I begged that my letters might be forwarded under cover to the postmistress at Shoxford, and bearing my initials. For now I had made up my mind to let Mrs. Busk know whatever I could tell her. I had found her a cross and well-educated woman, far above her neighbors, and determined to remain so. Gossip, that universal leveler, theoretically she despised; and she had that magnificent esteem for rank which works so beautifully in England. And now when my good nurse reasonably said that, much as she loved to be with me, her business would allow that delight no longer, and it also came home to my own mind that money would be running short again, and small hope left in this dreadful civil war of our nugget escaping pillage (which made me shudder horribly at internal discord), I just did this—I dismissed Betsy, or rather I let her dismiss herself, which she might not have altogether meant to do, although she threatened it so often. For here she had nothing to do but live well, and protest against tricks of her own profession which she practiced as necessary laws at home; and so, with much affection, for the time we parted.

Mrs. Busk was delighted at her departure, for she never had liked to be criticised so keenly while she was doing her very best. And as soon as the wheels of Betsy's fly had shown their last spoke at the corner, she told me, with a smile, that her mind had been made up to give us notice that very evening to seek for better lodgings. But she could not wish for a quieter, pleasanter, or more easily pleased young lady than I was without any mischief-maker; and so, on the spur of the moment, I took her into my own room, while her little girl minded the shop, and there and then I told her who I was, and what I wanted.

And now she behaved most admirably. Instead of expressing surprise, she assured me that all along she had felt there was something, and that I must be somebody. Lovely as my paintings were (which I never heard, before or since, from any impartial censor), she had known that it could not be that alone which had kept me so long in their happy valley. And now she did hope I would do her the honor to stay beneath her humble roof, though entitled to one so different. And was the fairy ring in the church-yard made of all my family?

I replied that too surely this was so, and that nothing would please me better than to find, according to my stature, room to sleep inside it as soon as ever I should have solved the mystery of its origin. At the moment this was no exaggeration, so depressing was the sense of fighting against the unknown so long, with scarcely any one to stand by me, or avenge me if I fell. And Betsy's departure, though I tried to take it mildly, had left me with a readiness to catch my breath.

But to dwell upon sadness no more than need be (a need as sure as hunger), it was manifest now to my wondering mind that once more I had chanced upon a good, and warm, and steadfast heart. Every body is said to be born, whether that happens by night or day, with a certain little widowed star, which has lost its previous mortal, concentrating from a billion billion of miles, or leagues, or larger measure, intense, but generally invisible, radiance upon him or her; and to take for the moment this old fable as of serious meaning, my star was to find bad facts at a glance, but no bad folk without long gaze.

CHAPTER XL
THE MAN AT LAST

This new alliance with Mrs. Busk not only refreshed my courage, but helped me forward most importantly. In truth, if it had not been for this I never could have borne what I had to bear, and met the perils which I had to meet. For I had the confidence of feeling now that here was some one close at hand, an intelligent person, and well acquainted with the place and neighborhood, upon whom I could rely for warning, succor, and, if the worst should come to the very worst, revenge. It is true that already I had Jacob Rigg, and perhaps the protector promised by my cousin; but the former was as ignorant as he was honest, and of the latter, as he made no sign, how could I tell any thing?

Above all things, Mrs. Busk's position, as mistress of the letters, gave me very great advantage both for offense and defense. For without the smallest breach of duty or of loyal honor she could see that my letters passed direct to me or from me, as the case might be, at the same time that she was bound to observe all epistles addressed to strangers or new-comers in her district, which extended throughout the valley. And by putting my letters in the Portsmouth bag, instead of that for Winchester, I could freely correspond with any of my friends without any one seeing name or postmark in the neighboring villages.

It is needless to say that I had long since explored and examined with great diligence that lonely spot where my grandfather met his terrible and mysterious fate. Not that there seemed to be any hope now, after almost nineteen years, of finding even any token of the crime committed there. Only that it was natural for me, feeling great horror of this place, to seek to know it thoroughly.

For this I had good opportunity, because the timid people of the valley, toward the close of day, would rather trudge another half mile of the homeward road than save brave legs at the thumping cost of hearts not so courageous. For the planks were now called "Murder-bridge;" and every body knew that the red spots on it, which could never be seen by daylight, began to gleam toward the hour of the deed, and glowed (as if they would burn the wood) when the church clock struck eleven.

This phenomenon was beyond my gifts of observation; and knowing that my poor grandfather had scarcely set foot on the bridge, if ever he set foot there at all—which at present was very doubtful—also that he had fallen backward, and only bled internally, I could not reconcile tradition (however recent) with proven truth. And sure of no disturbance from the step of any native, here I often sat in a little bowered shelter of my own, well established up the rise, down which the path made zigzag, and screened from that and the bridge as well by sheaf of twigs and lop of leaves. It was a little forward thicket, quite detached from the upland copse, to which perhaps it had once belonged, and crusted up from the meadow slope with sod and mould in alternate steps. And being quite the elbow of a foreland of the meadow-reach, it yielded almost a "bird's-eye view" of the beautiful glade and the wandering brook.

One evening when I was sitting here, neither drawing, nor working, nor even thinking with any set purpose, but idly allowing my mind to rove, like the rivulet, without any heed, I became aware of a moving figure in the valley. At first it did not appear to me as a thing at all worth notice; it might be a very straightforward cow, or a horse, coming on like a stalking-horse, keeping hind-legs strictly behind, in direct desire of water. I had often seen those sweet things that enjoy four legs walking in the line of distance as if they were no better off than we are, kindly desiring, perhaps, to make the biped spectator content with himself. And I was content to admire this cow or horse, or whatever it might be, without any more than could be helped of that invidious feeling which has driven the human race now to establish its right to a tail, and its hope of four legs. So little, indeed, did I think of what I saw, that when among the hazel twigs, parted carelessly by my hand, a cluster of nuts hung manifest, I gathered it, and began to crack and eat, although they were scarcely ripe yet.

But while employed in this pleasant way, I happened to glance again through my leafy screen, and then I distinguished the figure in the distance as that of a man walking rapidly. He was coming down the mill-stream meadow toward the wooden bridge, carrying a fishing rod, but clearly not intent on angling. For instead of following the course of the stream, he was keeping quite away from it, avoiding also the footpath, or, at any rate, seeming to prefer the long shadows of the trees and the tufted places. This made me look at him, and very soon I shrank into my nest and watched him.

As he came nearer any one could tell that he was no village workman, bolder than the rest, and venturesome to cross the "Murder-bridge" in his haste to be at home. The fishing rod alone was enough to show this when it came into clearer view; for our good people, though they fished sometimes, only used rough rods of their own making, without any varnish or brass thing for the line. And the man was of different height and walk and dress from any of our natives.

"Who can he be?" I whispered to myself, as my heart began to beat heavily, and then seemed almost to stop, as it answered, "This is the man who was in the churchyard." Ignoble as it was, and contemptible, and vile, and traitorous to all duty, my first thought was about my own escape; for I felt that if this man saw me there he would rush up the hill and murder me. Within pistol-shot of the very place where my grandfather had been murdered—a lonely place, an unholy spot, and I was looking at the hand that did it.

The thought of this made me tremble so, though well aware that my death might ensue from a twig on the rustle, or a leaf upon the flutter, that my chance of making off unseen was gone ere I could seize it. For now the man was taking long strides over the worn-out planks of the bridge, disdaining the hand-rail, and looking upward, as if to shun sight of the footing. Advancing thus, he must have had his gaze point-blank upon my lair of leafage; but, luckily for me, there was gorse upon the ridge, and bracken and rag-thistles, so that none could spy up and through the footing of my lurking-place. But if any person could have spied me, this man was the one to do it. So carefully did he scan the distance and inspect the foreground, as if he were resolved that no eye should be upon him while he was doing what he came to do. And he even drew forth a little double telescope, such as are called "binoculars," and fixed it on the thicket which hid me from him, and then on some other dark places.

No effort would compose or hush the heavy beating of my heart; my lips were stiffened with dread of loud breath, and all power of motion left me. For even a puff of wind might betray me, the ruffle of a spray, or the lifting of a leaf, or the random bounce of a beetle. Great peril had encompassed me ere now, but never had it grasped me as this did, and paralyzed all the powers of my body. Rather would I have stood in the midst of a score of Mexican rovers than thus in the presence of that one man. And yet was not this the very thing for which I had waited, longed, and labored? I scorned myself for this craven loss of nerve, but that did not enable me to help it. In this benumbed horror I durst not even peep at the doings of my enemy; but presently I became aware that he had moved from the end of the planks (where he stood for some time as calmly as if he had done nothing there), and had passed round the back of the hawthorn-tree, and gone down to the place where the body was found, and was making most narrow and minute search there. And now I could watch him without much danger, standing as I did well above him, while his eyes were steadfastly bent downward. And, not content with eyesight only, he seemed to be feeling every blade of grass or weed, every single stick or stone, craning into each cranny of the ground, and probing every clod with his hands. Then, after vainly searching with the very utmost care all the space from the hawthorn trunk to the meadow-leet (which was dry as usual), he ran, in a fury of impatience, to his rod, which he had stuck into the bank, as now I saw, and drew off the butt end, and removed the wheel, or whatever it is that holds the fishing line; and this butt had a long spike to it, shining like a halberd in a picture.

This made me shudder; but my spirit was returning, and therewith my power of reasoning, and a deep stir of curiosity. After so many years and such a quantity of searching, what could there still be left to seek for in this haunted and horrible place? And who was the man that was looking for it?

The latter question partly solved itself. It must be the murderer, and no other, whoever he might be among the many black spots of humanity. But as to the other point, no light could be thrown upon it, unless the search should be successful, and perhaps not even then. But now this anxiety, and shame of terror, made me so bold—for I can not call it brave—that I could not rest satisfied where I was, and instead of blessing every leaf and twig that hid me from the enemy, nothing would do for me but to creep nearer, in spite of that truculent long bright spike.

I thought of my father, and each fibre of my frame seemed to harden with vigor and fleetness. Every muscle of my body could be trusted now. I had always been remarkably light of foot. Could a man of that age catch me? It was almost as much as Firm Gundry could do, as in childish days I had proved to him. And this man, although his hair was not gray, must be on the slow side of fifty now, and perhaps getting short of his very wicked breath. Then I thought of poor Firm, and of good Uncle Sam, and how they scorned poltroonery; and, better still, I thought of that great Power which always had protected me: in a word, I resolved to risk it.

But I had not reckoned upon fire-arms, which such a scoundrel was pretty sure to have; and that idea struck cold upon my valor. Nevertheless, I would not turn back. With no more sound than a field-mouse makes in the building of its silken nest, and feet as light as the step of the wind upon the scarcely ruffled grass, I quitted my screen, and went gliding down a hedge, or rather the residue of some old hedge, which would shelter me a little toward the hollow of the banks. I passed low places, where the man must have seen me if he had happened to look up; but he was stooping with his back to me, and working in the hollow of the dry water trough. He was digging with the long spike of his rod, and I heard the rattle of each pebble that he struck.

Before he stood up again, to ease his back and to look at the ground which he still had to turn, I was kneeling behind a short, close-branched holly, the very last bush of the hedge-row, scarcely fifteen yards from the hawthorn-tree. It was quite impossible to get nearer without coming face to face with him. And now I began again to tremble, but with a great effort conquered it.

The man was panting with his labor, and seemed to be in a vile temper too. He did not swear, but made low noises full of disappointment. And then he caught up his tool, with a savage self-control, and fell to again.

Now was my time to see what he was like, and engrave him on my memory. But, lo! in a moment I need not do that. The face was the bad image of my father's. A lowered, and vicious, and ill-bred image of a noble countenance—such as it was just possible to dream that my dear father's might have fallen to, if his mind and soul had plunged away from the good inborn and implanted in them. The figure was that of a tall strong man, with shoulders rather slouching, and a habit of keeping his head thrown back, which made a long chin look longer. Altogether he seemed a perilous foe, and perhaps a friend still more perilous.

Be he what he might, he was working very hard. Not one of all Uncle Sam's men, to my knowledge, least of all Martin, would have worked so hard. With his narrow and ill-adapted tool he contrived to turn over, in less than twenty minutes, the entire bed of the meadow-leet, or trough, for a length of about ten yards. Then he came to the mouth, where the water of the main stream lapped back into it, and he turned up the bottom as far as he could reach, and waited for the mud he had raised to clear away. When this had flowed down with the stream, he walked in for some little distance till the pool grew deep; but in spite of all his labor, there was nothing.

Meanwhile the sunset glow was failing, and a gray autumnal haze crept up the tranquil valley. Shadows waned and faded into dimness more diffuse, and light grew soft and vague and vaporous. The gleam of water, and the gloss of grass, and deep relief of trees, began to lose their several phase and mingle into one large twilight blend. And cattle, from their milking sheds, came lowing for more pasture; and the bark of a shepherd's dog rang quick, as if his sheep were drowsy.

In the midst of innocent sights and sounds that murderer's heart misgave him. He left his vain quest off, and gazed, with fear and hate of nature's beauty, at the change from day to night which had not waited for him. Some touch of his childhood moved him perhaps, some thought of times when he played "I spy," or listened to twilight ghost tales; at any rate, as he rose and faced the evening, he sighed heavily.

Then he strode away; and although he passed me almost within length of his rod, there was little fear of his discovering me, because his mind was elsewhere.

It will, perhaps, be confessed by all who are not as brave as lions that so far I had acquitted myself pretty well in this trying matter. Horribly scared as I was at first, I had not allowed this to conquer me, but had even rushed into new jeopardy. But now the best part of my courage was spent; and when the tall stranger refixed his rod and calmly recrossed those ominous planks, I durst not set forth on the perilous errand of spying out his ways and tracking him. A glance was enough to show the impossibility in those long meadows of following without being seen in this stage of the twilight. Moreover, my nerves had been tried too long, and presence of mind could not last forever. All I could do, therefore, was to creep as far as the trunk of the hawthorn-tree, and thence observe that my enemy did not return by the way he had come, but hastened down the dusky valley.

One part of his labors has not been described, though doubtless a highly needful one. To erase the traces of his work, or at least obscure them to a careless eye, when he had turned as much ground as he thought it worth his while to meddle with, he trod it back again to its level as nearly as might be, and then (with a can out of his fishing basket) sluiced the place well with the water of the stream. This made it look to any heedless person, who would not descend to examine it, as if there had been nothing more than a little reflux from the river, caused by a flush from the mill-pond. This little stratagem increased my fear of a cunning and active villain.

CHAPTER XLI
A STRONG TEMPTATION

Now it will be said, and I also knew, that there was nothing as yet, except most frail and feeble evidence, to connect that nameless stranger with the crime charged upon my father. Indeed, it might be argued well that there was no evidence at all, only inference and suspicion. That, however, was no fault of mine; and I felt as sure about it as if I had seen him in the very act. And this conclusion was not mine alone; for Mrs. Busk, a most clever woman, and the one who kept the post-office, entirely agreed with me that there could be no doubt on earth about it.

But when she went on to ask me what it was my intention to do next, for the moment I could do nothing more than inquire what her opinion was. And she told me that she must have a good night's rest before advising any thing. For the thought of having such a heinous character in her own delivery district was enough to unhinge her from her postal duties, some of which might be useful to me.

With a significant glance she left me to my own thoughts, which were sad enough, and too sad to be worth recording. For Mrs. Busk had not the art of rousing people and cheering them, such as Betsy Strouss, my old nurse, had, perhaps from her knowledge of the nursery. My present landlady might be the more sagacious and sensible woman of the two, and therefore the better adviser; but for keeping one up to the mark she was not in any way equal to Betsy.

There is no ingratitude in saying this, because she herself admitted it. A clever woman, with a well-balanced mind, knows what she can do, and wherein she fails, better than a man of her own proportion does. And Mrs. Busk often lamented, without much real mortification, that she had not been "born sympathetic."

All the more perhaps for that, she was born sagacious, which is a less pleasing, but, in a bitter pinch, a more really useful, quality. And before I had time to think much of her defects, in the crowd of more important thought, in she came again, with a letter in her hand, and a sparkle of triumph in her small black eyes. After looking back along the passage, and closing my door, she saw that my little bay-window had its old-fashioned shutters fastened, and then, in a very low whisper, she said, "What you want to know is here, miss."

"Indeed!" I answered, in my usual voice. "How can you know that? The letter is sealed."

"Hush! Would you have me ruined for your sake? This was at the bottom of the Nepheton bag. It fell on the floor. That was God's will, to place it in your power."

"It is not in my power," I answered, whispering in my turn, and staring at it, in the strong temptation. "I have no right even to look at it. It is meant for some one else, and sealed."

"The seal is nothing. I can manage that. Another drop of wax—and I strike our stamp by accident over the breakage. I refuse to know any thing about it. I am too busy with the other letters. Five minutes—lock the door—and I will come again."

This was a desperate conflict for me, worse even than bodily danger. My first impulse was to have nothing to do with it—even to let the letter lie untouched, and, if possible, unglanced at. But already it was too late for the eyes to turn away. The address had flashed upon me before I thought of any thing, and while Mrs. Busk held it up to me. And now that address was staring at me, like a contemptuous challenge, while the seal, the symbol of private rights and deterrent honor, lay undermost. The letter was directed to "H. W. C., Post-office, Newport, Sussex." The writing was in round hand, and clear, so as not to demand any scrutiny, and to seem like that of a lawyer's clerk, and the envelope was of thin repellent blue.

My second impulse was to break the letter open and read it without shrinking. Public duty must conquer private scruples. Nothing but the hand of Providence itself could have placed this deadly secret in my power so amazingly. Away with all squeamishness, and perhaps prevent more murder.

But that "perhaps" gave me sudden pause. I had caught up the letter, and stood near the candle to soften the wax and lift the cover with a small sharp paper-knife, when it flashed on my mind that my cousin would condemn and scorn what I was doing. Unconsciously I must have made him now my standard of human judgment, or what made me think of him at that moment? I threw down the letter, and then I knew. The image of Lord Castlewood had crossed my mind, because the initials were his own—those of Herbert William Castlewood. This strange coincidence—if it were, indeed, an accident—once more set me thinking. Might not this letter be from his agent, of whom he had spoken as my protector here, but to whom as all unseen I scarcely ever gave a thought? Might not young Stixon, who so often was at Bruntsea, be employed to call at Newport for such letters, and return with them to his master? It was not very likely, for my cousin had the strongest contempt of anonymous doings. Still it was possible, and the bare possibility doubled my reluctance to break the seal.

For one minute longer I stood in doubt, and then honor and candor and truth prevailed. If any other life had been in peril but my own, duty to another might have overridden all. But duty to one's self, if overpushed in such a case, would hold some taint of cowardice. So I threw the letter, with a sense of loathing, on a chair. Whatever it might contain, it should pass, at least for me, inviolate.

Now when Mrs. Busk came to see what I had done, or rather left undone, she flew into a towering passion, until she had no time to go on with it. The rattle of the rickety old mail-cart, on its way to Winchester that night, was heard, and the horn of the driver as he passed the church.

"Give it me. 'A mercy! A young natural, that you are!" the good woman cried, as she flung out of the room to dash her office stamp upon that hateful missive, and to seal the leathern bag. "Seal, indeed! Inviolate! How many seals have I got to make every day of my life?"

I heard a great thump from the corner of the shop where the business of the mails was conducted; and she told me afterward that she was so put out, that broken that seal should be—one way or another. Accordingly she smashed it with the office stamp, which was rather like a woman's act, methought; and then, having broken it, she never looked inside—which, perhaps, was even more so.

When she recovered her leisure and serenity, and came in, to forgive me and be forgiven, we resolved to dismiss the moral aspect of the question, as we never should agree about it, although Mrs. Busk was not so certain as she had been, when she found that the initials were the initials of a lord. And then I asked her how she came to fix upon that letter among so many others, and to feel so sure that it came from my treacherous enemy.

"In the first place, I know every letter from Nepheton," she answered, very sensibly. "There are only fourteen people that write letters in the place, and twelve of those fourteen buy their paper in my shop—there is no shop at all at Nepheton. In the next place, none of them could write a hand like that, except the parson and the doctor, who are far above disguise. And two other things made me certain as could be. That letter was written at the 'Green Man' ale-house; not on their paper, nor yet with their ink; but being in great hurry, it was dusted with their sand—a sand that turns red upon ink, miss. And the time of dispatch there is just what he would catch, by walking fast after his dig where you saw him, going in that direction too, and then having his materials ready to save time. And if all that is not enough to convince you, miss—you remember that you told me our old sexton's tale?"

"To be sure I do. The first evening I was left alone here. And you have been so kind, there is nothing I would hide from you."

"Well, miss, the time of old Jacob's tale is fixed by the death of poor old Sally Mock; and the stranger came again after you were here, just before the death of the miller's eldest daughter, and you might almost have seen him. Poor thing! we all called her the 'flower of the Moon,' meaning our little river. What a fine young woman she was, to be sure! Whenever we heard of any strangers about, we thought they were prowling after her. I was invited to her funeral, and I went, and nothing could be done nicer. But they never will be punctual with burials here; they like to dwell on them, and keep the bell going, for the sake of the body, and the souls that must come after it. And so, when it was done, I was twenty minutes late for the up mail and the cross-country post, and had to move my hands pretty sharp, I can assure you. That doesn't matter; I got through it, with the driver of the cart obliging, by means of some beer and cold bacon. But what I feared most was the Nepheton bag, having seen the old man at the funeral, and knowing what they do afterward. I could not return him 'too late' again, or he would lose his place for certain, and a shilling a day made all the difference to him, between wife and no wife. The old pair without it must go to the workhouse, and never see one another. However, when I was despairing quite of him, up he comes with his bag quite correct, but only one letter to sort in it, and that letter was, miss, the very identical of the one you held in your hands just now. And a letter as like it as two peas had come when we buried old Sally. It puzzled me then, but I had no clew to it; only now, you see, putting this and that together, the things we behold must have some meaning for us; and to let them go without it is against the will of God; especially when at the bottom of the bag."

"If you hear so soon of any stranger in the valley," I asked, to escape the re-opening of the opening question, "how can that man come and go—a man of remarkable stature and appearance—without any body asking who he is?"

"You scarcely could have put it better, miss, for me to give the answer. They do ask who he is, and they want to know it, and would like any body to tell them. But being of a different breed, as they are, from all outside the long valley, speaking also with a different voice, they fear to talk so freely out of their own ways and places. Any thing they can learn in and out among themselves, they will learn; but any thing out of that they let go, in the sense of outlandish matter. Bless you, miss, if your poor grandfather had been shot any where else in England, how different it would have been for him!"

"For us, you mean, Mrs. Busk. Do you think the man who did it had that in his mind?"

"Not unless he knew the place, as few know it. No, that was an accident of his luck, as many other things have been. But the best luck stops at last, Miss Erema; and unless I am very much mistaken, you will be the stop of his. I shall find out, in a few days, where he came from, where he staid, and when he went away. I suppose you mean to let him go away?"

"What else am I to do?" I asked. "I have no evidence at all against him; only my own ideas. The police would scarcely take it up, even if—"

"Oh, don't talk of them. They spoil every thing. And none of our people would say a word, or care to help us, if it came to that. The police are all strangers, and our people hate them. And, indeed, I believe that the worst thing ever done was the meddling of that old Jobbins. The old stupe is still alive at Petersfield, and as pompous-headed as ever. My father would have been the man for your sad affair, miss, if the police had only been invented in his time. Ah, yes, he was sharp! Not a Moonstock man—you may take your oath of that, miss—but a good honest native from Essex. But he married my mother, a Moonstock woman; or they would not put up with me here at all. You quality people have your ideas to hold by, and despise all others, and reasonable in your opinions; but you know nothing—nothing—nothing—of the stiffness of the people under you."

"How should I know any thing of that?" I answered; "all these things are new to me. I have not been brought up in this country, as you know. I come from a larger land, where your stiffness may have burst out into roughness, from having so much room suddenly. But tell me what you think now your father would have done in such a case as mine is."

"Miss Erema, he was that long-headed that nobody could play leap-frog with him. None of them ever cleared over his barrel. He walked into this village fifty-five years back, this very month, with his spade upon his shoulder and the knowledge of every body in his eye. They all put up against him, but they never put him down; and in less than three months he went to church, I do assure you, with the only daughter of the only baker. After that he went into the baking line himself; he turned his spade into a shovel, as he said, and he introduced new practices."

"Oh, Mrs. Busk, not adulteration?"

"No, miss, no! The very last thing he would think of. Only the good use of potatoes in the bread, when flour was frightful bad and painful dear. What is the best meal of the day? he used to reason. Dinner. And why? Why, because of the potatoes. If I can make people take potato for their breakfast, and potato for their supper too, I am giving them three meals a day instead of one. And the health of the village corresponded to it."

"Oh, but, Mrs. Busk, he might have made them do it by persuasion, or at least with their own knowledge—"

"No, miss, no! The whole nature of our people, Moonstock or out of it, is never to take victuals by any sort of persuasion. If St. Paul was to come and preach, 'Eat this or that,' all I had of it in the shop would go rotten. They hate any meddling with their likings, and they suspect doctor's rubbish in all of it."

"I am quite of their opinion," I replied; "and I am glad to hear of their independence. I always used to hear that in England none of the poor people dared have a will of their own."

Mrs. Busk lifted up her hands to express amazement at my ignorance, and said that she "must run away and put the shutters up, or else the policeman would come rapping, and look for a glass of beer, which he had no right to till it came to the bottom of the firkin; and this one was only tapped last Sunday week. Don't you ever think of the police, miss."

Probably this was good advice, and it quite agreed with the opinions of others, and my own impressions as to the arrogant lethargy of "the force," as they called themselves, in my father's case. Mrs. Busk had more activity and intelligence in her little head than all the fat sergeants and inspectors of the county, helmet, belt, and staff, and all.

CHAPTER XLII
MASTER WITHYPOOL

At first I was much inclined to run for help, or at least for counsel, either to Lord Castlewood or to Major Hockin; but further consideration kept me from doing any thing of the kind. In the first place, neither of them would do much good; for my cousin's ill health would prevent him from helping me, even if his strange view of the case did not, while the excellent Major was much too hot and hasty for a delicate task like this. And, again, I might lose the most valuable and important of all chances by being away from the spot just now. And so I remained at Shoxford for a while, keeping strict watch upon the stranger's haunt, and asking about him by means of Mrs. Busk.

"I have heard more about him, miss," she said one day, when the down letters had been dispatched, which happened about middle-day. "He has been here only those three times this summer, upon excuse of fishing always. He stays at old Wellham, about five miles down the river, where the people are not true Moonites. And one thing that puzzles them is, that although he puts up there simply for the angling, he always chooses times when the water is so low that to catch fish is next to impossible. He left his fishing quarters upon the very day after you saw him searching so; and he spoke as if he did not mean to come again this season. And they say that they don't want him neither, he is such a morose, close-fisted man; and drinking nothing but water, there is very little profit with him."

"And did you find out what his name is? How cleverly you have managed!"

"He passes by the name of 'Captain Brown;' but the landlord of his inn, who has been an old soldier, is sure he was never in the army, nor any other branch of the service. He thinks that he lives by inventing things, for he is always at some experiments, and one of his great points is to make a lamp that will burn and move about under water. To be sure you see the object of that, miss?"

"No, really, Mrs. Busk, I can not. I have not your penetration."

"Why, of course, to find what he can not find upon land. There is something of great importance there, either for its value or its meaning. Have you ever been told that your poor grandfather wore any diamonds or precious jewels?"

"No. I have asked about that most especially. He had nothing about him to tempt a robber. He was a very strong-willed man, and he hated outward trumpery."

"Then it must be something that this man himself has dropped, unless it were a document, or any other token, missing from his lordship. And few things of that sort would last for twenty years almost."

"Nineteen years the day after to-morrow," I answered, with a glance at my pocket-book. "I determined to be here on that very day. No doubt I am very superstitious. But one thing I can not understand is this—what reason can there have been for his letting so many years pass, and then hunting like this?"

"No one can answer that question, miss, without knowing more than we know. But many reasons might be supposed. He might have been roving abroad, for instance, just as you and your father have been. Or he might not have known that the thing was there; or it might not have been of importance till lately; or he might have been afraid, until something else happened. Does he know that you are now in England?"

"How can I possibly tell, Mrs. Busk? He seems to know a great deal too much. He found me out when I was at Colonel Gundry's. At least I conclude so, from what I know now; but I hope he does not know"—and at such a dreadful idea I shuddered.

"I am almost sure that he can not know it," the good postmistress answered, "or he would have found means to put an end to you. That would have been his first object."

"But, Mrs. Busk," I said, being much disturbed by her calmness, "surely, surely he is not to be allowed to make an end of every one! I came to this country with the full intention of going into every thing. But I did not mean at all, except in my very best moments, to sacrifice myself. It seems too bad—too bad to think of."

"So it is, Miss Erema," Mrs. Busk replied, without any congenial excitement. "It does seem hard for them that have the liability on them. But still, miss, you have always shown such a high sense of duty, and of what you were about—"

"I can't—I can not. There are times, I do assure you, when I am fit for nothing, Mrs. Busk, and wish myself back in America. And if this man is to have it all his own way—"

"Not he, miss—not he. Be you in no hurry. Could he even have his way with our old miller? No; Master Withypool was too many for him."

"That is a new thing. You never told me that. What did he try to do with the miller?"

"I don't justly know what it was, Miss Erema. I never spoke to miller about it, and, indeed, I have had no time since I heard of it. But those that told me said that the tall strange gentleman was terribly put out, and left the gate with a black cloud upon his face, and the very next day the miller's daughter died, quite sudden and mysterious."

"How very strange! But now I have got a new idea. Has the miller a strong high dam to his pond, and a good stout sluice-gate at the end!"

"Yes, miss, to be sure he has," said Mrs. Busk; "otherwise how could he grind at all, when the river is so low as it is sometimes?"

"Then I know what he wanted, and I will take a leaf out of his own book—the miscreant! He wanted the miller to stop back the water and leave the pool dry at the 'Murder-bridge.' Would it be possible for him to do that?"

"I can not tell you, miss; but your thought is very clever. It is likely enough that he did want that, though he never would dare to ask without some pretense—some other cause I mean, to show for it. He may have been thinking that whatever he was wanting was likely to be under water. And that shows another thing, if it is so."

"Mrs. Busk, my head goes round with such a host of complications. I do my best to think them out—and then there comes another!"

"No, miss; this only clears things up a little. If the man can not be sure whether what he is looking for is on land or under water, it seems to me almost to show that it was lost at the murder time in the dark and flurry. A man would know if he dropped any thing in the water by daylight, from the splash and the ripple, and so on, for the stream is quite slow at that corner. He dropped it, miss, when he did the deed, or else it came away from his lordship."

"Nothing was lost, as I said before, from the body of my grandfather, so far at least as our knowledge goes. Whatever was lost was the murderer's. Now please to tell me all about the miller, and how I may get round him."

"You make me laugh in the middle of black things, miss, by the way you have of putting them. But as to the miller—Master Withypool is a wonder, as concerns the ladies. He is one of those men that stand up for every thing when a man tries upper side of them. But let a woman come, and get up under, and there he is—a pie crust lifted. Why, I, at my age, could get round him, as you call it. But you, miss—and more than that, you are something like his daughter; and the old man frets after her terrible. Go you into his yard, and just smile upon him, miss, and if the Moon River can be stopped, he'll stop it for you."

This seemed a very easy way to do it. But I told Mrs. Busk that I would pay well also, for the loss of a day's work at the mill was more than fifty smiles could make up.

But she told me, above all things, not to do that. For old Master Withypool was of that sort that he would stand for an hour with his hands in his pocket for a half-penny, if not justly owing from him. But nothing more angered him than a bribe to step outside of his duty. He had plenty of money, and was proud of it. But sooner would he lose a day's work to do a kindness, when he was sure of having right behind it, than take a week's profit without earning it. And very likely that was where the dark man failed, from presuming that money would do every thing. However, there was nothing like judging for one's self; and if I would like to be introduced, she could do it for me with the best effect; taking as she did a good hundred-weight of best "households" from him every week, although not herself in the baking line, but always keeping quartern bags, because the new baker did adulterate so.

I thought of her father, and how things work round; but that they would do without remarks of mine. So I said nothing on that point, but asked whether Master Withypool would require any introduction. And to this Mrs. Busk said, "Oh dear, no!" And her throat had been a little rough since Sunday, and the dog was chained tight, even if any dog would bite a sweet young lady; and to her mind the miller would be more taken up and less fit to vapor into obstacles, if I were to hit upon him all alone, just when he came out to the bank of his cabbage garden, not so very long after his dinner, to smoke his pipe and to see his things a-growing.

It was time to get ready if I meant to catch him then, for he always dined at one o'clock, and the mill was some three or four meadows up the stream; therefore as soon as Mrs. Busk had re-assured me that she was quite certain of my enemy's departure, I took my drawing things and set forth to call upon Master Withypool.

Passing through the church-yard, which was my nearest way, and glancing sadly at the "fairy ring," I began to have some uneasiness about the possible issue of my new scheme. Such a thing required more thinking out than I had given to it. For instance, what reason could I give the miller for asking so strange a thing of him? And how could the whole of the valley be hindered from making the greatest talk about the stoppage of their own beloved Moon, even if the Moon could be stopped without every one of them rushing down to see it? And if it was so talked of, would it not be certain to come to the ears of that awful man? And if so, how long before he found me out, and sent me to rejoin my family?

These thoughts compelled me to be more discreet; and having lately done a most honorable thing, in refusing to read that letter, I felt a certain right to play a little trick now of a purely harmless character. I ran back therefore to my writing-desk, and took from its secret drawer a beautiful golden American eagle, a large coin, larger and handsomer than any in the English coinage. Uncle Sam gave it to me on my birthday, and I would not have taken 50 pounds for it. With this I hurried to that bridge of fear, which I had not yet brought myself to go across; and then, not to tell any story about it, I snipped a little hole in the corner of my pocket, while my hand was still steady ere I had to mount the bridge. Then pinching that hole up with a squeeze, I ran and got upon that wicked bridge, and then let go. The heavy gold coin fell upon the rotten plank, and happily rolled into the water, as if it were glad not to tempt its makers to any more sin for the sake of it.

Shutting up thought, for fear of despising myself for the coinage of such a little trick, I hurried across the long meadow to the mill, and went through the cow-gate into the yard, and the dog began to bark at me. Seeing that he had a strong chain on, I regarded him with lofty indignation. "Do you know what Jowler would do to you?" I said; "Jowler, a dog worth ten of you. He would take you by the neck and drop you into that pond for daring to insult his mistress!" The dog appeared to feel the force of my remarks, for he lay down again, and with one eye watched me in a manner amusing, but insidious. Then, taking good care to keep out of his reach, I went to the mill-pond and examined it.

It looked like a very nice pond indeed, long, and large, and well banked up, not made into any particular shape, but producing little rushy elbows. The water was now rather low, and very bright (though the Moon itself is not a crystal stream), and a school of young minnows, just watching a water-spider with desirous awe, at sight of me broke away, and reunited, with a speed and precision that might shame the whole of our very best modern fighting. Then many other things made a dart away, and furrowed the shadow of the willows, till distance quieted the fear of man—that most mysterious thing in nature—and the shallow pool was at peace again, and bright with unruffled reflections.

"What ails the dog?" said a deep gruff voice; and the poor dog received a contemptuous push, not enough to hurt him, but to wound his feelings for doing his primary duty. "Servant, miss. What can I do for you? Foot-path is t'other side of that there hedge."

"Yes, but I left the foot-path on purpose. I came to have a talk with you, if you will allow me."

"Sartain! sartain," the miller replied, lifting a broad floury hat and showing a large gray head. "Will you come into house, miss, or into gearden?"

I chose the garden, and he led the way, and set me down upon an old oak bench, where the tinkle of the water through the flood-gates could be heard.

"So you be come to paint the mill at last," he said. "Many a time I've looked out for you. The young leddy down to Mother Busk's, of course. Many's the time we've longed for you to come, you reminds us so of somebody. Why, my old missus can't set eyes on you in church, miss, without being forced to sit down a'most. But we thought it very pretty of you not to come, miss, while the trouble was so new upon us."

Something in my look or voice made the old man often turn away, while I told him that I would make the very best drawing of his mill that I could manage, and would beg him to accept it.

"Her ought to 'a been on the plank," he said, with trouble in getting his words out. "But there! what good? Her never will stand on that plank no more. No, nor any other plank."

I told him that I would put her on the plank, if he had any portrait of her showing her dress and her attitude. Without saying what he had, he led me to the house, and stood behind me, while I went inside. And then he could not keep his voice as I went from one picture of his darling to another, not thinking (as I should have done) of what his feelings might be, but trying, as no two were at all alike, to extract a general idea of her.

"Nobody knows what her were to me," the old man said, with a quiet little noise and a sniff behind my shoulder. "And with one day's illness her died—her died."

"But you have others left. She was not the only one. Please, Mr. Withypool, to try to think of that. And your dear wife still alive to share your trouble. Just think for a moment of what happened to my father. His wife and six children all swept off in a month—and I just born, to be brought up with a bottle!"

I never meant, of course, to have said a word of this, but was carried away by that common old idea of consoling great sorrow with a greater one. And the sense of my imprudence broke vexatiously upon me when the old man came and stood between me and his daughter's portraits.

"Well, I never!" he exclaimed, with his bright eyes steadfast with amazement. "I know you now, miss. Now I knows you. To think what a set of blind newts us must be! And you the very moral of your poor father, in a female kind of way! To be sure, how well I knew the Captain! A nicer man never walked the earth, neither a more unlucky one."

"I beg you—let me beg you," I began to say; "since you have found me out like this—"

"Hush, miss, hush! Not my own wife shall know, unless your own tongue telleth her. A proud man I shall be, Miss Raumur," he continued, with emphasis on my local name, "if aught can be found in my power to serve you. Why, Lord bless you, miss," he whispered, looking round, "your father and I has spent hours together! He were that pleasant in his ways and words, he would drop in from his fishing, when the water was too low, and sit on that very same bench where you sat, and smoke his pipe with me, and tell me about battles, and ask me about bread. And many a time I have slipped up the gate, to give him more water for his flies to play, and the fish not to see him so plainly. Ah, we have had many pleasant spells together; and his eldest boy and girl, Master George and Miss Henrietta, used to come and fetch our eggs. My Polly there was in love with him, we said; she sat upon his lap so, when she were two years old, and played with his beautiful hair, and blubbered—oh, she did blubber, when the Captain went away!"

This invested Polly with new interest for me, and made me determine to spare no pains in putting her pretty figure well upon the plank. Then I said to the miller, "How kind of you to draw up your sluice-gates to oblige my father! Now will you put them down and keep them down, to do a great service both to him and me?"

Without a moment's hesitation, he promised that any thing he could do should be done, if I would only tell him what I wanted. But perhaps it would be better to have our talk outside. Taking this hint, I followed him back to the bench in the open garden, and there explained what I wished to have done, and no longer concealed the true reason. The good miller answered that with all his heart he would do that much to oblige me, and a hundred times more than that; but some little thought and care were needful. With the river so low as it was now, he could easily stop the back-water, and receive the whole of the current in his dam, and keep it from flowing down his wheel trough, and thus dry the lower channel for perhaps half an hour, which would be ample for my purpose. Engineering difficulties there were none; but two or three other things must be heeded. Miller Sims, a mile or so down river, must be settled with, to fill his dam well, and begin to discharge, when the upper water failed, so as not to dry the Moon all down the valley, which would have caused a commotion. Miller Sims being own brother-in-law to Master Withypool, that could be arranged easily enough, after one day's notice. But a harder thing to manage would be to do the business without rousing curiosity, and setting abroad a rumor which would be sure to reach my enemy. And the hardest thing of all, said Master Withypool, smiling as he thought of what himself had once been, would be to keep those blessed boys away, who find out every thing, and go every where. Not a boy of Shoxford but would be in the river, or dancing upon its empty bed, screeching and scolloping up into his cap any poor bewildered trout chased into the puddles, if it were allowed to leak out, however feebly, that the Moon water was to stop running. And then how was I to seek for any thing?

This was a puzzle. But, with counsel, we did solve it. And we quietly stopped the Moon, without man or boy being much the wiser.

CHAPTER XLIII
GOING TO THE BOTTOM

It is not needful to explain every thing, any more than it was for me to tell the miller about my golden eagle, and how I had managed to lose it in the Moon—a trick of which now I was heartily ashamed, in the face of honest kindness. So I need not tell how Master Withypool managed to settle with his men, and to keep the boys unwitting of what was about to come to pass. Enough that I got a note from him to tell me that the little river would be run out, just when all Shoxford was intent upon its dinner, on the second day after I had seen him. And he could not say for certain, but thought it pretty safe, that nobody would come near me, if I managed to be there at a quarter before one, when the stream would begin to run dry, and I could watch it. I sent back a line by the pretty little girl, a sister of poor Polly, to say how much I thanked him, and how much I hoped that he himself would meet me there, if his time allowed. For he had been too delicate to say a word of that; but I felt that he had a good right to be there, and, knowing him now, I was not afraid.

Nearly every thing came about as well as could be wished almost. Master Withypool took the precaution, early in the morning, to set his great fierce bull at large, who always stopped the foot-path. This bull knew well the powers of a valley in conducting sound; and he loved to stand, as if at the mouth of a funnel, and roar down it to another bull a mile below him, belonging to his master's brother-in-law. And when he did this, there was scarcely a boy, much less a man or woman, with any desire to assert against him the public right of thoroughfare. Throughout that forenoon, then, this bull bellowed nobly, still finding many very wicked flies about, so that two mitching boys, who meant to fish for minnows with a pin, were obliged to run away again.

However, I was in the dark about him, and as much afraid of him as any body, when he broke into sight of me round a corner, without any tokens of amity. I had seen a great many great bulls before, including Uncle Sam's good black one, who might not have meant any mischief at all, and atoned for it—if he did—by being washed away so.

And therefore my courage soon returned, when it became quite clear that this animal now had been fastened with a rope, and could come no nearer. For some little time, then, I waited all alone, as near that bridge as I could bring myself to stand, for Mrs. Busk, my landlady, could not leave the house yet, on account of the mid-day letters. Moreover, she thought that she had better stay away, as our object was to do things as quietly as could be.

Much as I had watched this bridge from a distance, or from my sheltering-place, I had never been able to bring myself to make any kind of sketch of it, or even to insert it in a landscape, although it was very well suited and expressive, from its crooked and antique simplicity. The overhanging, also, of the hawthorn-tree (not ruddy yet, but russety with its coloring crop of coral), and the shaggy freaks of ivy above the twisted trunk, and the curve of the meadows and bold elbow of the brook, were such as an artist would have pitched his tent for, and tantalized poor London people with a dream of cool repose.

As yet the little river showed no signs of doing what the rustic—or surely it should have been the cockney—was supposed to stand still and wait for. There was no great rush of headlong water, for that is not the manner of the stream in the very worst of weather; but there was the usual style of coming on, with lips and steps at the sides, and cords of running toward the middle. Quite enough, at any rate, to make the trout jump, without any omen of impending drought, and to keep all the play and the sway of movement going on serenely.

I began to be afraid that the miller must have failed in his stratagem against the water-god, and that, as I had read in Pope's Homer, the liquid deity would beat the hero, when all of a sudden there were signs that man was the master of this little rustic. Broadswords of flag and rapiers of water-grass, which had been quivering merrily, began to hang down and to dip themselves in loops, and the stones of the brink showed dark green stripes on their sides as they stood naked. Then fine little cakes of conglomerated stuff, which only a great man of nature could describe, came floating about, and curdling into corners, and holding on to one another in long-tailed strings. But they might do what they liked, and make their very best of it, as they fell away to nothing upon stones and mud. For now more important things began to open, the like of which never had been yielded up before— plots of slimy gravel, varied with long streaks of yellow mud, dotted with large double shells, and parted into little oozy runs by wriggling water-weeds. And here was great commotion and sad panic of the fish, large fellows splashing and quite jumping out of water, as their favorite hovers and shelves ran dry, and darting away, with their poor backs in the air, to the deepest hole they could think of. Hundreds must have come to flour, lard, and butter if boys had been there to take advantage. But luckily things had been done so well that boys were now in their least injurious moment, destroying nothing worse than their own dinners.

A very little way below the old wooden bridge the little river ran into a deepish pool, as generally happens at or near a corner, especially where there is a confluence sometimes. And seeing nothing, as I began to search intently, stirring with a long-handled spud which I had brought, I concluded that even my golden eagle had been carried into that deep place. However, water or no water, I resolved to have it out with that dark pool as soon as the rest of the channel should be drained, which took a tormenting time to do; and having thick boots on, I pinned up my skirts, and jumping down into the shoals, began to paddle in a fashion which reminded me of childish days passed pleasantly in the Blue River.

Too busy thus to give a thought to any other thing, I did not even see the miller, until he said,

"Good-day, miss," lifting his hat, with a nice kind smile. "Very busy, miss, I see, and right you are to be so. The water will be upon us again in less than half an hour. Now let me clear away they black weeds for you. I brought this little shivel a-purpose. If I may make so bold, miss, what do 'e look to find here?"

"I have not the very smallest notion," I could only answer; "but if there is any thing, it must be in that hole. I have searched all the shallow part so closely that I doubt whether even a sixpence could escape me, unless it were buried in the mud or pebbles. Oh, how can I manage to search that hole? There must be a yard of water there."

"One thing I ought to have told 'e for to do," Master Withypool whispered, as he went on shoveling—"to do what the boys do when they lose a farden—to send another after un. If so be now, afore the water was run out, you had stood on that there bridge, and dropped a bright coin into it, a new half crown or a two-shilling piece, why, the chances would be that the run of the current would 'a taken it nigh to the likeliest spot for holding any other little matter as might 'a dropped, permiskous, you might say, into this same water."

"I have done so," I answered; "I have done that very thing, though not at all with that object. The day before yesterday a beautiful coin, a golden eagle of America, fell from my pocket on that upper plank, and rolled into the water. I would not lose it for a great deal, because it was given to me by my dearest friend, the greatest of all millers."

"And ha'n't you found it yet, miss? Well, that is queer. Perhaps we shall find it now, with something to the back of it. I thought yon hole was too far below the bridge. But there your gold must be, and something else, most likely. Plaise to wait a little bit, and us 'll have the wet out of un. I never should 'a thought of that but for your gold guinea, though."

With these words Master Withypool pulled his coat off and rolled up his shirt sleeves, displaying arms fit to hold their own even with Uncle Sam's almost; and then he fell to with his shovel and dug, while I ran with my little spud to help.

"Plaise keep out of way, miss; I be afeard of knocking you. Not but what you works very brave indeed, miss."

Knowing what men are concerning "female efforts," I got out of the strong man's way, although there was plenty of room for me. What he wanted to do was plain enough—to dig a trench down the empty bed of the Moon River, deep enough to drain that pit before the stream came down again.

"Never thought to run a race against my own old dam," he said, as he stopped for a moment to recover breath. "Us never knows what us may have to do. Old dam must be a'most busting now. But her's sound enough, till her beginneth to run over."

I did not say a word, because it might have done some mischief, but I could not help looking rather anxiously up stream, for fear of the water coming down with a rush, as it very soon must do. Master Withypool had been working, not as I myself would have done, from the lips of the dark pit downward, but from a steep run some twenty yards below, where there was almost a little cascade when the river was full flowing; from this he had made his channel upward, cutting deeper as he came along, till now, at the brink of the obstinate pool, his trench was two feet deep almost. I had no idea that any man could work so with a shovel, which seems such a clumsy tool compared with a spade: but a gentleman who knows the country and the people told me that, with their native weapon, Moonites will do as much digging in an hour as other folk get through in an hour and a half with a spade. But this may be only, perhaps, because they are working harder.

"Now," said Master Withypool at last, standing up, with a very red face, and desiring to keep all that unheeded—"now, miss, to you it belongeth to tap this here little cornder, if desirable. Plaise to excoose of me going up of bank to tell 'e when the wet cometh down again."

"Please to do nothing of the sort," I answered, knowing that he offered to stand out of sight from a delicate dread of intrusion. "Please to tap the pool yourself, and stay here, as a witness of what we find in it."

"As you plaise, miss, as you plaise. Not a moment for to lose in arguing. Harken now, the water is atopping of our dam. Her will be here in five minutes."

With three or four rapid turns of his shovel, which he spun almost as fast as a house-maid spins a mop, he fetched out the plug of earth severing his channel from the deep, reluctant hole. And then I saw the wisdom of his way of working: for if he had dug downward from the pool itself, the water would have followed him all the way, and even drowned his tool out of its own strokes; whereas now, with a swirl and a curl of ropy mud, away rushed the thick, sluggish, obstinate fluid, and in less than two minutes the hole was almost dry.

The first thing I saw was my golden eagle, lodged about half-way down the slope on a crust of black sludge, from which I caught it up and presented it to Master Withypool, as a small token and record of his kindness; and to this day he carries it upon his Sunday watch chain.

"I always am lucky in finding things," I exclaimed, while he watched me, and the up stream too, whence a babble of water was approaching. "As sure as I live I have found it!"

"No doubt about your living, miss. And the Captain were always lively. But what have your bright eyes hit upon? I see nort for the life of me."

"Look there," I cried, "at the very bottom of it—almost under the water. Here, where I put my spud—a bright blue line! Oh, can I go down, or is it quicksand?"

"No quicksand in our little river, miss. But your father's daughter shannot go into the muck, while John Withypool stands by. I see un now, sure enough; now I see un! But her needeth care, or her may all goo away in mullock. Well, I thought my eyes was sharp enough; but I'm blest if I should have spied that, though. A bit of flint, mebbe, or of blue glass bottle. Anyhow, us will see the bottom of un."

He was wasting no time while he spoke, but working steadfastly for his purpose, fixing the blade of his shovel below the little blue line I was peering at, so that no slip of the soft yellow slush should bury it down, and plunge over it. If that had once happened, good-by to all chance of ever beholding this thing again, for the river was coming, with fury and foam, to assert its ancient right of way.

With a short laugh the miller jumped down into the pit. "Me to be served so, by my own mill-stream! Lor', if I don't pay you out for this!"

His righteous wrath failed to stop the water from pouring into the pit behind him; and, strong as he was, he nearly lost his footing, having only mud to stand upon. It seemed to me that he was going to be drowned, and I offered him the handle of my spud to help him; but he stopped where he was, and was not going to be hurried.

"I got un now," he said; "now I don't mind coming out. You see if I don't pay you out for this! Why, I always took you for a reasonable hanimal."

He shook his fist strongly at the river, which had him well up to the middle by this time; and then he disdainfully waded out, with wrath in all his countenance.

"I've a great mind to stop there, and see what her would do," he said to me, forgetting altogether what he went for. "And I would, if I had had my dinner. A scat of a thing as I can manage with my thumb! Ah, you have made a bad day of it."

"But what have you found, Mr. Withypool?" I asked, for I could not enter into his wrath against the water, wet as he was to the shoulders. "You have something in your hand. May I see it, if you please? And then do please to go home and change your clothes."

"A thing I never did in my life, miss, and should be ashamed to begin at this age. Clothes gets wet, and clothes dries on us, same as un did on the sheep afore us; else they gets stiff and creasy. What this little thing is ne'er a body may tell, in my line of life—but look'th aristocratic."

The "mullock," as he called it, from his hands, and from the bed where it had lain so long, so crusted the little thing which he gave me, that I dipped it again in the swelling stream, and rubbed it with both hands, to make out what it was. And then I thought how long it had lain there; and suddenly to my memory it came, that in all likelihood the time of that was nineteen years this very day.

"Will another year pass," I cried, "before I make out all about it? What are you, and who, now looking at me with such sad, sad eyes?"

For I held in my hand a most handsome locket, of blue enamel and diamonds, with a back of chased gold, and in front the miniature of a beautiful young woman, done as they never seem to do them now. The work was so good, and the fitting so close, that no drop of water had entered, and the face shone through the crystal glass as fresh as the day it was painted. A very lovely face it was, yet touched with a shade of sadness, as the loveliest faces generally are; and the first thought of any beholder would be, "That woman was born for sorrow."

The miller said as much when I showed it to him.

"Lord bless my heart! I hope the poor craitur' hathn't lasted half so long as her pictur' hath."

CHAPTER XLIV
HERMETICALLY SEALED

The discovery which I have described above (but not half so well as the miller tells it now) created in my young heart a feeling of really strong curiosity. To begin with, how could this valuable thing have got into the Moon-stream, and lain there so long, unsought for, or at best so unskillfully sought for? What connection could it have with the tragic death of my grandfather? Why was that man so tardily come to search for it, if he might do so without any body near him? Again, what woman was this whose beauty no water or mud could even manage to disguise? That last was a most disturbing question to one's bodily peace of mind. And then came another yet more urgent—what was in the inside of this tight case?

That there was something inside of it seemed almost a certainty. The mere value of the trinket, or even the fear that it ever might turn up as evidence, would scarcely have brought that man so often to stir suspicion by seeking it; though, after so long a time, he well might hope that suspicion was dead and buried. And being unable to open this case—after breaking three good nails over it, and then the point of a penknife—I turned to Master Withypool, who was stamping on the grass to drain himself.

"What sort of a man was that," I asked, "who wanted you to do what now you have so kindly done for me? About a month or six weeks ago? Do please to tell me, as nearly as you can."

If Mrs. Withypool had been there, she might have lost all patience with me for putting long questions so selfishly to a man who had done so much for me, and whose clothes were now dripping in a wind which had arisen to test his theory of drying. He must have lost a large quantity of what scientific people call "caloric." But never a shiver gave he in exchange.

"Well, miss," he said, "I was thinking a'most of speaking on that very matter. More particular since you found that little thing, with the pretty lady inside of it. It were borne in on my mind that thissom were the very thing he were arter."

"No doubt of it," I answered, with far less patience, though being comparatively dry. "But what was he like? Was he like this portrait?"

"This picture of the lady? No; I can't say that he were, so much. The face of a big man he hath, with short black fringes to it. Never showeth to my idea any likeliness of a woman. No, no, miss; think you not at all that you have got him in that blue thing. Though some of their pictures is like men, the way they dress up nowadays."

"I did not mean that it was meant for him; what I mean is, do you see any sign of family likeness? Any resemblance about the eyes, or mouth, or forehead?"

"Well, now, I don't know but what I might," replied Master Withypool, gazing very hard; "if I was to look at 'un long enough, a' might find some'at favoring of that tall fellow, I do believe. Indeed, I do believe the more I look, the more I diskivers the image of him."

The good and kind miller's perception of the likeness strengthened almost too fast, as if the wish were father to the thought, until I saw clearly how selfish I was in keeping him in that state so long; for I knew, from what Mrs. Busk had told me, that in spite of all his large and grand old English sentiments about his clothes, his wife would make him change them all ere ever she gave him a bit of dinner, and would force him then to take a glass of something hot. So I gave him a thousand thanks, though not a thousandth part of what he deserved, and saw him well on his homeward way before I went back to consider things.

As soon as my landlady was at leisure to come in and talk with me, and as soon as I had told her how things happened, and shown her our discovery, we both of us did the very same thing, and said almost the very same words. Our act was, with finger and nail and eye, to rime into every jot of it; and our words were,

"I am sure there is something inside. If not, it would open sensibly."

In the most senseless and obstinate manner it refused not only to open, but to disclose any thing at all about itself. Whether it ever had been meant to open, and if so, where, and by what means; whether, without any gift of opening, it might have a hidden thing inside; whether, when opened by force or skill, it might show something we had no business with, or (which would be far worse) nothing at all—good Mrs. Busk and myself tested, tapped, and felt, and blew, and listened, and tried every possible overture, and became at last quite put out with it.

"It is all of a piece with the villains that owned it," the postmistress exclaimed at last. "There is no penetrating either it or them. Most likely they have made away with this beautiful lady on the cover. Kill one, kill fifty, I have heard say. I hope Master Withypool will let out nothing, or evil it will be for you, miss. If I was you, I would carry a pistol."

"Now please not to frighten me, Mrs. Busk. I am not very brave at the best of times, and this has made me so nervous. If I carried a pistol, I should shoot myself the very first hour of wearing it. The mere thought of it makes me tremble. Oh, why was I ever born, to do man's work?"

"Because, miss, a man would not have done it half so well. When you saw that villain digging, a man would have rushed out and spoiled all chance. And now what man could have ever found this? Would Master Withypool ever have emptied the Moon River for a man, do you think? Or could any man have been down among us all this time, in this jealous place, without his business being long ago sifted out and scattered over him? No, no, miss; you must not talk like that—and with me as well to help you. The rogues will have reason to wish, I do believe, that they had only got a man to deal with."

In this argument there were points which had occurred to me before; but certainly it is a comfort to have one's own ideas in a doubtful matter reproduced, and perhaps put better, by a mind to which one may have lent them, perhaps, with a loan all unacknowledged. However, trouble teaches care, and does it so well that the master and the lesson in usage of words are now the same; therefore I showed no sign of being suggested with my own suggestions, but only asked, quietly, "What am I to do?"

"My dear young lady," Mrs. Busk replied, after stopping some time to think of it, "my own opinion is, for my part, that you ought to consult somebody."

"But I am, Mrs. Busk. I am now consulting you."

"Then I think, miss, that this precious case should be taken at once to a jeweler, who can open it without doing any damage, which is more than we can do."

"To be sure; I have thought of that," I replied. "But how can that be done without arousing curiosity?—without the jeweler seeing its contents, if indeed it has any? And in that case the matter would be no longer at our own disposal, as now it is. I have a great mind to split it with a hammer. What are the diamonds to me?"

"It is not the diamonds, but the picture, miss, that may be most important. And more than that, you might ruin the contents, so as not to make head or tale of them. No, no; it is a risk that must be run; we must have a jeweler, but not one of this neighborhood."

"Then I shall have to go to London again, and perhaps lose something most important here. Can you think of no other way out of it?"

"No, miss, at present I see nothing else. Unless you will place it all in the hands of the police."

"Constable Jobbins, to wit, or his son! No, thank you, Mrs. Busk, not yet. Surely we are not quite reduced to such a hopeless pass as that. My father knew what the police were worth, and so does Betsy, and so does Major Hockin. 'Pompous noodles,' the Major calls them, who lay hold of every thing by the wrong end."

"Then if he can lay hold of the right end, miss, what better could you do than consult him?"

I had been thinking of this already, and pride alone debarred me. That gentleman's active nature drove him to interfere with other people's business, even though he had never heard of them; and yet through some strange reasoning of his own, or blind adoption of public unreason, he had made me dislike, or at any rate not like, him, until he began to show signs at last of changing his opinion. And now the question was, had he done that enough for me, without loss of self-respect, to open my heart to him, and seek counsel?

In settling that point the necessity of the case overrode, perhaps, some scruples; in sooth, I had nobody else to go to. What could I do with Lord Castlewood? Nothing; all his desire was to do exactly what my father would have done: and my father had never done any thing more than rove and roam his life out. To my mind this was dreadful now, when every new thing rising round me more and more clearly to my mind established what I never had doubted—his innocence. Again, what good could I do by seeking Betsy's opinion about it, or that of Mrs. Price, or Stixon, or any other person I could think of? None whatever—and perhaps much harm. Taking all in all, as things turn up, I believed myself to be almost equal to the cleverest of those three in sense, and in courage not inferior. Moreover, a sort of pride—perhaps very small, but not contemptible—put me against throwing my affairs so much into the hands of servants.

For this idea Uncle Sam, no doubt the most liberal of men, would perhaps condemn me. But still I was not of the grand New World, whose pedigrees are arithmetic (at least with many of its items, though the true Uncle Sam was the last for that); neither could I come up to the largeness of universal brotherhood. That was not to be expected of a female; and few things make a man more angry than for his wife to aspire to it. No such ideas had ever troubled me; I had more important things to think of, or, at any rate, something to be better carried out. And of all these desultory thoughts it came that I packed up that odious but very lovely locket, without further attempt to unriddle it, and persuaded my very good and clever Mrs. Busk to let me start right early. By so doing I could have three hours with a good gentleman always in a hurry, and yet return for the night to Shoxford, if he should advise me so.

Men and women seem alike to love to have their counsels taken; and the equinox being now gone by, Mrs. Busk was ready to begin before the tardy sun was up, who begins to give you short measure at once when he finds the weights go against him. Mrs. Busk considered not the sun, neither any of his doings. The time of day was more momentous than any of the sun's proceedings. Railway time was what she had to keep (unless a good customer dropped in), and as for the sun—"clock slow, clock fast," in the almanacs, showed how he managed things; and if that was not enough, who could trust him to keep time after what he had done upon the dial of Ahaz? Reasoning thus—if reason it was—she packed me off in a fly for the nearest railway station, and by midday I found the Major laboring on his ramparts.

After proper salutations, I could not help expressing wonder at the rapid rise of things. Houses here and houses there, springing up like children's teeth, three or four in a row together, and then a long gap, and then some more. And down the slope a grand hotel, open for refreshment, though as yet it had no roof on; for the Major, in virtue of his charter, defied all the magistrates to stop him from selling whatever was salable on or off the premises. But noblest and grandest of all to look at was the "Bruntsea Athenaeum, Lyceum, Assembly-Rooms, Institution for Mutual Instruction, Christian Young Men's Congress, and Sanitary, Saline, Hydropathic Hall, at nominal prices to be had gratis."

"How you do surprise me!" I said to Major Hockin, after reading all that, which he kindly requested me to do with care; "but where are the people to come from?"

"Erema," he replied, as if that question had been asked too often, "you have not had time to study the laws of political economy—the noblest of noble sciences. The first of incontrovertible facts is that supply creates demand. Now ask yourself whether there could even be a Yankee if ideas like yours had occurred to Columbus?"

This was beyond me; for I never could argue, and strove to the utmost not to do so. "You understand those things, and I do not," said I, with a smile, which pleased him. "My dear aunt Mary always says that you are the cleverest man in the world; and she must know most about it."

"Partiality! partiality!" cried the Major, with a laugh, and pulling his front hair up. "Such things pass by me like the idle wind; or rather, perhaps, they sadden me, from my sense of my own deficiencies. But, bless me! dinner must be waiting. Look at that fellow's trowel—he knows: he turns up the point of it like a spoon. They say that he can smell his dinner two miles off. We all dine at one o'clock now, that I may rout up every man-Jack of them."

The Major sounded a steam-guard's whistle, and led me off in the rapidly vanishing wake of his hungry workmen.

CHAPTER XLV
CONVICTION

Sir Montague Hockin, to my great delight, was still away from Bruntsea. If he had been there, it would have been a most awkward thing for me to meet him, or to refuse to do so. The latter course would probably have been the one forced upon me by self-respect and affection toward my cousin; and yet if so, I could scarcely have avoided an explanation with my host. From the nature of the subject, and several other reasons, this would have been most unpleasant; and even now I was haunted with doubts, as I had been from the first, whether I ought not to have told Mrs. Hockin long ago what had been said of him. At first sight that seemed the honest thing to do; but three things made against it. It might seem forward and meddlesome; it must be a grievous thing to my cousin to have his sad story discussed again; and lastly, I had promised Mrs. Price that her words should go no further. So that on the whole perhaps I acted aright in keeping that infamous tale to myself as long as ever it was possible.

But now ere ever I spoke of him—which I was always loath to do—Mrs. Hockin told me that he very seldom came to see them now, and when he did come he seemed to be uneasy and rather strange in his manners. I thought to myself that the cause of this was clear. Sir Montague, knowing that I went to Castlewood, was pricked in his conscience, and afraid of having his vile behavior to my cousin disclosed. However, that idea of mine was wrong, and a faulty conception of simple youth. The wicked forgive themselves so quickly, if even they find any need of it, that every body else is supposed to do the same. With this I have no patience. A wrong unrepented of and unatoned gathers interest, instead of getting discount, from lost time. And so I hated that man tenfold.

Good Mrs. Hockin lamented his absence not only for the sake of her darling fowls, but also because she considered him a check upon the Major's enterprise. Great as her faith was in her husband's ability and keenness, she was often visited with dark misgivings about such heavy outlay. Of economy (as she often said) she certainly ought to know something, having had to practice it as strictly as any body in the kingdom, from an age she could hardly remember. But as for what was now brought forward as a great discovery—economy in politics—Mrs. Hockin had tried to follow great opinions, but could only find, so far, downright extravagance. Supply (as she had observed fifty times with her own butcher and fishmonger), instead of creating demand, produced a lot of people hankering round the corner, till the price came down to nothing. And if it were so with their institutions—as her dear husband called his new public-house—who was to find all the interest due to the building and land societies? Truly she felt that Sir Rufus Hockin, instead of doing any good to them, had behaved very badly in leaving them land, and not even a shilling to work it with.

It relieved her much to tell me this, once for all and in strict confidence; because her fine old-fashioned (and we now may say quite obsolete) idea of duty toward her husband forbade her ever to say to him, or about him, when it could be helped, any thing he might not like, any thing which to an evil mind might convey a desire on her part to meddle with—with—

"Political economy," I said; and she laughed, and said, Yes, that was just it. The Major of course knew best, and she ought with all her heart to trust him not to burden their old days with debt, after all the children they had brought up and fairly educated upon the professional income of a distinguished British officer, who is not intended by his superiors to provide successors.

"Perhaps it is like the boiled eggs they send me," the old lady said, with her soft sweet smile, "for my poor hens to sit upon. Their race is too good to be made common. So now they get tinkers' and tailors' boys, after much competition, and the crammed sons of cooks. And in peace-time they do just as well."

Of such things I knew nothing; but she seemed to speak with bitterness, the last thing to be found in all her nature, yet discoverable—as all bad things (except its own) are—by the British government. I do not speak from my own case, in which they discovered nothing.

By the time these things had been discussed, my host (who was always particular about his dress) came down to dinner, and not until that was over could I speak of the subject which had brought me there. No sooner had I begun my tale than they both perceived that it must neither be flurried nor interrupted, least of all should it be overheard.

"Come into my lock-up," cried the Major; "or, better still, let us go out of doors. We can sit in my snuggery on the cliff, with only gulls and jackdaws to listen, and mount my telescope and hoist my flag, and the men know better than to skulk their work. I can see every son of a gun of them as clearly as if I had them on parade. You wish Mrs. Hockin to come, I suppose. Very well, let us be off at once. I shall count my fellows coming back from dinner."

With a short quick step the Major led the way to a beautifully situated outpost at a corner of the cliff, where land and sea for many a fair league rolled below. A niche of the chalk had been cleverly enlarged and scooped into a shell-shaped bower, not, indeed, gloriously overhung, as in the far West might have been, but broken of its white defiant glare by climbing and wandering verdure. Seats and slabs of oak were fixed to check excess of chalkiness, and a parapet of a pattern which the Major called Egyptian saved fear of falling down the cliff, and served to spread a paper on, or to rest a telescope.

"From this point," said the Major, crossing wiry yet substantial legs, "the whole of my little domain may be comprised as in a bird's-eye view. It is nothing, of course, much less than nothing, compared with the Earl of Crowcombe's, or the estate of Viscount Gamberley; still, such as it is, it carries my ideas, and it has an extent of marine frontage such as they might envy. We are asked 5 pounds per foot for a thread of land fronting on a highway, open to every kind of annoyance, overlooked, without any thing to look at. How much, then, per fathom (or measure, if you please, by cable-lengths) is land worth fronting the noble, silent, uncontaminating, healthful sea? Whence can come no coster-mongers' cries, no agitating skir of bagpipes or the maddening hurdy-gurdy, no German band expecting half a crown for the creation of insanity; only sweet murmur of the wavelets, and the melodious whistle of a boatman catching your breakfast lobster. Where, again, if you love the picturesque—"

"My dear," said Mrs. Hockin, gently, "you always were eloquent from the first day I saw you; and if you reconstitute our borough, as you hope, and enter Parliament for Bruntsea, what a sensation you will create! But I wished to draw your attention to the fact that Erema is waiting to tell her tale."

"To be sure. I will not stop her. Eloquence is waste of time, and I never yet had half a second to spare. Fear no eloquence from me; facts and logic are my strong points. And now, Erema, show what yours are."

At first this made me a little timid, for I had never thought that any strong points would be needed for telling a simple tale. To my mind the difficulty was, not to tell the story, but to know what to make of it when told; and soon I forgot all about myself in telling what I had seen, heard, and found.

The Major could not keep himself from stamping great holes through his—something I forget the name of, but people sow it to make turf of chalk—and dear "Aunt Mary's" soft pink cheeks, which her last grandchild might envy, deepened to a tone of rose; while her eyes, so full of heavenly faith when she got upon lofty subjects, took a most human flash and sparkle of hatred not theological.

"Seven!" she cried; "oh, Nicholas, Nicholas, you never told me there were seven!"

"There were not seven graves without the mother," the Major answered, sternly. "And what odds whether seven or seventy? The criminality is the point, not the accumulation of results. Still, I never heard of so big a blackguard. And what did he do next, my dear?"

The way in which they took my story was a great surprise to me, because, although they were so good, they had never paid any attention to it until it became exciting. They listened with mere politeness until the scent of a very wicked man began to taint my narrative; but from that moment they drew nearer, and tightened their lips, and held their breath, and let no word escape them. It made me almost think that people even of pure excellence, weaned as they are from wicked things by teaching and long practice, must still retain a hankering for them done at other people's cost.

"And now," cried the Major, "let us see it"—even before I had time to pull it out, though ready to be quick, from a knowledge of his ways. "Show it, and you shall have my opinion. And Mary's is certain to agree with mine. My dear, that makes yours so priceless."

"Then, Nicholas, if I retain my own, yours is of no value. Never mind that. Now don't catch words, or neither opinion will be worth a thought. My dear, let us see it and then judge."

"My own idea, but not so well expressed," Major Hockin answered, as he danced about, while I with stupid haste was tugging at my package of the hateful locket. For I had not allowed that deceitful thing any quarters in my pocket, where dear little relics of my father lay, but had fastened it under my dress in a manner intended in no way for gentlemen to think about. Such little things annoy one's comfort, and destroy one's power of being quite high-minded. However, I got it out at last, and a flash of the sun made the difference.

"Brilliants, Mary!" the Major cried; "brilliants of first water; such as we saw, you know where; and any officer in the British army except myself, I do believe, would have had them at once in his camlet pouch—my dear, you know all about it. Bless my heart, how slow you are! Is it possible you have forgotten it? There came out a fellow, and I cut him down, as my duty was, without ceremony. You know how I used to do it, out of regulation, with a slash like this—"

"Oh, Nicholas, you will be over the cliff! You have shown me how you used to do it, a thousand times—but you had no cricks in your back then: and remember how brittle the chalk is."

"The chalk may be brittle, but I am tough. I insist upon doing every thing as well as I did it forty years ago. Mary, you ought not to speak to me like that. Eighteen, nineteen, twenty brilliants, worth twenty pounds apiece upon an average, I do believe. Four hundred pounds. That would finish our hotel."

"Nicholas!"

"My dear, I was only in fun. Erema understands me. But who is this beautiful lady?"

"The very point," I exclaimed, while he held it so that the pensive beauty of the face gleamed in soft relief among bright blue enamel and sparkling gems. "The very thing that I must know—that I would give my life to know—that I have fifty thousand fancies—"

"Now don't be excited, Erema, if you please. What will you give me to tell you who it is?"

"All those diamonds, which I hate the sight of, and three-quarters of my half nugget; and if that is not enough—"

"It is a thousand times too much; I will tell you for just one smile, and I know it, will be a smile of unbelief."

"No, no; I will believe it, whoever you say," with excitement superior to grammar, I cried; "only tell me at once—don't be so long."

"But then you won't believe me when I do tell you," the Major replied, in the most provoking way. "I shall tell you the last person you would ever think of, and then you will only laugh at me."

"I won't laugh; how can I laugh in such a matter? I will believe you if you say it is—Aunt Mary."

"My dear, you had better say at once that it is I, and have no more mystery about it." Mrs. Hockin was almost as impatient as myself.

"Mrs. Hockin, you must indeed entertain an exalted idea of your own charms. I knew that you were vain, but certainly did not—Well, then, if you will allow me no peace, this is the lady that lives down in the ruin, and stands like a pillar by my pillar-box."

"I never thought you would joke like that," I cried, with vexation and anger. "Oh, is it a subject to be joked about?"

"I never was graver in my life; and you promised implicitly to believe me. At any rate, believe that I speak in earnest."

"That I must believe, when you tell me so. But what makes you think such a wonderful thing? I should have thought nothing more impossible. I had made up my mind that it was Flittamore who lived down here; but this can not be she. Flittamore was unheard of at the time of my grandfather's death. Moreover, her character was not like this; she was giddy and light and heartless. This lady had a heart—good or bad, a deep one. Most certainly it is not Flittamore."

"Flittamore! I do not remember that name. You should either tell us all or tell us nothing." The Major's tone was reproachful, and his eyes from their angular roofs looked fierce.

"I have not told you," I said, "because it can have nothing to do with it. The subject is a painful one, and belongs to my family only."

"Enough. I am not inquisitive—on the other hand, too forgetful. I have an appointment at 3.25. It takes me seven minutes and a quarter to get there. I must be two minutes and three-quarters late. Mrs. Hockin, mount the big telescope and point it at the ramparts; keep the flag up also. Those fellows will be certain that I am up here, while I enfilade them from the western end with this fine binocular. Surprises maintain discipline. Good-by, my dear, and, Miss Castlewood, good-by. Tea at 6.30, and not too much water."

CHAPTER XLVI
VAIN ZEAL

Leaving his telescope leveled at the men, the Major marched off with his opera-glass in a consciously provoking style, and Mrs. Hockin most heartily joined me in condemning such behavior. In a minute or two, however, she would not have one word said against him, and the tide of her mind (as befits a married woman) was beyond all science; so that the drift of all words came back to her husband's extraordinary merits. And certainly these, if at all like her description, deserved to be dwelt upon at very precious periods.

However, I had heard enough of them before; for the Major himself was not mute upon this point, though comparatively modest, and oftentimes deprecating praise ere ever he received it. And so I brought Mrs. Hockin back at last to talk about the lady who was living in the ruin.

"It is not quite a ruin," she said. "My dear husband is fond of picturesque expressions. However, it is not in very good repair; and being unable to get possession of it, through some legal quibble, possibly he may look at it from a rather unfavorable point of view. And for the same reason—though he is so purely just—he may have formed a bad opinion of the strange individual who lives there. What right has she to be living without his leave upon his own manor? But there she is, and she does not care for us or any body. She fetches all she wants, she speaks to none, and if any body calls for rates or taxes, or any other public intrusion, they may knock and knock, but never get in, and at last they go away again."

"But surely that can not go on forever. Bruntsea is such an enlightened place."

"Our part of it is, but the rest quite benighted. As the man says—I forget his name, but the man that misunderstands us so—his contention is that 'Desolate Hole,' as the Major calls it, although in the middle of our land, is entirely distinct from it. My husband never will put up with that—his love of justice is far too strong—and he means to have a lawsuit. But still he has reasons for not beginning yet; and he puts up with a great deal, I am sure. It is too bad for them to tease him so."

"It does seem a very sad thing," I replied; "and the poor soul living there all alone! Even in the summer it is bad enough; but whatever will she do when the winter comes? Why, the sea in bad weather must be almost in upon her. And the roar of the pebbles all night! Major Hockin will never allow her to stay there."

"What can he do, when he can not get in, and they even deny his title? I assure you, Erema, I have sent down cream, and even a dozen of my precious eggs, with the lady of the manor's compliments; but instead of being grateful, they were never taken in; and my Polly—'Miss Polly Hopkins,' you know—very wisely took it all to her grandmother."

"To her grandmother instead of mine, as the Major facetiously calls her. And now he says this is her portrait; and instead of giving his reasons, runs away! Really you must excuse me, Aunt Mary, for thinking that your good husband has a little too much upon his mind sometimes."

The old lady laughed, as I loved to see her do. "Well, my dear, after that, I think you had better have it out with him. He comes home to tea at 6.30, which used to be half past six in my days. He is very tired then, though he never will allow it, and it would not be fair to attack him. I give him a mutton-chop, or two poached eggs, or some other trifle of nourishment. And then I make him doze for an hour and a half, to soothe his agitated intellect. And when he wakes he has just one glass of hot water and sugar, with a little Lochnagar. And then he is equal to any thing—backgammon, bezique, or even conversation."

Impatient as I was, I saw nothing better; and by this time I was becoming used to what all of us must put up with—the long postponement of our heavy cares to the light convenience of others. Major Hockin might just as well have stopped, when he saw how anxious I was. Uncle Sam would have stopped the mill itself, with a dozen customers waiting; but no doubt he had spoiled me; and even that should not make me bitter. Aunt Mary and I understood one another. We gazed away over the breadth of the sea and the gleam of its texture, and we held our peace.

Few things are more surprising than the calm way in which ripe age looks on at things which ought to amaze it. And yet any little one of its own concerns grows more important, perhaps, than ever as the shadow of the future dwindles. Major Hockin had found on the beach a pebble with a streak of agate in it. He took it as the harbinger of countless agates, and resolved to set up a lapidary, with a tent, or even a shop, perhaps—not to pay, but to be advertised, and catch distinguished visitors.

"Erema, you are a mighty finder; you found the biggest nugget yet discovered. You know about stones from the Rocky Mountains, or at least the Sierra Nevada. You did not discover this beautiful agate, but you saw and greatly admired it. We might say that a 'young lady, eminent for great skill in lithology, famed as the discoverer,' etc. Hold it between your eyes and this candle, but wet it in the slop-basin first; now you see the magnificent veins of blue."

"I see nothing of the kind," I said; for really it was too bad of him. "It seems to me a dirty bit of the commonest flint you could pick up."

This vexed him more than I wished to have done, and I could not help being sorry; for he went into a little fit of sulks, and Aunt Mary almost frowned at me. But he could not stay long in that condition, and after his doze and his glass he came forth as lively and meddlesome as ever. And the first thing he did was to ask me for the locket.

"Open it?" he cried; "why, of course I can; there is never any difficulty about that. The finest workmanship in the world is that of the Indian jewelers. I have been among them often; I know all their devices and mechanism, of which the European are bad copies. I have only to look round this thing twice, and then pronounce my Sesame."

"My dear, then look round it as fast as you can," said his wife, with a traitorous smile at me, "and we won't breathe a Sess till it flies asunder."

"Mary, Miss Castlewood makes you pert, although herself so well conducted. However, I do not hesitate to say that I will open this case in two minutes."

"Of course you will, dear," Mrs. Hockin replied, with provoking acquiescence. "The Major never fails, Erema, in any thing he is so sure about; and this is a mere child's toy to him. Well, dear, have you done it? But I need not ask. Oh, let us see what is inside of it!"

"I have not done it yet, Mrs. Hockin; and if you talk with such rapidity, of course you throw me out. How can I command my thoughts, or even recall my experience?"

"Hush! now hush, Erema! And I myself will hush most reverently."

"You have no reverence in you, and no patience. Do you expect me to do such a job in one second? Do you take me for a common jeweler? I beg you to remember—"

"Well, my dear, I remember only what you told us. You were to turn it round twice, you know, and then cry Sesame. Erema, was it not so?"

"I never said any thing of the sort. What I said was simply this— However, to reason with ladies is rude; I shall just be off to my study."

"Where you keep your tools, my darling," Mrs. Hockin said, softly, after him: "at least, I mean, when you know where they are."

I was astonished at Aunt Mary's power of being so highly provoking, and still more at her having the heart to employ it. But she knew best what her husband was; and to worship forever is not wise.

"Go and knock at his door in about five minutes," Mrs. Hockin said to me, with some mischief in her eyes. "If he continues to fail, he may possibly take a shorter way with it. And with his tools so close at hand—"

"Oh," I exclaimed, "his geological hammer—that dreadful crusher! May I go at once? I detest that thing, but I can not have it smashed."

"He will not break it up, my dear, without your leave. He never would think of such a thing, of course. However, you may as well go after him."

It was wrong of Mrs. Hockin to make me do this; and I felt quite ashamed of myself when I saw the kind old Major sitting by his lamp, and wrinkling his forehead into locks and keys of puzzle, but using violence to his own mind alone. And I was the more ashamed when, instead of resenting my intrusion, he came to meet me, and led me to his chair, and placed the jeweled trinket in my hand, and said, "My dear, I give it up. I was wrong in taking it away from you. You must consult some one wiser."

"That odious thing!" I answered, being touched by this unusual humility of his; "you shall not give it up; and I know no wiser person. A lapidary's tricks are below your knowledge. But if you are not tired of me and offended, may I leave it to you to get it opened?"

"I would like nothing better," he replied, recovering his natural briskness and importance; "but you ought to be there, my dear; you must be there. Are you sure that you ought not rather to take it to your good cousin Lord Castlewood? Now think before you answer."

"I need not think twice of that, Major Hockin. Good and learned as my father's cousin is, he has distinctly refused to help me, for some mysterious reason of his own, in searching into this question. Indeed, my great hope is to do it without him: for all that I know, he might even wish to thwart me."

"Enough, my dear; it shall be just as you wish. I brought you to England, and I will stand by you. My cousin, Colonel Gundry, has committed you to me. I have no patience with malefactors. I never took this matter up, for very many reasons; and among them not the least was that Sampson, your beloved 'Uncle Sam,' thought it better not to do so. But if you desire it, and now that I feel certain that an infamous wrong has been done to you—which I heartily beg your pardon for my doubt of—by the Lord of all justice, every thing else may go to the devil, till I see it out. Do you desire it, Erema?"

"I certainly do not wish that any of your great works should be neglected. But if, without that, you can give me your strong help, my only difficulty will be to thank you."

"I like plain speaking, and you always speak plainly; sometimes too plainly," he said, recollecting little times when he had the worst of it. "How far do you trust me now?"

"Major Hockin, I trust you altogether. You may make mistakes, as all men do—"

"Yes, yes, yes. About my own affairs; but I never do that for other people. I pay a bill for twopence, if it is my own. If I am trustee of it, I pay three half-pence."

His meaning was a little beyond me now; but it seemed better not to tell him so; for he loved to explain his own figures of speech, even when he had no time to spare for it. And he clearly expected me to ask him to begin; or at least it seemed so from his eyebrows. But that only came home to me afterward.

"Please not to speak of my affairs like that," I said, as if I were quite stupid; "I mean to pay fourpence for every twopence—both to friends and enemies."

"You are a queer girl; I have always said so. You turn things to your own ideas so. However, we must put up with that, though none of my daughters have ever done it; for which I am truly thankful. But now there is very little time to lose. The meaning of this thing must be cleared up at once. And there is another thing to be done as well, quite as important, in my opinion. I will go to London with you to-morrow, if you like. My clever little Cornishman will see to things here—the man that sets up all the angles."

"But why should I hurry you to London so?" I asked. "Surely any good country jeweler could manage it? Or let us break it open."

"On no account," he answered; "we might spoil it all; besides the great risk to the diamonds, which are very brittle things. To London we must take it, for this reason—the closure of this case is no jeweler's work; of that I have quite convinced myself. It is the work of a first-rate lapidary, and the same sort of man must undo it."

To this I agreed quite readily, because of such things I knew nothing; whereas my host spoke just as if he had been brought up to both those walks of art. And then I put a question which had long been burning on my tongue.

"What made you imagine, Major Hockin, that this very beautiful face could have ever been that of the old lady living in the ruin?"

"In Desolate Hole? I will tell you at once; and then call it, if you like, an imagination. Of all the features of the human face there is none more distinctive than the eyebrow. 'Distinctive' is not exactly what I mean—I mean more permanently marked and clear. The eyes change, the nose changes, so does the mouth, and even the shape of the forehead sometimes; but the eyebrows change very little, except in color. This I have noticed, because my own may perhaps be a little peculiar; and they have always been so. At school I received a nickname about it, for boys are much sharper than men about such things; and that name after fifty years fits as well as ever. You may smile, if you like; I shall not tell you what it was, but leave you to re-invent it, if you can. Now look at this first-rate miniature. Do you see an unusual but not uncomely formation of the eyebrows?"

"Certainly I do; though I did not observe it until you drew my attention. I had only regarded the face, as a whole."

"The face, as a whole, is undoubtedly fine. But the eyebrows have a peculiar arch, and the least little turn at the lower end, as if they designed to rise again. The lady of Desolate Hole has the same."

"But how can you tell? How very strange! I thought she let nobody see her face."

"You are perfectly right about that, Erema; so far at least as she has vouchsafed to exhibit her countenance to me. Other people may be more fortunate. But when I met her for the second time, being curious already about her, I ventured to offer my services, with my inborn chivalry, at a place where the tide was running up, and threatened to surround her. My politeness was not appreciated, as too often is the case; for she made me a very stiff bow, and turned away. Her face had been covered by the muffler of her cloak, as if the sea-breeze were too much for her; and she did not even raise her eyes. But before she turned away, I obtained a good glance at her eyebrows—and they were formed like these."

"But her age, Major Hockin! Her age—what is it?"

"Upon that proverbially delicate point I can tell you but little, Erema. Perhaps, however, I may safely say that she can not be much under twenty."

"It is not right to provoke me so. You call her 'the old woman,' and compare her to your letter-box. You must have some idea—is she seventy?" "Certainly not, I should say; though she can not expect me to defend her, when she will not show her face to me; and what is far worse, at my time of life, she won't even pay me a half-penny of rent. Now let us go back to Aunt Mary, my dear; she always insists upon packing overnight."

CHAPTER XLVII
CADMEIAN VICTORY

Before two o'clock of the following day Major Hockin and myself were in London, and ready to stay there for two or three days, if it should prove needful. Before leaving Bruntsea I had written briefly to Lord Castlewood, telling him that important matters had taken me away from Shoxford, and as soon as I could explain them, I would come and tell him all about it. This was done only through fear of his being annoyed at my independence.

From London Bridge the Major took a cab direct to Clerkenwell; and again I observed that of all his joys one of the keenest was to match his wits against a cabman's. "A regular muff, this time," he said, as he jerked up and down with his usual delight in displaying great knowledge of London; "no sport to be had out of him. Why, he stared at me when I said 'Rosamond Street,' and made me stick on 'Clerkenwell.' Now here he is taking us down Snow Hill, when he should have been crossing Smithfield. Smithfield, cabby, Smithfield!"

"Certain, Sir, Smiffle, if you gives the order;" and he turned the poor horse again, and took us up the hill, and among a great number of barriers. "No thoroughfare," "No thoroughfare," on all hands stretched across us; but the cabman threaded his way between, till he came to the brink of a precipice. The horse seemed quite ready, like a Roman, to leap down it, seeing nothing less desirable than his present mode of life, till a man with a pickaxe stopped him.

"What are you at?" cried the Major, with fury equalled by nothing except his fright. "Erema, untie my big rattan. Quick—quick—"

"Captain," said the cabman, coolly, "I must have another shilling for this job. A hextra mile and a quarter, to your orders. You knows Lunnon so much better. Smiffle stopped—new railway—new meat market—never heered of that now, did you?"

"You scoundrel, drive straight to the nearest police office."

"Must jump this little ditch, then, Captain. Five pun' fine for you, when we gets there. Hold on inside, old gentleman. Kuck, kuck, Bob, you was a hunter once. It ain't more than fifty feet deep, my boy."

"Turn round! turn round, I tell you! turn round! If your neck is forfeit, you rogue, mine is not. I never was so taken in in my life!" Major Hockin continued to rave, and amid many jeers we retreated humbly, and the driver looked in at us with a gentle grin. "And I thought he was so soft, you know! Erema, may I swear at him?"

"On no account," I said. "Why, after all, it is only a shilling, and the loss of time. And then, you can always reflect that you have discharged, as you say, a public duty, by protesting against a vile system."

"Protesting is very well, when it pays," the Major answered, gloomily; "but to pay for protesting is another pair of shoes."

This made him cross, and he grew quite fierce when the cabman smote him for eight-pence more. "Four parcels on the roof, Captain," he said, looking as only a cabman can look at his money, and spinning his extra shilling. "Twopence each under new hact, you know. Scarcely thought a hofficer would 'a tried evasion."

"You consummate scoundrel—and you dress yourself like a countryman! I'll have your badge indorsed—I'll have your license marked. Erema, pay the thief; it is more than I can do."

"Captain, your address, if you please; I shall summon you for scurrilous language, as the hact directs. Ah, you do right to be driven to a pawn shop."

Triumphantly he drove off, while the Major cried, "Never tie up my rattan again. Oh, it was Mrs. Hockin, was it? What a fool I was not to stop on my own manor!"

"I pray you to disdain such low impudence," I said, for I could not bear to see him shake like that, and grieved to have brought him into it. "You have beaten fifty of them—a hundred of them—I have heard you say."

"Certainly I have, my dear; but I had no Bruntsea then, and could not afford to pay the rogues. That makes me feel it so bitterly, so loftily, and so righteously. To be treated like this, when I think of all my labors for the benefit of the rascally human race! my Institute, my Lyceum, my Mutual Improvement Association, and Christian Young Men's something. There is no institution, after all, to be compared to the tread-mill."

Recovering himself with this fine conclusion, he led me down a little sloping alley, scarcely wide enough for a wheelbarrow, to an old black door, where we set down our parcels; for he had taken his, while I carried mine, and not knowing what might happen yet, like a true peace-maker I stuck to the sheaf of umbrellas and the rattan cane. And thankful I was, and so might be the cabman, to have that weapon nicely sheathed with silk.

Major Hockin's breath was short, through too much talking without action, and he waited for a minute at this door, to come back to his equanimity. And I thought that our female breath falls short for the very opposite reason—when we do too much and talk too little; which happily seldom happens.

He was not long in coming back to his usual sprightliness and decision. And it was no small relief to me, who was looking at him miserably, and longing that his wife was there, through that very sad one-and-eightpence, when he pulled out a key, which he always carried as signer and lord of Bruntsea, the key of the town-hall, which had survived lock, door, and walls by centuries, and therewith struck a door which must have reminded that key of its fine old youth.

Before he had knocked so very many times, the door was opened by a young man wearing an apron and a brown paper cap, who knew Major Hockin at once, and showed us up stairs to a long low workshop. Here were many wheels and plates and cylinders revolving by energy of a strap which came through the floor and went through the ceiling. And the young man told us to be careful how we walked, for fear of getting entangled. Several men, wearing paper caps and aprons of leather or baize, were sitting doing dextrous work, no doubt, and doing it very easily, and the master of them all was hissing over some fine touch of jewel as a groom does at a horse. Then seeing us, he dropped his holders, and threw a leather upon his large lens, and came and took us to a little side room.

"Are you not afraid to leave them?" asked the Major. "They may secrete some gems, Mr. Handkin."

"Never," said the lapidary, with some pride. "I could trust these men with the Koh-i-noor; which we could have done better, I believe, than it was done by the Hollanders. But we don't get the chance to do much in diamonds, through the old superstition about Amsterdam, and so on. No, no; the only thing I can't trust my men about is to work as hard when I am away as when I am there. And now, Sir, what can I do for you? Any more Bruntsea pebbles? The last were not worth the cutting."

"So you said; but I did not think so. We have some agates as good as any from Aberystwith or Perthshire. But what I want now is to open this case. It must be done quite privately, for a most particular reason. It does open, doesn't it? I am sure it does."

"Certainly it opens," Mr. Handkin answered, while I trembled with anxiety as he lightly felt it round the edges with fingers engrained with corundum. "I could open it in one instant, but the enamel might fly. Will you risk it?"

The Major looked at me, and I said, "Oh no; please not to risk any thing, if any slower process will do it without risk. We want it done without injury."

"Then it will cost a good bit," he replied. "I can open it for five shillings, if you run the risk; if that rests with me, I must charge five pounds."

"Say three," cried the Major. "Well, then, say four guineas: I have a lot of work in store for you."

"I never overcharge, and I never depart from my figures," the lapidary answered. "There is only one other man in London who knows the secret of this enamel, and he is my brother. They never make such enamel now. The art is lost, like that of the French paste of a hundred years ago, which almost puzzles even me until I go behind it. I will give you my brother's address if you like; but instead of five pounds, he will charge you ten guineas—if it must be done in private. Without that condition, I can do it for two pounds. You wish to know why that should make such a difference. Well, for this simple reason: to make sure of the job, it must be done by daylight; it can be done only in my chief work-room; if no one is to see what I am about (and my men have sharp eyes, I can tell you), all my hands must be sacked for the afternoon, but not without their wages. That alone would go far toward the difference, and then there is the dropping of the jobs in hand, and waste of power, and so on. I have asked you too little, Major Hockin, I assure you; but having said, I will stick to it, although I would much rather you would let me off."

"I have known you for many years," the Major answered—"ever since you were a boy, with a flat box, working at our Cornish opals. You would have done a lot of work for five pounds then. But I never knew you overcharge for any thing. We agree to your terms, and are obliged to you. But you guarantee no damage?"

"I will open this locket, take out its contents, whatever they may be, and reclose it so that the maker, if still alive—which is not very probable—should not know that it had been meddled with."

"Very well; that is exactly what we want; for I have an idea about it which I may try to go on with afterward. And for that it is essential to have no symptom that it ever has been opened. What are these brilliants worth, Mr. Handkin?"

"Well, Sir, in the trade, about a hundred and fifty, though I dare say they cost three hundred. And the portrait is worth another hundred, if I find on the back the marks I expect."

"You do not mean to say that you know the artist?" I could not help exclaiming, though determined not to speak. "Oh, then, we shall find out every thing!"

"Erema, you are a—well, you are a silly!" Major Hockin exclaimed, and then colored with remembering that rather he should have let my lapse pass. But the lapidary seemed to pay no attention, only to be calling down to some one far below. "Now mind what you say," the Major whispered to me, just as if he were the essence of discretion.

"The work-room is clear now," Mr. Handkin said; "the fellows were delighted to get their afternoon. Now you see that I have to take off this hoop, and there lies the difficulty. I could have taken out the gold back, as I said, with very little trouble, by simply cutting it. But the locket would never have been quite the same, though we put a new back; and, more than that, the pressure of the tool might flaw the enamel, or even crack the portrait, for the make of this thing is peculiar. Now first I submit the rim or verge, without touching the brilliants, mind you, to the action of a little preparation of my own—a gentle but penetrative solvent. You are welcome to watch me; you will be none the wiser; you are not in the trade, though the young lady looks as if she would make a good polisher. Very well: if this were an ordinary closure, with two flat surfaces meeting, the solvent would be absorbed into the adhesion, expansion would take place, and there we have it. But this is what we call a cyme-joint, a cohesion of two curved surfaces, formed in a reflex curve which admits the solvent most reluctantly, or, indeed, not at all, without too long application. For that, then, another kind of process is needful, and we find it in frictional heat applied most gradually and judiciously. For that I must have a buff-leather wheel, whose revolutions are timed to a nicety, and that wheel I only have in this room. Now you see why I sent the men away."

Though I watched his work with great interest, it is out of my power to describe it now, and, moreover, it is not needful. Major Hockin, according to his nature, grew quite restless and impatient, and even went out for a walk, with his cane unpacked and unsheathed against cabmen. But I was content to wait and watch, having always heard and thought that good work will not do itself, but must have time and skill to second it. And Mr. Handkin, moving arms, palms, and fingers beautifully, put the same thought into words.

"Good work takes a deal of time to do; but the man that does it all the time knows well that it will take long to undo. Here it comes undone at last!"

As he spoke, the excitable Major returned.

"Done it, eh? Well, you are a clever fellow. Now don't look inside it; that is no part of your business, nor mine either, unless this young lady desires it. Hand it to her first, my friend."

"Wait half a minute," said the lapidary; "it is so far opened that the hoop spins round, but it must not be taken off until it cools. The lady may lift it then with care. I have done this job as a piece of fine art; I have no wish to see any more of it."

"Handkin, don't you be so touchy to a brother Cornishman. I thought that I was Cornish enough, but you go cliffs beyond me."

"Well, Major Hockin," the lapidary answered, "I beg your pardon, if I said harm. But a man doing careful and skilled work—and skilled work it is, at every turn of the hand, as miss can bear witness, while you walked off—he don't care who it is, Major Hockin, he would fight his own brother to maintain it."

"Very well, very well. Let us come away. I always enter into every body's feelings. I see yours as clearly, Handkin, as if you had laid them open on that blessed wheel. My insight has always been remarkable. Every one, without exception, says that of me. Now come away, come away—will you never see?"

Intent as I was upon what lay in my left palm relaxing itself, I could not help being sorry for the way in which the man of art, after all his care, was ground down by his brother Cornishman. However, he had lived long enough in the world to feel no surprise at ingratitude.

Now I went to one of the windows, as the light (which had been very good) began to pale from its long and labored sufferance of London, and then, with soft and steady touch, I lifted off the loosened hoop. A smell of mustiness—for smells go through what nothing else can—was the first thing to perceive, and then, having moved the disk of gold, I found a piece of vellum. This was doubled, and I opened it, and read, in small clear writing:

"May 7, 1809 A.D., George, Lord Castlewood, married Winifred, only child of Thomas Hoyle, as this his signature witnesseth.

"CASTLEWOOD.

"(Witness) THOMAS HOYLE."

There was nothing more inside this locket, except two little wisps of hair tied with gold thread, and the miniature upon ivory, bearing on the back some anagram, probably that of the artist.

Already had I passed through a great many troubles, changes, chances, and adventures which always seem strange (when I come to look back), but never surprised me at the moment. Indeed, I might almost make bold to pronounce that not many persons of my age and sex have been visited, wholly against their own will, by such a series of incidents, not to say marvelous, but at any rate fairly to be called unusual. And throughout them perhaps it will be acknowledged by all who have cared to consider them, that up to the present time I did not fail more than themselves might have done in patience. And in no description of what came to pass have I colored things at all in my own favor—at least so far as intention goes—neither laid myself out to get sympathy, though it often would have done me a world of good.

But now I am free to confess that my patience broke down very sadly. Why, if what was written on that vellum was true, and Major Hockin correct as well, it came to no less than this, that my own dear father was a base-born son, and I had no right to the name I was so proud of! If, moreover, as I now began to dream, that terrible and mysterious man did not resemble my father so closely without some good reason, it seemed too likely that he might be his elder brother and the proper heir.

This was bad enough to think of, but an idea a thousandfold worse assailed me in the small hours of the night, as I lay on Mrs. Strouss's best bed, which she kept for consuls, or foreign barons, or others whom she loved to call "international notorieties." Having none of these now, she assigned me that bed after hearing all I had to say, and not making all that she might have done of it, because of the praise that would fall to Mrs. Busk.

However, she acknowledged that she knew nothing of the history of "the poor old lord." He might have carried on, for all she could tell, with many wives before his true one—a thing she heard too much of; but as for the Captain not being his true son and the proper heir to the peerage, let any one see him walk twice, and then have a shadow of a doubt about it!

This logic pleased but convinced me not, and I had to go to bed in a very unhappy, restless, and comfortless state of mind.

I hope that, rather than myself, that bed, full of international confusion, is to blame for the wicked ideas which assailed me while I could not even try to sleep. One of them—and a loyal daughter could scarcely have a worse one—was that my own dear father, knowing Lord Castlewood's bad behavior, and his own sad plight in consequence, and through that knowledge caring little to avenge his death, for wife and children's sake preferred to foil inquiry rather than confront the truth and challenge it. He might not have meant to go so far, at first beginning with it; but, starting once, might be driven on by grievous loss, and bitter sense of recreant friends, and the bleak despair of a homeless world before him. And serving as the scape-goat thus, he might have received from the real culprit a pledge for concealment of the family disgrace.

CHAPTER XLVIII
A RETURN CALL

In the morning I labored to dismiss these thoughts, these shameful suspicions, almost as injurious to my father's honor as it was to suspect him of the crime itself. And calling back my memories of him, and dwelling on what Mr. Shovelin said, and Uncle Sam and others, I became quite happy in the firm conviction that I ought to be put upon bread and water for having such vile visions. Then suddenly a thing came to my mind which shattered happy penitence.

Major Hockin had spoken of another purpose which he had in store while bringing me thus to London—another object, that is to say, besides the opening of the trinket. And this his second intention was to "have it out," as he expressed it, "with that league of curs and serpents, Vypan, Goad, and Terryer." This was the partnership whose card of business had been delivered at the sawmills under circumstances which, to say the least, required explanation. And the Major, with strong words and tugs of his head-crest, had vowed to get that explanation, or else put the lot of them into a police dock.

Moreover, when, at the opening of the locket, I did not think fit to show the lapidary what I had found inside it, except the painting on ivory (which proved to be as he expected), and when my companion suppressed curiosity at the risk of constitution, and while I could scarcely tell what I was about (through sudden shock and stupidity), I must have been hurried on to tell Major Hockin the whole of the private things I had discovered. For, in truth, there was scarcely any time to think; and I was afraid of giving way, which must have befallen me without relief of words; and being so much disturbed I may, in the cab, have rushed off for comfort to the Major, sitting so close to me. No doubt I did so, from what happened afterward; but in the morning, after such a night, I really could not be certain what I had said to Betsy, and what to him.

A large mind would have been steady throughout, and regarded the question of birth as a thing to which we, who are not consulted about it, should bear ourselves indifferently. And gladly would I have done so, if I could, but the power was not in me. No doubt it served me right for having been proud about such a trifle; but though I could call it a trifle as long as it seemed to be in my favor, my strength of mind was not enough to look at it so when against me.

Betsy told me not to be like that, for I had a great deal to go through yet, and must not be drawing on my spirit so, every atom of which would be needful. For the General—as she called the Major—was coming to fetch me at eleven o'clock to face some abominable rascals, and without any breakfast how could I do it? Then I remembered all about the appointment to go to Messrs. Vypan, Goad, and Terryer, and beginning to think about them, I saw sad confirmation of my bad ideas. My father's wicked elder brother by another mother had left his own rights pending, as long as my father lived, for good reason. For if the latter had turned against him, through a breach of compact, things might go ill in a criminal court; but having him silenced now by death, this man might come forward boldly and claim estates and title. His first point would be to make sure as sure could be of the death of my father, to get hold of his private papers, and of me, who might possess dangerous knowledge. And if this were so, one could understand at once Mr. Goad's attempt upon Uncle Sam.

"Now none of this! none of this, I say, Erema!" Major Hockin exclaimed, as he ran in and saw me scarcely even caring to hold my own with the gentle Maximilian—to which name Mr. Strouss was promoted from the too vernacular "Hans." "My dear, I never saw you look ill before. Why, bless my heart, you will have crows'-feet! Nurse, what are you doing with her? Look at her eyes, and be ashamed of yourself. Give her goulard, tisane, tiffany—I never know what the proper word is—something, any thing, volatile Sally, hartshorn, ammonia, aromatic vinegar, saline draught, or something strong. Why, I want her to look at her very, very best."

"As if she was a-going to a ball, poor dear!" Betsy Strouss replied, with some irony. "A young lady full of high spirits by nature, and have never had her first dance yet! The laws and institutions of this kingdom is too bad for me, General. I shall turn foreigner, like my poor husband."

"It is vere goot, vere goot always," said the placid Maximilian; "foreigner dis way, foreigner dat way; according to de hills, or de sea, or de fighting, or being born, or someting else."

"Hold your tongue, Hans," cried his Wilhelmina; "remember that you are in England now, and must behave constitutionally. None of your loose outlandish ideas will ever get your bread in England. Was I born according to fighting, or hills, or sea, or any thing less than the will of the Lord, that made the whole of them, and made you too? General, I beg you to excuse him, if you can. When he gets upon such things, he never can stop. His goodness is very great; but he must have a firm hand put upon his 'philosophy.' Maximilian, you may go and smoke your pipe for an hour and a quarter, and see where the cheapest greens and oil are, for his Excellence is coming in to-night; and mind you get plenty of stump in them. His Excellence loves them, and they fill the dish, besides coming cheaper. Now, Miss Erema, if you please, come here. Trust you in me, miss, and soon I will make you a credit to the General."

I allowed her to manage my dress and all that according to her own ideas; but when she entreated to finish me up with the "leastest little touch of red, scarcely up to the usual color, by reason of not sleeping," I stopped her at once, and she was quite content with the color produced by the thought of it. Meanwhile Major Hockin, of course, was becoming beyond all description impatient. He had made the greatest point of my being adorned, and expected it done in two minutes! And he hurried me so, when I did come down, that I scarcely noticed either cab or horse, and put on my new gloves anyhow.

"My dear, you look very nice," he said at last, when thoroughly tired of grumbling. "That scoundrel of a Goad will be quite amazed at sight of the child he went to steal."

"Mr. Goad!" I replied, with a shudder, caused, perhaps, by dark remembrance; "if we go to the office, you surely will not expect me to see Mr. Goad himself?"

"That depends, as the Frenchmen say. It is too late now to shrink back from any thing. If I can spare you, I will. If not, you must not be ashamed to show yourself."

"I am never ashamed to show myself. But I would rather not go to that place at all. If things should prove to be as I begin to think, I had better withdraw from the whole of it, and only lament that I ever began. My father was right; after all, my father was wise; and I ought to have known it. And perhaps Uncle Sam knew the truth, and would not tell me, for fear of my rushing to the Yosemite. Cabman, please to turn the horse and go in the opposite direction." But the Major pulled me back, and the driver lifted his elbow and said, "All right."

"Erema," the Major began, quite sternly, "things are gone a little too far for this. We are now embarked upon a most important investigation"—even in my misery I could scarce help smiling at his love of big official words—"an investigation of vast importance. A crime of the blackest dye has been committed, and calmly hushed up, for some petty family reason, for a period of almost twenty years. I am not blaming your father, my dear;

you need not look so indignant. It is your own course of action, remember, which has led to the present—the present—well, let us say imbroglio. A man of honor and an officer of her Majesty's service stands now committed at your request—mind, at your own request—"

"Yes, yes, I know; but I only meant you to—to go as far as I should wish."

"Confidential instructions, let us say; but there are times when duty to society overrides fine feeling. I have felt that already. The die is cast. No half-and-half measures, no beating about the bush, for me. After what I saw yesterday, and the light that burst upon me, I did not act hastily—I never do, though slow coaches may have said so. I put this and that together carefully, and had my dinner, and made up my mind. And you see the result in that man on the box."

"The cabman? Oh yes, you resolved to have a cab, and drive to those wicked informers."

"Where are your eyes? You are generally so quick. This morning you are quite unlike yourself—so weak, so tearful, and timorous. Have you not seen that by side of the cabman there sits another man altogether? One of the most remarkable men of the age, as your dear Yankees say."

"Not a policeman in disguise, I hope. I saw a very common, insignificant man. I thought he was the driver's groom, perhaps."

"Hush! he hears every thing, even on this granite. He is not a policeman; if he were, a few things that disgrace the force never would happen. If the policemen of England did their duty as our soldiers do, at once I would have gone to them; my duty would have been to do so. As it is, I go to our private police, who would not exist if the force were worth a rap. Vypan, Goad, and Terryer, in spite of Goad's clumsiness, rank second. I go to the first of all these firms, and I get their very cleverest rascal."

Major Hockin, speaking in this hoarse whisper—for he could not whisper gently—folded his arms, and then nodded his head, as much as to say, "I have settled it now. You have nothing to do but praise me." But I was vexed and perplexed too much to trust my voice with an answer.

"The beauty of this arrangement is," he continued, with vast complacency, "that the two firms hate one another as the devil hates—no, that won't do; there is no holy water to be found among them—well, as a snake hates a slow-worm, let us say. 'Set a thief to catch a thief' is a fine old maxim; still better when the two thieves have robbed one another."

As he spoke, the noble stranger slipped off the driving seat without troubling the cabman to stop his jerking crawl, and he did it so well that I had no chance of observing his nimble face or form. "You are disappointed," said the Major, which was the last thing I would have confessed. "You may see that man ten thousand times, and never be able to swear to him. Ha! ha! he is a oner!"

"I disdain such mean tricks beyond all expression," I exclaimed, as was only natural, "and every thing connected with them. It is so low to talk of such things. But what in the world made him do it? Where does he come from, and what is his name?"

"Like all noble persons, he has got so many names that he does not know which is the right one; only his are short and theirs are long. He likes 'Jack' better than any thing else, because it is not distinctive. 'Cosmopolitan Jack,' some call him, from his combining the manners and customs, features and figures, of nearly all mankind. He gets on with every one, for every one is gratified by seeing himself reflected in him. And he can jump from one frame to another as freely as Proteus or the populace. And yet, with all that, he is perfectly honest to any allegiance he undertakes. He would not betray us to Vypan, Goad, and Terryer for your great nugget and the Castlewood estates."

"I have heard that there are such people," I said; "but what can he possibly know about me? And what is he coming to do for us now?"

"He knows all about you, for a very simple reason. That you do not know him, is a proof of his ability. For you must have met him times out of number. This is the fellow employed by your good but incapable cousin, Lord Castlewood."

"He is not incapable; he is a man of great learning, and noble character—"

"Well, never mind that; you must not be so hot. What I mean is that he has done nothing for you beyond providing for your safety. And that he certainly did right well, and at considerable expense, for this man can't be had for nothing. You need have been under no terror at all in any of the scenes you have been through. Your safety was watched for continually."

"Then why did he not come and help me? Why did he not find out that horrible man?"

"Because it was not in his orders, and Jack is the last man to go beyond those. He is so clever that the stupid Moonites took him for a stupid Moonite. You should have employed him yourself, Erema; but you are so proud and independent."

"I should hope so, indeed. Should I put up with deceit? If the truth is not to be had without falsehood, it is not worth having. But what is this man to do here now?"

"That depends upon circumstances. He has better orders than I could give, for I am no hand at scheming. Here we are; or here we stop. Say nothing till I tell you. Pray allow me the honor. You keep in the background, remember, with your veil, or whatever you call it, down. Nobody stops at the very door. Of course that is humbug—we conform to it."

With a stiff inclination, the gallant Major handed me out of the cab in a quiet corner of a narrow street, then paid the driver with less fuss than usual, and led me into a queer little place marked in almost illegible letters, "Little England Polygon." "You have the card, my dear?" he whispered; "keep it till I call you in. But be ready to produce it in a moment. For the rest, I leave you to your own wit. Jack is on the watch, mind."

There were two doors near together, one a brave door with a plate, and swung on playing hinges, the other of too secluded a turn to even pronounce itself "private." We passed through the public door, and found only a lobby, with a boy on guard. "Mr. Goad? Yes, Sir. This way, Sir," cried the boy. "Lady stay? Yes, Sir; waiting-room for ladies. Chair, miss; here, if you please—first right. Mr. Goad, second on the left. Knock twice. Paper, miss? Poker chained at this time of year. Bell A, glass of water. Bell B, cup of tea, if ladies grows impatient."

If I had been well, I might have reduced this boy to his proper magnitude, for I never could endure young flippancy; but my spirits were so low that the boy banged the door with a fine sense of having vanquished me. And before there was any temptation to ring Bell A, not to mention Bell B, the sound of a wrathful voice began coming. Nearer and nearer it came, till the Major strode into the "ladies' waiting-room," and used language no ladies should wait for.

"Oh, don't!" I said; "what would Mrs. Hockin say? And consider me too, Major Hockin, if you please."

"I have considered you, and that makes me do it. Every body knows what I am. Did I ever exaggerate in all my life? Did I ever say any thing without just grounds? Did I ever take any distorted views? Did I ever draw upon my imagination? Erema, answer me this instant!"

"I do not remember a single instance of your drawing upon your imagination," I answered, gravely, and did not add, "because there is none to draw upon."

"Very well. I was sure of your concurrence. Then just come with me. Take my arm, if you please, and have the thief's card ready. Now keep your temper and your self-command."

With this good advice, the Major, whose arm and whole body were jerking with wrath, led me rapidly down the long passage and through a door, and my eyes met the eyes of the very man who had tried to bribe Uncle Sam of me. He never saw me then, and he did not know me now; but his insolent eyes fell under mine. I looked at him quietly, and said nothing.

"Now, Mr. Goad, you still assert that you never were in California—never even crossed the Atlantic. This young lady under my protection—don't you be afraid, my dear—is the Honorable Erema Castlewood, whom you, in the pay of a murderer, went to fetch, and perhaps to murder. Now, do you acknowledge it? You wrote her description, and ought to know her. You double-dyed villain, out with it!"

"Major Hockin," said Mr. Goad, trying to look altogether at his ease, but failing, and with his bull-dog forehead purple, "if indeed you are an officer—which I doubt for the credit of her Majesty's service—if the lady were not present, I should knock you down." And the big man got up as if to do it.

"Never mind her," my companion answered, in a magnanimous manner; "she has seen worse than that, poor thing. Here I am—just come and do it."

The Major was scarcely more than half the size of Mr. Goad in mere bodily bulk, and yet he defied him in this way. He carefully took his blue lights off, then drew up the crest of his hair, like his wife's most warlike cock a-crowing, and laid down his rattan upon a desk, and doubled his fists, and waited. Then he gave a blink from the corner of his gables, clearly meaning, "Please to stop and see it out." It was a distressing thing to see, and the Major's courage was so grand that I could not help smiling. Mr. Goad, however, did not advance, but assumed a superior manner.

"Major," he said, "we are not young men; we must not be so hasty. You carry things with too high a hand, as veteran officers are apt to do. Sir, I make allowance for you; I retract my menace, and apologize. We move in different spheres of life, Sir, or I would offer you my hand."

"No, thank you!" the Major exclaimed, and then looked sorry for his arrogance. "When a man has threatened me, and that man sees the mistake of doing so, I am pacified, Sir, in a moment; but it takes me some time to get over it. I have served his Gracious Majesty, and now hers, in every quarter of the civilized globe, with distinction, Sir—with distinction, and thanks, and no profit to taint the transaction, Sir. In many battles I have been menaced with personal violence, and have received it, as in such positions is equitable. I am capable, Sir, of receiving it still, and repaying it, not without interest."

"Hang it, Major, if a man is sorry, a soldier forgives him frankly. You abused me, and I rashly threatened you. I beg your pardon, as a man should do, and that should be an end to it."

"Very well, very well; say no more about it. But am I to understand that you still deny in that barefaced manner, with my witness here, the fact of your having been at Colonel Gundry's—my cousin, Sir, and a man not to be denied, without an insult to myself—a man who possesses ingots of gold, ingots of gold, enough to break the Bank of England, and a man whose integrity doubles them all. Have you not heard of the monster nugget, transcending the whole of creation, discovered by this young lady looking at you, in the bed of the saw-mill river, and valued at more than half a million?"

"You don't mean to say so? When was it? Sylvester never said a word about it—the papers, I mean, never mentioned it."

"Try no more—well, I won't say lies, though they are confounded lies—what I mean is, no further evasion, Mr. Goad. Sylvester's name is enough, Sir. Here is the card of your firm, with your own note of delivery on the back, handed by you to my cousin, the Colonel. And here stands the lady who saw you do it."

"Major, I will do my very best to remember. I am here, there, every where—China one day, Peru the next, Siberia the day after. And this young lady found the nugget, did she? How wonderfully lucky she must be!"

"I am lucky; I find out every thing; and I shall find out you, Mr. Goad." Thus I spoke on the spur of the moment, and I could not have spoken better after a month of consultation. Rogues are generally superstitious. Mr. Goad glanced at me with a shudder, as I had gazed at him some three years back; and then he dropped his bad, oily-looking eyes.

"I make mistakes sometimes," he said, "as to where I have been and where I have not. If this young lady saw me there, it stands to reason that I may have been there. I have a brother extremely similar. He goes about a good deal also. Probably you saw my brother."

"I saw no brother of yours, but yourself. Yourself—your mean and cowardly self—and I shall bring you to justice."

"Well, well," he replied, with a poor attempt to turn the matter lightly; "I never contradict ladies; it is an honor to be so observed by them. Now, Major, can you give me any good reason for drawing upon a bad memory? My time is valuable. I can not refer to such by-gone matters for nothing."

"We will not bribe you, if that is what you mean," Major Hockin made answer, scornfully. "This is a criminal case, and we have evidence you little dream of. Our only offer is—your own safety, if you make a clean breast of it. We are on the track of a murderer, and your connection with him will ruin you. Unless you wish to stand in the dock at his side, you will tell us every thing."

"Sir, this is violent language."

"And violent acts will follow it: if you do not give up your principal, and every word you know about him, you will leave this room in custody. I have Cosmopolitan Jack outside, and the police at a sign from him will come."

"Is this job already in the hands of the police, then?"

"No, not yet. I resolved to try you first. If you refuse, it will be taken up at once; and away goes your last chance, Sir."

Mr. Goad's large face became like a field of conflicting passions and low calculations. Terror, fury, cupidity, and doggedness never had a larger battle-field.

"Allow me at least to consult my partners," he said, in a low voice and almost with a whine; "we may do things irregular sometimes, but we never betray a client."

"Either betray your client or yourself," the Major answered, with a downright stamp. "You shall consult no one. You have by this watch forty-five seconds to consider it."

"You need not trouble yourself to time me," the other answered, sulkily; "my duty to the firm overrides private feeling. Miss Castlewood, I call you to witness, since Major Hockin is so peppery—"

"Peppery, Sir, is the very last word that ever could be applied to me. My wife, my friends, every one that knows me, even my furthest-off correspondents, agree that I am pure patience."

"It may be so, Major; but you have not shown it. Miss Castlewood, I have done you no harm. If you had been given up to me, you would have been safer than where you were. My honor would have been enlisted. I now learn things which I never dreamed of—or, at least—at least only lately. I always believed the criminality to be on the other side. We never ally ourselves with wrong. But lately things have come to my knowledge which made me doubtful as to facts. I may have been duped—I believe I have been: I am justified, therefore, in turning the tables."

"If you turn tables," broke in the Major, who was grumbling to himself at the very idea of having any pepper in his nature—"Goad, if you turn tables, mind you, you must do it better than the mesmerists. Out of this room you do not stir; no darkness—no bamboozling! Show your papers, Sir, without sleight of hand. Surrender, or you get no quarter."

To me it was quite terrifying to see my comrade thus push his victory. Mr. Goad could have killed him at any moment, and but for me perhaps would have done so. But even in his fury he kept on casting glances of superstitious awe at me, while I stood quite still and gazed at him. Then he crossed the room to a great case of drawers, unlocked something above the Major's head, made a sullen bow, and handed him a packet.

CHAPTER XLIX
WANTED, A SAWYER

To judge Mr. Goad by his own scale of morality and honor, he certainly had behaved very well through a trying and unexpected scene. He fought for his honor a great deal harder than ever it could have deserved of him; and then he strove well to appease it with cash, the mere thought of which must have flattered it. However, it was none the worse for a little disaster of this kind. At the call of duty it coalesced with interest and fine sense of law, and the contact of these must have strengthened it to face any future production.

For the moment he laid it aside in a drawer—and the smallest he possessed would hold it—and being compelled to explain his instructions (partly in short-hand and partly in cipher), he kindly, and for the main of it truly, interpreted them as follows:

"July 31, 1858.—Received directions from M. H. to attend without fail, at whatever expense, to any matter laid before us by a tall, dark gentleman bearing his card. M. H. considerably in our debt; but his father can not last long. Understand what he means, having dealt with this matter before, and managed well with it.

"August 2.—Said gentleman called, gave no name, and was very close. Had experienced some great wrong. Said that he was true heir to the C. estates now held by Lord C. Only required a little further evidence to claim them; and some of this was to be got through us. Important papers must be among the effects of the old lord's son, lately dead in California, the same for whom a reward had been offered, and we had been employed about it. Must get possession of those papers, and of the girl, if possible. Yankees to be bribed, at whatever figure, and always stand out for a high one. Asked where funds were to come from; gave good reference, and verified it. To be debited to the account of M. H. Said we would have nothing to do with it without more knowledge of our principal. Replied, with anger, that he himself was Lord C., ousted by usurpers. Had not the necessary proofs as yet, but would get them, and blast all his enemies. Had doubts about his sanity, and still greater about his solvency. Resolved to inquire into both points.

"August 3.—M. H. himself, as cool as ever, but shammed to be indignant. Said we were fools if we did not take it up. Not a farthing would he pay of his old account, and fellows like us could not bring actions. Also a hatful of money was to be made of this job, managed snugly. Emigrants to California were the easiest of all things to square up. A whole train of them disappeared this very year, by Indians or Mormons, and no bones made. The best and most active of us must go—too ticklish for an agent. We must carry on all above-board out there, and as if sent by British government. In the far West no one any wiser. Resolved to go myself, upon having a certain sum in ready.

"August 5.—The money raised. Start for Liverpool to-morrow. Require a change, or would not go. May hit upon a nugget, etc., etc."

Mr. Goad's memoranda of his adventures, and signal defeat by Uncle Sam, have no claim to be copied here, though differing much from my account. With their terse unfeeling strain, they might make people laugh who had not sadder things to think of. And it matters very little how that spy escaped, as such people almost always seem to do.

"Two questions, Goad, if you please," said Major Hockin, who had smiled sometimes, through some of his own remembrances; "what has happened since your return, and what is the name of the gentleman whom you have called 'M.H.?'"

"Is it possible that you do not know, Sir? Why, he told us quite lately that you were at his back! You must know Sir Montague Hockin."

"Yes, yes; certainly I do," the old man said, shortly, with a quick gleam in his eyes; "a highly respected gentleman now, though he may have sown his wild oats like the rest. To be sure; of course I know all about it. His meaning was good, but he was misled."

In all my little experience of life nothing yet astonished me more than this. I scarcely knew whom to believe, or what. That the Major, most upright of men, should take up his cousin's roguery—all new to him—and speak of him thus! But he gave me a nudge; and being all confusion, I said nothing, and tried to look at neither of them, because my eyes must always tell the truth.

"As to the other point," Mr. Goad went on; "since my embassy failed, we have not been trusted with the confidence we had the right to expect. Ours is a peculiar business, Sir: 'Trust me in all, or trust me not at all,' as one of our modern poets says, is the very essence of it. And possibly, Major, if that had been done, even your vigor and our sense of law might not have extorted from me what you have heard. Being cashiered, as we are, we act according to the strictest honor in divulging things no longer confided to us."

"Goad, you have done yourself the utmost credit, legally, intellectually, and—well, I will not quite say morally. If I ever have a nasty job to do—at least I mean a stealthy one—which God, who has ever kept me straight, forbid!—I will take care not to lose your address. I have a very queer thing occurring on my manor—I believe it is bound up with this affair—never mind; I must think—I hate all underhanded work."

"Major, our charges are strictly moderate. We do in a week what takes lawyers a twelvemonth. Allow me to hand you one of our new cards."

"No, no. My pockets are all full. And I don't want to have it found among my papers. No offense, Mr. Goad, no offense at all. Society is not as it was when I was young. I condemn no modern institutions, Sir, though the world gets worse every day of its life."

In terror of committing himself to any connection with such a firm, the Major put on his dark lights again, took up his cane, and let every body know, with a summary rap on the floor, that he might have relaxed, but would not allow any further liberty about it. And as he marched away, not proudly, yet with a very nice firmness, I was almost afraid to say any thing to him to disturb his high mental attitude. For Mrs. Hockin must have exclaimed that here was a noble spectacle.

"But one thing," I forced myself to suggest; "do ask one thing before we go. That strange man who called himself 'Lord Castlewood' here, and 'Captain Brown' at Soberton—have they any idea where to find him now? And why does he not come forward?"

My comrade turned back, and put these questions; and the private inquirer answered that they had no idea of his whereabouts, but could easily imagine many good reasons for his present reserve of claim. For instance, he might be waiting for discovery of further evidence; or (which was even more likely) for the death of the present Lord Castlewood, which could not be very far distant, and would remove the chief opponent. It grieved me deeply to find that my cousin's condition was so notorious, and treated of in such a cold-blooded way, like a mule fallen lame, or a Chinaman in Frisco.

"My dear, you must grow used to such things," Major Hockin declared, when he saw that I was vexed, after leaving those selfish premises. "If it were not for death, how could any body live? Right feeling is shown by considering such points, and making for the demise of others even more preparation than for our own. Otherwise there is a selfishness about it by no means Christian-minded. You look at things always from such an intense and even irreligious point of view. But such things are out of my line altogether. Your Aunt Mary understands them best."

"Would you be able," I said, "to account to Aunt Mary conscientiously for that dreadful story which I heard you tell? I scarcely knew where I stood, Major Hockin."

"You mean about Montague? Family honor must be defended at any price. Child, I was greatly pained to go beyond the truth; but in such a case it is imperative. I was shocked and amazed at my cousin's conduct; but how could I let such a fellow know that? And think what I owe to his father, Sir Rufus? No, no; there are times when Bayard himself must stretch a point. Honor and religion alike demand it; and Mrs. Hockin need never hear of it."

"Certainly I shall not speak of it," I answered, though a little surprised at his arguments; "but you mean, of course, to find out all about it. It seems to me such a suspicious thing. But I never could bear Sir Montague."

The Major smiled grimly, and, perceiving that he wished to drop the subject, I said no more. He had many engagements in London always, and I must not attempt to engross his time. However, he would not for a moment hear of leaving me any where but with Betsy, for perhaps he saw how strange I was. And, being alone at last with her, I could keep up my pride no longer.

Through all that had happened, there never had been such a dreadful trial as I had borne this day without a word to any one. Danger and loss and sad dreariness of mind, from want of young companionship; mystery also, and obscurity of life, had always been my fortune. With all of these I had striven, to the best of my very small ability, having from nature no gift except the dull one of persistence. And throughout that struggle I had felt quite sure that a noble yearning for justice and a lofty power of devotion were my two impelling principles. But now, when I saw myself sprung of low birth, and the father of my worship base-born, down fell all my arduous castles, and I craved to go under the earth and die.

For every word of Mr. Goad, and every crooked turn of little things in twist against me—even the Major's last grim smile—all began to work together, and make up a wretched tumult, sounding in my ears like drums. Where was the use of going on, of proving any body's guilt or any body's innocence, if the utmost issue of the whole would be to show my father an impostor? Then, and only then, I knew that love of abstract justice is to little minds impossible, that sense of honor is too prone to hang on chance of birth, and virtue's fountain, self-respect, springs but ill from parental taint.

When I could no longer keep such bitter imaginings to myself, but poured them forth to Betsy, she merely laughed, and asked me how I could be such a simpleton. Only to think of my father in such a light was beyond her patience! Where was my pride, she would like to know, and my birth, and my family manners? However, she did believe there was something in my ideas, if you turned them inside out, and took hold of them by the other end. It was much more likely, to her mind, that the villain, the unknown villain at the bottom of all the misery, was really the son born out of wedlock, if any such there were at all, and therefore a wild harum-scarum fellow like Ishmael in the Book of Genesis. And it would be just of a piece, she thought, with the old lord's character to drive such a man to desperation by refusing to give him a farthing.

"All that might very well be," I answered; "but it would in no way serve to explain my father's conduct, which was the great mystery of all." Nevertheless, I was glad to accept almost any view of the case rather than that which had forced itself upon me since the opening of the locket. Any doubt of that most wretched conclusion was a great relief while it lasted; and, after so long a time of hope and self-reliance, should I cast away all courage through a mere suspicion?

While I was thus re-assuring myself, and being re-assured by my faithful nurse, sad news arrived, and drove my thoughts into another crooked channel. Mrs. Hockin, to meet my anxiety for some tidings from California, had promised that if any letter came, she would not even wait for the post, but forward it by special messenger. And thus, that very same evening, I received a grimy epistle, in an unknown hand, with the postmark of Sacramento. Tearing it open, I read as follows:

"MISS 'REMA,—No good luck ever came, since you, to this Blue River Station, only to be washed away, and robbed by greasers, and shot through the ribs, and got more work than can do, and find an almighty nugget sent by Satan. And now the very worst luck of all have come, wholly and out of all denial, by you and your faces and graces and French goings on. Not that I do not like you, mind; for you always was very polite to me, and done your best when you found me trying to put up with the trials put on me. But now this trial is the worst of all that ever come to my establishings; and to go away now as I used to think of doing when tyrannized upon is out of my way altogether, and only an action fit for a half-breed. Sawyer Gundry hath cut and run, without a word behind him—no instructions for orders in hand, and pouring in—no directions where to find him, not even 'God bless you' to any one of the many hands that looked up to him. Only a packet of dollars for me to pay the wages for two months to come, and a power of lawyer to receive all debts, and go on anyhow just the same. And to go on just the same is more than the worst of us has the heart for, without the sight of his old red face. He may have been pretty sharp, and too much the master now and then, perhaps; but to do without him is a darned sight worse, and the hands don't take to me like him. Many's the time I have seen his faults, of having his own way, and such likes, and paying a man beyond his time if his wife was out of order. And many's the time I have said myself I was fitter to be at the head of it.

"About that I was right enough, perhaps, if I had started upon my own hook; but to stand in the tracks he has worn to his own foot is to go into crooked compasses. There is never a day without some hand threatening to strike and to better himself, as if they were hogs to come and go according to the acorns; and such low words I can never put up with, and packs them off immediate. No place can be carried on if the master is to shut up his lips to impudence. And now I have only got three hands left, with work enough for thirty, and them three only stopped on, I do believe, to grumble of me if the Sawyer do come home!

"But what we all want to know—and old Suan took a black stick to make marks for you—is why the old man hath run away, and where. Young Firm, who was getting a sight too uppish for me to have long put up with him, he was going about here, there, and every where, from the very first time of your going away, opening his mouth a deal too much, and asking low questions how long I stopped to dinner. Old Suan said he was troubled in his mind, as the pale-faces do about young girls, instead of dragging them to their wigwams; and she would give him a spell to get over it. But nothing came of that; and when the war broke out, he had words with his grandfather, and went off, so they said, to join the rebels.

"Sawyer let him go, as proud as could be, though he would sooner have cut his own head off; and the very same night he sat down by his fire and shammed to eat supper as usual. But I happened to go in to get some orders, and, my heart, I would never wish to see such things again!

"The old man would never waste a bit of victuals, as you know, Miss 'Rema; and, being acquaint with Suan's way of watching, he had slipped all his supper aside from his plate, and put it on a clean pocket-handkerchief to lock it in the press till his appetite should serve; and I caught him in the act, and it vexed him. 'Ha'n't you the manners to knock at the door?' he said; and I said, 'Certainly,' and went back and done it; and, troubled as he was, he grinned a bit. Then he bowed his great head, as he always did when he knew he had gone perhaps a trifle too far with a man in my position. I nodded to forgive him, and he stood across, and saw that he could do no less than liquor me, after such behavior. But he only brought out one glass; and I said, 'Come, Colonel, square is square, you know.' 'Excuse of me, Martin,' he said; 'but no drop of strong drink passes the brim of my mouth till this gallivanting is done with. I might take too much, as the old men do, to sink what they don't want to think on.' 'You mean about bully-cock Firm,' says I; 'rebel Firm—nigger-driver Firm.' 'Hush!' he said; 'no bad words about it. He has gone by his conscience and his heart. What do we know of what come inside of him?'

"This was true enough, for I never did make that boy out to my liking: and the old man now was as stiff as a rock, and pretty nigh as peculiar. He made me a cocktail of his own patent, to show how firm his hand was; but the lines of his face was like wainscot mouldings, and the cords of his arm stood out like cogs. Then he took his long pipe, as he may have done perhaps every blessed night for the last fifty years; but that length of time ought to have learned him better than to go for to fill it upside down. 'Ha, ha!' he said; 'every thing is upside down since I was a man under heaven—countries and nations and kindreds and duties; and why not a old tobacco-pipe? That's the way babies blow bubbles with them. We shall all have to smoke 'em that way if our noble republic is busted up. Fill yours, and try it, Martin.'

"Instead of enjoying my cocktail, Miss 'Rema, I never was so down at mouth; for, to my mind, his old heart was broken while he carried on so. And let every body say what they will, one thing there is no denying of. Never was seen on this side of the big hills a man fit to walk in the tracks of Uncle Sam, so large and good-hearted according to his lights, hard as a grizzly bear for a man to milk him, but soft in the breastbone as a young prairie-hen for all folk down upon their nine-pins.

"You may be surprised, miss, to find me write so long. Fact is, the things won't go out of my mind without it. And it gives me a comfort, after all I may have said, to put good opinions upon paper. If he never should turn up again, my language will be to his credit; whereas if he do come back, with the betting a horse to a duck against it, to his pride he will read this testimonial of yours, faithfully, MARTIN CLOGFAST.

"P.S.—Can't carry on like this much longer. Enough to rip one's heart up. You never would know the old place, miss. The heads of the horses is as long as their tails with the way they carry them; the moss is as big as a Spaniard's beard upon the kitchen door-sill; and the old dog howls all day and night, like fifty thousand scalpers. Suan saith, if you was to come back, the lad might run home after you. 'Tisn't the lad I cares about so much, but poor old Sawyer, at his time of life, swallowed up in the wilderness."

CHAPTER L
THE PANACEA

As if my own trouble were not enough, so deeply was I grieved by this sad news that I had a great mind to turn back on my own and fly to far-off disasters. To do so appeared for the moment a noble thing, and almost a duty; but now, looking back, I perceive that my instinct was right when it told me to stay where I was, and see out my own sad story first. And Betsy grew hot at the mere idea of my hankering after a miller's affairs, as she very rudely expressed it. To hear about lords and ladies, and their crimes and adventures, was lovely; but to dwell upon people of common birth, and in trade, was most unbeseeming. A man who mended his own mill, and had hands like horn—well, even she was of better blood than that, she hoped.

Before these large and liberal views had fairly been expounded, Major Hockin arrived, with his mind in such a state that he opened his watch every second.

"Erema, I must speak to you alone," he cried; "no, not even you, Mrs. Strouss, if you please. If my ward likes to tell you, why, of course she can; but nobody shall say that I did. There are things that belong to the family alone. The most loyal retainers—you know what I mean."

"General, I was not aware that you belonged to the family. But this way, Sir; this way, if you please. There is lath and plaster to that wall, and a crack in the panel of the door, Sir. But here is a room where I keep my jams, with double brick and patent locks, from sweet-toothed lodgers. The 'scutcheon goes over the key-hole, General. Perhaps you will see to that, while I roll up the carpet outside; and then, if any retainers come, you will hear their footsteps."

"Bless the woman, what a temper she has!" whispered the Major, in dread of her ears. "Is she gone, Erema? She wants discipline."

"Yes, she is gone," I said, trying to be lightsome; "but you are enough to frighten any one."

"So far from that, she has quite frightened me. But never mind such trifles. Erema, since I saw you I have discovered, I may almost say, every thing."

Coming upon me so suddenly, even with all allowance made for the Major's sanguine opinion of his own deeds, this had such effect upon my flurried brain that practice alone enabled me to stand upright and gaze at him.

"Perhaps you imagined when you placed the matter in my hands, Miss Castlewood," he went on, with sharp twinkles from the gables of his eyes, but soft caresses to his whiskers, "that you would be left in the hands of a man who encouraged a crop of hay under his feet. Never did you or any body make a greater mistake. That is not my character, Miss Castlewood."

"Why do you call me 'Miss Castlewood' so? You quite make me doubt my own right to the name."

Major Hockin looked at me with surprise, which gladdened even more than it shamed me. Clearly his knowledge of all, as he described it, did not comprise the disgrace which I feared.

"You are almost like Mrs. Strouss to-day," he answered, with some compassion. "What way is the wind? I have often observed that when one female shows asperity, nearly all the others do the same. The weather affects them more than men, because they know nothing about it. But to come back—are you prepared to hear what I have got to tell you?"

I bowed without saying another word. For he should be almost the last of mankind to give a lecture upon irritation.

"Very well; you wish me to go on. Perceiving how sadly you were upset by the result of those interviews, first with Handkin, and then with Goad, after leaving you here I drove at once to the office, studio, place of business, or whatever you please to call it, of the famous fellow in the portrait line, whose anagram, private mark, or whatever it is, was burned into the back of the ivory. Handkin told me the fellow was dead, or, of course, his work would be worth nothing; but the name was carried on, and the register kept, at a little place somewhere in Soho, where, on the strength of his old repute, they keep up a small trade with inferior hands. I gave them a handsome order for a thing that will never be handsome, I fear—my old battered physiognomy. And then I produced the locket which in some queer state of mind you had given me, and made them hunt out their old books, and at last discovered the very entry. But to verify it I must go to Paris, where his son is living."

"Whose son? Lord Castlewood's?"

"Erema, have you taken leave of your senses? What son has Lord Castlewood? The artist's son, to be sure; the son of the man who did the likeness. Is it the vellum and the stuff upon it that has so upset your mind? I am glad that you showed it to me, because it would have been mean to do otherwise. But show it to no one else, my dear, except your cousin, Lord Castlewood. He has the first right of all to know it, though he will laugh at it as I do. Trumpery of that sort! Let them produce a certified copy of a register. If they could do that, need they ever have shot that raffish old lord—I beg pardon, my dear—your highly respected grandfather? No, no; don't tell me. Nicholas Hockin was never in any way famous for want of brains, my dear, and he tells you to keep your pluck up."

"I never can thank you enough," I replied, "for such inspiriting counsel. I have been rather miserable all this day. And I have had such a letter from America!"

Without my intending any offer of the kind, or having such idea at the furthest tip of any radius of mind, I found myself under a weight about the waist, like the things the young girls put on now. And this was the arm of the Major, which had been knocked about in some actions, but was useful still to let other people know, both in this way and that, what he thought of them. And now it let me know that he pitied me.

This kindness from so old a soldier made me partial to him. He had taken an age to understand me, because my father was out of the army almost before I was born, and therefore I had no traditions. Also, from want of drilling, I had been awkward to this officer, and sometimes mutinous, and sometimes a coward. All that, however, he forgave me when he saw me so downhearted; and while I was striving to repress all signs, the quivering of my lips perhaps suggested thoughts of kissing. Whereupon he kissed my forehead with nice dry lips, and told me not to be at all afraid.

"How many times have you been brave?" he inquired, to set me counting, knowing from all his own children, perhaps, that nothing stops futile tears and the waste of sobs like prompt arithmetic. "Six, if not seven, times you have displayed considerable valor. Are you going to fall away through some wretched imagination of your own? Now don't stop to argue—time will not allow it. I have put Cosmopolitan Jack as well upon the track of Captain Brown. I have not told you half of what I could tell, and what I am doing; but never mind, never mind; it is better that you should not know too much, my dear. Young minds, from their want of knowledge of the world, are inclined to become uneasy. Now go to bed and sleep soundly, Erema, for we have lots to do to-morrow, and you have had a most worrying day to-day. To-morrow, of course, you must come with me to Paris. You can parleyvoo better than I can."

However, as it happened, I did nothing of the kind, for when he came back in the morning, and while he was fidgeting and hurrying me, and vowing that we should lose the tidal train, a letter from Bruntsea was put into my hand. I saw Mrs. Price's clear writing, followed by good Aunt Mary's crooked lines, and knew that the latter must have received it too late to be sent by her messenger. In few words it told me that if I wished to see my cousin alive, the only chance was to start immediately.

Shock and self-reproach and wonder came (as usual) before grief, which always means to stay, and waits to get its mourning ready. I loved and respected my cousin more deeply than any one living, save Uncle Sam; and now to lose them both at once seemed much too dreadful to be true. There was no time to think. I took the Major's cab, and hurried off to Paddington, leaving him to catch his tidal train.

Alas! when I got to Castlewood, there was but a house of mourning! Faithful Stixon's eyes were dim, and he pointed upward and said, "Hush!" I entered with great awe, and asked, "How long?" And he said, "Four-and-twenty hours now; and a more peacefuller end was never seen, and to lament was sinful; but he was blessed if he could help it." I told him, through my tears, that this was greatly to his credit, and he must not crush fine feelings, which are an honor to our nature. And he said that I was mistress now, and must order him to my liking.

I asked him to send Mrs. Price to me, if she was not too busy; and he answered that he believed her to be a very good soul, and handy. And if he ever had been thought to speak in a sense disparishing of her, such things should not be borne in mind, with great afflictions over us. Mrs. Price, hearing that I was come, already was on her way to me, and now glanced at the door for Mr. Stixon to depart, in a manner past misunderstanding.

"He gives himself such airs!" she said; "sometimes one would think—but I will not trouble you now with that, Miss Castlewood, or Lady Castlewood—which do you please to be called, miss? They say that the barony goes on, when there is no more Viscount."

"I please to be called 'Miss Castlewood,' even if I have any right to be called that. But don't let us talk of such trifles now. I wish to hear only of my cousin."

"Well, you know, ma'am, what a sufferer he has been for years. If ever an angel had pains all over, and one leg compulsory of a walking-stick, that angel was his late lordship. He would stand up and look at one, and give orders in that beautiful silvery voice of his, just as if he was lying on a bed of down. And never a twitch, nor a hitch in his face, nor his words, nor any other part of him. I assure you, miss, that I have been quite amazed and overwhelmed with interest while looking at his poor legs, and thinking—"

"I can quite enter into it. I have felt the same. But please to come to what has happened lately."

"The very thing I was at the point of doing. Then last Sunday, God alone knows why, the pain did not come on at all. For the first time for seven years or more the pain forgot the time-piece. His lordship thought that the clock was wrong; but waited with his usual patience, though missing it from the length of custom, instead of being happy. But when it was come to an hour too late for the proper attack of the enemy, his lordship sent orders for Stixon's boy to take a good horse and ride to Pangbourne for a highly respectable lawyer. There was no time to fetch Mr. Spines, you see, miss, the proper solicitor, who lives in London. The gentleman from Pangbourne was here by eight o'clock; and then and there his lordship made his will, to supersede all other wills. He put it more clearly, the lawyer said, than he himself could have put it, but not, of course, in such legal words, but doubtless far more beautiful. Nobody in the house was forgotten; and the rule of law being, it seems, that those with best cause to remember must not witness, two of the tenants were sent for, and wrote down their names legitimate. And then his lordship lay back and smiled, and said, 'I shall have no more pain.'

"All that night and three days more he slept as sound as a little child, to make up for so many years. We called two doctors in; but they only whispered and looked dismal, and told us to have hot water ready at any hour of the day or night. Nobody loved him as I did, miss, from seeing so much of his troubles and miraculous way of bearing them; and I sat by the hour and hour, and watched him, trusting no paid nurses.

"It must have been eight o'clock on Wednesday morning—what is to-day? Oh, Friday—then Thursday morning it must have been, when the clouds opened up in the east, and the light of the sun was on the window-sill, not glaring or staring, but playing about, with patterns of leaves between it; and I went to screen it from his poor white face; but he opened his eyes, as if he had been half awake, half dreaming, and he tried to lift one of his thin, thin hands to tell me not to do it. So I let the curtain stay as it was, and crept back, and asked, very softly, 'Will your lordship have some breakfast?'

"He did not seem to comprehend me, but only watched the window; and if ever a blessed face there was, looking toward heaven's glory, his lordship had it, so that I could scarcely keep from sobbing. For I never had seen any living body die, but knew that it must be so. He heard me catching my breath, perhaps, or at any rate he looked at me; and the poor angel knew that I was a woman; and being full of high respect, as he always was for females—in spite of the way they had served him—it became apparent to his mind that the pearl button of his neck was open, as ordered by the doctors. And he tried to lift his hand to do it; and then he tried to turn away, but could not manage either. Poor dear! the only movement he could make was to a better world.

"Then I drew the sheet across his chest, and he gave me a little smile of thanks, and perhaps he knew whose hand it was. But the look of his kind soft eyes was flickering—not steady, I mean, miss—but glancing and stopping and going astray, as drops of rain do on the window-glass. But I could not endure to examine him much; at such a holy time I felt that to watch death was unholy.

"Perhaps I ought to have rung the bell for others to be present. But his lordship was always shy, you know, miss; and with none of his kindred left, and no wife to say 'good-by' to him, right or wrong I resolved alone to see him depart to his everlasting rest. And people may talk about hirelings, but I think nobody loved him as I did."

Here Mrs. Price broke fairly down, and I could not help admiring her. To a faithful servant's humility and duty she had added a woman's pure attachment to one more gifted than herself, and ruined for life by her own sex. But she fell away frightened and ashamed beneath my look, as if I had caught her in sacrilege.

"Well, miss, we all must come and go," she began again, rather clumsily; "and, good and great as he was, his lordship has left few to mourn for him. Only the birds and beasts and animals that he was so good to; they will miss him, if men don't. There came one of his favorite pigeons, white as snow all over, and sat on the sill of the window, and cooed, and arched up its neck for his fingers. And he tried to put his fingers out, but they were ice already. Whether that or something else brought home his thoughts, who knows, miss? but he seemed to mix the pigeon up with some of his own experience.

"'Say that I have forgiven her, if ever she did harm to me,' he whispered, without moving lips. 'Times and times, when I was young, I was not always steady;' and then he seemed to wander in his mind among old places; and he would have laughed at something if his voice had been sufficient.

"'Bitter grief and pain shall never come again,' he seemed to breathe, with a calm, soft smile, like a child with its rhyme about the rain when the sun breaks out; and sure enough, the sun upon the quilt above his heart was shining, as if there could be no more clouds. Then he whispered a few short words to the Lord, more in the way of thanks than prayer, and his eyes seemed to close of their own accord, or with some good spirit soothing them. And when or how his sleep passed from this world into the other there was scarcely the flutter of a nerve to show. There he lies, like an image of happiness. Will you come and see him?"

I followed her to the bedroom, and am very glad that I did so; for it showed me the bliss of a good man's rest, and took away my fear of death.

CHAPTER LI
LIFE SINISTER

When business and the little cares of earthly life awoke again, every one told me (to my great surprise and no small terror at first, but soon to increasing acquiescence) that I was now the mistress of the fair estates of Castlewood, and, the male line being extinct, might claim the barony, if so pleased me; for that, upon default of male heirs, descended by the spindle. And as to the property, with or without any will of the late Lord Castlewood, the greater part would descend to me under unbarred settlement, which he was not known to have meddled with. On the contrary, he confirmed by his last will the settlement—which they told me was quite needless—and left me all that he had to leave, except about a thousand pounds distributed in legacies. A private letter to me was sealed up with his will, which, of course, it would not behoove me to make public. But thus much—since our family history is, alas! so notorious—in duty to him I should declare. He begged me, if his poor lost wife—of whom he had never spoken to me—should reappear and need it, to pay her a certain yearly sum, which I thought a great deal too much for her, but resolved to obey him exactly.

Neither the will nor the letter contained any reference to my grandfather, or the possibility of an adverse claim. I could not, however, be quit of deep uneasiness and anxiety, but stanchly determined that every acre should vanish in folds of "the long robe" rather than pass to a crafty villain who had robbed me of all my kindred. My hatred of that man deepened vastly, as he became less abstract, while my terror decreased in proportion. I began to think that, instead of being the reckless fiend I had taken him for, he was only a low, plotting, cold-blooded rogue, without even courage to save him. By this time he must have heard all about me, my pursuit of him, and my presence here—then why not come and shoot me, just as he shot my grandfather?

The idea of this was unwelcome; still, I felt no sort of gratitude, but rather a lofty contempt toward him for not having spirit to try it. In Shoxford church-yard he had expressed (if Sexton Rigg was not then deceived) an unholy wish to have me there, at the feet of my brothers and sisters. Also he had tried to get hold of me—doubtless with a view to my quietude—when

I was too young to defend myself, and left at haphazard in a lawless land. What was the reason, if his mind was still the same, for ceasing to follow me now? Was I to be treated with contempt as one who had tried her best and could do nothing, as a feeble creature whose movements were not even worth inquiry? Anger at such an idea began to supersede fear, as my spirits returned.

Meanwhile Major Hockin was making no sign as to what had befallen him in Paris, or what Cosmopolitan Jack was about. But, strangely enough, he had sent me a letter from Bruntsea instead of Paris, and addressed in grand style to no less a person than "The right honorable Baroness Castlewood"—a title which I had resolved, for the present, neither to claim nor acknowledge. In that letter the Major mingled a pennyweight of condolence with more congratulation than the post could carry for the largest stamp yet invented. His habit of mind was to magnify things; and he magnified my small grandeur, and seemed to think nothing else worthy of mention.

Through love of the good kind cousin I had lost, even more than through common and comely respect toward the late head of the family, I felt it impossible to proceed, for the present, with any inquiries, but left the next move to the other side. And the other side made it, in a manner such as I never even dreamed of.

About three weeks after I became, in that sad way, the mistress, escaping one day from lawyers and agents, who held me in dreary interview, with long computations of this and of that, and formalities almost endless, I went, for a breath of good earnest fresh air, beyond precinct of garden or shrubbery. To me these seemed in mild weather to temper and humanize the wind too strictly, and take the wild spirit out of it; and now, for the turn of the moment, no wind could be too rough to tumble in. After long months of hard trouble, and worry, and fear, and sad shame, and deep sorrow, the natural spring of clear youth into air and freedom set me upward. For the nonce there was nothing upon my selfish self to keep it downward; troubles were bubbles, and grief a low thief, and reason almost treason. I drank the fine fountain of air unsullied, and the golden light stamped with the royalty of sun.

Hilarious moments are but short, and soon cold sense comes back again. Already I began to feel ashamed of young life's selfish outburst, and the vehement spring of mere bodily health. On this account I sat down sadly in a little cove of hill, whereto the soft breeze from the river came up, with a tone of wavelets, and a sprightly water-gleam. And here, in fern and yellow grass and tufted bights of bottom growth, the wind made entry for the sun, and they played with one another.

Besting here, and thinking, with my face between my hands, I wondered what would be the end. Nothing seemed secure or certain, nothing even steady or amenable to foresight. Even guess-work or the wider cast of dreams was always wrong. To-day the hills and valleys, and the glorious woods of wreathen gold, bright garnet, and deep amethyst, even that blue river yet unvexed by autumn's turbulence, and bordered with green pasture of a thousand sheep and cattle—to-day they all were mine (so far as mortal can hold ownership)—to-morrow, not a stick, or twig, or blade of grass, or fallen leaf, but might call me a trespasser. To see them while they still were mine, and to regard them humbly, I rose and took my black hat off—a black hat trimmed with mourning gray. Then turning round, I met a gaze, the wildest, darkest, and most awful ever fixed on human face.

"Who are you? What do you want here?" I faltered forth, while shrinking back for flight, yet dreading or unable to withdraw my gaze from his. The hollow ground barred all escape; my own land was a pit for me, and I must face this horror out. Here, afar from house or refuge, hand of help, or eye of witness, front to front I must encounter this atrocious murderer.

For moments, which were ages to me, he stood there without a word; and daring not to take my eyes from his, lest he should leap at me, I had no power (except of instinct), and could form no thought of him, for mortal fear fell over me. If he would only speak, would only move his lips, or any thing!

"The Baroness is not brave," he said at last, as if reproachfully; "but she need have no fear now of me. Does her ladyship happen to know who I am?"

"The man who murdered my grandfather."

"Yes, if you put a false color on events. The man who punished a miscreant, according to the truer light. But I am not here to argue points. I intend to propose a bargain. Once for all, I will not harm you. Try to listen calmly. Your father behaved like a man to me, and I will be no worse to you. The state of the law in this country is such that I am forced to carry fire-arms. Will it conduce to your peace of mind if I place myself at your mercy?"

I tried to answer; but my heart was beating so that no voice came, only a flutter in my trembling throat. Wrath with myself for want of courage wrestled in vain with pale, abject fear. The hand which offered me the pistol seemed to my dazed eyes crimson still with the blood of my grandfather.

"You will not take it? Very well; it lies here at your service. If your father's daughter likes to shoot me, from one point of view it will be just; and but for one reason, I care not. Don't look at me with pity, if you please. For what I have done I feel no remorse, no shadow of repentance. It was the best action of my life. But time will fail, unless you call upon your courage speedily. None of your family lack that; and I know that you possess it. Call your spirit up, my dear."

"Oh, please not to call me that! How dare you call me that?"

"That is right. I did it on purpose. And yet I am your uncle. Not by the laws of men, but by the laws of God—if there are such things. Now, have you the strength to hear me?"

"Yes; I am quite recovered now. I can follow every word you say. But—but I must sit down again."

"Certainly. Sit there, and I will stand. I will not touch or come nearer to you than a story such as mine requires. You know your own side of it; now hear mine.

"More than fifty years ago there was a brave young nobleman, handsome, rich, accomplished, strong, not given to drink or gambling, or any fashionable vices. His faults were few, and chiefly three—he had a headstrong will, loved money, and possessed no heart at all. With chances in his favor, this man might have done as most men do who have such gifts from fortune. But he happened to meet with a maiden far beneath him in this noble world, and he set his affections—such as they were—upon that poor young damsel.

"This was Winifred Hoyle, the daughter of Thomas Hoyle, a farmer, in a lonely part of Hampshire, and among the moors of Rambledon. The nobleman lost his way, while fishing, and being thirsty, went to ask for milk. What matter how it came about? He managed to win her heart before she heard of his rank and title. He persuaded her even to come and meet him in the valley far from her father's house, where he was wont to angle; and there, on a lonely wooden bridge across a little river, he knelt down (as men used to do) and pledged his solemn truth to her. His solemn lie—his solemn lie!

"Such love as his could not overleap the bars of rank or the pale of wealth—are you listening to me carefully?—or, at any rate, not both of them. If the poor farmer could only have given his Winifred 50,000 pounds, the peer would have dropped his pride, perhaps, so far as to be honest. But farmers in that land are poor, and Mr. Hoyle could give his only child his blessing only. And this he did in London, where his simple mind was all abroad, and he knew not church from chapel. He took his daughter for the wife of a lord, and so she took herself, poor thing! when she was but his concubine. In 1809 such tricks were easily played by villains upon young girls so simple.

"But he gave her attestation and certificate under his own hand; and her poor father signed it, and saw it secured in a costly case, and then went home as proud as need be for the father of a peer, but sworn to keep it three years secret, till the king should give consent. Such foul lies it was the pride of a lord to tell to a farmer.

"You do not exclaim—of course you do not. The instincts of your race are in you, because you are legitimate. Those of the robbed side are in me, because I am of the robbed. I am your father's elder brother. Which is the worse, you proud young womam, the dastard or the bastard?"

"You have wrongs, most bitter wrongs," I answered, meeting fierce eyes mildly; "but you should remember that I am guiltless of those wrongs, and so was my father. And I think that if you talk of birth so, you must know that gentlemen speak quietly to ladies."

"What concern is that of mine? A gentleman is some one's son. I am the son of nobody. But to you I will speak quietly, for the sake of your poor father. And you must listen quietly. I am not famous for sweet temper. Well, this great lord took his toy to Paris, where he had her at his mercy. She could not speak a word of French; she did not know a single soul. In vain she prayed him to take her to his English home; or, if not that, to restore her to her father. Not to be too long about it—any more than he was—a few months were enough for him. He found fault with her manners, with her speech, her dress, her every thing—all which he had right, perhaps, to do, but should have used it earlier. And she, although not born to the noble privilege of weariness, had been an old man's darling, and could not put up with harshness. From words they came to worse, until he struck her, told her of her shame, or rather his own infamy, and left her among strangers, helpless, penniless, and brokenhearted, to endure the consequence.

"There and thus I saw the light beneath most noble auspices. But I need not go on with all that. As long as human rules remain, this happy tale will always be repeated with immense applause. My mother's love was turned to bitter hatred of his lordship, and, when her father died from grief, to eager thirst for vengeance. And for this purpose I was born.

"You see that—for a bastard—I have been fairly educated; but not a farthing did his lordship ever pay for that, or even to support his casual. My grandfather Hoyle left his little all to his daughter Winifred; and upon that, and my mother's toil and mine, we have kept alive. Losing sight of my mother gladly—for she was full of pride, and hoped no more to trouble him, after getting her father's property—he married again, or rather he married for the first time without perjury, which enables the man to escape from it. She was of his own rank—as you know—the daughter of an earl, and not of a farmer. It would not have been safe to mock her, would it? And there was no temptation.

"The history of my mother and myself does not concern you. Such people are of no account until they grow dangerous to the great. We lived in cheap places and wandered about, caring for no one, and cared for by the same. Mrs. Hoyle and Thomas Hoyle we called ourselves when we wanted names; and I did not even know the story of our wrongs till the heat and fury of youth were past. Both for her own sake and mine my mother concealed it from me. Pride and habit, perhaps, had dulled her just desire for vengeance; and, knowing what I was, she feared—the thing which has befallen me. But when I was close upon thirty years old, and my mother eight-and-forty—for she was betrayed in her teens—a sudden illness seized her. Believing her death to be near, she told me, as calmly as possible, every thing, with all those large, quiet views of the past, which at such a time seem the regular thing, but make the wrong tenfold blacker. She did not die; if she had, it might have been better both for her and me, and many other people. Are you tired of my tale? Or do you want to hear the rest?"

"You can not be asking me in earnest," I replied, while I watched his wild eyes carefully. "Tell me the rest, if you are not afraid."

"Afraid, indeed! Then, for want of that proper tendance and comfort which a few pounds would have brought her, although she survived, she survived as a wreck, the mere relic and ruin of her poor unhappy self. I sank my pride for her sake, and even deigned to write to him, in rank and wealth so far above me, in every thing else such a clot below my heel. He did the most arrogant thing a snob can do—he never answered my letter.

"I scraped together a little money, and made my way to England, and came to that house—which you now call yours—and bearded that noble nobleman—that father to be so proud of! He was getting on now in years, and growing, perhaps, a little nervous, and my first appearance scared him. He got no obeisance from me, you may be certain, but still I did not revile him. I told him of my mother's state of mind, and the great care she required, and demanded that, in common justice, he, having brought her to this, should help her. But nothing would he promise, not a sixpence even, in the way of regular allowance. Any thing of that sort could only be arranged by means of his solicitors. He had so expensive a son, with a very large and growing family, that he could not be pledged to any yearly sum. But if I would take a draft for 100 pounds, and sign an acquittance in full of all claims, I might have it, upon proving my identity.

"What identity had I to prove? He had taken good care of that. I turned my back on him and left the house, without even asking for his curse, though as precious as a good man's blessing.

"It was a wild and windy night, but with a bright moon rising, and going across this park—or whatever it is called—I met my brother. At a crest of the road we met face to face, with the moon across our foreheads. We had never met till now, nor even heard of one another; at least he had never heard of me. He started back as if at his own ghost; but I had nothing to be startled at, in this world or the other.

"I made his acquaintance, with deference, of course, and we got on very well together. At one time it seemed good luck for him to have illegitimate kindred; for I saved his life when he was tangled in the weeds of this river while bathing. You owe me no thanks. I thought twice about it, and if the name would have ended with him, I would never have used my basket-knife. By trade I am a basket-maker, like many another 'love-child.'

"However, he was grateful, if ever any body was, for I ran some risk in doing it; and he always did his very best for me, and encouraged me to visit him. Not at his home—of course that would never do—but when he was with his regiment. Short of money as he always was, through his father's nature and his own, which in some points were the very opposite, he was even desirous to give me some of that; but I never took a farthing from him. If I had it at all, I would have it from the proper one. And from him I resolved to have it.

"How terrified you look! I am coming to it now. Are you sure that you can bear it? It is nothing very harrowing; but still, young ladies—"

"I feel a little faint," I could not help saying; "but that is nothing. I must hear the whole of it. Please to go on without minding me."

"For my own sake I will not, as well as for yours. I can not have you fainting, and bringing people here. Go to the house and take food, and recover your strength, and then come here again. I promise to be here, and your father's daughter will not take advantage of my kindness."

Though his eyes were fierce (instead of being sad) and full of strange tempestuous light, they bore some likeness to my father's, and asserted power over me. Reluctant as I was, I obeyed this man, and left him there, and went slowly to the house, walking as if in a troubled dream.

CHAPTER LII
FOR LIFE, DEATH

Upon my return, I saw nothing for a time but fans and feathers of browning fern, dark shags of ling, and podded spurs of broom and furze, and wisps of grass. With great relief (of which I felt ashamed while even breathing it), I thought that the man was afraid to tell the rest of his story, and had fled; but ere my cowardice had much time for self-congratulation a tall figure rose from the ground, and fear compelled me into courage. For throughout this long interview more and more I felt an extremely unpleasant conviction. That stranger might not be a downright madman, nor even what is called a lunatic; but still it was clear that upon certain points—the laws of this country, for instance, and the value of rank and station—his opinions were so outrageous that his reason must be affected. And, even without such proofs as these, his eyes and his manner were quite enough. Therefore I had need of no small caution, not only concerning my words and gestures, but as to my looks and even thoughts, for he seemed to divine these last as quickly as they flashed across me. I never had learned to conceal my thoughts, and this first lesson was an awkward one.

"I hope you are better," he said, as kindly as it was possible for him to speak. "Now have no fear of me, once more I tell you. I will not sham any admiration, affection, or any thing of that kind; but as for harming you—why, your father was almost the only kind heart I ever met!"

"Then why did you send a most vile man to fetch me, when my father was dead in the desert?"

"I never did any thing of the sort. It was done in my name, but not by me; I never even heard of it until long after, and I have a score to settle with the man who did it."

"But Mr. Goad told me himself that you came and said you were the true Lord Castlewood, and ordered him at once to America. I never saw truth more plainly stamped on a new situation—the face of a rogue—than I saw it then on the face of Mr. Goad."

"You are quite right; he spoke the truth—to the utmost of his knowledge. I never saw Goad, and he never saw me. I never even dreamed of pretending to the title. I was personated by a mean, low friend of Sir Montague Hockin; base-born as I am, I would never stoop to such a trick. You will find out the meaning of that by-and-by. I have taken the law into my own hands—it is the only way to work such laws—I have committed what is called a crime. But, compared with Sir Montague Hockin, I am whiter than yonder shearling on his way to the river for his evening drink."

I gazed at his face, and could well believe it. The setting sun shone upon his chin and forehead—good, resolute, well-marked features; his nose and mouth were keen and clear, his cheeks curt and pale (though they would have been better for being a trifle cleaner). There was nothing suggestive of falsehood or fraud, and but for the wildness of the eyes and flashes of cold ferocity, it might have been called a handsome face.

"Very well," he began again, with one of those jerks which had frightened me, "your father was kind to me, very kind indeed; but he knew the old lord too well to attempt to interpose on my behalf. On the other hand, he gave no warning of my manifest resolve; perhaps he thought it a woman's threat, and me no better than a woman! And partly for his sake, no doubt, though mainly for my mother's, I made the short work which I made; for he was horribly straitened—and in his free, light way he told me so—by his hard curmudgeon of a father.

"To that man, hopeless as he was, I gave fair grace, however, and plenty of openings for repentance. None of them would he embrace, and he thought scorn of my lenity. And I might have gone on with such weakness longer, if I had not heard that his coach-and-four was ordered for the Moonstock Inn.

"That he should dare thus to pollute the spot where he had so forsworn himself! I resolved that there he should pay justice, either with his life or death. And I went to your father's place to tell him to prepare for disturbances; but he was gone to see his wife, and I simply borrowed a pistol.

"Now you need not be at all afraid nor shrink away from me like that. I was bound upon stricter justice than any judge that sets forth on circuit; and I meant to give, and did give, what no judge affords to the guilty—the chance of leading a better life. I had brought my mother to England, and she was in a poor place in London; her mind was failing more and more, and reverting to her love-time, the one short happiness of her life. 'If I could but see him, if I could but see him, and show him his tall and clever son, he would forgive me all my sin in thinking ever to be his wife. Oh, Thomas! I was too young to know it. If I could but see him once, just once!'

"How all this drove me no tongue can tell. But I never let her know it; I only said, 'Mother, he shall come and see you if he ever sees any body more!'

And she trusted me and was satisfied. She only said, 'Take my picture, Thomas, to remind him of the happy time, and his pledge to me inside of it.' And she gave me what she had kept for years in a bag of chamois leather, the case of which I spoke before, which even in our hardest times she would never send to the pawn-shop.

"The rest is simple enough. I swore by the God, or the Devil, who made me, that this black-hearted man should yield either his arrogance or his life. I followed him to the Moon valley, and fate ordained that I should meet him where he forswore himself to my mother; on that very plank where he had breathed his deadly lies he breathed his last. Would you like to hear all about it?"

For answer I only bowed my head. His calm, methodical way of telling his tale, like a common adventure with a dog, was more shocking than any fury.

"Then it was this. I watched him from the Moonstock Inn to a house in the village, where he dined with company; and I did not even know that it was the house of his son, your father—so great a gulf is fixed between the legitimate and the bastard! He had crossed the wooden bridge in going, and was sure to cross it in coming back. How he could tread those planks without contrition and horror—but never mind. I resolved to bring him to a quiet parley there, and I waited in the valley.

"The night was soft, and dark in patches where the land or wood closed in; and the stream was brown and threw no light, though the moon was on the uplands. Time and place alike were fit for our little explanation. The path wound down the meadow toward me, and I knew that he must come. My firm intention was to spare him, if he gave me a chance of it; but he never had the manners to do that.

"Here I waited, with the cold leaves fluttering around me, until I heard a firm, slow step coming down the narrow path. Then a figure appeared in a stripe of moonlight, and stopped, and rested on a staff. Perhaps his lordship's mind went back some five-and-thirty years, to times when he told pretty stories here; and perhaps he laughed to himself to think how well he had got out of it. Whatever his meditations were, I let him have them out, and waited.

"If he had even sighed, I might have felt more kindness toward him; but he only gave something between a cough and a grunt, and I clearly heard him say, 'Gout to-morrow morning! what the devil did I drink port-wine for!' He struck the ground with his stick and came onward, thinking far more of his feet than heart.

"Then, as he planted one foot gingerly on the timber and stayed himself, I leaped along the bridge and met him, and without a word looked at him. The moon was topping the crest of the hills and threw my shadow upon him, the last that ever fell upon his body to its knowledge.

"'Fellow, out of the way!' he cried, with a most commanding voice and air, though only too well he knew me; and my wrath against him began to rise.

"'You pass not here, and you never make another live step on this earth,' I said, as calmly as now I speak, 'unless you obey my orders.'

"He saw his peril, but he had courage—perhaps his only virtue. 'Fool! whoever you are,' he shouted, that his voice might fetch him help; 'none of these moon-struck ways with me! If you want to rob me, try it!'

"'You know too well who I am,' I answered, as he made to push me back. 'Lord Castlewood, here you have the choice—to lick the dust, or be dust! Here you forswore yourself; here you pay for perjury. On this plank you knelt to poor Winifred Hoyle, whom you ruined and cast by; and now on this plank you shall kneel to her son and swear to obey him—or else you die!'

"In spite of all his pride, he trembled as if I had been Death himself, instead of his own dear eldest son.

"'What do you want!' As he asked, he laid one hand on the rickety rail and shook it, and the dark old tree behind him shook. 'How much will satisfy you?'

"'Miser, none of your money for us! it is too late for your half crowns! We must have a little of what you have grudged—having none to spare—your honor. My demands are simple, and only two. My mother is fool enough to yearn for one more sight of your false face; you will come with me and see her.'

"'And if I yield to that, what next?'

"'The next thing is a trifle to a nobleman like you. Here I have, in this blue trinket (false gems and false gold, of course), your solemn signature to a lie. At the foot of that you will have the truth to write, "I am a perjured liar!" and proudly sign it "Castlewood," in the presence of two witnesses. This can not hurt your feelings much, and it need not be expensive.'

"Fury flashed in his bright old eyes, but he strove to check its outbreak. The gleaning of life, after threescore years, was better, in such lordly fields, than the whole of the harvest we got. He knew that I had him all to myself, to indulge my filial affection.

"'You have been misled; you have never heard the truth; you have only heard your mother's story. Allow me to go back and to sit in a dry place; I am tired, and no longer young; you are bound to hear my tale as well. I passed a dry stump just now; I will go back: there is no fear of interruption.' My lord was talking against time.

"'From this bridge you do not budge until you have gone on your knees and sworn what I shall dictate to you; this time it shall be no perjury. Here I hold your cursed pledge—'

"He struck at me, or at the locket—no matter which—but it flew away. My right arm was crippled by his heavy stick; but I am left-handed, as a bastard should be. From my left hand he took his death, and I threw the pistol after him: such love had he earned from his love-child!"

Thomas Castlewood, or Hoyle, or whatever else his name was, here broke off from his miserable words, and, forgetting all about my presence, set his gloomy eyes on the ground. Lightly he might try to speak, but there was no lightness in his mind, and no spark of light in his poor dead soul. Being so young, and unacquainted with the turns of life-worn mind, I was afraid to say a word except to myself, and to myself I only said, "The man is mad, poor fellow; and no wonder!"

The sun was setting, not upon the vast Pacific from desert heights, but over the quiet hills and through the soft valleys of tame England; and, different as the whole scene was, a certain other sad and fearful sunset lay before me: the fall of night upon my dying father and his helpless child, the hour of anguish and despair! Here at last was the cause of all laid horribly before me; and the pity deeply moving me passed into cold abhorrence. But the man was lost in his own visions.

"So in your savage wrath," I said, "you killed your own father, and in your fright left mine to bear the brunt of it."

He raised his dark eyes heavily, and his thoughts were far astray from mine. He did not know what I had said, though he knew that I had spoken. The labor of calling to mind and telling his treatment of his father had worked upon him so much that he could not freely shift attention.

"I came for something, something that can be only had from you," he said, "and only since your cousin's death, and something most important. But will you believe me? it is wholly gone, gone from mind and memory!"

"I am not surprised at that," I answered, looking at his large wan face, and while I did so, losing half my horror in strange sadness. "Whatever it is, I will do it for you; only let me know by post."

"I see what you mean—not to come any more. You are right about that, for certain. But your father was good to me, and I loved him, though I had no right to love any one. My letter will show that I wronged him never. The weight of the world is off my mind since I have told you every thing; you can send me to the gallows, if you think fit, but leave it till my mother dies. Good-by, poor child. I have spoiled your life, but only by chance consequence, not in murder-birth—as I was born."

Before I could answer or call him back, if I even wished to do so, he was far away, with his long, quiet stride; and, like his life, his shadow fell, chilling, sombre, cast away.

CHAPTER LIII
BRUNTSEA DEFIANT

Thus at last—by no direct exertion of my own, but by turn after turn of things to which I blindly gave my little help—the mystery of my life was solved. Many things yet remained to be fetched up to focus and seen round; but the point of points was settled.

Of all concerned, my father alone stood blameless and heroic. What tears of shame and pride I shed, for ever having doubted him!—not doubting his innocence of the crime itself, but his motives for taking it upon him. I had been mean enough to dream that my dear father outraged justice to conceal his own base birth!

That ever such thought should have entered my mind may not make me charitable to the wicked thoughts of the world at large, but, at any rate, it ought to do so. And the man in question, my own father, who had starved himself to save me! Better had I been the most illegal child ever issued into this cold world, than dare to think so of my father, and then find him the model of every thing.

To hide the perjury, avarice, and cowardice of his father, and to appease the bitter wrong, he had even bowed to take the dark suspicion on himself, until his wronged and half-sane brother (to whom, moreover, he owed his life) should have time to fly from England. No doubt he blamed himself as much as he condemned the wretched criminal, because he had left his father so long unwarned and so unguarded, and had thoughtlessly used light words about him, which fell not lightly on a stern, distempered mind. Hence, perhaps, the exclamation which had told against him so.

And then when he broke jail—which also told against him terribly—to revisit his shattered home, it is likely enough that he meant after that to declare the truth, and stand his trial as a man should do. But his wife, perhaps, in her poor weak state, could not endure the thought of it, knowing how often jury is injury, and seeing all the weight against him. She naturally pledged him to pursue his flight, "for her sake," until she should be better able to endure his trial, and until he should have more than his own pure word and character to show. And probably if he had then been tried, with so many things against him, and no production of that poor brother, his tale would have seemed but a flimsy invention, and "Guilty" would have been the verdict. And they could not know that, in such case, the guilty man would have come forward, as we shall see that he meant to do.

When my father heard of his dear wife's death, and believed, no doubt, that I was buried with the rest, the gloom of a broken and fated man, like polar night, settled down on him. What matter to him about public opinion or any thing else in the world just now? The sins of his father were on his head; let them rest there, rather than be trumpeted by him. He had nothing to care for; let him wander about. And so he did for several years, until I became a treasure to him—for parental is not intrinsic value—and then, for my sake, as now appeared, he betook us both to a large kind land.

Revolving these things sadly, and a great many more which need not be told, I thought it my duty to go as soon as possible to Bruntsea, and tell my good and faithful friends what I was loath to write about. There, moreover, I could obtain what I wanted to confirm me—the opinion of an upright, law-abiding, honorable man about the course I proposed to take. And there I might hear something more as to a thing which had troubled me much in the deepest of my own troubles—the melancholy plight of dear Uncle Sam. Wild, and absurd as it may appear to people of no gratitude, my heart was set upon faring forth in search of the noble Sawyer, if only it could be reconciled with my duty here in England. That such a proceeding would avail but little, seemed now, alas! too manifest; but a plea of that kind generally means that we have no mind to do a thing.

Be that as it will, I made what my dear Yankees—to use the Major's impertinent phrase—call "straight tracks" for that ancient and obsolete town, rejuvenized now by its Signor. The cause of my good friend's silence— not to use that affected word "reticence"—was quite unknown to me, and disturbed my spirit with futile guesses.

Resolute, therefore, to pierce the bottom of every surviving mystery, I made claim upon "Mr. Stixon, junior"—as "Stixon's boy" had now vindicated his right to be called, up to supper-time—and he with high chivalry responded. Not yet was he wedded to Miss Polly Hopkins, the daughter of the pickled-pork man; otherwise would he or could he have made telegraphic blush at the word "Bruntsea?" And would he have been quite so eager to come?

Such things are trifling, compared to our own, which naturally fill the universe. I was bound to be a great lady now, and patronize and regulate and drill all the doings of nature. So I durst not even ask, though desiring much to do so, how young Mr. Stixon was getting on with his delightful

Polly. And his father, as soon as he found me turned into the mistress, and "his lady" (as he would have me called thenceforth, whether or no on my part), not another word would he tell me of the household sentiments, politics, or romances. It would have been thought a thing beneath me to put any nice little questions now, and I was obliged to take up the tone which others used toward me. But all the while I longed for freedom, Uncle Sam, Suan Isco, and even Martin of the Mill.

Law business, however, and other hinderances, kept me from starting at once for Bruntsea, impatient as I was to do so. Indeed, it was not until the morning of the last Saturday in November that I was able to get away. The weather had turned to much rain, I remember, with two or three tempestuous nights, and the woods were almost bare of leaves, and the Thames looked brown and violent.

In the fly from Newport to Bruntsea I heard great rollers thundering heavily upon the steep bar of shingle, and such a lake of water shone in the old bed of the river that I quite believed at first that the Major had carried out his grand idea, and brought the river back again. But the flyman shook his head, and looked very serious, and told me that he feared bad times were coming. What I saw was the work of the Lord in heaven, and no man could prevail against it. He had always said, though no concern of his—for he belonged to Newport—that even a British officer could not fly in the face of the Almighty. He himself had a brother on the works, regular employed, and drawing good money, and proud enough about it; and the times he had told him across a pint of ale—howsomever, our place was to hope for the best; but the top of the springs was not come yet, and a pilot out of Newport told him the water was making uncommon strong; but he did hope the wind had nigh blowed itself out; if not, they would have to look blessed sharp tomorrow. He had heard say that in time of Queen Elizabeth sixscore of houses was washed clean away, and the river itself knocked right into the sea; and a thing as had been once might just come to pass again, though folk was all so clever now they thought they wor above it. But, for all that, their grandfathers' goggles might fit them. But here we was in Bruntsea town, and, bless his old eyes—yes! If I pleased to look along his whip, I might see ancient pilot come, he did believe, to warn of them!

Following his guidance, I descried a stout old man, in a sailor's dress, weather-proof hat, and long boots, standing on a low seawall, and holding vehement converse with some Bruntsea boatmen and fishermen who were sprawling on the stones as usual.

"Driver, you know him. Take the lower road," I said, "and ask what his opinion is."

"No need to ask him," the flyman answered; "old Banks would never be here, miss, if he was of two opinions. He hath come to fetch his daughter out of harm, I doubt, the wife of that there Bishop Jim, they call him—the chap with two nails to his thumb, you know. Would you like to hear how they all take it, miss?"

With these words he turned to the right, and drove into Major Hockin's "Sea Parade." There we stopped to hear what was going on, and it proved to be well worth our attention. The old pilot perhaps had exhausted reason, and now was beginning to give way to wrath. The afternoon was deepening fast, with heavy gray clouds lowering, showing no definite edge, but streaked with hazy lines, and spotted by some little murky blurs or blots, like tar pots, carried slowly.

"Hath Noah's Ark ever told a lie?" the ancient pilot shouted, pointing with one hand at these, and with a clinched fist at the sea, whence came puffs of sullen air, and turned his gray locks backward. "Mackerel sky when the sun got up, mermaiden's eggs at noon, and now afore sunset Noah's Arks! Any of them breweth a gale of wind, and the three of them bodes a tempest. And the top of the springs of the year to-morrow. Are ye daft, or all gone upon the spree, my men? Your fathers would 'a knowed what the new moon meant. Is this all that cometh out of larning to read?"

"Have a pinch of 'bacco, old man," said one, "to help you off with that stiff reel. What consarn can he be of yourn?"

"Don't you be put out, mate," cried another. "Never came sea as could top that bar, and never will in our time. Go and calk your old leaky craft, Master Banks."

"We have rode out a good many gales without seeking prophet from Newport—a place never heerd on when this old town was made."

"Come and wet your old whistle at the 'Hockin Arms,' Banks. You must want it, after that long pipe."

"'Hockin Arms,' indeed!" the pilot answered, turning away in a rage from them. "What Hockin Arms will there be this time to-morrow? Hockin legs wanted, more likely, and Hockin wings. And you poor grinning ninnies, as ought to have four legs, ye'll be praying that ye had them to-morrow. However, ye've had warning, and ye can't blame me. The power of the Lord is in the air and sea. Is this the sort of stuff ye trust in?"

He set one foot against our Major's wall—an action scarcely honest while it was so green—and, coming from a hale and very thickset man, the contemptuous push sent a fathom of it outward. Rattle, rattle went the new patent concrete, starting up the lazy-pated fellows down below.

"You'll try the walls of a jail," cried one. "You go to Noah's Ark," shouted another. The rest bade him go to a place much worse; but he buttoned his jacket in disdain, and marched away, without spoiling the effect by any more weak words.

"Right you are," cried my flyman—"right you are, Master Banks. Them lubbers will sing another song to-morrow. Gee up, old hoss, then!"

All this, and the ominous scowl of the sky and menacing roar of the sea (already crowding with black rollers), disturbed me so that I could say nothing, until, at the corner of the grand new hotel, we met Major Hockin himself, attired in a workman's loose jacket, and carrying a shovel. He was covered with mud and dried flakes of froth, and even his short white whiskers were incrusted with sparkles of brine; but his face was ruddy and smiling, and his manner as hearty as ever.

"You here, Erema! Oh, I beg pardon—Baroness Castlewood, if you please. My dear, again I congratulate you."

"You have as little cause to do that as I fear I can find in your case. You have no news for me from America? How sad! But what a poor plight you yourself are in!"

"Not a bit of it. At first sight you might think so; and we certainly have had a very busy time. Send back the fly. Leave your bag at our hotel. Porter, be quick with Lady Castlewood's luggage. One piece of luck befalls me—to receive so often this beautiful hand. What a lot of young fellows now would die of envy—"

"I am glad that you still can talk nonsense," I said; "for I truly was frightened at this great lake, and so many of your houses even standing in the water."

"It will do them good. It will settle the foundations and crystallize the mortar. They will look twice as well when they come out again, and never have rats or black beetles. We were foolish enough to be frightened at first; and there may have been danger a fortnight ago. But since that tide we have worked day and night, and every thing is now so stable that fear is simply ridiculous. On the whole, it has been a most excellent thing—quite the making, in fact, of Bruntsea."

"Then Bruntsea must be made of water," I replied, gazing sadly at the gulf which parted us from the Sea Parade, the Lyceum, and Baths, the Bastion Promenade, and so on; beyond all which the streaky turmoil and misty scud of the waves were seen.

"Made of beer, more likely," he retorted, with a laugh. "If my fellows worked like horses—which they did—they also drank like fishes. Their mouths were so dry with the pickle, they said. But the total abstainers were the worst, being out of practice with the can. However, let us make no complaints. We ought to be truly thankful; and I shall miss the exercise. That is why you have heard so little from me. You see the position at a glance. I have never been to Paris at all, Erema. I have not rubbed up my parleywoo, with a blast from Mr. Bellows. I was stopped by a telegram about this job—acrior illum. I had some Latin once, quite enough for the House of Commons, but it all oozed out at my elbows; and to ladies (by some superstition) it is rude—though they treat us to bad French enough. Never mind. What I want to say is this, that I have done nothing, but respected your sad trouble; for you took a wild fancy to that poor bedridden, who never did you a stroke of good except about Cosmopolitan Jack, and whose removal has come at the very nick of time. For what could you have done for money, with the Yankees cutting each other's throats, and your nugget quite sure to be annexed, or, at the very best, squared up in greenbacks?"

"You ought not to speak so, Major Hockin. If all your plans were not under water, I should be quite put out with you. My cousin was not bedridden; neither was he at all incapable, as you have called him once or twice. He was an infinitely superior man to—to what one generally sees; and when you have heard what I have to tell, in his place you would have done just as he did. And as for money, and 'happy release'—as the people who never want it for themselves express it—such words simply sicken me; at great times they are so sordid."

"What is there in this world that is not sordid—to the young in one sense, and to the old in another?"

Major Hockin so seldom spoke in this didactic way, and I was so unable to make it out, that, having expected some tiff on his part at my juvenile arrogance, I was just in the mould for a deep impression from sudden stamp of philosophy. I had nothing to say in reply, and he went up in my opinion greatly.

He knew it; and he said, with touching kindness, "Erema, come and see your dear aunt Mary. She has had an attack of rheumatic gout in her thimble-finger, and her maids have worried her out of her life, and by far the most brilliant of her cocks (worth 20 pounds they tell me) breathed his last on Sunday night, with gapes, or croup, or something. This is why you have not heard again from her. I have been in the trenches day and night, stoning out the sea with his own stones, by a new form of concrete discovered by myself. And unless I am very much mistaken—in fact, I do not hesitate to say—But such things are not in your line at all. Let us go up to the house. Our job is done, and I think Master Neptune may pound away in vain. I have got a new range in the kitchen now, partly of my own invention; you can roast, or bake, or steam, or stew, or frizzle kabobs—all by turning a screw. And not only that, but you can keep things hot, piping hot, and ripening, as it were, better than when they first were done. Instead of any burned iron taste, or scum on the gravy, or clottiness, they mellow by waiting, and make their own sauce. If I ever have time I shall patent this invention; why, you may burn brick-dust in it, Bath-brick, hearth-stone, or potsherds! At any hour of the day or night, while the sea is in this condition, I may want my dinner; and there we have it. We say grace immediately, and down we sit. Let us take it by surprise, if it can be taken so. Up through my chief drive, instanter! I think that I scarcely ever felt more hungry. The thought of that range always sets me off. And one of its countless beauties is the noble juicy fragrance."

Major Hockin certainly possessed the art—so meritorious in a host—of making people hungry; and we mounted the hill with alacrity, after passing his letter-box, which reminded me of the mysterious lady. He pointed to "Desolate Hole," as he called it, and said that he believed she was there still, though she never came out now to watch their house. And a man of dark and repelling aspect had been seen once or twice by his workmen, during the time of their night relays, rapidly walking toward Desolate Hole. How any one could live in such a place, with the roar and the spray of the sea, as it had been, at the very door, and through the windows, some people might understand, but not the Major.

Good Mrs. Hockin received me with her usual warmth and kindness, and scolded me for having failed to write more to her, as all people seem to do when conscious of having neglected that duty themselves. Then she showed me her thimble-finger, which certainly was a little swollen; and then she poured forth her gratitude for her many blessings, as she always did after any little piece of grumbling. And I told her that if at her age I were only a quarter as pleasant and sweet of temper, I should consider myself a blessing to any man.

After dinner my host produced the locket, which he had kept for the purpose of showing it to the artist's son in Paris, and which he admired so intensely that I wished it were mine to bestow on him. Then I told him that, through a thing wholly unexpected—the confession of the criminal himself—no journey to Paris was needful now. I repeated that strange and gloomy tale, to the loud accompaniment of a rising wind and roaring sea, while both my friends listened intently.

"Now what can have led him so to come to you?" they asked; "and what do you mean to do about it?"

"He came to me, no doubt, to propose some bargain, which could not be made in my cousin's lifetime. But the telling of his tale made him feel so strange that he really could not remember what it was. As to what I am to do, I must beg for your opinion; such a case is beyond my decision." Mrs. Hockin began to reply, but stopped, looking dutifully at her lord.

"There is no doubt what you are bound to do, at least in one way," the Major said. "You are a British subject, I suppose, and you must obey the laws of the country. A man has confessed to you a murder—no matter whether it was committed twenty years ago or two minutes; no matter whether it was a savage, cold-blooded, premeditated crime, or whether there were things to palliate it. Your course is the same; you must hand him over. In fact, you ought never to have let him go."

"How could I help it?" I pleaded, with surprise. "It was impossible for me to hold him."

"Then you should have shot him with his own pistol. He offered it to you. You should have grasped it, pointed it at his heart, and told him that he was a dead man if he stirred."

"Aunt Mary, would you have done that?" I asked. "It is so easy to talk of fine things! But in the first place, I had no wish to stop him; and in the next, I could not if I had."

"My dear," Mrs. Hockin replied, perceiving my distress at this view of the subject, "I should have done exactly what you did. If the laws of this country ordain that women are to carry them out against great strong men, who, after all, have been sadly injured, why, it proves that women ought to make the laws, which to my mind is simply ridiculous."

CHAPTER LIV
BRUNTSEA DEFEATED

Little sleep had I that night. Such conflict was in my mind about the proper thing to be done next, and such a war of the wind outside, above and between the distant uproar of the long tumultuous sea. Of that sound much was intercepted by the dead bulk of the cliff, but the wind swung fiercely over this, and rattled through all shelter. In the morning the storm was furious; but the Major declared that his weather-glass had turned, which proved that the gale was breaking. The top of the tide would be at one o'clock, and after church we should behold a sight he was rather proud of—the impotent wrath of the wind and tide against his patent concrete.

"My dear, I scarcely like such talk," Mrs. Hockin gently interposed. "To me it seems almost defiant of the power of the Lord. Remember what happened to poor Smeaton—at least I think his name was Smeaton, or Stanley, was it? But I dare say you know best. He defied the strength of the Lord, like the people at the mouth of their tent, and he was swallowed up."

"Mary, my dear, get your prayer-book. Rasper's fly is waiting for us, and the parson has no manners. When he drops off, I present to the living; and I am not at all sure that I shall let George have it. He is fond of processions, and all that stuff. The only procession in the Church of England is that of the lord of the manor to his pew. I will be the master in my own church."

"Of course, dear, of course; so you ought to be. It always was so in my father's parish. But you must not speak so of our poor George. He may be 'High-Church,' as they call it; but he knows what is due to his family, and he has a large one coming."

We set off hastily for the church, through blasts of rain and buffets of wind, which threatened to overturn the cab, and the seaward window was white, as in a snowstorm, with pellets of froth, and the drift of sea-scud. I tried to look out, but the blur and the dash obscured the sight of every thing. And though in this lower road we were partly sheltered by the pebble ridge, the driver was several times obliged to pull his poor horse up and face the wind, for fear of our being blown over.

That ancient church, with its red-tiled spire, stands well up in the good old town, at the head of a street whose principal object now certainly is to lead to it. Three hundred years ago that street had business of its own to think of, and was brave perhaps with fine men and maids at the time of the Spanish Armada. Its only bravery now was the good old church, and some queer gables, and a crypt (which was true to itself by being buried up to the spandrels), and one or two corners where saints used to stand, until they were pelted out of them, and where fisher-like men, in the lodging season, stand selling fish caught at Billingsgate. But to Bruntsea itself the great glory of that street was rather of hope than of memory. Bailiff Hopkins had taken out three latticed windows, and put in one grand one of plate-glass, with "finishing" blinds all varnished. And even on a Sunday morning Bruntsea wanted to know what ever the bailiff was at behind them. Some said that he did all his pickling on a Sunday; and by putting up "spectacle glass" he had challenged the oldest inhabitant to come and try his focus.

Despite all the rattle and roar of the wind, we went on in church as usual. The vicar had a stout young curate from Durham, who could outshout any tempest, with a good stone wall between them; and the Bruntsea folk were of thicker constitution than to care an old hat for the weather. Whatever was "sent by the Lord" they took with a grumble, but no excitement. The clock in front of the gallery told the time of the day as five minutes to twelve, when the vicar, a pleasant old-fashioned man, pronounced his text, which he always did thrice over to make us sure of it. And then he hitched up his old black gown, and directed his gaze at the lord of the manor, to impress the whole church with authority. Major Hockin acknowledged in a proper manner this courtesy of the minister by rubbing up his crest, and looking even more wide-awake than usual; whereas Aunt Mary, whose kind heart longed to see her own son in that pulpit, calmly settled back her shoulders, and arranged her head and eyes so well as to seem at a distance in rapt attention, while having a nice little dream of her own. But suddenly all was broken up. The sexton (whose license as warden of the church, and even whose duty it was to hear the sermon only fitfully, from the tower arch, where he watched the boys, and sniffed the bakehouse of his own dinner)—to the consternation of every body, this faithful man ran up the nave, with his hands above his head, and shouted,

"All Brownzee be awash, awash"—sounding it so as to rhyme with "lash"—"the zea, the zea be all over us!"

The clergyman in the pulpit turned and looked through a window behind him, while all the congregation rose.

"It is too true," the preacher cried; "the sea is in over the bank, my friends. Every man must rush to his own home. The blessing of the Lord be on you through His fearful visitation!"

He had no time to say more; and we thought it very brave of him to say that, for his own house was in the lower village, and there he had a wife and children sick. In half a minute the church was empty, and the street below it full of people, striving and struggling against the blast, and breasting it at an incline like swimmers, but beaten back ever and anon and hurled against one another, with tattered umbrellas, hats gone, and bonnets hanging. And among them, like gulls before the wind, blew dollops of spray and chunks of froth, with every now and then a slate or pantile.

All this was so bad that scarcely any body found power to speak, or think, or see. The Major did his very best to lead us, but could by no means manage it. And I screamed into his soundest ear to pull Aunt Mary into some dry house—for she could not face such buffeting—and to let me fare for myself as I might. So we left Mrs. Hockin in the bailiff's house, though she wanted sadly to come with us, and on we went to behold the worst. And thus, by running the byes of the wind, and craftily hugging the corners, we got to the foot of the street at last, and then could go no further.

For here was the very sea itself, with furious billows panting. Before us rolled and ran a fearful surf of crested whiteness, torn by the screeching squalls, and tossed in clashing tufts and pinnacles. And into these came, sweeping over the shattered chine of shingle, gigantic surges from the outer deep, towering as they crossed the bar, and combing against the sky-line, then rushing onward, and driving the huddle of the ponded waves before them.

The tide was yet rising, and at every blow the wreck and the havoc grew worse and worse. That long sweep of brick-work, the "Grand Promenade," bowed and bulged, with wall and window knuckled in and out, like wattles; the "Sea Parade" was a parade of sea; and a bathing-machine wheels upward lay, like a wrecked Noah's Ark, on the top of the "Saline-Silico-Calcareous Baths."

The Major stood by me, while all his constructions "went by the board," as they say at sea; and verily every thing was at sea. I grieved for him so that it was not the spray alone that put salt drops on my cheeks. And I could not bear to turn and look at his good old weather-beaten face. But he was not the man to brood upon his woes in silence. He might have used nicer language, perhaps, but his inner sense was manful.

"I don't care a damn," he shouted, so that all the women heard him. "I can only say I am devilish glad that I never let one of those houses."

There was a little band of seamen, under the shelter of a garden wall, crouching, or sitting, or standing (or whatever may be the attitude, acquired by much voyaging and experience of bad weather, which can not be solved, as to centre of gravity, even by the man who does it), and these men were so taken with the Major's manifesto, clinched at once and clarified to them by strong, short language, that they gave him a loud "hurrah," which flew on the wings of the wind over house-tops. So queer and sound is English feeling that now Major Hockin became in truth what hitherto he was in title only—the lord and master of Bruntsea.

"A boat! a boat!" he called out again. "We know not who are drowning. The bank still breaks the waves; a stout boat surely could live inside it."

"Yes, a boat could live well enough in this cockle, though never among them breakers," old Barnes, the fisherman, answered, who used to take us out for whiting; "but Lord bless your honor, all the boats are thumped to pieces, except yonner one, and who can get at her?"

Before restoring his hands to their proper dwelling-place—his pockets—he jerked his thumb toward a long white boat, which we had not seen through the blinding scud. Bereft of its brethren, or sisters—for all fluctuating things are feminine—that boat survived, in virtue of standing a few feet higher than the rest. But even so, and mounted on the last hump of the pebble ridge, it was rolling and reeling with stress of the wind and the wash of wild water under it.

"How nobly our Lyceum stands!" the Major shouted, for any thing less than a shout was dumb. "This is the time to try institutions. I am proud of my foundations."

In answer to his words appeared a huge brown surge, a mountain ridge, seething backward at the crest with the spread and weight of onset. This great wave smote all other waves away, or else embodied them, and gathered its height against the poor worn pebble bank, and descended. A roar distinct above the universal roar proclaimed it; a crash of conflict shook the earth, and the shattered bank was swallowed in a world of leaping whiteness. When this wild mass dashed onward into the swelling flood before us, there was no sign of Lyceum left, but stubs of foundation, and a mangled roof rolling over and over, like a hen-coop.

"Well, that beats every thing I ever saw," exclaimed the gallant Major. "What noble timber! What mortise-work! No London scamping there, my lads. But what comes here? Why, the very thing we wanted! Barnes, look alive, my man. Run to your house, and get a pair of oars and a bucket."

It was the boat, the last surviving boat of all that hailed from Bruntsea. That monstrous billow had tossed it up like a school-boy's kite, and dropped it whole, with an upright keel, in the inland sea, though nearly half full of water. Driven on by wind and wave, it labored heavily toward us; and more than once it seemed certain to sink as it broached to and shipped seas again. But half a dozen bold fishermen rushed with a rope into the short angry surf—to which the polled shingle bank still acted as a powerful breakwater, else all Bruntsea had collapsed—and they hauled up the boat with a hearty cheer, and ran her up straight with, "Yo—heave—oh!" and turned her on her side to drain, and then launched her again, with a bucket and a man to bail out the rest of the water, and a pair of heavy oars brought down by Barnes, and nobody knows what other things.

"Naught to steer with. Rudder gone!" cried one of the men, as the furious gale drove the boat, athwart the street, back again.

"Wants another oar," said Barnes. "What a fool I were to bring only two!"

"Here you are!" shouted Major Hockin. "One of you help me to pull up this pole."

Through a shattered gate they waded into a little garden, which had been the pride of the season at Bruntsea; and there from the ground they tore up a pole, with a board at the top nailed across it, and the following not rare legend: "Lodgings to let. Inquire within. First floor front, and back parlors."

"Fust-rate thing to steer with! Would never have believed you had the sense!" So shouted Barnes—a rough man, roughened by the stress of storm and fright. "Get into starn-sheets if so liketh. Ye know, ye may be useful."

"I defy you to push off without my sanction. Useful, indeed! I am the captain of this boat. All the ground under it is mine. Did you think, you set of salted radicals, that I meant to let you go without me? And all among my own houses!"

"Look sharp, governor, if you has the pluck, then. Mind, we are more like to be swamped than not."

As the boat swung about, Major Hockin jumped in, and so, on the spur of the moment, did I. We staggered all about with the heave and roll, and both would have fallen on the planks, or out over, if we had not tumbled, with opposite impetus, into the arms of each other. Then a great wave burst and soaked us both, and we fell into sitting on a slippery seat.

Meanwhile two men were tugging at each oar, and Barnes himself steering with the sign-board; and the head of the boat was kept against the wind and the billows from our breakwater. Some of these seemed resolved (though shorn of depth and height in crossing) to rush all over us and drown us in the washer-women's drying ground. By skill and presence of mind, our captain, Barnes, foiled all their violence, till we got a little shelter from the ruins of the "Young Men's Christian Institute."

"Hold all!" cried Barnes; "only keep her head up, while I look about what there is to do."

The sight was a thing to remember; and being on the better side now of the scud, because it was flying away from us, we could make out a great deal more of the trouble which had befallen Bruntsea. The stormy fiord which had usurped the ancient track of the river was about a furlong in width, and troughed with white waves vaulting over. And the sea rushed through at the bottom as well, through scores of yards of pebbles, as it did in quiet weather even, when the tide was brimming. We in the tossing boat, with her head to the inrush of the outer sea, were just like people sitting upon the floats or rafts of a furious weir; and if any such surge had topped the ridge as the one which flung our boat to us, there could be no doubt that we must go down as badly as the Major's houses. However, we hoped for the best, and gazed at the desolation inland.

Not only the Major's great plan, but all the lower line of old Bruntsea, was knocked to pieces, and lost to knowledge in freaks of wind-lashed waters. Men and women were running about with favorite bits of furniture, or feather-beds, or babies' cradles, or whatever they had caught hold of. The butt ends of the three old streets that led down toward the sea-ground were dipped, as if playing seesaw in the surf, and the storm made gangways of them and lighthouses of the lamp-posts. The old public-house at the corner was down, and the waves leaping in at the post-office door, and wrecking the globes of the chemist.

"Drift and dash, and roar and rush, and the devil let loose in the thick of it. My eyes are worn out with it. Take the glass, Erema, and tell us who is next to be washed away. A new set of clothes-props for Mrs. Mangles I paid for the very day I came back from town."

With these words, the lord of the submarine manor (whose strength of spirit amazed me) offered his pet binocular, which he never went without upon his own domain. And fisherman Barnes, as we rose and fell, once more saved us from being "swamped" by his clever way of paddling through a scallop in the stern, with the board about the first floor front to let.

The seamen, just keeping way on the boat, sheltered their eyes with their left hands, and fixed them on the tumultuous scene.

I also gazed through the double glass, which was a very clear one; but none of us saw any human being at present in any peril.

"Old pilot was right, after all," said one; "but what a good job as it come o' middle day, and best of all of a Sunday!"

"I have heered say," replied another, "that the like thing come to pass nigh upon three hunder years agone. How did you get your things out, Jem Bishop?"

Jem, the only one of them whose house was in the havoc, regarded with a sailor's calmness the entry of the sea through his bedroom window, and was going to favor us with a narrative, when one of his mates exclaimed,

"What do I see yonner, lads? Away beyond town altogether. Seemeth to me like a fellow swimming. Miss, will you lend me spy-glass? Never seed a double-barreled one before. Can use him with one eye shut, I s'pose?"

"No good that way, Joe," cried Barnes, with a wink of superior knowledge, for he often had used this binocular. "Shut one eye for one barrel—stands to reason, then, you shut both for two, my son."

"Stow that," said the quick-eyed sailor, as he brought the glass to bear in a moment. "It is a man in the water, lads, and swimming to save the witch, I do believe."

"Bless me!" cried the Major; "how stupid of us! I never thought once of that poor woman. She must be washed out long ago. Pull for your lives, my friends. A guinea apiece if you save her."

"And another from me," I cried. Whereupon the boat swept round, and the tough ash bent, and we rushed into no small danger. For nearly half a mile had we to pass of raging and boisterous water, almost as wild as the open sea itself at the breaches of the pebble ridge. And the risk of a heavy sea boarding us was fearfully multiplied by having thus to cross the storm instead of breasting it. Useless and helpless, and only in the way, and battered about by wind and sea, so that my Sunday dress was become a drag, what folly, what fatuity, what frenzy, I might call it, could ever have led me to jump into that boat? "I don't know. I only know that I always do it," said my sensible self to its mad sister, as they both shut their eyes at a great white wave. "If I possibly survive, I will try to know better. But ever from my childhood I am getting into scrapes."

The boat labored on, with a good many grunts, but not a word from any one. More than once we were obliged to fetch up as a great billow topped the poor shingle bank; and we took so much water on board that the men said afterward that I saved them. I only remember sitting down and working at the bucket with both hands, till much of the skin was gone, and my arms and many other places ached. But what was that to be compared with drowning?

At length we were opposite "Desolate Hole," which was a hole no longer, but filled and flooded with the churning whirl and reckless dominance of water. Tufts and tussocks of shattered brush and rolling wreck played round it, and the old gray stone of mullioned windows split the wash like mooring-posts. We passed and gazed; but the only sound was the whistling of the tempest, and the only living sight a sea-gull, weary of his wings, and drowning.

"No living creature can be there," the Major broke our long silence. "Land, my friends, if land we may. We risk our own lives for nothing."

The men lay back on their oars to fetch the gallant boat to the wind again, when through a great gap in the ruins they saw a sight that startled manhood. At the back of that ruin, on the landward side, on a wall which, tottered under them, there were two figures standing. One a tall man, urging on, the other a woman shrinking. At a glance, or with a thought, I knew them both. One was Lord Castlewood's first love, the other his son and murderer.

Our men shouted with the whole power of their hearts to tell that miserable pair to wait till succor should be brought to them. And the Major stood up and waved his hat, and in doing so tumbled back again. I can not tell—how could I tell in the thick of it?—but an idea or a flit of fancy touched me (and afterward became conviction) that while the man heard us not at all, and had no knowledge of us, his mother turned round and saw us all, and faced the storm in preference.

Whatever the cause may have been, at least she suddenly changed her attitude. The man had been pointing to the roof, which threatened to fall in a mass upon them, while she had been shuddering back from the depth of eddying waves below her. But now she drew up her poor bent figure, and leaned on her son to obey him.

Our boat, with strong arms laboring for life, swept round the old gable of the ruin; but we were compelled to "give it wide berth," as Captain Barnes shouted; and then a black squall of terrific wind and hail burst forth. We bowed our heads and drew our bodies to their tightest compass, and every rib of our boat vibrated as a violin does; and the oars were beaten flat, and dashed their drip into fringes like a small-toothed comb.

That great squall was either a whirlwind or the crowning blast of a hurricane. It beat the high waves hollow, as if it fell from the sky upon them; and it snapped off one of our oars at the hilt, so that two of our men rolled backward. And when we were able to look about again the whole roof of "Desolate Hole" was gone, and little of the walls left standing. And how we should guide our course, or even save our lives, we knew not.

We were compelled to bring up—as best we might—with the boat's head to the sea, and so to keep it by using the steering gear against the surviving oar. As for the people we were come to save, there was no chance whatever of approaching them. Even without the mishap to the oar, we never could have reached them.

And indeed when first we saw them again they seemed better off than ourselves were. For they were not far from dry land, and the man (a skillful and powerful swimmer) had a short piece of plank, which he knew how to use to support his weak companion.

"Brave fellow! fine fellow!" the Major cried, little knowing whom he was admiring. "See how he keeps up his presence of mind! Such a man as that is worth any thing. And he cares more for her than he does for himself. He shall have the Society's medal. One more long and strong stroke, my noble friend. Oh, great God! what has befallen him?"

In horror and pity we gazed. The man had been dashed against something headlong. He whirled round and round in white water, his legs were thrown up, and we saw no more of him. The woman cast off the plank, and tossed her helpless arms in search of him. A shriek, ringing far on the billowy shore, declared that she had lost him; and then, without a struggle, she clasped her hands, and the merciless water swallowed her.

"It is all over," cried Major Hockin, lifting his drenched hat solemnly. "The Lord knoweth best. He has taken them home."

CHAPTER LV
A DEAD LETTER

With that great tornado, the wind took a leap of more points of the compass than I can tell. Barnes, the fisherman, said how many; but I might be quite wrong in repeating it. One thing, at any rate, was within my compass—it had been blowing to the top of its capacity, direct from the sea, but now it began to blow quite as hard along the shore. This rough ingratitude of wind to waves, which had followed each breath of its orders, produced extraordinary passion, and raked them into pointed wind-cocks.

"Captain, we can't live this out," cried Barnes; "we must run her ashore at once; tide has turned; we might be blown out to sea, with one oar, and then the Lord Himself couldn't save us."

Crippled as we were, we contrived to get into a creek, or backwater, near the Major's gate. Here the men ran the boat up, and we all climbed out, stiff, battered, and terrified, but doing our best to be most truly thankful.

"Go home, Captain, as fast as you can, and take the young lady along of you," said Mr. Barnes, as we stood and gazed at the weltering breadth of disaster. "We are born to the drip, but not you, Sir; and you are not so young as you was, you know."

"I am younger than ever I was," the lord of the manor answered, sternly, yet glancing back to make sure of no interruption from his better half—who had not even heard of his danger. "None of that nonsense to me, Barnes. You know your position, and I know mine. On board of that boat you took the lead, and that may have misled you. I am very much obliged to you, I am sure, for all your skill and courage, which have saved the lives of all of us. But on land you will just obey me."

"Sartinly, Captain. What's your orders?"

"Nothing at all. I give no orders. I only make suggestions. But if your experience sees a way to recover those two poor bodies, let us try it at once—at once, Barnes. Erema, run home. This is no scene for you. And tell Margaret to put on the double-bottomed boiler, with the stock she made on

Friday, and a peck of patent pease. There is nothing to beat pea soup; and truly one never knows what may happen."

This was only too evident now, and nobody disobeyed him.

Running up his "drive" to deliver that message, at one of the many bends I saw people from Bruntsea hurrying along a footpath through the dairy-farm. While the flood continued this was their only way to meet the boat's crew. On the steps of "Smuggler's Castle" (as Bruntlands House was still called by the wicked) I turned again, and the new sea-line was fringed with active searchers. I knew what they were looking for, but, scared and drenched and shivering as I was, no more would I go near them. My duty was rather to go in and comfort dear Aunt Mary and myself. In that melancholy quest I could do no good, but a great deal of harm, perhaps, if any thing was found, by breaking forth about it.

Mrs. Hockin had not the least idea of the danger we had encountered. Bailiff Hopkins had sent her home in Rasper's fly by an inland road, and she kept a good scolding quite ready for her husband, to distract his mind from disaster. That trouble had happened she could not look out of her window without knowing; but could it be right, at their time of life, to stand in the wet so, and challenge Providence, and spoil the first turkey-poult of the season?

But when she heard of her husband's peril, in the midst of all his losses, his self-command, and noble impulse first of all to rescue life, she burst into tears, and hugged and kissed me, and said the same thing nearly fifty times.

"Just like him. Just like my Nicholas. You thought him a speculative, selfish man. Now you see your mistake, Erema."

When her veteran husband came home at last (thoroughly jaded, and bringing his fishermen to gulp the pea soup and to gollop the turkey), a small share of mind, but a large one of heart, is required to imagine her doings. Enough that the Major kept saying, "Pooh-pooh!" and the more he said, the less he got of it.

When feelings calmed down, and we returned to facts, our host and hero (who, in plain truth, had not so wholly eclipsed me in courage, though of course I expected no praise, and got none, for people hate courage in a lady), to put it more simply, the Major himself, making a considerable fuss, as usual—for to my mind he never could be Uncle Sam—produced from the case of his little "Church Service," to which he had stuck like a Briton, a sealed and stamped letter, addressed to me at Castlewood, in Berkshire—"stamped," not with any post-office tool, but merely with the red thing which pays the English post.

Sodden and blurred as the writing was, I knew the clear, firm hand, the same which on the envelope at Shoxford had tempted me to meanness. This letter was from Thomas Hoyle; the Major had taken it from the pocket of his corpse; all doubt about his death was gone. When he felt his feet on the very shore, and turned to support his mother, a violent wave struck the back of his head upon Major Hockin's pillar-box.

Such sadness came into my heart—though sternly it should have been gladness—that I begged their pardon, and went away, as if with a private message. And wicked as it may have been, to read was more than once to cry. The letter began abruptly:

"You know nearly all my story now. I have only to tell you what brought me to you, and what my present offer is. But to make it clear, I must enlarge a little.

"There was no compact of any kind between your father and myself. He forbore at first to tell what he must have known, partly, perhaps, to secure my escape, and partly for other reasons. If he had been brought to trial, his duty to his family and himself would have led him, no doubt, to explain things. And if that had failed, I would have returned and surrendered myself. As things happened, there was no need.

"Through bad luck, with which I had nothing to do, though doubtless the whole has been piled on my head, your father's home was destroyed, and he seems to have lost all care for every thing. Yet how much better off was he than I! Upon me the curse fell at birth; upon him, after thirty years of ease and happiness. However, for that very reason, perhaps, he bore it worse than I did. He grew imbittered against the world, which had in no way ill-treated him; whereas its very first principle is to scorn all such as I am. He seems to have become a misanthrope, and a fatalist like myself. Though it might almost make one believe the existence of such a thing as justice to see pride pay for its wickedness thus—the injury to the outcast son recoil upon the pampered one, and the family arrogance crown itself with the ignominy of the family.

"In any case, there was no necessity for my interference; and being denied by fate all sense of duty to a father, I was naturally driven to double my duty to my mother, whose life was left hanging upon mine. So we two for many years wandered about, shunning islands and insular prejudice. I also shunned your father, though (so far as I know) he neither sought me nor took any trouble to clear himself. If the one child now left him had been a son, heir to the family property and so on, he might have behaved quite otherwise, and he would have been bound to do so. But having only a female child, who might never grow up, and, if she did, was very unlikely to succeed, he must have resolved at least to wait. And perhaps he confirmed himself with the reflection that even if people believed his tale (so long after date and so unvouched), so far as family annals were concerned, the remedy would be as bad as the disease. Moreover, he owed his life to me, at great risk of my own; and to pay such a debt with the hangman's rope would scarcely appear quite honorable, even in the best society.

"It is not for me to pretend to give his motives, although from my knowledge of his character I can guess them pretty well, perhaps. We went our several ways in the world, neither of us very fortunate.

"One summer, in the Black Forest, I fell in with an outcast Englishman, almost as great a vagabond as myself. He was under the ban of the law for writing his father's name without license. He did not tell me that, or perhaps even I might have despised him, for I never was dishonest. But one great bond there was between us—we both detested laws and men. My intimacy with him is the one thing in life which I am ashamed of. He passed by a false name then, of course. But his true name was Montague Hockin. My mother was in very weak health then, and her mind for the most part clouded; and I need not say that she knew nothing of what I had done for her sake. That man pretended to take the greatest interest in her condition, and to know a doctor at Baden who could cure her.

"We avoided all cities (as he knew well), and lived in simple villages, subsisting partly upon my work, and partly upon the little income left by my grandfather, Thomas Hoyle. But, compared with Hockin, we were well off; and he did his best to swindle us. Luckily all my faith in mankind was confined to the feminine gender, and not much even of that survived. In a very little time I saw that people may repudiate law as well from being below as from being above it.

"Then he came one night, with the finest style and noblest contempt of every thing. We must prepare ourselves for great news, and all our kindness to him would be repaid tenfold in a week or two. Let me go into Freyburg that time to-morrow night, and listen. I asked him nothing as to what he meant, for I was beginning to weary of him, as of every body. However, I thought it just worth while, having some one who bought my wicker-work, to enter the outskirts of the town on the following evening, and wait to be told if any news was stirring. And the people were amazed at my not knowing that last night the wife of an English lord—for so they called him, though no lord yet—had run away with a golden-bearded man, believed to be also English.

"About that you know more, perhaps, than I do. But I wish you to know what that Hockin was, and to clear myself of complicity. Of Herbert

Castlewood I knew nothing, and I never even saw the lady. And to say (as Sir Montague Hockin has said) that I plotted all that wickedness, from spite toward all of the Castlewood name, is to tell as foul a lie as even he can well indulge in.

"It need not be said that he does not know my story from any word of mine. To such a fellow I was not likely to commit my mother's fate. But he seems to have guessed at once that there was something strange in my history; and then, after spying and low prying at my mother, to have shaped his own conclusion. Then, having entirely under his power that young fool who left a kind husband for him, he conceived a most audacious scheme. This was no less than to rob your cousin, the last Lord Castlewood, not of his wife and jewels and ready money only, but also of all the disposable portion of the Castlewood estates. For the lady's mother had taken good care, like a true Hungarian, to have all the lands settled upon her daughter, so far as the husband could deal with them. And though, at the date of the marriage, he could not really deal at all with them—your father being still alive—it appears that his succession (when it afterward took place) was bound, at any rate, as against himself. A divorce might have canceled this—I can not say—but your late cousin was the last man in the world to incur the needful exposure. Upon this they naturally counted.

"The new 'Lady Hockin' (as she called herself, with as much right as 'Lady Castlewood') flirted about while her beauty lasted; but even then found her master in a man of deeper wickedness. But if her poor husband desired revenge—which he does not seem to have done, perhaps—he could not have had it better. She was seized with a loathsome disease, which devoured her beauty, like Herod and his glory. I believe that she still lives, but no one can go near her; least of all, the fastidious Montague."

At this part of the letter I drew a deep breath, and exclaimed, "Thank God!" I know not how many times; and perhaps it was a crime of me to do it even once.

"Finding his nice prospective game destroyed by this little accident—for he meant to have married the lady after her husband's death, and set you at defiance; but even he could not do that now, little as he cares for opinion—what did he do but shift hands altogether? He made up his mind to confer the honor of his hand on you, having seen you somewhere in London, and his tactics became the very opposite of what they had been hitherto. Your father's innocence now must be maintained instead of his guiltiness.

"With this in view, he was fool enough to set the detective police after me—me, who could snap all their noses off! For he saw how your heart was all set on one thing, and expected to have you his serf forever, by the simple expedient of hanging me. The detectives failed, as they always do. He also failed in his overtures to you.

"You did your utmost against me also, for which I bear you no ill-will, but rather admire your courage. You acted in a straightforward way, and employed no dirty agency. Of your simple devices I had no fear. However, I thought it as well to keep an eye upon that Hockin, and a worthy old fool, some relation of his, who had brought you back from America. To this end I kept my head-quarters near him, and established my mother comfortably. She was ordered sea air, and has had enough. To-morrow I shall remove her. By the time you receive this letter we shall both be far away, and come back no more; but first I shall punish that Hockin. Without personal violence this will be done.

"Now what I propose to you is simple, moderate, and most strictly just. My mother's little residue of life must pass in ease and comfort. She has wronged no one, but ever been wronged. Allow her 300 pounds a year, to be paid as I shall direct you. For myself I will not take a farthing. You will also restore, as I shall direct, the trinket upon which she sets great value, and for which I sought vainly when we came back to England. I happen to know that you have it now.

"In return for these just acts, you have the right to set forth the whole truth publicly, to proclaim your father's innocence, and (as people will say) his chivalry; and, which will perhaps rejoice you also, to hear no more of

"THOMAS HOYLE.

"P.S.—Of course I am trusting your honor in this. But your father's daughter can be no sneak; as indeed I have already proved."

CHAPTER LVI
WITH HIS OWN SWORD

"What a most wonderful letter!" cried the Major, when, after several careful perusals, I thought it my duty to show it to him. "He calls me a 'worthy old fool,' does he? Well, I call him something a great deal worse—an unworthy skulk, a lunatic, a subverter of rank, and a Radical! And because he was a bastard, is the whole world base? And to come and live like that in a house of mine, and pay me no rent, and never even let me see him! Your grandfather was quite right, my dear, in giving him the cold shoulder. Of course you won't pay him a farthing."

"You forget that he is dead," I answered, "and his poor mother with him. At least he behaved well to his mother. You called him a hero—when you knew not who he was. Poor fellow, he is dead! And, in spite of all, I can not help being very sorry for him."

"Yes, I dare say. Women always are. But you must show a little common-sense, Erema. Your grandfather seems to have had too much, and your father far too little. We must keep this matter quiet. Neither the man nor the woman must we know, or a nice stir we shall have in all the county papers. There must be an inquest, of course, upon them both; but none of the fellows read this direction, for the admirable reason that they can not read. Our coming forward could do no good, and just now Bruntsea has other things to think of; and, first and foremost, my ruin, as they say."

"Please not to talk of that," I exclaimed. "I can raise any quantity of money now, and you shall have it without paying interest. You wanted the course of the river restored, and now you have more—you have got the very sea. You could float the Bridal Veil itself, I do believe, at Bruntsea."

"You have suggested a fine idea," the Major exclaimed, with emphasis. "You certainly should have been an engineer. It is a thousand times easier—as every body knows—to keep water in than to keep it out. Having burst my barricade, the sea shall stop inside and pay for it. Far less capital will be required. By Jove, what a fool I must have been not to see the hand of Providence in all this! Mary, can you spare me a minute, my dear? The noblest idea has occurred to me. Well, never mind, if you are busy; perhaps I had better not state it crudely, though it is not true that it happens every hour. I shall turn it over in my mind throughout the evening service. I mean to be there, just to let them see. They think that I am crushed, of course. They will see their mistake; and, Erema, you may come. The gale is over, and the evening bright. You sit by the fire, Mary, my dear; I shall not let you out again; keep the silver kettle boiling. In church I always think more clearly than where people talk so much. But when I come home I require something. I see, I see. Instead of an idle, fashionable lounging-place for nincompoops from London, instead of flirtation and novel-reading, vulgarity, show, and indecent attire, and positively immoral bathing, we will now have industry, commerce, wealth, triumph of mechanism, lofty enterprise, and international good-will. A harbor has been the great want of this coast; see what a thing it is at Newport! We will now have a harbor and floating docks, without any muddy, malarious river—all blue water from the sea; and our fine cliff range shall be studded with good houses. And the whole shall be called 'Erema-port.'"

Well, Erema must be getting very near her port, although it was not at Bruntsea. Enough for this excellent man and that still more excellent woman that there they are, as busy and as happy as the day is long—which imposes some limit upon happiness, perhaps, inasmuch as to the busy every day is short. But Mrs. Hockin, though as full of fowls as ever, gets no White Sultans nor any other rarity now from Sir Montague Hockin. That gentleman still is alive—so far, at least, as we have heard of; but no people owning any self-respect ever deal with him, to their knowledge. He gambled away all his father's estates, and the Major bought the last of them for his youngest son, a very noble Captain Hockin (according to his mother's judgment), whom I never had the honor of seeing. Sir Montague lives in a sad plight somewhere, and his cousin still hopes that he may turn honest.

But as to myself and far greater persons, still there are a few words to be said. As soon as all necessary things were done at Bruntsea and at Castlewood, and my father's memory cleared from all stain, and by simple truth ennobled, in a manner strictly legal and consistent with heavy expenses, myself having made a long deposition and received congratulations—as soon as it was possible, I left them all, and set sail for America.

The rashness of such a plan it is more easy for one to establish than two to deny. But what was there in it of peril or of enterprise compared with what I had been through already? I could not keep myself now from going, and reasoned but little about it.

Meanwhile there had been no further tidings of Colonel Gundry or Firm, or even Martin of the Mill himself. But one thing I did which showed some little foresight. As soon as my mind was made up, and long before ever I could get away, I wrote to Martin Clogfast, telling him of my intention, and begging him, if he had any idea of the armies, or the Sawyer, or even Firm, or any thing whatever of interest, to write (without losing a day) to me, directing his letter to a house in New York whose address Major Hockin gave me.

So many things had to be done, and I listened so foolishly to the Major (who did his very best to stop me), that it came to be May, 1862 (nearly four years after my father's death), before I could settle all my plans and start. For every body said that I was much too young to take such a journey all by myself, and "what every body says must be right," whenever there is no exception to prove the rule. "Aunt Marys" are not to be found every day, nor even Major Hockins; and this again helped to throw me back in getting away from England. And but for his vast engineering ideas, and another slight touch of rheumatic gout (brought upon herself by Mrs. Hockin through setting seven hens in one evening), the Major himself might have come with me, "to observe the new military tactics," as well as to look for his cousin Sampson.

In recounting this I seem to be as long as the thing itself was in accomplishing. But at last it was done, and most kindly was I offered the very thing to suit me—permission to join the party of a well-known British officer, Colonel Cheriton, of the Engineers. This gentleman, being of the highest repute as a writer upon military subjects, had leave from the Federal government to observe the course of this tremendous war. And perhaps he will publish some day what seems as yet to be wholly wanting—a calm and impartial narrative of that unparalleled conflict. At any rate, he meant to spare no trouble in a matter so instructive, and he took his wife and two daughters—very nice girls, who did me a world of good—to establish them in Washington, or wherever the case might require.

Lucky as this was for me, I could not leave my dear and faithful friends without deep sorrow; but we all agreed that it should be only for a very little time. We landed first at New York, and there I found two letters from Martin of the Mill. In the first he grumbled much, and told me that nothing was yet known about Uncle Sam; in the second he grumbled (if possible) more, but gave me some important news. To wit, he had received a few lines from the Sawyer, who had failed as yet to find his grandson, and sadly lamented the misery he saw, and the shocking destruction of God's good works. He said that he could not bring himself to fight (even if he were young enough) against his own dear countrymen, one of whom was his own grandson; at the same time he felt that they must be put down for trying to have things too much their own way. About slavery, he had seen too much of niggers to take them at all for his equals, and no white man with any self-respect would desire to be their brother. The children of Ham were put down at the bottom, as their noses and their lips pronounced, according to Divine revelation; and for sons of Japheth to break up the noblest nation in the world, on their account, was like rushing in to inherit their curse. As sure as his name was Sampson Gundry, those who had done it would get the worst, though as yet they were doing wonders. And there could be no doubt about one thing—which party it was that began it. But come what would of it, here he was; and never would Saw-mills see him again unless he brought Firm Gundry. But he wanted news of poor Miss 'Rema; and if any came to the house, they must please to send it to the care of Colonel Baker, headquarters of the Army of the Potomac.

This was the very thing I wished to know, and I saw now how stupid I must have been not to have thought of it long ago. For Colonel Baker was, to my knowledge, an ancient friend of Uncle Sam, and had joined the national army at the very outbreak of the war. Well known not only in California, but throughout the States, for gallantry and conduct, this officer had been a great accession to the Federal cause, when so many wavered, and so he was appointed to a good command. But, alas! when I told Colonel Cheriton my news, I learned from him (who had carefully watched all the incidents of the struggle) that Uncle Sam's noble friend had fallen in the battle of Ball's Bluff, while charging at the head of his regiment.

Still, there was hope that some of the officers might know where to find Uncle Sam, who was not at all a man to be mislaid; and being allowed to accompany my English friends, I went on to Washington. We found that city in a highly nervous state, and from time to time ready to be captured. General Jackson was almost at the gates, and the President every day was calling out for men. The Army of Virginia had been beaten back to intrenchments before the capital, and General Lee was invading Maryland. Battle followed battle, thick as blows upon a threshing-floor, and though we were always said to be victorious, the enemy seemed none the more to run away. In this confusion, what chance had I of discovering even the Sawyer?

Colonel Cheriton (who must have found me a dreadful thorn in the flank of his strategy) missed no opportunity of inquiry, as he went from one valley to another. For the war seemed to run along the course of rivers, though it also passed through the forests and lakes, and went up into the mountains. Our wonderfully clever and kind member of the British army was delighted with the movements of General Lee, who alone showed scientific elegance in slaying his fellow-countrymen; and the worst of it was that instead of going after my dear Uncle Sam, Colonel Cheriton was always rushing about with maps, plans, and telescopes, to follow the tracery of Lee's campaign. To treat of such matters is far beyond me, as I am most thankful to confess. Neither will I dare to be sorry for a great man doing what became his duty. My only complaint against him is that he kept us in a continual fright.

However, this went by, and so did many other things, though heavily laden with grief and death; and the one thing we learned was to disbelieve ninety-nine out of every hundred. Letters for the Sawyer were dispatched by me to every likely place for him, and advertisements put into countless newspapers, but none of them seemed to go near him. Old as he was, he avoided feather-beds, and roamed like a true Californian. But at last I found him, in a sad, sad way.

It was after the battle of Chancellorsville, and our army had been driven back across the Rappahannock. "Our army," I call it, because (although we belonged to neither party) fortune had brought us into contact with these, and knowing more about them, we were bound to take their side. And not only that, but to me it appeared altogether beyond controversy that a man of large mind and long experience (such as Uncle Sam had) should know much better than his grandson which cause was the one to fight for. At the same time Firm was not at all to be condemned. And if it was true, as Martin Clogfast said, that trouble of mind at my absence had driven him into a prejudiced view, nothing could possibly be more ungracious than for me to make light of his judgment.

Being twenty years old by this time, I was wiser than I used to be, and now made a practice of thinking twice before rushing into peril, as I used to do in California, and to some extent also in England. For though my adventures might not have been as strange as many I myself have heard of (especially from Suan Isco), nevertheless they had comprised enough of teaching and suffering also to make me careful about having any more. And so for a long time I kept at the furthest distance possible, in such a war, from the vexing of the air with cannons, till even Colonel Cheriton's daughters—perfectly soft and peaceful girls—began to despise me as a coward. Knowing what I had been through, I indulged their young opinions.

Therefore they were the more startled when I set forth under a sudden impulse, or perhaps impatience, for a town very near the head-quarters of the defeated General Hooker. As they were so brave, I asked them whether they would come with me; but although their father was known to be there, they turned pale at the thought of it. This pleased me, and made me more resolute to go; and in three days' time I was at Falmouth, a town on our side of the Rappahannock.

Here I saw most miserable sights that made me ashamed of all trifling fear. When hundreds and thousands of gallant men were dying in crippled agony, who or what was I to make any fuss about my paltry self? Clumsy as I was, some kind and noble ladies taught me how to give help among the sufferers.

At first I cried so at every body's pain, while asking why ever they should have it, that I did some good by putting them up to bear it rather than distress me so. And when I began to command myself (as custom soon enabled me), I did some little good again by showing them how I cared for them. Their poor weak eyes, perhaps never expecting to see a nice thing in the world again, used to follow me about with a faint, slow roll, and a feeble spark of jealousy.

That I should have had such a chance of doing good, onefold to others and a thousandfold to self, at this turn of life, when I was full of little me, is another of the many most clear indications of a kind hand over me. Every day there was better than a year of ordinary life in breaking the mind from its little selfish turns, and opening the heart to a larger power. And all this discipline was needed.

For one afternoon, when we all were tired, with great heat upon us suddenly, and the flies beginning to be dreadful, our chief being rather unwell and fast asleep, the surgeons away, and our beds as full as they could be, I was called down to reason with an applicant who would take no denial. "A rough man, a very rough old man, and in a most terrible state of mind," said the girl who brought the message; "and room he would have, or he would know the reason."

"The reason is not far to seek," I answered, more to myself than her, as I ran down the stairs to discomfit that old man. At the open door, with the hot wind tossing worn white curls and parching shriveled cheeks, now wearily raising his battered hat, stood my dear Uncle Sam, the Sawyer.

"Lor' a massy! young lady, be you altogether daft? In my best of days, never was I lips for kissing. And the bootifulest creatur—Come now, I ain't saved your life, have I now?"

"Yes, fifty times over—fifty thousand times. Uncle Sam, don't you know Erema?"

"My eyes be dashed! And dashed they be, to forget the look of yours, my dearie. Seven days have I marched without thanking the Lord; and hot coals of fire has He poured upon me now, for His mercy endureth forever. To think of you—to think of you—as like my own child as could be—only of more finer breed—here standing in front of me, like this here! There! I never dreamed to do that again, and would scorn a young man at the sight of it."

The Sawyer was too honest to conceal that he was weeping. He simply turned his tanned and weathered face toward the door-post, not to hide his tears, but reconcile his pride by feigning it. I felt that he must be at very low ebb, and all that I had seen of other people's sorrow had no power to assuage me. Inside the door, to keep the hot wind out and hide my eyes from the old man's face, I had some little quiet sobs, until we could both express ourselves.

"It is poor Firm, the poor, poor lad!—oh, what hath happened him? That I should see the day!"

Uncle Sam's deep voice broke into a moan, and he bowed his rough forehead on his arm, and shook. Then I took him by the sleeve and brought him in.

"Not dead—poor Firm, your only one—not dead?" as soon as words would come, I asked, and trembled for the opening of his lips.

"Not dead—not quite; but ten times worse. He hath flown into the face of the Lord, like Saul and his armor-bearer; he hath fallen on his own sword; and the worst of it is that the darned thing won't come out again."

"Firm—the last person in the world to do it! Oh, Uncle Sam, surely they have told you—"

"No lies—no lie at all, my dear. And not only that, but he wanteth now to die—and won't be long first, I reckon. But no time to lose, my dear. The Lord hath sent you to make him happy in his leaving of the world. Can 'e raise a bed and a doctor here? If he would but groan, I could bear it a bit, instead of bleeding inward. And for sartin sure, a' would groan nicely, if only by force of habit, at first sight of a real doctor."

"There are half a dozen here," I said; "or at least close by. He shall have my own bed. But where is he?"

"We have laid 'un in the sand," he answered, simply, "for to dry his perspiration. That weak the poor chap is that he streameth night and day, miss. Never would you know him for our Firm now, any more than me for Sampson Gundry. Ah me! but the Lord is hard on us!"

Slowly and heavily he went his way to fetch poor Firm to the hospital; while, with light feet but a heavy heart, I returned to arouse our managers. Speedily and well were all things done; and in half an hour Finn lay upon my bed, with two of the cleverest surgeons of New York most carefully examining his wasted frame. These whispered and shook their heads, as in such a case was indispensable; and listening eagerly, I heard the senior surgeon say, "No, he could never bear it." The younger man seemed to think otherwise, but to give way to the longer experience. Then dear Uncle Sam, having bought a new hat at the corner of the street, came forward. Knowing too well what excitement is, and how it changes every one, I lifted my hand for him to go back; but he only put his great hot web of fingers into mine, and drew me to him softly, and covered me up with his side. "He heareth nort, nort, nort," he whispered to me; and then spoke aloud:

"Gentlemen and ladies—or ladies and gentlemen, is the more correct form nowadays—have I leave to say a word or two? Then if I have, as your manner to me showeth, and heartily thanking you for that same, my words shall go into an acorn-cup. This lad, laid out at your mercy here, was as fine a young fellow as the West hath ever raised—straight and nimble, and could tell no lie. Family reasons, as you will excoose of, drew him to the arms of rebellion. I may have done, and overdone it myself, in arguing cantrips and convictions, whereof to my knowledge good never came yet. At any rate, off he went anyhow, and the force of nature drew me after him. No matter that to you, I dare say; but it would be, if you was in it.

"Ladies and gentlemen, here he is, and no harm can you make out of him. Although he hath fought for the wrong side to our thinking, bravely hath he fought, and made his way to a colonelship, worth five thousand dollars, if ever they pay their wages. Never did I think that he would earn so much, having never owned gifts of machinery; and concerning the handling of the dollars, perhaps, will carry my opinion out. But where was I wandering of a little thing like that?

"It hath pleased the Lord, who doeth all things well, when finally come to look back upon—the Lord hath seen fit to be down on this young man for going agin his grandfather. From Californy—a free State, mind you—he come away to fight for slavery. And how hath he magnified his office? By shooting the biggest man on that side, the almighty foe of the Union, the foremost captain of Midian—the general in whom they trusted. No bullets of ours could touch him; but by his own weapons he hath fallen. And soon as Ephraim Gundry heard it, he did what you see done to him."

Uncle Sam having said his say—which must have cost him dearly—withdrew from the bed where his grandson's body lay shrunken, lax, and grimy. To be sure that it was Firm, I gave one glance—for Firm had always been straight, tall, and large—and then, in a miserable mood, I stole to the Sawyer's side to stand with him. "Am I to blame? Is this my fault? For even this am I to blame?" I whispered; but he did not heed me, and his hands were like hard stone.

After a long, hot, heavy time, while I was laboring vainly, the Sawyer also (through exhaustion of excitement) weary, and afraid to begin again with new bad news, as beaten people expect to do, the younger surgeon came up to him, and said, "Will you authorize it?"

"To cut 'un up? To show your museums what a Western lad is? Never. By the Blue River he shall have a good grave. So help me God, to my own, my man!"

"You misunderstand me. We have more subjects now than we should want for fifty years. War knocks the whole of their value on the head. We have fifty bodies as good as this, and are simply obliged to bury them. What I mean is, shall we pull the blade out?"

"Can he do any thing with that there blade in him? I have heard of a man in Kentucky once—"

"Yes, yes; we know all those stories, Colonel—suit the newspapers, not the journals. This fellow has what must kill him inside; he is worn to a shadow already. If there it is left, die he must, and quick stick; inflammation is set up already. If we extract it, his chance of surviving is scarcely one in a hundred."

"Let him have the one, then, the one in the hundred, like the ninety and nine lost sheep. The Lord can multiply a hundredfold—some threescore, and some an hundredfold. I will speak to Him, gentlemen, while you try the job."

CHAPTER LVII
FEMALE SUFFRAGE

All that could be done by skill and care and love, was done for Firm. Our lady manager and head nurse never left him when she could be spared, and all the other ladies vied in zeal for this young soldier, so that I could scarcely get near him. His grandfather's sad and extraordinary tale was confirmed by a wounded prisoner. Poor Ephraim Gundry's rare power of sight had been fatal perhaps to the cause he fought for, or at least to its greatest captain. Returning from desperate victory, the general, wrapped in the folds of night, and perhaps in the gloom of his own stern thoughts, while it seemed quite impossible that he should be seen, encountered the fire of his own troops; and the order to fire was given by his favorite officer, Colonel Firm Gundry. When the young man learned that he had destroyed, by a lingering death, the chief idol of his heart, he called for a rifle, but all refused him, knowing too well what his purpose was. Then under the trees, without a word or sigh, he set the hilt of his sword upon the earth, and the point to his heart—as well as he could find it. The blade passed through him, and then snapped off—But I can not bear to speak of it.

And now, few people might suppose it, but the substance of which he was made will be clear, when not only his own knowledge of his case but also the purest scientific reasoning established a truth more frankly acknowledged in the New World than in the Old one. It was proved that, with a good constitution, it is safer to receive two wounds than one, even though they may not be at the same time taken. Firm had been shot by the captain of Mexican robbers, as long ago related. He was dreadfully pulled down at the time, and few people could have survived it. But now that stood him in the very best stead, not only as a lesson of patience, but also in the question of cartilage. But not being certain what cartilage is, I can only refer inquirers to the note-book of the hospital, which has been printed.

For us it was enough to know that (shattered as he was and must be) this brave and single-minded warrior struggled for the time successfully with that great enemy of the human race, to whom the human race so largely consign one another and themselves. But some did say, and emphatically Uncle Sam, that Colonel Firm Gundry—for a colonel he was now, not by courtesy, but commission—would never have held up his head to do it, but must have gone on with his ravings for death, if somebody had not arrived in the nick of time, and cried over him—a female somebody from old England.

And, even after that, they say that he never would have cared to be a man again, never would have calmed his conscience with the reflection, so commonplace and yet so high—that having done our best according to our lights, we must not dwell always on our darkness—if once again, and for the residue of life, there had not been some one to console him—a consolation that need not have, and is better without, pure reason, coming, as that would come, from a quarter whence it is never quite welcome. Enough for me that he never laid hand to a weapon of war again, and never shall unless our own home is invaded.

For after many months—each equal to a year of teaching and of humbling—there seemed to be a good time for me to get away and attend to my duties in England. Of these I had been reminded often by letters, and once by a messenger; but all money matters seemed dust in the balance where life and death were swinging. But now Uncle Sam and his grandson, having their love knit afresh by disaster, were eager to start for the Sawmill, and trust all except their own business to Providence.

I had told them that, when they went westward, my time would be come for starting eastward; and being unlikely to see them again, I should hope for good news frequently. And then I got dear Uncle Sam by himself, and begged him, for the sake of Firm's happiness, to keep him as far as he could from Pennsylvania Sylvester. At the same time I thought that the very nice young lady who jumped upon his nose from the window, Miss Annie—I forgot her name, or at any rate I told him so—would make him a good straightforward wife, so far as one could tell from having seen her. And that seemed to have been settled in their infancy. And if he would let me know when it was to be, I had seen a thing in London I should like to give them.

When I asked the Sawyer to see to this, instead of being sorry, he seemed quite pleased, and nodded sagaciously, and put his hat on, as he generally did, to calculate.

"Both of them gals have married long ago," he said, looking at me with a fine soft gaze; "and bad handfuls their mates have got of them. But what made you talk of them, missy—or 'my lady,' as now you are in old country, I hear—what made you think of them like that, my dearie?"

"I can't tell what made me think of them. How can I tell why I think of every thing?"

"Still, it was an odd thing for your ladyship to say."

"Uncle Sam, I am nobody's ladyship, least of all yours. What makes you speak so? I am your own little wandering child, whose life you saved, and whose father you loved, and who loses all who love her. Even from you I am forced to go away. Oh, why is it always my fate—my fate?"

"Hush!" said the old man; and I stopped my outburst at his whisper. "To talk of fate, my dearie, shows either one thing or the other—that we have no will of our own, or else that we know not how to guide it. I never knew a good man talk of fate. The heathens and the pagans made it. The Lord in heaven is enough for me; and He always hath allowed me my own free-will, though I may not have handled 'un cleverly. And He giveth you your own will now, my missy—to go from us or to stop with us. And being as you are a very grand young woman now, owning English land and income paid in gold instead of greenbacks—the same as our nugget seems likely—to my ideas it would be wrong if we was so much as to ask you."

"Is that what you are full of, then, and what makes you so mysterious? I did think that you knew me better, and I had a right to hope so."

"Concerning of yourself alone is not what we must think of. You might do this, or you might do that, according to what you was told, or, even more, according to what was denied you. For poor honest people, like Firm and me, to deal with such a case is out of knowledge. For us it is—go by the will of the Lord, and dead agin your own desires."

"But, dear Uncle Sam," I cried, feeling that now I had him upon his own tenterhooks, "you rebuked me as sharply as lies in your nature for daring to talk about fate just now; but to what else comes your own conduct, if you are bound to go against your own desire? If you have such a lot of freewill, why must you do what you do not like to do?"

"Well, well, perhaps I was talking rather large. The will of the world is upon us as well. And we must have respect for its settlements."

"Now let me," I said, with a trembling wish to have every thing right and maidenly. "I have seen so much harm from misunderstandings, and they are so simple when it is too late—let me ask you one or two questions, Uncle Sam. You always answer every body. And to you a crooked answer is impossible."

"Business is business," the Sawyer said. "My dear, I contract accordingly."

"Very well. Then, in the first place, what do you wish to have done with me? Putting aside all the gossip, I mean, of people who have never even heard of me."

"Why, to take you back to Saw-mill with us, where you always was so natural."

"In the next place, what does your grandson wish?"

"To take you back to Saw-mill with him, and keep you there till death do you part, as chanceth to all mortal pairs."

"And now, Uncle Sam, what do I wish? You say we all have so much free-will."

"It is natural that you should wish, my dear, to go and be a great lady, and marry a nobleman of your own rank, and have a lot of little noblemen."

"Then I fly against nature; and the fault is yours for filling me so with machinery."

The Sawyer was beaten, and he never said again that a woman can not argue.

CHAPTER LVIII
BEYOND DESERT, AND DESERTS

From all the carnage, havoc, ruin, hatred, and fury of that wicked war we set our little convoy forth, with passes procured from either side. According to all rules of war, Firm was no doubt a prisoner; but having saved his life, and taken his word to serve no more against them, remembering also that he had done them more service than ten regiments, the Federal authorities were not sorry to be quit of him.

He, for his part, being of a deep, retentive nature, bore in his wounded breast a sorrow which would last his lifetime. To me he said not a single word about his bitter fortune, and he could not bring himself to ask me whether I would share it. Only from his eyes sometimes I knew what he was thinking; and having passed through so much grief, I was moved with deep compassion. Poor Firm had been trained by his grandfather to a strong, earnest faith in Providence, and now this compelled him almost to believe that he had been specially visited. For flying in the face of his good grandfather, and selfishly indulging his own stiff neck, his punishment had been hard, and almost heavier than he could bear. Whatever might happen to him now, the spring and the flower of his life were gone; he still might have some calm existence, but never win another day of cloudless joy. And if he had only said this, or thought about it, we might have looked at him with less sadness of our own.

But he never said any thing about himself, nor gave any opening for our comfort to come to him. Only from day to day he behaved gently and lovingly to both of us, as if his own trouble must be fought out by himself, and should dim no other happiness. And this kept us thinking of his sorrow all the more, so that I could not even look at him without a flutter of the heart, which was afraid to be a sigh.

At last, upon the great mountain range, through which we now were toiling, with the snow little more than a mantle for the peaks, and a sparkling veil for sunrise, dear Uncle Sam, who had often shown signs of impatience, drew me apart from the rest. Straightforward and blunt as he generally was, he did not seem altogether ready to begin, but pulled off his hat, and then put it on again, the weather being now cold and hot by turns. And while he did this he was thinking at his utmost, as every full vein of his forehead declared. And being at home with his ways, I waited.

"Think you got ahead of me? No, not you," he exclaimed at last, in reply to some version of his own of my ideas, which I carefully made a nonentity under the scrutiny of his keen blue eyes. "No, no, missy; you wait a bit. Uncle Sam was not hatched yesterday, and it takes fifty young ladies to go round him."

"Is that from your size, Uncle Sam, or your depth?"

"Well, a mixture of both, I do believe. Now the last thing you ever would think of, if you lived to be older than Washington's nurse, is the very thing I mean to put to you. Only you must please to take it well, according to my meaning. You see our Firm going to a shadow, don't you? Very well; the fault of that is all yourn. Why not up and speak to him?"

"I speak to him every day, Uncle Sam, and I spare no efforts to fatten him. I am sure I never dreamed of becoming such a cook. But soon he will have Suan Isco."

"Old Injun be darned! It's not the stomach, it's the heart as wants nourishment with yon poor lad. He looketh that pitiful at you sometimes, my faith, I can hardly tell whether to laugh at his newings or cry at the lean face that does it."

"You are not talking like yourself, Uncle Sam. And he never does any thing of the kind. I am sure there is nothing to laugh at."

"No, no; to be sure not. I made a mistake. Heroic is the word, of course— every thing is heroic."

"It is heroic," I answered, with some vexation at his lightness. "If you can not see it, I am sorry for you. I like large things; and I know of nothing larger than the way poor Firm is going on."

"You to stand up for him!" Colonel Gundry answered, as if he could scarcely look at me. "You to talk large of him, my Lady Castlewood, while you are doing of his heart into small wittles! Well, I did believe, if no one else, that you were a straightforward one."

"And what am I doing that is crooked now?"

"Well, not to say crooked, Miss 'Rema; no, no. Only onconsistent, when squared up."

"Uncle Sam, you're a puzzle to me to-day. What is inconsistent? What is there to square up?"

He fetched a long breath, and looked wondrous wise. Then, as if his main object was to irritate me, he made a long stride, and said, "Soup's a-bilin now."

"Let it boil over, then. You must say what you mean. Oh, Uncle Sam, I only want to do the right!"

"I dessay. I dessay. But have you got the pluck, miss? Our little missy would 'a done more than that. But come to be great lady—why, they take another tune. With much mind, of course it might be otherwise. But none of 'em have any much of that to spare."

"Your view is a narrow one," I replied, knowing how that would astonish him. "You judge by your own experience only; and to do that shows a sad want of breadth, as the ladies in England express it."

The Sawyer stared, and then took off his hat, and then felt all about for his spectacles. The idea of being regarded by a "female" from a larger and loftier point of view, made a new sensation in his system.

"Yes," I continued, with some enjoyment, "let us try to look largely at all things, Uncle Sam. And supposing me capable of that, what is the proper and the lofty course to take?"

He looked at me with a strange twinkle in his eyes, and with three words discomfited me—"Pop the question."

Much as I had heard of woman's rights, equality of body and mind with man, and superiority in morals, it did not appear to me that her privilege could be driven to this extent. But I shook my head till all my hair came down; and so if our constitutional right of voting by color was exercised, on this occasion it claimed the timid benefit of ballot.

With us a suggestion, for the time discarded, has often double effect by-and-by; and though it was out of my power to dream of acting up to such directions, there could be no possible harm in reviewing such a theory theoretically.

Now nothing beyond this was in my thoughts, nor even so much as that (safely may I say), when Firm and myself met face to face on the third day after Uncle Sam's ideas. Our little caravan, of which the Sawyer was the captain, being bound for Blue River and its neighborhood, had quitted the Sacramento track by a fork on the left not a league from the spot where my father had bidden adieu to mankind. And knowing every twist and turn of rock, our drivers brought us at the camping-time almost to the verge of chaparral.

I knew not exactly how far we were come, but the dust-cloud of memory was stirring, and though mountains looked smaller than they used to look, the things done among them seemed larger. And wandering forth from the camp to think, when the evening meal was over, lo! there I stood in that selfsame breach or portal of the desert in which I stood once by my father's side, with scared and weary eyes, vainly seeking safety's shattered landmark. The time of year was different, being the ripe end of October now; but though the view was changed in tint, it was even more impressive. Sombre memories, and deep sense of grandeur, which is always sad, and solemn lights, and stealing shadows, compassed me with thoughtfulness. In the mouth of the gorge was a gray block of granite, whereupon I sat down to think.

Old thoughts, dull thoughts, thoughts as common as the clouds that cross the distant plain, and as vague as the wind that moves them—they please and they pass, and they may have shed kindly influence, but what are they? The life that lies before us is, in some way, too, below us, like yon vast amplitude of plain; but it must be traversed foot by foot, and laboriously travailed, without the cloudy vaporing or the high-flown meditation. And all that must be done by me, alone, with none to love me, and (which for a woman is so much worse) nobody ever to have for my own, to cherish, love, and cling to.

Tier upon tier, and peak over peak, the finest mountains of the world are soaring into the purple firmament. Like northern lights, they flash, or flush, or fade into a reclining gleam; like ladders of heaven, they bar themselves with cloudy air; and like heaven itself, they rank their white procession. Lonely, feeble, puny, I look up with awe and reverence; the mind pronounces all things small compared with this magnificence. Yet what will all such grandeur do—the self-defensive heart inquires—for puny, feeble, lonely me?

Before another shadow deepened or another light grew pale, a slow, uncertain step drew near, and by the merest chance it happened to be Ephraim Gundry's. I was quite surprised, and told him so; and he said that he also was surprised at meeting me in this way. Remembering how long I had been here, I thought this most irrational, but checked myself from saying so, because he looked so poorly. And more than that, I asked him kindly how he was this evening, and smoothed my dress to please his eye, and offered him a chair of rock. But he took no notice of all these things.

I thought of the time when he would have behaved so very differently from this, and nothing but downright pride enabled me to repress vexation. However, I resolved to behave as kindly as if he were his own grandfather.

"How grand these mountains are!" I said. "It must do you good to see them again. Even to me it is such a delight. And what must it be to you, a native?"

"Yes, I shall wander from them no more. How I wish that I had never done so?"

"Have men less courage than women?" I asked, with one glance at his pale worn face. "I owe you the debt of life; and this is the place to think and speak of it. I used to talk freely of that, you know. You used to like to hear me speak; but now you are tired of that, and tired of all the world as well, I fear."

"No, I am tired of nothing, except my own vile degradation. I am tired of my want of spirit, that I can not cast my load. I am tired of my lack of reason, which should always guide a man. What is the use of mind or intellect, reasoning power, or whatever it is called, if the whole of them can not enable a man to hold out against a stupid heart?"

"I think you should be proud," I said, while trembling to approach the subject which never had been touched between us, "at having a nature so sensitive. Your evil chance might have been any body's, and must of course have been somebody's. But nobody else would have taken it so—so delightfully as you have done!"

"Delightfully! Is that the word you use? May I ask who gets any delight from it?"

"Why, all who hate the Southern cause," I replied, with a sudden turn of thought, though I never had meant to use the word. "Surely that needs no explanation."

"They are delighted, are they? Yes, I can very well believe it. Narrow-minded bigots! Yes, they are sure to be delighted. They call it a just visitation, of course, a righteous retribution. And they hope I may never get over it."

"I pray you to take it more gently," I said; "they are very good men, and wish you no harm. But they must have their own opinions; and naturally they think them just."

"Then all their opinions are just wrong. They hope to see me go down, to my grave. They shall not have that pleasure. I will outlive every old John Brown of them. I did not care two cents to live just now. Henceforth I will make a point of it. If I cannot fight for true freedom any more, having ruined it perhaps already, the least I can do is to give no more triumph to its bitter enemies. I will eat and drink, and begin this very night. I suppose you are one of them, as you put their arguments so neatly. I suppose you consider me a vile slave-driver?"

"You are very ill," I said, with my heart so full of pity that anger could not enter; "you are very ill, and very weak. How could you drive the very best slave now—even such a marvel as Uncle Tom?"

Firm Gundry smiled; on his lean dry face there shone a little flicker, which made me think of the time when he bought a jest-book, published at Cincinnati, to make himself agreeable to my mind. And little as I meant it, I smiled also, thinking of the way he used to come out with his hard-fought jokes, and expect it.

"I wish you were at all as you used to be," he said, looking at me softly through the courage of his smile, "instead of being such a grand lady."

"And I wish you were a little more like yourself," I answered, without thinking; "you used to think always there was nobody like me."

"Suppose that I am of the same opinion still? Tenfold, fiftyfold, a millionfold?"

"To suppose a thing of that sort is a little too absurd, when you have shown no sign of it."

"For your own dear sake I have shown no sign. The reason of that is too clear to explain."

"Then how stupid I must be not to see an atom of it!"

"Why, who would have any thing to say to me—a broken-down man, a fellow marked out for curses, one who hates even the sight of himself? The lowest of the low would shun me."

He turned away from me, and gazed back toward the dismal, miserable, spectral desert; while I stood facing the fruitful, delicious, flowery Paradise of all the world. I thought of the difference in our lots, and my heart was in misery about him. Then I conquered my pride and my littleness and trumpery, and did what the gentle sweet Eve might have done. And never have I grieved for that action since.

With tears on my cheeks quite undissembled, and a breast not ashamed of fluttering, I ran to Firm Gundry, and took his right hand, and allowed him no refuge from tender wet eyes. Then before he could come to see the meaning of this haste—because of his very high discipline—I was out of his distance, and sitting on a rock, and I lifted my eyes, full of eloquence, to his; then I dropped them, and pulled my hat forward, and said, as calmly as was possible, "I have done enough. The rest remains with you, Firm Gundry."

The rest remained with him. Enough that I was part of that rest; and if not the foundation or crown of it, something desirous to be both, and failing (if fail it ever does) from no want of trial. Uncle Sam says that I never fail at all, and never did fail in any thing, unless it was when I found that blamed nugget, for which we got three wagon-loads of greenbacks; which (when prosperity at last revives) will pay perhaps for greasing all twelve wheels.

Jowler admits not that failure even. As soon as he recovered from canine dementia, approaching very closely to rabies, at seeing me in the flesh once more (so that the Sierra Nevada rang with avalanches of barking), he tugged me to the place where his teeth were set in gold, and proved that he had no hydrophobia. His teeth are scanty now, but he still can catch a salmon, and the bright zeal and loyalty of his soft brown eyes and the sprightly elevation of his tail are still among dogs as pre-eminent as they are to mankind inimitable.

Now the war is past, and here we sit by the banks of the soft Blue River. The early storm and young conflict of a clouded life are over. Still out of sight there may be yet a sea of troubles to buffet with; but it is not merely a selfish thought that others will face it with me. Dark mysteries have been cleared away by being confronted bravely; and the lesson has been learned that life (like California flowers) is of infinite variety. This little river, ten steps wide, on one side has all lupins, on the other side all larkspurs. Can I tell why? Can any body? Can even itself, so full of voice and light, unroll the reason?

Behind us tower the stormy crags, before us spread soft tapestry of earth and sweep of ocean. Below us lies my father's grave, whose sin was not his own, but fell on him, and found him loyal. To him was I loyal also, as a daughter should be; and in my lap lies my reward—for I am no more Erema.